BLACK

"YOU'RE NOT GOING TO PUT IT DOWN."
—NELSON DEMILLE

WATER

"A NERVE-JANGLING THRILL RIDE."
—HARLAN COBEN

TRANSIT

"SUSPENSE FICTION AT ITS FINEST."
—JONATHAN KELLERMAN

CARSTEN STROUD
NEW YORK TIMES BESTSELLING AUTHOR OF CLOSE PURSUIT

ALSO BY
CARSTEN STROUD

CLOSE PURSUIT

*DEADLY FORCE

LIZARDSKIN

SNIPER'S MOON

*IRON BRAVO

***Available from
Bantam Books**

Dell

ISBN 0-440-23709-2

9 780440 237099

50699

US $6.99 / $10.99 CAN

S

BLACK WATER TRANSIT

A NOVEL

CARSTEN STROUD

A DELL BOOK

A Dell Book
Published by
Dell Publishing
a division of
Random House, Inc.
1540 Broadway
New York, New York 10036

Library of Congress Catalog Card Number: 2001017480

ISBN: 0-440-23709-2

Reprinted by arrangement with Delacorte Press

MANUFACTURED IN THE UNITED STATES OF AMERICA
PUBLISHED SIMULTANEOUSLY IN CANADA

August 2002

OPM 10 9 8 7 6 5 4 3 2 1

Dedicated to the memory of

BEVERLY LEWIS

my friend and my editor for fifteen years,
and to

CATHERINE AMANDA STROUD

my mother.

Both of these graceful,
intelligent, and compassionate women
died during the year this book
was being written.

And to

KATIE HALL

my editor,
who loved Beverly
as much as I did.

A sigh can break a man in two.

—**THE TALMUD**

Thanks are also due to, among many other people, Irwyn Applebaum, for being patient with a very complicated book, to Barney Karpfinger, for being patient with a very stressed-out writer, and to John Flicker, for helping me get the Barrett Fifty right. And finally, my thanks to Howard Hardwick and a couple of NYPD detectives, who made the book possible in the first place.

BLACK
WATER
TRANSIT

PART ONE

EARL V. PIKE

It's the first day of summer, New York State—a hot clear sun and the trees all greening out under a sky as blue as Bombay gin—this hard case named Pike—Earl V. Pike— he's doing ninety in a big navy-blue Benz 600, north-bound in the cruise lane of the Taconic, listening to a tape of African drums, has it cranked up so loud the windows are vibrating—it doesn't bother him because his hearing is totally shot—too many years of small-arms fire popping off right next to his skull. The trees and the towns are just black-and-green blurs racing past his window, the incoming lane markers are hot yellow bars that make him think of tracer rounds. Pike is look-ing at his rearview mirror again, he's been checking it every few seconds, thinking very hard about a black GMC truck, windows tinted dark, hanging there in the cruise lane, rock steady, floating there like a big fat deer-fly in the mirror, seven cars back. He speeds up, the Jimmy speeds up. He slows, the Jimmy slows. Earl Pike does not like this.

He takes a deep breath, lets it out slow, shifts his po-sition. Under the blue dress shirt, plates of heavy chest muscle flex as he moves. He's got five circular scars big as silver dollars stitched across his belly in an arc from right to left. He can feel them tug like fishhooks in the muscle. His blunt face is seamed and cracked, his white hair short, a military cut, and his hands on the leather-wrapped wheel are corded and thick, the forearms ropy, veined, bared to his rolled-up sleeves. He has the build of a guy who works against the weight of things, but he's older now and the wear and tear is showing.

As he reaches the Gallatin exit brake lights flash on up ahead, hundreds of ruby lights against the forest green. The cars and vans back up fast and now he's down to a crawl in a mile-long caravan of cars and trucks. He pulls to the right far enough to get a view up the parkway. All he can see is an endless chain of traffic. Some feckless mutt in a fender-bender, he figures, and then he sees the exit sign for Highway 82. Maybe he can flank this tangle, go north on the back roads, get onto the Taconic somewhere farther on. A man named Jack Vermillion was going to be at the Frontenac Hotel just outside of Albany in the early afternoon. Pike had a four-hour safety zone, but he was a meticulous man, and it has been his experience that the devil who lives in the details never sleeps.

Pike cuts the wheel of the Benz hard and bounces over the curb, accelerates up the ramp. As he reaches the top of the exit and comes to a stop, he sees the same black Jimmy pulling up quickly behind him, a brand-new SLT. It's up too close for him to get the plates. The windshield is filled with a reflection of leafy branches from the trees all around them. All he can see through the tint are two vague shapes. He has no particular reason to be worried, but it's an operational habit with him. He tended to notice things like that. The Jimmy has no signal on. Pike waits at the stop sign for a flatbed trailer to pass through and then signals a left turn onto 82 in the direction of Blue Stores. He watches the Jimmy's lights and sees the turn signals come on. He's also making a left.

Pike thinks some more about the black Jimmy as he pulls out onto Highway 82 and crosses over the Taconic. The northbound traffic on the parkway was jammed solid as far as he could see. He moves out fast, passing the flatbed in a quarter mile.

In a few minutes he's far from the sound of the highway and traveling at a steady seventy down a two-lane blacktop that curves and twists over rolling countryside. The Jimmy has also passed the flatbed truck and is now a half-mile back, speeding, closing fast.

Pike keeps his left hand on the wheel and disconnects his seat belt, leans across the center console, flips open the glove compartment, pulls out a worn leather shaving kit, sets it down on the passenger seat. The Jimmy is now less than a hundred feet back.

He zips the kit bag open and lifts out a gray steel Smith and Wesson with his right hand, rebuckles his belt, and holds the Smith on his thigh. The Jimmy is now signaling a pass, so close to his bumper now that all he can see are headlights. There's a flat stretch coming up fast, and then a long left curve running through a tree-lined section. There is no one else on the road. Pike lifts his foot off the accelerator, lets the Benz slow.

He can hear the Jimmy's engine wind out as the driver guns it. The Jimmy pulls out and comes up beside him, the engine a dull roar through the thick glass of the Benz's window. There's movement up ahead, a pale-blue pickup pulling onto the highway. It makes a right turn that puts it directly into the path of the Jimmy. The driver floors it, gaining speed. The pickup truck coming in fast, the Jimmy parallel with his car now, Pike looks up at the passenger window, a shiny black screen, now rolling down, the blue pickup flashing its headlights, the driver punching the horn. Pike looks back up at the Jimmy. A young woman, blonde, maybe nineteen, her lips are moving, she's swearing at him, her face bright red and her mouth twisted and ugly. Pike hits his brakes and opens up the lane, the Jimmy driver cuts the wheel hard, just catching the left front fender of the Benz as he cuts in front, and now Pike sees the Jimmy's brake lights come on.

The suicidal son of a bitch. He locks up the Benz, the scene bright and clear in his mind, his heart rate steady, no panic. There's a pale-blue streak at his left shoulder and he hears the horn on the pickup blaring as it goes by. Fifty feet ahead the Jimmy is now pulling away, the driver's arm is coming out of the window, the fuck-you finger raised, and Pike gets the New Jersey plate number—IMA DV8—"I'm a deviate"?—but now the Jimmy's brake lights come on again, and he sees smoke coming from the tires—it veers and comes to a full stop in the middle of the highway. Pike hits the brakes harder, his shaving kit flies into the passenger well, the Smith comes off his lap, lands with a thump beside the brake pedal. He brings the car to a halt less than four feet off the Jimmy's tailgate.

The driver's door pops open and a young man wearing a white tank top and tan slacks jumps out of the truck and comes back toward the Benz. His head is shaved and his body packed to bursting with muscle and sinew, a bony Italian face swollen with anger. He comes jogging in, much too fast for Pike to get out of the car and deal with him. As the man clears the left fender, he kicks the Benz hard and Pike hears glass shattering. The man—no older than nineteen or twenty—reaches the side window of the Benz, slams it hard with the flat of his hand. The Benz rocks from the blow. Pike locks eyes with the kid, who leans down into the window space and screams directly onto the glass, his breath clouding on it. Pike sees that the man has several of his rear molars capped, around his thick neck there's a gold chain with a scapular medal of Saint Christopher hanging on it. The kid's eyes are very blue, although his skin is olive and his shaved head is tinged with black bristles. His mouth is as ugly as the girl's. Pike isn't really listening to the words. He's busy processing a tactical shift. This is just a random contact with a civilian. This has nothing to do with his work. It looks like the kid has convinced himself that the near miss was Pike's fault, and is now communicating his displeasure to Pike using all the hip-hop gangster slang his sluggish cortex can process. This element of the contact pisses Pike off. Was this fool so degraded he couldn't even curse in his own fucking idiom? How did nigger thugs get to dominate the insult landscape in America? Pike feels his temper starting to slip some cables.

He watches the veins pulsing in the kid's neck. The kid is likely a lifter or some kind of jock and could be in the middle of some sort of steroidal episode. Or he is just a complete asshole. Pike is making a concerted effort to leave the kid alone. He has business to take care of at the Frontenac. He has no time for this jerk. Just move away, he is saying to himself, almost like a prayer. The kid sees his lips forming words, steps back, kicks out at the glass. His sandal slips on the tarmac, he falls on his ass. Hard. This does not improve his mood in any visible way. Pike watches him spring up, approach the car again. This is bullshit, Pike is thinking.

He'll give the boy one more chance. He knows exactly where the pistol is, down by the brake pedal. One more kick and it's a nine-mill head canoe coming right up and the carnival band plays a requiem for this buffed-out moron. Then ten minutes for the blonde with the ugly mouth. Maybe less. The kid has more to say, he says it some more, but no more kicks seem to be in the works. The boy is breathing very hard now. He makes another war face at Pike, shakes himself like a dog coming out of the water, walks away, glaring over his shoulder at Pike. Pike, maybe for amusement, at any rate against his own better judgment, gives him a finger-flutter wave, a big happy smile.

The kid stops so fast he skids on his sandals, comes back toward the front windshield, leans far over the hood, works his throat and mouth for a few seconds, and spits onto the glass, directly over Pike's face. Now there's a shrill call, and the kid turns away. The blonde girl is out of the car, yelling at him.

He looks back down at Pike, makes a kissy face, and walks away with his shoulders rolling and his arms spread out so Pike can see how big his deltoids are. Pike watches through the dribble of lumpy brown and yellow spit running down the windshield as the kid gets back into the Jimmy and slams the door so hard dust bounces off the roof. The blonde looks at Pike blankly for another few seconds and then she gets back inside the truck, the Jimmy's engine roars and the tires smoke, and the truck accelerates away from the Benz.

Pike looks down at his watch. The whole incident has taken less than two minutes. The ribbon of greasy mucus reaches the wiper blade. He flicks on the blade and a pale amber smear tinged with red blood and solid matter spreads across the windshield. He presses the spray button and watches as the blades work back and forth. The Jimmy is now a quarter mile away, moving very fast, snaking through a tree-lined avenue toward a crest of hill.

In a little while the windshield is almost clear of the boy's spit. Pike stops the blades, sits for another twenty seconds, listening to the engine muttering and burbling. He hears a deep brassy wail and sees the flatbed trailer coming up behind him. The wall of wind it's pushing rocks the Benz on its springs. Pike watches the flatbed grow smaller in the distance. Something spidery twitches in his left cheek. He sighs deeply, collects his Smith and the kit bag from the floor wells, puts the Smith carefully back inside the kit bag, replaces the bag in the glove compartment, closes the latch very gently. Then he puts the Benz in gear, lets out another deep breath, and now he feels something feathery and light moving on his upper lip.

He leans forward to look at his reflection in the rearview mirror. A tiny spot of ochre-red is moving downward from his left nostril. As he watches, the dot changes direction and begins to crawl sideways across his upper lip. Another tiny red dot crawls out of his right eye, very near the tear duct, and moves over the bridge of his nose. Then another. The car begins to roll forward. Pike closes his eyes, presses hard on the brake, the Benz lurches to a stop.

More tiny red spiders crawl across the insides of his lids, black silhouettes against the sun glare. They float in his vision, a constellation of pinpricks. They begin to pour out of his ears. He can feel them in their thousands as they race across his skull. He opens his eyes and studies his face in the rearview mirror. Nothing. Still, they are there. This is a thing he knows. He can feel them, thousands of them, a tide of little red spiders the size of pinpoints, crawling along the dome of his skull, moving in steady columns under his skin.

Pike had been told by men he respected—army shrinks at the rehab center in Bethesda—that the spiders weren't real, that they were a kind of post-traumatic stress reaction to the thing that happened in Ecuador, but right now he still has to deal with the distraction they present. He reaches into his pocket and pulls out a plastic container of small orange-and-blue caplets, pops the lid, dry-swallowing two, and then two more. They go down slowly, scraping at his throat: he wishes for water. The Jimmy reaches the crest and disappears. Two more minutes pass. He takes his foot off the brake, exhales and then inhales, rubs the bullet wounds in his belly, and presses down hard on the gas. In less than fifteen seconds he's doing eighty miles an hour, and ninety by the time he clears the crest of the hill and comes down onto the straightaway on the far side. The flatbed trailer is up ahead.

He tops ninety as he overtakes it and now he sees the black Jimmy far up the road. It's just a tiny little spot in the hazy blue distance, no bigger than a spider, but at this point it has filled up Earl Pike's mind completely.

HARLEM

NEW YORK CITY

1015 HOURS

On the same lovely day, the very first day of summer, down in Harlem, in a shaft of sunlight cutting through a space between two project towers, a girl in a bottle-green dress and ruby-red sneakers got pulled right off the sidewalk in front of the Wagner Houses on Paladino. Two—maybe three—white males in a rusted, navy-blue van. A witness got a partial on a Jersey marker. The girl's name was Shawana Coryell. She was nine. Cassandra Spandau was catching for the Two Five Sex Crimes squad that morning.

Cassandra—known as Casey—was just another black PW—a policewoman—but people remembered these strange Chinese eyes she had, pale amber with tiny slivers of gold, and high cheekbones, skin as brown as a gun dog's eye. She wasn't what you'd call a beauty—way too tight around the eyes and her lips were too thin— but when you met her, she stayed with you: how she moved, her voice, and the way a vein in her neck pulsed when she spoke. She had what the academy boys called command presence, but she wore her skin like an armadillo, had nothing outside of business with any of the white cops at the Two Five, male or female. She would tell you, if you let her, that the DEA ran the crack trade and that AIDS was a CIA plot to kill blacks and that Maya Angelou was a great American poet. But she was young, and the young have always been a pain in the ass.

The point here is, the Two Five CO liked her anyway—who knows why—but it turned out to be important later. About where she came from or what her childhood had been like, the guys at the Two Five never heard a word from her, but her sheet from the academy had her down as born upstate, some little town called Carthage, and the space for the father's name had *deceased* scrawled across it in big blunt letters, an angry scrawl, somebody pissed off just at the thought.

Now the Two Five Sex Crimes Unit worked out of a puke-green and baby-shit yellow squad room at the top of a flight of wooden stairs in the back of the house. It had no windows, so it was always lit by two banks of fluorescent tubes. All the white folks looked lime-green and all the black folks looked purple. Sex Crimes at the Two Five was eight guys and two women, all white shields, a couple or more years out of the academy.

Casey and her partner—a no-neck ex-linebacker named Levon Jamal, who had washed out of a Jets walk-on four years back—were on a domestic dispute at the Taft Houses when they got a 10-10 call just after ten o'clock, a male witness had just seen a young black girl get snatched, nine, he knew her, said her name was Shawana Coryell.

He had watched her from his third-floor window as she walked along Paladino by the Wagner Houses, green dress, red Keds sneakers, and a baggy black silk windbreaker with a Yankees logo, lugging a huge sack of groceries, apparently on her way back from the corner market near Guvillier Park. It was a load no nine-year-old would have been asked to carry in a decent neighborhood, but her mother was doing a court-ordered tour in detox and her aunt was in a wheelchair, dying of HIV picked up off a grubby spike; her little brother Antowain had the flu and needed some baby aspirin, and the fridge was empty, and there was nobody else, so there you go.

Anyway, she's on the street and this is when two—maybe three—men in a rusted blue van, partial plates from Jersey, Whisky X ray Nevada something, ducked out of the traffic and pulled up alongside the little girl, and then—for some insane reason—Harlem kids are as street sharp as cats—little Shawana Coryell steps right up to the passenger side window. Ba-bing. She's gone.

Six seconds for the hook, maybe less. The blue van then bolts northbound before the witness can get out of his chair. But the witness, a security guard at Gondorff Jewels on 125th Street, got a good look at the whole thing, including the partial, and called it in to 911, where it was patched through to the Two Five, who handed it straight off to Casey Spandau.

Casey and Levon moved on the 10-10 fast. While all the Two Five RMPs—radio motor patrol cars—hit the streets looking for the rolling blue van, she and Levon scooped the witness up at the Wagner project and took him straight into the station, where he described the takers as white males, the driver hard to see, a blur inside the tinted windshield, but the guy who snagged her, he had to lean out of the window, and the witness pegged him in the shaft of sunlight, a guy maybe in his early thirties, pale skin, almost an albino, buggy eyes, with shiny black hair hanging down past his shoulders.

Casey and Levon got right back on the street and went north, looking hard for that partial marker, and Casey said later she knew it in her belly that they'd see it just around the next curve. She wanted that marker so hard it was hurting her throat. But they missed it. Somehow the Jersey marker flanks the cordon.

It happens. They go to ground, or make it to one of the bridges. New York's a big town. So now Casey and Levon go totally postal, they spend the next two hours ripping up the streets and shaking down the sex-trade crowd—what they liked to call a WHAM tour—winning hearts and minds—and by one o'clock they managed to connect with a baby-faced hustler named Two-Pack, looked to be maybe eleven but wasn't, worked the short-eyes beat—the pedophile market—doing stuff that would make a hyena gag all along West 125th Street. Casey put the witness sketch of the guy with the long black hair down in front of Two-Pack and—bingo—they got a name out of him. Tony. Last name sounds like "gash."

Two-Pack paints a picture of a wiry little guy, late twenties, has an Italian accent, and it matches the witness ID right down to the waist-length black hair. Word is that Tony no-name was in and out of Rikers like a swinging gate and last year got sent upstate for a sex beef. Tony the Gash was known to be hanging with a pair of brothers whose names Two-Pack cannot remember, they're heavy into the kiddie-sex circuit, always cruising for prospects on the Net or trading deeply twisted videos.

"But never the real thing?" asked Levon.

Two-Pack seems to think it over while Casey and the linebacker do silent inner work on their personal anger management issues in the front seat of the DT car.

Finally, he says that the last time he was with Tony . . . guy was sort of a regular customer . . . maybe he heard

Tony say something about nailing the real thing, about having "a fresh mango."

"What did he say, exactly?" says Casey.

"Hard to say," says Two-Pack. "I was upside down. I had my face up against the door. A lot was going on at the time."

"These brothers got names?"

Two-Pack has no idea.

"Where do we find this Tony mutt?"

"You guys know a place in the Village, no nameplate, a walk-down in an alleyway off Gansevoort? Kind of a water sports club? Private?"

They had heard about it.

"Could be, you go there tonight, you look around, maybe you'll see this guy there. Like I said, short, wiry, really pale, almost an albino, but has long black hair, never in a ponytail, likes to let it hang way down his back. Shiny black hair, looks blue under a street lamp. He'll be in the back. Way in the back there. You won't miss him."

Levon sat in the DT car—a detective car—this one is an unmarked dark-blue Crown Victoria—he stays there with Two-Pack, waiting while Casey, whose cell phone battery was dead, went off to make a phone call to the assistant district attorney assigned to Harlem and the Uptown Sex Crimes Task Force. The ADA was a woman named Veronica Stein, mid-twenties, Upper East Side background, black hair in a tricky razor cut, always dressed in pinstripe suits and sneakers, and Casey loved her because she hated sex offenders very deeply and always made a project out of the ones she could get a net around. Casey laid out the state of the case so far. A confidential informant with corroborative information that supports a warrant for the suspect.

"What would that corroborative information be?" she asks.

"Pattern of behavior. Verbally expressed a pedophile kidnap fantasy to the informant." Casey knew that was weak.

"Under what circumstances?" she asks.

"Ah, under . . . during a sexual contact."

"So your informant is a hooker?"

"Yes."

"Okay. What did you get out of NCIC?"

They had run a search on the National Crime Information Computer database and got a hit on a Tony LoGascio—pronounced "lo-gashio"—DOB October 18, 1969, place called Agrigento, in Sicily. Naturalized in 1978. Got right into crime. Popped for Section 130 beefs, also a history of drugs and violence. Got a 120 for assault police too. His intake photo matched the witness ID eight points out of ten.

"Not enough for an arrest warrant," says the ADA.

Casey thinks about case law.

"How about something under Section 130 of the code?"

"What have you got?"

"Our CI says that this LoGascio guy had consensual sodomy with him last week."

"Your CI under seventeen?"

"Yeah."

"You say LoGascio has a date of birth of October eighteenth, 1969? He's thirty-one, then. So that's a class E felony. Will your CI support the charge? Lay an information?"

"Yes. If I tell him to."

"We'll run it by a judge," says Veronica Stein. "Where'll you be?"

Casey says she and Levon will go downtown and locate the place on Gansevoort, and they'll get the snitch to lay the information in front of the duty desk at the Sixth and she'll fax Stein the sheets. They'll wait for

Stein's call at the Sixth Precinct on West Tenth, phone number there is 741-4811. Okay? Okay.

Then on the way downtown, the Sex Crimes Unit CO from the Two Five gets on the radio to say that Shawana Coryell has been found and would Casey or Levon call him on a land line. Casey pulled over at Third and Forty-ninth and made the call from a booth inside Smith and Wollensky. She listened to the CO as he described the condition of the victim. What had been done. The damage. Little Shawana Coryell would live, but her childhood was now officially over.

Back in the cruiser, Levon gives her a look. She sends it back and he sighs. They go down to the Sixth Precinct and wait. Thirty-seven minutes later the phone rings at the desk sergeant's post.

It's Stein. They have the warrant.

ALBANY

NEW YORK STATE

1300 HOURS

Earlier the same day, at around the same hour that Casey and Levon first connected with Two-Pack down in Harlem, a few miles down the Hudson from Albany, in a place called Castleton, on one of those shining days where the trees are all greened out and a smoky haze is drifting in the air, making everything glow like you were seeing it through stained glass, we're at the Frontenac Hotel, right on the river, in an old wood-paneled room called the Long Bar, with a man named Jack Vermillion, a sort of western look to him: deep lines around the eyes, a white cowhand mustache, his hair white, wears it long and brushed back, big chest, and a flat belly like a drumhead.

On this particular day he's wearing a pair of creased blue jeans, a white T-shirt, blue blazer, light-brown cowboy boots. He's here with Raleigh "Creek" Johnson, his business partner, they're leaning back in those big leather sofas with the brass buttons stuck all over them, mahogany paneling on the walls, rose glass shades, a tall and frosty waitress with hair like the meringue on a lemon pie. What he's doing, he's listening to an aerodynamic little mook named Martin Glazer.

Jack is staring at Martin Glazer, at these three guys from Galitzine Sheng and Munro, this private investment bank from down on Wall Street, here to make a pitch to take over the employee pension fund, manage it better, make it even fatter—he's watching them over the marble coffee table, over the coffee cups and heavy glasses full of single-malt scotch, thinking—these three guys remind him of something. But he can't figure what. He can't quite get the answer. Martin Glazer is prosing on about "P-and-E ratio" and "no-load mutuals" with his rounded-off head and his hair gelled right back and his soft brown eyes behind the wire frames and his weird habit of barking out critical statistics in short sharp yelps.

His assistants, the veeps, Kuhlman and Bern, little goatees, crew cuts like boot camp pukes, only they're in two-thousand-dollar Armani suits, wing tips wider than shovel blades, they're sitting up ramrod straight with tumblers of Glenfiddich in their hands and staring at him so hard that Jack feels he ought to throw them a—and then Jack gets it.

Seals.

They look like harbor seals.

He grins to himself at the picture. Glazer sees this, it puzzles him, he hesitates, and then he starts in again. Yap yap. Bark bark. The services they offer . . . how they can make Black Water Transit a better company . . .

growth funds . . . employee share plans . . . payroll deductions . . . global investment management . . . dotcoms . . . the NASDAQ . . . operational streamlining . . . Jack finds he has to work very hard just to follow the man.

He cares, he knows this is important, he wants the deal. Black Water Transit has over eighteen hundred employees. Dockworkers, drivers, barge pilots, warehouse staff, office people. He had big trouble with the Teamsters last year, a union takeover bid, very aggressive, and only got out of it by offering his employees, who were all market-struck just like the rest of the country, a great pension package and a chance to make regular stock investments through a payroll deduction plan. Out of nowhere, while he was still thinking about this project but doing nothing solid about it, he gets a call from Galitzine Sheng and Munro, offering exactly that kind of pension fund service.

Jack figured somebody on the inside had given them a heads-up, but he could never find out who. It didn't seem to matter. Now they were here at the Frontenac and Glazer was making an impressive pitch.

It looks like a great business opportunity. Good for the workers, good for Black Water Transit, even good for Jack and his only partner, Creek Johnson, since they would also share in the market investment program.

He stretches, looks left at Creek, who seems to be taking in Glazer's pitch with a wary look in his watery blue eyes, his hands folded across his big belly. He's saying nothing, his thin blond hair is combed back, his skin is sunburned from the golf course. Around his eyes Jack can see a fan of white lines on the tanned skin. His hands are bumpy and knotted and the veins in his thick forearms are bulging. Creek always had good hands for work. Not that he ever used them.

Creek had been real active in Black Water Transit

Systems in the early years after Vietnam, he'd drive all day and load all night, a bear for the heavy work. But then he got lazy. Lately it seemed to Jack that Creek had spent most of the last ten years cheering him on from the nineteenth hole, while Jack built Black Water Transit from a two-truck outfit hauling clean fill out of Rochester all the way up to the point where they're both sitting here listening to Martin Glazer tell them how Galitzine Sheng and Munro can make their employees rich.

Well, that was okay with Jack, Creek being a little to the left of the big picture, because Jack wasn't a man who had a strong need to consult with anybody. Black Water Transit was totally private, owned by just the two of them, no shares, no IPOs, no public involvement at all—other than the federal regs he had to live with—and that was how it was going to stay if Jack had anything to say about it. Creek had effectively retired from the day-to-day operations of the company and was here mainly because Jack liked him and wanted him to have a say in the matter.

Creek had shown up for this meet in tan Dockers and a pink polo shirt, white socks and Sperry Top-Siders, which indicated just how seriously he was taking this whole proposition. Has his cleats and his clubs in the trunk, Jack figured. Creek will be on the links as soon as this is over.

Glazer's voice is like a busy signal, like a very stupid bee bumping into a window over and over again, and in a little while Jack begins to drift. He looks out the leaded-glass window at the big willows on the river's edge, they're swaying in a summer wind off the river, the long narrow leaves showing silvery undersides, and he gets this image in his head, the way he used to see big schools of amberjack on those gunship sweeps down from Soc Trang. From a thousand feet up they looked like silver ribbons in the blue water. This is in the South China Sea, maybe a mile off the Ca Mau Point, southern tip of Vietnam. Anyway, Glazer's into an aria now. Jack's eyes begin to close.

"So what do you think?" somebody asks him.

He's thinking about the Corps, Parris Island, Camp Lejeune, the sand ticks they had there, a month at Quantico, and then the 121st Helicopter Assault Team. RVN. Thirty-five years ago? Couldn't be. Otts. Gorman, the door gunner . . . who the hell was—

"Mr. Vermillion?"

Jack came back, blinked at them all.

Damn, he thinks. This won't do.

He shakes his head, sits up straight, puts his glass down hard.

"Sorry . . . the heat."

"It is warm," said Glazer, his eyes flat as little pebbles. There was something in there, and Jack considered it. Glazer was a touchy guy, had a mean streak. A guy to watch.

Creek looked at Jack and grinned at Glazer.

"Jackson here, he's old. He needs his nap," said Creek.

"I like it, Mr. Glazer," said Jack.

"*We* like it," said Creek, smiling the smile he had for people he didn't like very much but had to be nice to anyway.

"We do," said Jack. "I think we should do this thing."

"So do I," said Creek.

"Mr. Vermillion, I can't tell you how delighted we all are. This is going to be a very productive enterprise. I can assure you and your employees that no matter what your questions, we—all of us at Galitzine Sheng and Munro—are ready to help at any stage of the process. You won't regret this decision. It was the smart thing to do. In the current job market, keeping good employees happy and prosperous is a smart business move. You'll never regret it. We can make this pension fund a powerful instrument for Black Water Transit, for your people, even for you and your partner."

Jack smiled. Creek stood up. Glazer looked at his veeps.

"Gentlemen?"

The three of them rose together. The leather couch sighed. Big smiles and meaningful eye contact all around. Firm manly handshakes from the veeps.

"You take all the time you need, Mr. Vermillion."

"Call me Jack."

"Jack."

"Call me Creek," said Creek.

Glazer bobbed his seal head. Highlights moved across his polished cheeks. His wire frames glittered with gold light.

"Please call me Martin."

"I will, Martin," said Creek.

He turned to Jack, winked elaborately, did his trademark W. C. Fields finger twizzle.

"Walk with me, Jackson."

They left the Wall Street boys packing up their papers and poking at their Palm Pilots, the three of them chirping at each other, birds on a wire. The teak-lined hallway of the Frontenac was paved with flat granite blocks and the sunlight was so strong outside that the trees and the cars in the parking lot were bleached, colorless. The cicadas were droning and the air filled with drifting seed pods from a stand of cottonwoods. The Hudson was wide and mud-brown, but the sun on the water sparkled in a broad golden arc.

When they got outside, the heat was flat and strong on their faces. Creek was silent until they got to the valet stand and he handed the muscle-bound kid his ticket.

"The racing-green Corvette, sir. I hear screaming rubber, I will snap your collarbone like the celery stick in a Bloody Mary."

The kid grinned at him, jogged off. Creek scanned the parking lot, turned to Jack, shading his eyes in the hard white light.

"Where's your little torpedo of screaming doom?"

"In my pants. Where it belongs. But thanks for asking."

"Very amusing. Where is it?"

He was talking about Jack's 1967 Shelby Cobra, a jet-black roadster with a 427 mill capable of speeds in excess of all reason. The Cobra was one of Jack's three major vices, along with too much wine and too much work.

"Being detailed. At Frank's. I'll go pick it up today."

"How?"

"Cab. What's this? A sudden attack of courtesy?"

"Let me get it for you. I'm going that way anyway."

"Don't be considerate. It throws me off balance."

"I am always considerate. It's part of whom I am."

"Who."

"Who?"

"Not 'whom.' Who."

"As in 'whom's on first'? Okay, get your own damn car. Now, tell Uncle Raleigh. What did you think of them?"

"Glazer? There's a man who likes to talk."

"Whom likes to talk."

"Don't start. Did you notice they all looked like seals?"

Creek grinned. "Yeah. Now that you mention it. But the deal?"

"I like it. I told everybody we'd be reworking the fund. Now we are. It'll keep the Teamsters out at any rate."

"What about Dave at the bank? He's not going to be happy, you taking the pension fund away from Chase."

"Chase will still have the payroll operations. All Glazer's people are going to do is channel the investment strategy. That won't hurt Dave Fontenot. The market's going bats. Galitzine Sheng and Munro are right in the middle of it. They've been around for years."

"They're not going to be much fun to work with."

"That's not likely to bother you much, Creek. You haven't pulled a good day's duty since the Reagan administration."

"Once Ronnie was in, I figured my work here was done. Answer me one question?"

"I'll try."

"You don't really like letting go of it, do you?"

"I'm not. I never ran the fund. That was the problem."

"I mean the company itself. I watched you in there. You don't like anybody helping you out. Not even me. Black Water Transit is the only thing you've ever done. It's all you have. No offense, but your personal life sucks canal water. Streak's all you had, and look—"

"My son's name is Danny. Not Streak. Let's stay off that topic, okay? We're never gonna agree. We needed to work the pension fund better. Change is good, Creek. Change is good."

"Leave my underwear out of this. You were drifting back there. Where'd you go?"

Jack looked out to the parking lot.

"Soc Trang."

"Oh, jeez. Here we go. Down Memory Lane in my Cobra gunship. What did you do in Vietnam, Grandpop? Well, my boy, we lit up a boxcar full of dinks and we danced the Watusi on a mountain of blackened skulls. Care for a dried gook's ear, little fellow? They're just like Pringles, only crunchier."

"You're a sick bastard, Creek. Sometimes I miss the war."

"Mainly because you and me, we didn't get all shot to shit."

"Maybe. But it was something to remember. It held your attention. I almost fell asleep in there. Most of the time, I feel like I'm on Thorazine. I was wide awake and inside every minute of that war. A man needs to feel his life."

"Some men, Jackson. Shallow little men, mutts with no inner resources. It takes your man of character to do sweet dick every day and still have a rich inner life. That's why you have to work. Jeez, you're a wop. What's the phrase? *Il duce far niente?*"

"You mean *qui dolce far niente*. How sweet to do nothing."

"What did I say?"

"Basically you said, 'The leader does dick.' "

"Exactly my point!"

"I'll find something to do. Maybe I'll breed horses."

"Personally? This I got to watch."

"I like horses."

"Way too much. I can see that from here. Why not golf?"

"I'd rather stick hot needles in my eyes. Golf is a cult, like the Shriners, only the hats are sillier."

Creek's attention was elsewhere, out in the parking lot.

"Okay, now who's this mook in a suit coming up on us here?"

A mid-fifties-looking man had just gotten out of a dark-blue Mercedes 600 and was walking toward them, looking right at them, a big man shaped like a wheat barn, with wide sloping shoulders and a battered, rocky-looking face, his white hair shaved close to his skull. He was very well turned out in a lightweight navy suit, a pale-blue shirt open at the neck. When he got closer he nodded and smiled.

"Mr. Vermillion? Mr. Johnson?"

"Yes?" said Jack. Creek said nothing.

He reached them, nodded at Creek, and looked back at Jack.

"My name is Pike, Mr. Vermillion. Earl Pike. Have you got a minute?"

Jack assessed him. The guy looked . . . military, somehow. His skin was seamed and darkly tanned, as if he'd spent a lot of time in the Southwest. Age maybe fifty-five, maybe older. His carriage was very stiff. Jack could see him in full dress blues. Or maybe he just had a back problem. He could feel Creek peeling off.

"Jackson, my lad, I'll leave you with this gentleman. Mr. Pike, you have a good one."

Jack smiled at Creek, nodded. Creek stepped out into the parking lot just as his dark-green Corvette appeared. He overtipped the valet and climbed in, inclining his head to them both as he accelerated away. The Corvette throbbed and burbled and then they could hear the music playing, zydeco, Creek's favorite.

Earl Pike waited in silence until Creek reached the highway.

"I hope this isn't a bad time to talk a little business?"

He was smiling and looking as friendly as he could manage, but it didn't fit him. His eyes were off the power grid, a pair of dead sockets, and if he smiled much, it hadn't left any marks on his face. There was a jagged burn scar above the man's right eye. Jack figured he'd had a lot of surgery to cover it. He needed some more.

Pike offered Jack a hand and gave him a grip like getting your fingers caught in a car door. As he shook it, Jack saw that Pike's knuckles were bandaged. Pike looked down at his hand, smiled.

"Flat tire. On the Taconic. Had to change it myself, and the wrench slipped. Ripped up my knuckles pretty good. Sorry."

"What can I do for you, Mr. Pike?"

"You want to go in, get a drink?"

"No, I'm in a rush, actually. Sorry . . ."

"I'll take just a minute. I'm sorry to come in unexpectedly, but I've got to drive back down to New York this evening and this was the only chance I had to talk to you. I hate to impose. It's kind of urgent. Dave Fontenot suggested I meet you here. He said your meeting should be about over. I hope you don't mind?"

"Dave Fontenot? At Chase?"

"Yes. We had a foursome at Meadow Mills last week and I mentioned I needed to talk to someone in freight. I need some advice, actually. About a shipment. It's unusual. He said you were the best."

Dave Fontenot was the Chase Bank VP who handled all of Black Water Transit Systems' accounts. This wasn't the first time he'd sent business Jack's way. Personal connections made up most of the business world in Albany. Okay, Jack figured. I can see this.

"What can we do for you today, Mr. Pike?"

A thin smile from Earl.

"You ship, right?"

"That's what it says on the door."

"Containers? Sealed?"

"Yep, if you want. We have a bonded warehouse, we'll ship anywhere. Ground. Air. Down the Hudson. Up the Erie. The Saint Lawrence. I can have a rate card faxed—"

Earl Pike was nodding through this, something else showing in his face. Jack saw a caution light there and his silent alarm went off. Pike was looking over his shoulder. Glazer and Bern and Kuhlman came out into the parking lot, nodded at Jack, and moved away toward a large gray Fugazy limo. When they were far enough away Pike turned back to Jack and spoke softly.

"Dave says you were a marine. That right?"

"I was."

"See the show?"

"Some. Flew a Cobra gunship out of Soc Trang. You?"

"A little. I Corps. Up and down Thunder Road."

"That would count."

"Mind my asking, you own firearms?"

"A few. Nothing nuclear."

Earl Pike nodded and moved a little closer into Jack's space. Jack could smell the man's aftershave, something with lime in it. His voice was deep and he spoke in a hoarse whisper, which forced you to listen harder. It was an old DI trick Jack knew from Parris Island. But he had Jack's attention.

"You follow the firearms issues?"

"Not much."

"You've heard of the Violent Crime Control and Law Enforcement Act of 1994?"

"No. Gun politics aren't really my thing."

"It's a ban on all sorts of weapons, semiauto assault weapons, big magazines, that kind of thing."

"Well, sounds good to me. We got punk-ass kids in high school airing out the student body all over the country. We need more guns like we need more skin diseases. What's the problem?"

"We can disagree about that later. I have a . . . collection. Very unique. Irreplaceable pieces. Pieces of immense historical value. I can give you a complete description. You'd see what I mean. These are museum-quality weapons, weapons that helped make this country. This omnibus bill, it negated the grandfather clause and collector status. My collection was always intended for my children, had they lived, or perhaps for a museum. Now my children are gone, and this law makes it very difficult to manage the collection. So I'm thinking perhaps it's time to let it go."

"Your children are dead? I'm sorry. I really am."

Pike's face went through an alteration, and Jack saw a flash of grief, then something else. Ferocity. Rage. A murderous rage. Just beneath the man's skin. A death mask. Then it was gone.

"It was a long time ago. A fire. About the collection . . ."

"Why not donate it to a museum?"

Pike shook his head and gave Jack a thin smile.

"I'm a little short on altruism right now."

"You want to sell it, then?"

"Yes. There are good markets. And, to be frank, I resent the interference. I'm a good citizen, solid. I should have the freedom that I . . . that we fought for. But we have these . . . urban liberals. If I'm not careful, the ATF will just seize the collection."

"They'd compensate you."

Earl made a gesture with his huge right hand, moved a lot of air with it, moved it too close to Jack's face. Jack held his temper.

"Pennies. An insult. I've been contacted by a collector in Mexico, a retired Mexican cavalry officer. An old friend of the family. We've talked it over, and I know he'd value it, he'd ensure its intact survival for another hundred years. The problem is getting the collection to the buyer. It's rather large and needs to be shipped with care, by a professional."

"Large shipments of weapons must be reported to the ATF, even in-state. I keep them informed because they demand it. You do it or I do it. I won't ship weapons across the street without doing the paperwork. Mr. Pike, I sympathize. I don't like the nanny state any better than you do. But the law is clear. I break it, I get caught,

I lose my license, lose my business, maybe go to jail. Can't do it. Sorry."

Pike didn't seem fazed.

"I've done some research on the issue. Collections of historical pieces do not need to be completely itemized for the ATF. You can declare key elements of the collection and refer to other items as attachments and accessories. As long as the basic declaration is accurate in principle, the ATF will never question it. They're understaffed, anyway—they have less than two thousand agents nationwide, and few of them are field agents. Most of those have been directed to monitor gun shows and do random inspections on licensed dealers. The ATF management is busy supporting class-action suits against the gun manufacturers or helping to rape the cigarette companies. You could very accurately say that the attention of the ATF is likely to be elsewhere. And I am prepared to pay whatever is required to move this collection safely. Whatever."

Jack took a long calm look at the man's face. Pike did not flinch or break eye contact.

"What are we talking about here, Mr. Pike?"

"Business. Simply business. You have a service for which I am prepared to pay well. I would expect to pay an administrative fee. Well beyond the standard rates. You understand?"

Jack looked away from the man, scanned the parking lot. They were in the open, under a broad, arched wooden shelter in front of the Frontenac. The parking lot was full of cars. It was a bright clear day. Any one of those cars could be crammed with federal agents with minicams, directional mikes. Mr. Pike here could have more wiring in his underbra than Diane Sawyer. Jack felt his heartbeat increasing. This might be a federal sting. Or not.

"Maybe we should talk about this somewhere else?"

Earl's face grew redder, and his eyebrows knotted across his forehead. He squinted out at the sun-bleached lot.

"Yes. Perhaps we should."

GREENWICH VILLAGE
NEW YORK CITY
1710 HOURS

The place on Gansevoort was lit like an Anne Rice novel, but smelled worse. It was a little after five, but it was already packed. By the time Casey and Levon had extracted Tony LoGascio from the place, Two-Pack was bailing out of the neighborhood at a dead run.

They tossed Tony LoGascio into the back of the unit and threw him a blanket, since all he was wearing was a kind of black latex jockstrap and a pair of floppy rubber leggings tied to a belt around his waist. His torso was thin but well muscled, his skin milky white and covered with spidery veins. His hair was long and fine as black silk. He came across as a homeless ferret with a skin disorder.

"So what's this bullshit about a sodomy charge?" he says, taking a major attitude right off the mark.

"In a minute," says Casey. "While we're here, what can you tell us about a snatch, happened up in Harlem today?"

He made the kind of face you make when you're giving something very serious and intense thought. He shook his head, eyes very wide. The Wagner Houses thing? Oh goodness. He heard all about it on the radio. Terrible thing. Times we live in. Man, I really wish I could help, Officers. I mean, I feel for the little kid, you know?

Casey knew there was nothing in the department press releases about the victim's age. She let Levon deal with it.

Levon moved in the seat and flexed his shoulders. Heavy muscles jumped and rippled under his shirt.

"Let me put the question to you again another way," said Levon in a soft voice. "Where were you and what were you doing at the time this kidnap occurred in Harlem?"

They both watched as a cartoon "thinks" balloon appeared in the air over the guy's head.

"Golly. Let me see. Yes. I was in Flatbush. Playing soccer with some friends. In Prospect Park."

"You can prove this?"

"Sure. All afternoon. Let me make a call—"

"We'll do that for you. So maybe you can explain why a witness at the scene gave a description of one of the kidnappers and the description matches you perfectly?"

"Easy. He's wrong."

"How do you know the witness was a male?"

"I . . . I guessed. It's always gonna be fifty-fifty."

They show him the witness sketch. It's obviously Tony LoGascio. He stares at it for a while—they can both hear the gears in his skull grinding like a rusted gate—and then he shrugs.

"So you got a problem coming in and doing a lineup?"

"A lineup? For this witness?"

"No. A lineup for the victim."

"No way. Anyway, she can't."

"And why can't she?"

"The victim? I mean, well, she'd be all shook up there, not be able to make a good ID. And a little black kid, right? Hurt, like."

"How would you know that? We didn't release her

age. We never said she was black. Maybe she wasn't even a she, right?"

"Well, I just figured, you know, a sex thing. A kidnapping? That would probably be a sex thing. Right? A little girl. Anyway, it said on the news there that the vic was a nig—a black child, so, you know, I guess I just assumed that was what you were saying. And it's Harlem. So she's a little black kid, like."

"Of course," says Casey. "Everybody in Harlem is black, like. We all know that. Why do you think the victim couldn't, like, ID you?"

"I didn't say that. I mean, I did, but that's because it wasn't me."

Casey nodded. Raised a finger of caution and tapped her nose.

"Because she can, Tony. They picked her up a while ago. She's in rough shape, but she can do a lineup. She wants to do one real bad."

"Yeah? She can, hah? So, that's . . . that's good, okay? She's okay, huh? That's gotta be one tough little girl, hah? Assuming she is a little girl, I mean. No offense, right? But that's . . . that's good, hah?"

"Yeah. Okay, so you have no objection to the lineup, then? Be a good citizen, help us eliminate you as a suspect?"

"Oh yeah, and what if she does ID me as the guy? Banged up like that, what she's been through, maybe her head's all fucked up. She makes me anyway. Then I'm screwed."

"So you think she *might* ID you?"

"Well, you already said I looked like the composite, I mean."

"So you won't do the lineup, just to help out?"

"No. No way. Anyway, I wasn't there."

"Where?"

"Uptown. In Harlem. Anywhere. I didn't do anything

to anybody. Look, fuck this. What's all this got to do with a sodomy charge? Am I under arrest here? Or what?"

"For the sodomy thing? Not yet. Should you be?"

"Fuck that too. I saw that little shit, Two-Pack. He's a hustler. Everybody knows it. Charging me with sodomy for a meatpacker like that, why not beef an ATM for giving you cash. Look. You're not really serious about that charge. Even if I did pork the punk, he's a whore, it's just a misdemeanor, I won't do a day. So you can shove that where Two-Pack likes it. You just wanted an excuse to squeeze me about the Harlem thing. Am I right?"

"Hey, when you're right, you're right."

"So we go down to the station, you book me on consensual sodomy, I walk in three minutes on a desk appearance ticket, I'm back in the club an hour later, having a gin fizz. Right?"

"That's the way you want to play it?"

Tony nods, one short sharp jerk, and his lips thin out. Levon nods, grins.

"Yes? Okay, Casey. Anytime you're ready."

"One last thing, though?" says Casey.

"Yeah? What?" says Tony, now with a slight eye tic.

"Who says it's a misdemeanor?"

Tony takes a breath, speaks as if reciting a prayer.

"Consensual sodomy is a class B misdemeanor. Read the code, lady. No court in this town will bother with it."

"How old are you?"

"What? I'm . . . twenty-nine."

Casey noticed that Tony had knocked a couple of years off his age. It made her smile. He's in the back of a police car, he's going down for a felony kidnap charge, he's going to be in Attica or Ossining until Jesus gets a decent haircut, and he still has the idea that knocking a year or two off his age is a good public relations move. Ladies and gentlemen, please observe one Tony Lo-Gascio. Your complete criminal moron.

"So that's not a class B misdemeanor, then," says Levon. "It would be okay if you were, like, eleven years old."

"But you're not, are you?" says Casey. "At least not physically."

Tony's face muscles convulse. He looks pained. Thinking hurts.

"I don't get it. What are you saying?"

"Two-Pack," says Casey, the soul of patience, "is sixteen years old. Sixteen. Under Section 130.40 of the penal code, having consensual sodomy with a person less than seventeen years of age is in fact a class E felony, unless the perp is also underage, which you're not, and so it could get you a year in jail. And you've been popped under 130 a couple of times already, as well as— What is it, Officer Jamal? You got the sheet."

Levon makes a ceremony out of reading the LoGascio menu.

"Let's see . . . Section 220.46, criminal injection of a narcotic, 221.35, criminal sale of marijuana, *and* a big hit under 120.11, aggravated assault of a police officer—"

"That was dropped!"

"That was plea-bargained, as they usually are, Tony. So they still count as felony beefs. Anyway, add to all that this beef for Section 130 and you start to look like a Section 400 of the CPL. Persistent violent felony offender."

"I got suspended sentences on some of that shit."

Casey smiled sweetly at Tony.

"Section 70.06, Paragraph B3 of the code, even suspended sentences apply. You're still a predicate felony offender. So either way you're going away for a long—

Hey, are you okay there? You look all of a sudden kind of all pale and clammy. You want we should get you some water or something?"

"I'm okay. Jesus! No . . . hey. I'm fine. I'm . . . God*damn*! That little son of a bitch!"

"Yeah," said Levon, shaking his head. "Who knew?"

Tony LoGascio now began to look on the world as a very different place than he had imagined it to be, a place filled with duplicity and double dealing and faithless friends. Casey saw this inner change being manifested mainly as a slight greening under LoGascio's milk-white skin, concentrated chiefly under his jaw and around his eyes. Although work in the Sex Crimes Unit was nasty and brutal, every now and then it handed you a moment like this, and she was enjoying it very much.

RIVEREDGE PARK
KINDERHOOK, NEW YORK
1800 HOURS

Jack Vermillion and Earl Pike met again that same evening in a tourist park on the east side of the Hudson. The sun was much lower now and shadows were crossing the water. When Jack pulled in, Pike's big blue Mercedes 600 was already there. He noticed it had a broken left front headlamp and there was a scrape on the fender. Other than that, it was a mint vehicle, shining like a sapphire. Pike was standing at the river's edge, looking out at the opposite shore.

He turned and waited as Jack parked his black Cobra.

"Mr. Vermillion. That's a very fine vehicle. A real Shelby?"

"Yes. It's a nice ride. Look, can you do me a favor?"

"Sure."

"Can you take off your suit jacket?"

Pike frowned, and then his face cleared.

"You think I'm wired?"

"It occurred to me."

Pike took off his jacket. Under the pale-blue shirt, heavy muscles slithered and rippled. The man was built like an armored car. He patted his chest and thumped his flat belly twice, gave Jack a twisted smile.

"You want the shirt off, too?"

"Never mind. How about you tell me what you have in mind?"

Pike nodded and sketched out the details. The collection was already inside a sealed container, sitting in a freight yard in Oswego. One of Jack's truckers could pick it up as soon as Pike made the call. Jack would then ship the container by one of his river barges down the Hudson to the Red Hook Container Terminals in Brooklyn, to his freight storage yard there. From the Red Hook Terminal it would be transferred—still under a customs bond supplied by Jack's brokers—onto a freighter at the Jersey docks and take a seaboard route to Merida, on the Gulf of Mexico.

Upon the safe transfer of the container to the freighter, and as soon as the freighter reached international waters, Jack would receive $250,000 in negotiable instruments, delivered by Federal Express to a destination of his choosing. Jack listened, his face getting harder by the second.

"So we're clear on one thing, anyway. You're definitely offering me a bribe to ship this . . . collection?"

Pike gave him a stony look.

"This is an administrative fee. Standard practice. Maybe I should ask *you* to take off your jacket."

"I'm not wired. I'm confused."

"Don't be confused."

"I called Dave Fontenot."

"And?"

"He knows you. Says you're in the security business."

Pike reached into his shirt pocket and extracted a card, handed it to Jack.

CRISIS CONTROL SYSTEMS

CORPORATE CRISIS MANAGEMENT SERVICES

EARL V. PIKE, COL., U.S. ARMY (RET.)

"What does this mean?"

"What it says. CCS is an association of retired military professionals. We handle negative operational developments for a range of corporations across the United States, South America, Europe."

"Negative operational developments?"

"Kidnappings. Breaches of site security. Intellectual property protection. Civil unrest that affects a branch plant. Anything that a corporation wouldn't want handled by a federal agency. Anything that requires a tactful and extremely low-profile solution. Situations that the corporation wouldn't like to have tossed around on CNN."

"What's the V stand for?"

Pike didn't get it at once, and then he smiled.

"Varus. My father was a military historian."

"Didn't Varus lose his eagles?"

"Yes. To the Germans. My father fought in the Second World War. He thought it would be a cautionary reminder."

"The shipment. Why not use your own connections?"

"I did. I used Dave Fontenot."

"You do work for Chase?"

"I'm not in a position to confirm or deny that."

"So I'm still confused. Why run the risk of doing

business with me this way? The 'administrative fee'? The secrecy? You must know how to move . . . goods . . . without asking for help from a stranger."

"I don't care to involve my firm in this matter. My collection is a purely personal matter. I'm asking you because Dave Fontenot said you were a solid guy, you went your own way, had the balls I was looking for. Maybe he was wrong."

Jack watched his face. The guy was angry, but for some reason he was working hard to hold his temper. It made no sense to Jack. Here was a man with connections, a man who knew how to slip-slide down the back roads. Why was he working so hard to sell Jack on this stunt? Maybe Pike saw the look.

"Enough of this, okay? I'm being a pain. I'll tell you something I didn't think I'd have to say. I talked to one of Frank Torinetti's people about you. Guy named Carmine DaJulia."

Jack failed to hide the effect this had on him.

Pike watched him.

"How do you know Frank?"

"I don't. We know the same people, that's all. I helped Carmine with a problem in Central America. We had a good business relationship. Carmine mentioned that Frank has a firearms collection of his own. Carmine had a word with him, your name came up, among some others. You were first on my list. That's why I'm here today."

Jack was completely rocked and tried not to show it. But Earl Pike could read a man, and he spoke again more softly.

"Look, Jack . . . let's start fresh. I'm just a man trying to preserve a degree of personal freedom in the face of an intrusive firearms policy. I gotta tell you, as a man who knows them well, the feds mean none of us any good. They're screwing with gun owners today. Next week it could be you. Whoever gets their attention, whoever looks like they can be skinned alive to entertain the voters. I believe with all my heart that this government has become an enemy of the people. But that's not your problem. Not yet, anyway. The fee I was offering was merely a recognition of the enhanced service level I was asking for. If I expect you to maintain a degree of confidentiality concerning this shipment, then I should be prepared to compensate you for the extra work entailed. It's crazy that you see this as a bribe. You don't hit me as a guy into melodrama."

"Getting my corporate charter revoked isn't melodrama."

Pike nodded and let out a long breath.

"I see your point. I was trying to transport a firearms collection that is important to me, a collection the Pike family has spent six generations gathering together. People in my family died for some of these pieces, or in the getting of them, in places like Ciudad Juarez, Gettysburg, Belleau Woods, the Falaise Pocket, the Reservoir, LZ Bitch, Co Roc. I was a soldier, like my father and his father, all the way back. Two hundred years. That's what our family does. We soldier. How does the nation repay us? I have to get my collection out of the country just to keep it together. I don't want to see this inheritance— this blood gift from my ancestors—grubbed up or sold on the sly to ATF insiders or lost in a federal warehouse like Kane's wooden sleigh. My friend in Merida will cherish it. And I'd be happy for the money, to be honest. The collection is worth millions. And perhaps the relief from the burden. I have no . . . family . . . anymore. There's no one left in my line. I have to hand it on somehow. I admit this issue of my collection is irrational, emotional. I'm being a pest. I'll say good-bye."

Pike offered his hand and seemed ready to walk away.

Jack didn't take it.

"I'm not saying I won't do the work."

"What are you saying?"

"I suppose I'm saying I resent the offer of a personal fee."

"Then don't take it. I have already apologized for insulting you. Does this mean you'll consider the shipment?"

Jack said nothing for almost a minute. Pike waited in silence and showed no impatience in the waiting. He was a very self-possessed man. Finally Jack nodded.

"Yes. I'll consider it."

"I'll be in touch with you then? About the details?"

"Yes. But no 'administrative fee.' Understand?"

"Understood."

He offered his hand. Pike suddenly beamed at him like a boon companion. They shook on it. Jack watched him drive away, fired up his Cobra, picked up his cellular, thought about it, and two minutes later called Creek Johnson from a pay phone at an ARCO station a little outside Ravenna.

Creek picked up his cell phone on the fifth ring.

"Damn, Jackson—I got a ball hanging on the lip of the cup here. I get a good crosswind, that sucker's in for a birdie."

"It's a Mexican ball."

"What's that mean?"

"It needs one more revolution."

"I like that. Is it yours?"

"Creek, I gotta run something by you."

"Now?"

"Now."

"Okay. We're on the sixteenth. Meet me at my place. I'll cook up some steaks. Bring me one of your good old reds from out of that vault you got."

"What's this? A date?"

"One of the good ones, okay? Don't be bringing me none of that Sonoma crap. Frog's Leap or whatever. I want something French."

"I will. Creek, be alone, okay? No naked dental technicians in the swimming pool this time."

"You sound a tad intense, Jackson. Is this serious?"

"Yes. I think it's serious."

"I'll be there. Alone."

GREENWICH VILLAGE
NEW YORK CITY
1830 HOURS

They let Tony LoGascio think about the unpredictability of street life for an hour, sitting in the back of the cruiser while Levon went to a White Castle and got them all some burgers. While he was gone, Casey refused to respond to any conversational openers from LoGascio. Let him cook awhile longer.

Levon came back and handed LoGascio a burger and a Coke and they all ate in a heavy silence. When they were through, Levon gathered up the wrappers and tossed them, then climbed back into the cruiser. Tony was staring at his half-eaten burger with the look of an honest and good-hearted man deeply wounded by a trusted friend.

"So, now what?" said Levon, watching Tony LoGascio jump at the sound of his voice and go through more color changes than Michael Jackson.

"Now," said Casey, "we Mirandize Hopalong here and—"

Tony bounces off the seat.

"Wait a minute. Wait!"

Casey shook her head sadly.

"Too late. Can't wait. What you don't appreciate is, you get to stop talking and we read you your own personal rights. Officer Jamal, be my guest and read Mr. LoGascio his very own personal and totally custom-fitted rights."

"Thank you, Officer Spandau. It will be my pleasure. Mr. LoGascio? Listen up. You have the right to remain silent and refuse to answer questions. Do you understand?"

"I want to talk to the DA. I know some shit. Serious, heavy shit. We can do a deal. Listen to me."

"Now, if you plan to talk about some other crime," says Casey, "and I say this to you very sincerely, you keep it to yourself. Just answer the Miranda question. Now . . . anything you say may be used against you in a court of law. You follow this?"

"Yes."

"You have the right to consult an attorney and to have an attorney present during questioning. You understand?"

"Yeah, but—"

"Let the record show," says Levon, "that the subject replied in the affirmative."

"What's the charge? What am I charged with?"

"Like we said, sodomy with a minor, Section 130.40. Let us finish here, please? I lose track easy. If you cannot afford an attorney, we'll pay for one for you. If an attorney is not available, you have the right to remain silent until you can talk to one. You following? It's very important, Tony. Try to focus."

"Look . . . we can work this out. I can—"

"Shut up," said Levon. "Please? Now, Tony LoGascio, you have been advised of your rights. Do you want to answer questions at this time?"

"About what? No. I want a lawyer."

"Got anybody in mind?" asked Casey.

"No—yes. Maybe. I don't know. Shit."

"Okay, relax, we'll get you one at the station."

"This sucks, you know? This is wrong, what you're doing."

"Life is just one big Shop-Vac," said Casey. "But there's an upside. You get job skills training. Hell, by the time you get out of Sing Sing, you'll be able to suck-start a leaf blower. Shall we proceed, Officer Jamal?"

"Wait," says Tony. "There's gotta be something we can do here!"

"What's that, Tony? Not a thing, Tony. Now, you asked for a lawyer. Once you do that, there's nothing we got to say to each other. Nothing we can do. Out of our hands. We can't even ask you what day it is. Once you say that magic *lawyer* word, the whole thing runs on automatic pilot."

"I want a plea bargain. I can give you both of them."

"A plea bargain?" Casey shakes her head. "We can't discuss a plea bargain. We can't even *hint* at a plea bargain. To do so would be very wrong. Am I right, Officer Jamal?"

"It would be very wrong, Officer Spandau. It would be, like, totally wrongfully wrong. It would be . . . egregious."

"Egregious?" said Casey, raising an eyebrow.

Levon nodded.

"Egregious," he said again, savoring each syllable. It came out as "a-gree-juss." Casey fought against an outright laugh. In the meantime, Tony LoGascio's cup of sorrows ran over the brim. His voice reached a sort of strangled soprano squeal. Down the block, lapdogs were sitting up and cocking their pointy little heads. Bats became disoriented and flew into walls all along Gansevoort. Goldfish rolled over and died in their goldfish bowls. Casey watched with interest as a large purple vein began to bulge along the left side of

LoGascio's throat. It looked extremely promising. Casey hoped he'd have a massive stroke or at least pop a vasectomy clip.

"Rocco and Benno. I can take you right to them."

Casey shakes her head. She's baffled.

"Rocky and Bullwinkle? Don't know them. Never heard of them. I think I'm deaf. Let's go, Officer Jamal. Let's *roll* here. I need something more complicated than burgers. I'm thinking, after we drop Tony here in the shit, we go someplace nice, have some chorizos and ribs."

"I'm sick of chorizos, Officer Spandau. I am sick of all that Latin food. How about that place up at Third and Twenty-eighth? Jai-Ya something?"

"Now, Officer Jamal, you know very well that's Thai food. I hate that Oriental shit. Peanut shells in a gunpowder sauce. Dead leaves in a soup looks like an oil spill. Biscuits made out of bug bits."

Tony LoGascio now lost it. Officially.

"Look, willyajustwaitaminute? Willya just listen?"

"Your trouble there, Officer Spandau," says Levon, "is you never want to try anything new."

"They're brothers. The Scarpas. The Scarpa brothers!"

"I do *so*, Officer Jamal, I tried that Le Pesca dinkadoo place, off Prince there? Cost us a fortune and the food should have been served in an evidence bag. It's not that I don't want *new*, it's that I— Tony, will you shut the hell up? We're trying to plan a dinner here!"

"Christ, Officers, willya wait! *They* did it."

Casey shrugs, turns around to look at Tony in the backseat.

"Okay, Tony. You win. Who did it?"

"The *Scarpa* brothers. They did the thing!"

"*What* thing? Tony, what the heck *are* you going on about? I thought we were talking about your Section 130 beef. What are *you* talking about here? Make sense, okay? I'm hungry. Here you are, running off at the mouth about some Scarpa *thing*."

"In Harlem. The Shawana Coryell thing. I can give you those guys. They both did her. All I did was bag the little bitch."

Casey gives Levon a thin-lipped smile.

"Nice," says Levon, and he nods. "Very nice."

Casey Spandau gives him a prim little head bow.

"Thank you," she says.

Then a short pause.

"Egregious?"

"It pays to increase your word power," said Levon.

UNIVERSITY PARK TOWERS

ALBANY

1930 HOURS

Creek's top-floor condo in the University Park Towers had a huge terrace that overlooked the tree-covered grounds of the State University of New York at Albany. His suite was all white, with polished hardwood floors and a dark-gray marble gas fireplace. The massive kitchen was full of stainless-steel appliances and lit by halogen pots recessed into a polished copper ceiling. The overall look was accidental minimalist, because Creek didn't have too much in the way of furniture right now. His last girlfriend, a Lufthansa flight attendant named Zutzie, had made off with every last stick about a month ago, shortly after she had found a pair of shell-pink thong panties stuffed into the hip pocket of a pair of Creek's golfing slacks. Needless to say, not hers.

A few days later Creek had come back from a hectic weekend in Bermuda with a chakra manipulation therapist named Aurora Moonbeam and found the place completely bare except for his circular waterbed, which had been expertly gutted with a steak knife.

Creek knew it was done with a steak knife because Zutzie had left it sticking up out of a sodden tangle of black satin sheets. Zutzie had also hacked into Creek's Schwab.com account and shorted the Vancouver Stock Exchange and loaded him up with flaky dot-com futures on a lunatic margin call. Then she posted his e-mail address on a kiddie-porn site, unplugged the freezer, jammed his Cartier tank watch into the Cuisinart, poured bleach into his tropical fish tank, injected Krazy Glue into the frontdoor lock, and, as she was leaving, called an automated time-and-date service in Kyoto and left the line open. That was on Thursday night. Creek had come back late Monday afternoon. He had walked around the empty apartment awhile, and then he picked up the phone and listened to a sexy female voice speaking Japanese to him. Whatever she was saying, it grew rather repetitive, and he put the phone down after a few minutes.

Creek's relations with women were complex.

The sun was two fingers above the horizon by the time Jack let himself in and came out through the French doors onto the terrace. He found Creek by the rooftop pool, poking at the flaring coals inside the bowl of a huge Weber barbecue. He was still in his golf clothes and was wearing an apron that read KISS ME, I'M DELU-SIONAL.

He saw Jack coming, pulled a chilled Grolsch beer from a silver vase, and tossed it over to him. The evening was soft and warm under a pink-and-lime sky, and cozy yellow lights were blinking on all over the university grounds.

Jack popped the cap on the Grolsch and went over to the telescope Creek had mounted on a tripod by the terrace fence. He checked the view. The telescope was sighted on the window of an apartment block about a half mile away. Through the lens he could see a shimmering image of a group of young women in shorts and tank tops, sitting around on beanbag chairs. They were laughing and drinking from paper cups. A pizza box was open on the floor in front of them, next to a large bottle of white wine. As he watched, a girl emerged from a rear bedroom wearing pale-blue panties and a pink bra and rubbing her hair with a large white towel.

"Jesus, Creek. You're gonna get badly busted one day."

Creek looked up from the coals and grinned.

"They're my science project. Other people have ant farms and nobody objects. My interest in those fabulous young babes is purely anthropological. I may write a paper. How about the wine? Did you bring me something decent, you cheap dago bastard?"

Jack handed him a brown bag. Creek pulled the bottle of wine out and inspected the label.

"Mount Rat Shit. Excellent. Well done, Jackson. Pull up a pew and observe. I am performing a sacrament for carnivores here."

He had two thick sirloins on the grill. The scent was sharp and peppery. Onions and mushrooms were simmering on a side griddle. His face was bright and his eyes were watery from the charcoal smoke. Jack felt a sudden pang of real hunger.

Creek worked in silence for a while and they both watched a television on the edge of the swimming pool, the sound muted. A female news droid was talking rapidly, eyes bright, her lips working around a soundless crisis. A school picture flashed on, this little black girl, and the cut line *Kidnap in Harlem*. Then the screen jumped and another media zombie, a male this time, was pointing to a street map of Jerusalem and utilizing his Flexo-Feelings Model XD331 Frowny Face to communicate Serious Concern blended with Heartfelt Compassion.

Jack picked up the remote and clicked the set off. The visual silence was oddly soothing. He watched Creek work for a while and sipped at his Grolsch. Creek had good moves, a way of going about his business with calm and grace. Creek flipped the steaks carefully and then sat down on a deck chair beside Jack. He leaned back, raised a glass of the Montrachet, and sipped it with real enjoyment. There was a short silence while the two of them relaxed in the evening wind and watched the high clouds shining. After a minute Creek pushed Jack's knee with his sandal.

"Okay, Jackson. Tell Uncle Raleigh."

Jack sighed, looked at Creek for a while, and then laid out the entire conversation with Earl V. Pike, including the reference to the "administrative fee" and the call he made to Dave Fontenot to check Pike out.

"And Dave said he was a straight guy?"

"Yeah. Said he was in corporate security. I think Pike did some work for Chase, but Dave wouldn't admit to it."

"And neither did this Pike character?"

"He said he could neither confirm nor deny."

Creek looked at the business card.

"Crisis Control Systems. This Pike seem like a hard guy?"

"Machined in Dusseldorf and delivered in a crate."

"Legit military?"

"Oh yeah."

"Ours or somebody else's?"

"He said he worked Thunder Road."

"Out of Ahn Khe?"

"Didn't say. But it sounds like air cav to me."

"Those mutts. I'd watch him on that basis alone. You figure he knows who you know? Maybe that's where he got the idea. Some of your old Astoria street stickball buddies are into this kind of thing."

"Pike said he talked to Carmine DaJulia."

Creek was stunned into silence.

"Did Frank call you personally, tell you about this guy?"

"No. Neither did Carmine. Maybe I should call him."

Creek shook his head.

"Jackson. You're at this very moment trying to commission a Wall Street investment bank to pump up the pension plan and totally restructure your employee benefits package. If you have any contact with Frank or Carmine or any of his guys and it comes out in an SEC background check—which it will—there goes your deal with Galitzine Sheng and Munro and maybe worse. You follow?"

"So what do I do?"

Creek sipped at the wine and studied Pike's card.

"Jackson, my advice?"

"I'm not here for a lesson in covert surveillance."

"Put this Pike deal down gently and slowly back away. When you're about a mile out, turn your back and jog briskly into the rising sun. That's what I'd do. What I do wonder about?"

"What?"

"I wonder why you didn't just tell him to insert and twist as soon as he brought up the bribery shit. I know you, Jackson. You're a prideful rascal. If they still had duels, you'd have to wear a bell."

They heard a distant rumble and watched as a jetliner flew across the evening sky at thirty thousand feet. Sunlight glinted off the fuselage and the vapor trail sparkled and spread out like crystals behind a glass-cutter.

Soft music was floating up from the park, girls laughing, and the rolling racket of kids on skateboards.

Jack set the Grolsch bottle down and reached for another.

"So?" said Creek, lifting an eyebrow.

"You don't really want to know."

"Jackson, I had a date tonight. She's a lit major at McGill. It was a chance to have an orgasm with someone else in the room. I could have a half-naked lit major frolicking in the pool right now. She was a deconstructionist too. You know how nuts they are. But no, I called it off, and now here I am with you. So either you amuse me with your feckless numb-nuts entanglements or you get yourself into the master bedroom and prepare yourself."

"Danny."

"Danny? You mean Streak, the Lizard Boy?"

"I mean Danny, my son."

Creek was silent for another thirty seconds.

"Oh, jeez. Mary and Joseph too. Speak no more, Jackson. Let me guess. No, let me . . . infer. You figure this Pike guy, he's up to something . . . nefarious. Something illegal. And in what passes for a working cortex inside that vast echoing chamber where a normal human would have an actual brain, a tiny lever popped and a little spring went *bing* and there you were with the following thought: Well, by neddie-jingo, I'll just rat this Pike guy out to the feds—set up a sting of some sort—and then the feds will return the favor and get my reptilian little offspring out of Lompoc, where he just happens to be spending a richly deserved five-to-fifteen for assorted butt-wad offenses under the federal narcotics and armed robbery laws. Do I infer correctly?"

"I would never say 'by neddie-jingo.' And it sounded better when I was thinking it."

"Jackson, do you have a clear mind?"

"Reasonably."

"Then let's review. I am going to walk away and turn the steaks and jab away briskly at the onions in a master-chef-like manner, and while I do that you are going to sit quietly and do your best to remember the salient details of your life with Janice. I'll give you six minutes. You can skip the sex scenes, which ought to leave you with about ten full days to cover in depth. Focus mainly on what a wild-ass totally unredeemable lying sack of Dippity-Do she was, and then do some short-term comparative analysis of the nine hundred different ways in which Streak the Lizard Boy managed to surpass her in almost every area covered by the seven deadly sins. And we won't even get into the massive and possibly terminal consequences of embarrassing Frank or Carmine by fucking with one of their business associates. Okay? Pencils ready? Begin now. When I come back, I expect you to have achieved a cognitive epiphany."

"A cognitive epiphany?"

"A Gestalt. A revelation. Seen the light. If you have not done so by the time I return, I will strike you."

"Strike me?"

"Like a gong."

CENTRAL BOOKING
CENTRE STREET
MANHATTAN
2035 HOURS

Casey and Levon took Tony LoGascio to Central Booking at One Police and got a public defender for him. When Casey and Levon last saw him, he was in an interview room talking in a hoarse and panicky whisper with his PD, a mook named Eddie Rubinek, a reedy-looking pencil-neck with a felony haircut and a goatee beard that came over like a brown mold on his pinched little face and a clipboard with a Greenpeace sticker on the back. Rubinek was also wearing black socks with floppy brown Birkenstock sandals, one of the secret recognition signals of the Global Brotherhood of Stalinist Nimrods Everywhere. This was a portent.

Then Casey and Levon drove back up to the Two Five and Casey ran the names Rocco and Benno Scarpa on FINEST, the department's own computer database, and got color prints, full-face and profile, of Rocco and Benito Scarpa, a pair of genetically challenged louts with ragtag brown hair and bad skin, Rocco—Rocky to his friends—sporting a mandarin mustache and a wispy goatee, Benno balding with long stringy hair hanging over his ears and a comb-over that would make Homer Simpson cringe.

Both mutts had been popped for various misdemeanors, ranging from small-time drugs to theft and attempted armed robbery, as well as a recent charge of forcible confinement and sexual assault—dropped because the thirteen-year-old victim refused to testify—hence the recent photos. They were both, to say the least, ugly as star-nosed moles, and the only way either one of them would have qualified for a real live date with a willing adult female would have been to take up goat-herding in the Basque country.

Casey also got a current address, on Tinton Street in the South Bronx, which turned out to be a slate-rock dive not far from Mary's Park. The Scarpa brothers were lounging around in their shorts, slugging Thunderbird from a Tupperware container, passing a soggy spliff as big as a mackerel back and forth, and watching old *Mr. Rogers* programs on a hotwired DVD, when the door slammed open and Casey Spandau, Levon Jamal, and three other bulls from Sex Crimes exploded into the room like some sort of ugly mass hallucination. Rocco giggled out loud and Benno blinked at them for a couple of seconds before he was airborne in the grip of a highly pissed-off Casey Spandau and the rat-skin-gray shag rug on the floor was racing up at his face like an incoming asteroid.

As a part of the arrest procedure, Casey and Levon turned the Scarpa flat upside down and found a pair of bloody underpants stuck between the box spring and the mattress. Covered in little purple dinosaurs, they exactly matched the description of Shawana Coryell's underwear, part of the clothing list obtained from her aunt at the time of the kidnapping.

A field kit check showed semen stains mixed with the blood, and similar stains on the mattress itself. The Crime Scene Unit came in to do a complete workup on the secondary scene, and, barring a major screw-up, it looked like Casey Spandau and Levon Jamal had nailed three pederast sons-of-bitches to the main gate in Attica. So, at the end of the day, sweet victory? Not exactly.

Enter Euphonia Shabazz.

EASTBOUND I-90

ALBANY

2145 HOURS

Jack agreed with Earl Pike about his black Shelby Cobra; it was a hell of a ride. He liked the smell of the black leather interior, the simplicity of the analog tachometer, the honest brutality of the 427 turbo, the sound it made when cruising, a kind of muted growling purr. It was a head-turner, and Jack wasn't fond of attention, but the car was such a classic it was worth the distraction. It was one of the few things in his life that gave him unqualified satisfaction, and he was damn well keeping it.

He had on a CD, *Mule Variations,* by Tom Waits. The traffic around him was light and the downtown core of Albany glimmered softly in a heat haze. The interstate was smooth and he was rolling through it in an easy snaking line. When he crossed the Hudson into Rensselaer his tires drummed on the bridge deck, a syncopated booming reverberation that reminded him of his Huey, and thinking about his Huey made him think again about Creek's bleak view of Jack's ex-wife and his feckless kid. The trouble was, Creek was probably dead-right about both of them.

Pensacola Naval Air Station, back in 1966. She worked as a clerk in the base dry-cleaning shop. She said her name was Janice Cullitan. Creek used to say she probably wasn't allowed to tell her real name to potential victims. When she was on the hunt, she was quite a package, and covered the ground like a cat going down a drainpipe. Made love like one, too; upside down and sideways, she always knew where the ground was and how far to the door. She had perky little breasts that she had puppy names for. Jack could never remember which was which, and that bugged her. She talked baby talk during sex, and it still pained him that he used to like it. But the game had no goal line as far as he was concerned. It was just R-and-R in a precombat DMZ. He hadn't really given the future much thought because, as a jar-head grunt bound for Vietnam, he probably didn't have one. But Janice had an eye for quality and it had been love at first bite for her. If Jack made it through the war, Janice was sure he'd do something nice and profitable after it, and she wanted to be around for the cast party. She had all four fangs six inches deep in his carotid by the time he boarded the carrier for Three Corps, Republic of Vietnam.

He had written her a few times during the early months of his war and heard very little back from her, unless the Corps had screwed up his pay deposits. The first year in-country, after he'd been working as a crew chief on an extraction Huey—where he first met Creek—he'd caught a shrapnel fragment in his right knee and they sent him back to Pensacola for a rest and refit.

Janice rode him hard and put him away wet for six days straight, and each time they made love he lost a few more points off his IQ. By the time he left for Vietnam again, he was lucky to be able to tie his boots and respond to simple hand signals in exchange for a cube of sugar. Maybe that was why he never noticed that a lot of the REMFs—the rear-echelon motherfuckers—around Pensacola had practically no IQs at all, but seemed real happy in spite of it. It took him months to figure out that Janice was what you'd call these days fidelity-challenged. Their next meeting was a long while later; he'd been three years in-country, mainly flying Huey gunships out of Soc Trang with Creek Johnson, and Otts, and Gorman, and Jack Vermillion was not the same nice kid he'd been in 1966.

By the time they eventually split up, after a few more years of cheap red wine and heart-to-heart combat, Janice, until then childless, had presented him with a baby boy—Christ, but he had been a lovely one too, with huge brown eyes and a scent like dry hay and his breath on the back of Jack's hand warm and feathery— and Janice, hand on the place where a normal woman would have kept her soul, assured him that the child was truly his, swear to God.

Now and then it occurred to Jack that if he'd just killed her right at the start, he'd be out of prison by now.

Well, he hadn't, and the kid was his punishment. Whoever his daddy was, and maybe it *was* Jack, there was no doubt at all who his mother was.

They named him Danny, and yes he was a beautiful-looking child, but Christ, he seemed to be a bad-hearted little thing right out of the chute, and Jack's biggest fear in the later years was that Danny—not Streak, that was Creek Johnson's name for the boy—was only really happy when something small and furry was coughing up blood in a corner.

But the boy was his responsibility and Jack loved him as hard as he could. He was all the boy had, since Janice had finally bailed out on both of them when Danny was seven.

For some reason, maybe his Catholicism, Jack had never legally divorced Janice, so for years she had cruised into and out of their lives like a bad-luck comet, staying a few days, leaving radio static and bad weather in her wake, taking a purseful of cash and whatever else she could lever out of Jack, using Danny as the crowbar. Jack felt that Janice was the kind of mother who could damage the best of kids, and he had tried to be patient with Danny.

Jack had given fatherhood everything he had. Danny got the best schools Jack could afford, a different one almost every year, lots of athletics, work on the docks right alongside his daddy. He made sure that Danny stayed clear of the sons of his old friends, most of whom were already in crime and studying for their button-man finals. It was Jack's intention that Danny would become a full partner in Black Water Transit Systems as soon as he got himself straight.

Jack pumped so much positive affirmation and self-esteem into the kid, it was a wonder he hadn't exploded like an overheated spud. But Danny had a magnetic attraction for personal disasters, and in the latter years of their association his disaster *du jour* was drugs. Situations like this are what they call around the precinct "red-lined and ticking," and to nobody's surprise but Jack's, it all blew up one day when Jack found Danny in the Black Water Transit warehouse down in Red Hook, sitting next to a set of propane tanks, holding a Marine Corps Zippo lighter that Jack had thought he'd lost years ago.

Danny had it lit and was holding a spoon over it. He had a length of rubber tubing around his right elbow. When Jack walked in on him, first he saw the needle, then he saw a look in his son's eyes—those soft brown eyes that had once been so strong a pull on Jack that he stayed in a bad marriage just to be around them—well, that broke his heart. It took a couple of the dockworkers to drag Jack off his son, and the kid had spent two days in a Brooklyn hospital recuperating.

When Jack had gone to visit him the bed was empty. Danny was gone. So was the Day-Glo orange Camaro that Jack had leased for him. The next afternoon he got a call from a Key Bank branch in Passaic, a man he knew slightly, asking him about a check that had been presented for cash, made out to a Danny Vermillion, had Jack's signature on it. The manager recognized the name from other business with Jack and felt that the signature seemed shaky. Jack asked him how much.

Twenty-four thousand seven hundred and sixty-seven. And sixty cents.

One thousand for every year of Danny's life. He had probably thrown in the seven hundred and change to make the check look more plausible. Was Danny Vermillion there in the manager's office? He was. Did Jack want to talk to him? Yeah, he did.

But Danny refused. Jack could hear his voice over the

phone, a slate whine like somebody taking the rust off steel. The manager came back, asked Jack, what about the check?

It's good, he said. Give him the money.

Next time he heard from Danny it was indirectly, a call that was being made for him by a vice squad detective in Los Angeles, wanted to know if he'd take a call from a Danny Vermillion.

Jack accepted the call, listened to a series of bullshit excuse scenarios that were so poorly constructed they were an insult to criminal assholes everywhere, and then refused to send the bail, thinking a beef for cocaine possession would teach Danny a life lesson. And it did. It taught him to be more ambitious.

The next call was a year later, two weeks ago last Friday, from the prison clinic in Lompoc Correctional. The call came in after eleven at night. Jack had been sitting in the dark in the living room of his house in Rensselaer, listening to a Chopin nocturne and working through a bottle of Beringer's gamay. Two weeks later he could still play it back in his head word for word.

"Mr. Vermillion?"

"Yes?"

"Will you accept a collect call from a Daniello Vermillion in Lompoc, California?"

Jack had thought about it for a while. The nocturne floated through the darkened room and the gamay was in his bloodstream and he decided he was up to taking the call.

"Yes."

"Dad . . . it's Danny. Dad, don't hang up! Please!"

At first Jack didn't believe it really was Danny. He had never heard that quaver in his throat, never heard the panic.

"I won't."

"Please don't! Dad, I gotta get out of here. There's a

guy here, he's . . . he's trying to . . . I can't shake him. The guards won't help. I can't get him off me. I'm in isolation for another three weeks, but after that—"

"Why are you in isolation?"

"I cut myself. Cut my throat. Deep. I used a piece of sheet metal from the shop floor. I had to do something. I'm back in general population by the middle of July. There's no way I can take this guy. He's a freak with La Eme. They run the yard. Dad, you have to do something. I can't be a punk. I can't let that happen. I'd be better dead. I'll kill myself before I go back to gen pop. I swear, Dad. Please help me."

"Danny . . . I'll try. What can I do? I'll call the warden."

"That'll just make me a snitch. Don't call him. I can go to detox down in Fresno. I already asked my worker. They can do it, but they gotta have a recommendation for a transfer to medium security. My worker's a lady named Lucy Carillo-Vega. She's got it all set up. If you can get somebody in the Bureau of Prisons in DC to call her—"

"How can I make that happen, Danny? I don't know—"

"Fuck, Dad. You're a huge corporation. You gotta know somebody in Albany. Dad, I know I don't deserve any help. I know I've been . . . I know what I am. But I can change. Man, I can change. I had no fucking clue, but now, Dad, this place . . . Dad, please try!"

"Danny, I—"

"Dad. I gotta go. Dad . . . I love you. I gotta go!"

"Don't hang up."

"I gotta. Somebody's waiting. I can't hog the line. They shank you for that. I gotta go now. Do something fast, Dad. Please!"

Then he was gone.

Dad. Please help me.

But there was nothing Jack could do. Danny was in Lompoc for trafficking and weapons possession and attempted armed robbery. He would be in Lompoc for—at the least—ten more years.

Jack tried all the levers. Nothing worked. A state attorney in Albany explained it over a whisky sour. Jack had nothing to *trade*. Deals were always possible. If Jack wanted a medium-security bunk for the kid, maybe get him into a detox program, maybe some professional counseling, that could perhaps be done. But the feds would want something in return.

Like what?

The lawyer shrugged, tried to look casual, and said golly, he had no idea. Gee, wait a minute . . . what if? Maybe a lead on a big bust, something that would make the local U.S. attorney happy? That would be good, right? Something that came equipped with major headlines. Something conspiratorial and sexy.

Got anything like that? Jack?

Disarming smile, a sip of his whisky sour, and then he looked quickly away. Jack stared at the side of the man's head in silence and tried to keep his temper under control. The guy knew damn well that Jack had lines into the Italian community, that he knew people who were pulling the usual crimes, but he also knew that there was no proof whatever that Jack was a connected guy. No proof, because he wasn't. Not now. Not then. Not ever.

But around Albany the courthouse sharks were dead-bang certain there was no way a man like Jack Vermillion—a gutter wop from Astoria—could make Black Water Transit such a success without some kind of Mafia backing. How about the way those Teamsters backed off him last year? That had to be Jack's old school buddy, Frank Torinetti, now suspected of being a major figure in the local families. So naturally Jack was a source to be worked. And that wasn't going to happen, not even for Danny. Which meant that, other than being a rat to guys he grew up with, it was pretty clear that Jack Vermillion had nothing to offer the state or the feds by way of ransom for his kid, who, for some reason that Jack could not quite define, even to himself, was still his son, and whom Jack still wanted to protect, if there was any way on earth he could, because you don't throw away family, even if they deserve it, and you don't set a limit on forgiveness, because if you do, the time will come when you'll need it for yourself and it won't be there, because it comes from God, who remembers these sins like a Sicilian remembers an insult.

Danny had called two weeks ago. Jack had contacted his caseworker, Lucy Carillo-Vega, and she had confirmed that Danny was going back into general population next week. Was there anything Jack could do? If he was going to do something, it had to happen soon, she said. Jack had no answer. And then a total stranger named Earl Pike showed up at the Frontenac Hotel, and everything changed.

CENTRAL BOOKING

LOWER MANHATTAN

2150 HOURS

Euphonia Shabazz was actually the Honorable Euphonia Shabazz, known to the cops and the lawyers around Centre Street as the Eight Ball because she was round and shiny and black and had only three answers to any legal question—*yes, no,* and *reply hazy, ask again later.* Judge Shabazz was catching that very same evening when Eddie Rubinek filed an urgent request for dismissal of charges against Tony LoGascio on the grounds that the information provided by his client while in the back of the Sex Crimes DT car was wrongfully obtained under circumstances that constituted a clear violation of New York State's absolute right to counsel.

Ah yes, said Judge Shabazz, opening a yellow eye. She knew of this ruling. The absolute-right-to-counsel provision, known as ARC, states that a suspect may not be questioned until he waives his Miranda rights *in the physical presence of an attorney*.

Furthermore—Eddie Rubinek was a guy who liked to use that word—furthermore, if the suspect is in actual custody, under the control of a police officer and not free to leave of his own volition, then ARC applies for *all* matters and there may be no questioning about anything at all. As a result, information arising from the arrest and interrogation of his client, up to and including information leading to the arrests of the Scarpa brothers, was irrelevant and inadmissible since the information had come during an improper interrogation. Thus to use the information would, in the classic phrase, shock the conscience of the court.

Like there is such a thing. People have things stuck to the bottom of their shoes that have more conscience than a court of law. The law is a machine for processing and canning garbage meat.

Anyway, the assistant district attorney—Veronica Stein herself—comes right back with an impassioned assertion that, according to the records and the testimony of the arresting officers—Casey Spandau and Levon Jamal—LoGascio had *not* been formally arrested, had in fact *volunteered* relevant information about the Coryell kidnapping, and since he had not been charged with any involvement with the Coryell abduction at the time, he had no Miranda rights to waive.

This drew a squawk from Eddie Rubinek, who rose to proclaim that there *was* an accusatory instrument in effect at the time, a charge under Section 130, sodomy with a minor, a class E felony, so the defendant's absolute right to counsel had therefore been violated, and it followed that anything said even under a perception of a Miranda waiver in connection with any other matter did not alter the fact of the ARC violation, so whatever followed, however disconnected from the original charge, was tainted and was therefore absolutely inadmissible on technical grounds.

Nonsense, said the ADA. And even if there had been a violation of LoGascio's Miranda rights, those rights are not considered a constitutional guarantee, are in fact merely a prophylactic device to guard against self-incriminatory statements made involuntarily, and, for that matter, under *Harris v. New York,* the Supreme Court had ruled that even *intentional* violations of Miranda that resulted in inculpatory statements did not render those statements inadmissible.

Fah! observed Mr. Rubinek.

At this point Judge Shabazz leaned forward in her creaking leather chair and spread her hands across the jumble of candy wrappers and legal papers on her desk.

"I've heard enough. I intend to review the *Harris* decision and consider the relevant case law. I will render my decision in this matter in a few . . . in good time." She stopped Rubinek in mid-aria by raising her left hand and showing him a pink palm with stubby fingers spread wide.

"You can wait, Mr. Rubinek. I'll give you my decision in good time. Into the hall with you both."

In other words, *reply hazy, ask again later*. That's why they called her the Eight Ball.

Twenty-six minutes later, after a séance with a Moon Doggie and a Monster Big Gulp down in the cafeteria, Judge Euphonia Shabazz returned to her chambers, called in the combatants, and ruled that the LoGascio information, whatever it might have been, was inadmissible and that anything flowing from that information had therefore been obtained in a clear and *egregious*—that word was definitely making a comeback—violation of the suspect's ARC rights—including the inculpatory evidence obtained at the Scarpas' apartment, the underwear, the forensics—and was, under various loopholes in the Bonehead Justice Machine, totally inadmissible and tainted. As a direct result of this decision, Tony LoGascio and the Scarpa brothers hopped out of the holding cells on Centre Street before nine o'clock that very evening. They scrambled into a gypsy cab, and it was several months before they managed to attract the attention of the NYPD in any memorable way. Mind you, when they did, it was terminal. Now. Observe the following incident.

About an hour later, as he was walking home from the D train exit on Ninth Street, public defender Eddie Rubinek had his lights professionally punched out by an unknown but highly motivated assailant. The only description he was able to give the investigating officers from the Sixth Precinct, and this while sitting on the back steps of an EMS ambulance, talking through a purple face twice normal size and lips that looked like raw Polish sausages, was that she was female and black and built like an artillery shell.

"What millimeter?" asked a cop from the Sixth, a recon vet with four ugly years in Vietnam stuck deep into his ribs, who had early on in this case decided that whatever the victim had to say, he was certainly no judge of anything military and had probably spent the entire Vietnam War up in Toronto smoking ganja and spray-painting stupid Marxist slogans on the sides of public buildings.

"What do you mean?" says Rubinek, looking more than usually snitty. Blood was running from his nose down into his goatee and one of his eyes was puffed and half closed and the eyeball was bright red. He looked like the hand puppet from hell.

The cop sighed and repeated the question.

"You said she looked like a shell. I asked you what size."

Rubinek wiped some blood off his teeth with a swab of cotton and spat blood onto the sidewalk. Some of it hit the cop's boot. Eddie Rubinek was a guy who never knew when to quit. He's still at it, by the way; if you see him around Centre Street, ask him how's his nose. He never gets it. He never will.

Anyway, shortly after the report came in from the Sixth, the CO of the Two Five called the Sex Crimes section and told Casey Spandau to get her butt into his office right now. He then asked her where she had been and if she had anything to say about the incident.

Casey Spandau just sat in the wooden rail-back chair he kept in his office exactly for this purpose and she gives him back that Chinese stare and asks if she could have a member of the NYPD's black police officers association, the Guardians, as a witness to the meeting. The CO looked at her in silence for almost a full minute.

Then he asked her once again, straight out, had she in any way contributed to the thumping-out of Eddie Rubinek? She never broke her stare and never said a word. He fought back a red cloud around the edge of his vision and swallowed hard twice, told himself again that she was worth the effort.

"Spandau, can I ask you a hypothetical?"

"Yes, sir."

"Shawana Coryell is a little white kid and she's scooped by three black guys. Are you still on the case?"

"Yes, sir! Of course. It's not the kid's fault."

"Okay. And instead of Eddie Rubinek we have Johnny Cochran, and Johnny does his usual giant-squid act, sprays sticky black shit all over the courtroom, the jury goes stone-blind, achieves the approximate IQ of bark mulch. Bingo, the perps walk. Are you now waiting for Johnny Cochran outside the D train exit?"

"I firmly believe that O.J. was framed, sir."

"Yeah? So was Jesus Christ, but then he never took Mary Magdalene apart with a Swiss Army knife. Casey, spare me your totally fucked-in-the-head opinions on the Simpson case and answer my damned question."

"To answer that would . . . seem inculpatory, sir."

"Inculpatory! God's holy trousers! Now we got Kennesaw Mountain Clarence goddamn Darrow here. Okay. The Eight Ball is as black as dime-store licorice, Spandau. Does she get tuned-up for being the stupidest judge in Christendom?"

"She should be fired. She's a disgrace to her people."

"Oh man. What color *are* your people, Officer Spandau?"

"What color?"

"Never mind. I'll tell you. Your people are blue. There are thirty-one thousand of them in the city. Everybody else is and will forever be a total goddamn stranger. Now. Did you or didn't you tune-up Eddie Rubinek?"

"Sir, I can't answer that question."

"Why the *hell* not?"

"I . . . any answer I give you . . . would be dishonest."

"Spare me that condescending crap, kid. You know where this will go, don't you? Your badge is in the palm of my hand."

"I know that, sir. I know you have to do what you have to do."

"Spandau, you had the mojo. You could have gone anywhere."

"Thank you, sir. I appreciate that. It means a lot to me."

Then silence. So now what does he do?

He told her go wait in the hall and poured himself a belt of scotch from the bottle he kept in his drawer for occasions like this, when the burden of command got to be an unbearable pain in the neck, and then, after some further consultation with the Chivas, he has this, like, insight. A stroke of genius, he thinks.

He makes a call to One Police, gets a *possible maybe okay* from the personnel drone on the other end of the phone. He sits back in his chair and pops a Zoloft. Then he calls her back in, reads her the riot act from Section 9 of the administrative guide, and tells her to pack her gear and totally un-ass his area of operations in sixty seconds.

"Where to?" she asks, and he's pleased to see she's worried.

"JTF. The Jay Rats."

That stopped her. Casey had never heard of them.

"JTF? What do they do?"

"What it sounds like. Joint task force. They work with state and federal cops on cases that cross jurisdictional lines."

"Like what?"

"This isn't an audition, Casey."

"No. I'm sorry, sir. But . . ."

"Something happens in Poughkeepsie or Newark or Buffalo and a state cop thinks it connects to something going on in New York, he talks to the JTF guys. They help if they can, you follow? It's not complicated."

"Is this . . . you're serious? I'm not suspended?"

He was. She wasn't.

Jay Rats was a unit working out of an unmarked office in the Albee Square Mall over there in darkest Brooklyn. The boss of the Jay Rats is a gold-shield bull by the name of Vincent Zaragosa. The CO of the Two Five figured that if anybody could make a good cop out of Casey Spandau, Vince Zaragosa was the guy.

Casey Spandau lands on Vince Zaragosa's doorstep sixty-four minutes later, carrying a beat-up brown briefcase with a Patrolmen's Benevolent Association sticker on it. Zaragosa was sitting behind his desk—a huge rosewood number with a clipper ship inlaid in blond wood—and looking at her over the top of his gold-rimmed reading glasses. Zaragosa was huge, thick-necked and heavy-shouldered, a battered face and deep-set brown eyes, a nose that took the long way down his face and made two lane changes on the way. He was wearing a gray single-breasted suit and a pale-gray tie over a charcoal shirt. The tie was held in with a gold collar pin. On the ring finger of his right hand a heavy gold detective's ring glittered in the light from a green-glass reading lamp.

Casey sat down in front of him, balanced that pug-ugly briefcase on her lap like it held the secret to the meaning of the universe, and gave Zaragosa her Chinese eyes with her mouth thinned out and her back held so straight he could hear it creaking. Zaragosa took one long weary look at her and got right on the horn to her former CO at the Two Five.

"I got your package. She's here now. She's sitting in front of me. We're making meaningful eye contact. What the fuck am I supposed to do with her?"

He says, "You owe me, Vince."

"I owe you? You sick Irish mutt. For what?"

"Mulberry Street, you dumb guinea fuck."

"Mulberry Street? Where's that?"

"She's a good cop, Vince. I'm trying to keep her on the job."

"What'd she do at your house?"

"She allegedly kicked the living shit out of a PD name of Eddie Rubinek."

"Did he allegedly need it?"

"Desperately. You know the Coryell thing?"

"Yeah. That hers?"

"It was. The PD got them off."

"How?"

"The Eight Ball. Violation of ARC. She bought it."

"So they're back on the street?"

"Tonight. Even as we speak."

"Shit. Spandau likely to do this kind of thing again?"

"Which . . . tune-up a PD, or get caught for it?"

"Either one."

"No. I don't think so. I think she's pretty scared."

"Is she likely to get charged for the Rubinek beef?"

"Not if I can help it."

"You gonna mojo the beef?"

"I won't have to. There's not enough evidence to lay a charge. Don't tell her that. I want her to sweat this out for months."

"I won't. What else is wrong with her?"

"She's got attitude."

"No shit. I can see that from here. See? She's not smiling. I really hate that not-smiling-oppressed-black-woman-Oprah-book-club-my-daddy-was-emotionally-unavailable bullshit."

"She's young, Vince. She'll learn."

There was a long silence. Zaragosa could hear the CO breathing on the other end of the line. He's still making eye contact with Casey Spandau, watching her sit there hugging that stupid brown briefcase into her belly like it was a life preserver and the ship was already hard down by the bow with black ice on the promenade deck. He can see she's trying not to cry. There's no way she actually *will* cry. But the fact that she was close to it, okay, that made the difference for him.

"Okay, you Mick dick. I'm doing this for you. So remember. You owe me. I got just the guy for her."

Zaragosa said a couple more very bad words and hung up and then he slammed Casey directly—right the next thing—no nap—no tea and biscuits—dead-bang into a Jay Rats unit, a stakeout gig in Maspeth, run by this Irish gold shield by the name of Jimmy "Rock" Rule, who happens to be an outstanding street cop, but who is also a very intolerant guy on the issue of *the black thing* and its effect on the hiring and firing policies of the NYPD.

Anyway, here's where it gets weird.

THURSDAY, JUNE 22

HIGHWAY 82 NORTHBOUND

BLUE STORES, NEW YORK

MIDNIGHT

Nicky Cicero is working D watch—six at night to six in the morning—with the Highway Patrol section of the New York State Police. He's got six years in, he's unmarried, a man for the ladies, good-looking in a club-fighter kind of way, with a nice head of shiny black hair and, since he really is a club fighter but not too good at it, a nose pushed a little sideways and some scar tissue around his eyes. He's known around the station as an easygoing troop with a six-second delay, but when you hear the click, you better be elsewhere.

He's rolling west and north along Highway 82 listening to the cross talk on the radio and also listening to a Berlitz tape at the same time. He's going to Italy on a vacation next fall—see the old people in a place called Giarre, in Sicily, and he wants to be able to speak some real Italian to them. Nicky doesn't know there's a big difference between Sicilian and Italian. It got explained to him later, but that's another story.

He's conjugating the "to be" part of *tu sei molto*

bella, ragazzina mia and rolling up a dark stretch of the road when his headlight glare bounces off something that glitters bright glassy-red in a big stand of trees way off in the middle of a wheat field.

He stops the cruiser and moves his roof-rack searchlight. It dances around the woods for a while and he thinks, hey, nothing, a fox eye or a skunk eye or maybe a cat. And then he sees a reflection off a patch of shiny black metal and a section of a license plate. He moves the searchlight and it shows him two crushed-down tracks in the wheat field that start in the wooded area and come all the way back to the edge of the highway.

Or the other way around, right? From here to there. Somebody had a breakdown? But why park the vehicle way off there in the woods? He comes to a complete stop and turns on his roof-rack blue-and-reds. The disco lights bounce off the trees and he sees more reflections coming back from the vehicle. White, scattered, little diamond sparkles. Broken glass on the ground?

He picks up the radio.

"Echo One Four to base."

"Echo One Four?"

"Base, this is Echo One Four. I'm at mile marker three-four northbound on Highway Eighty-two. I'm out of the vehicle to look at a possible MVA here. Give me a time check."

"Ten-four, Echo One Four. Time is zero hour six minutes."

"I can never figure that out, Gracie."

The dispatcher's voice breaks, comes back.

"It's six minutes after midnight, Nicky. Take your portable."

"I don't have one. Pete LeTourneau has it in his lockbox."

"Then be careful."

"Thanks, Gracie. I know you want my body."

"That is so not happening, Nicky. I know where it's been."

He puts the handset away and shuts down the engine, leaving the roof lights churning red and blue. He takes his Maglite and, thinking about it, he also grabs his first-aid kit and some latex gloves. He locks the unit and sets out across the field. It's a starry night, but there's no moon. Maybe a mile away to the south he sees the yellow lights from a farmhouse. Other than that it's dark and still.

Nicky's a New York City kid—born in Far Rockaway—so it's not a happy walk for him. He's maybe twenty yards from the stand of trees when he hears something growling. This upsets him, he can tell, because he's experiencing an involuntary sex change and the air has gotten as thick as motor oil. He puts the Maglite on the trees. He can see a whole section of black tailgate now, and a Jersey plate: IMA DV8. "I'm a deviate"? Cute.

This doesn't help his mood. He thumbs the restraining flap off the butt of his Glock Ten and keeps his right hand on it. The growling is louder now. It's not a growling like a guard dog would make; it sounds different. Involved. Happy. Nicky doesn't want to speculate on what would make an animal like that happy. And there's something else. A tearing sound like something being ripped or tugged at.

"Police," says Nicky. It comes out a bit pinched. "Who's there?"

The growling stops at once. There's a short wait while Nicky listens to nothing hard enough to give himself a migraine, and then he sees a quick motion off to his right.

He lifts out the Glock and covers the area.

"State Police. Stand up and come out. Hands where I can see them. Now!"

Something large and dark bolts out of the wheat field at his right. Nicky jumps, steps back a yard, gets the light back on it, his Glock up and ready. His finger is on the blade. He can feel the serration on the trigger, and the three pale-green tritium dots—two on the foresight, one on the rear—are lined up in a perfect row. Beyond the foresight he sees a dog, some sort of mixed breed, part hound, part alligator. Its eyes catch the light and shine like bright red jewels. It stares back at him, jaws open, panting. There's something dark and sticky-looking all over its muzzle and chest. The dog's fur glistens.

Then it turns and . . . disappears. Nicky listens to the sound it makes as it huffs away through the wheat, a hissing rattle as it pushes through the wheat stalks. In a second he's alone with whatever is in the vehicle under the trees.

He comes up to it, a Jimmy SLT, shiny black, brand-new. The windows are heavily tinted. The passenger window is broken, and shattered glass lies all around in the long grass under the trees. He steps up to the passenger side and puts his light inside the Jimmy.

A young blonde girl is sprawled across the front seats. She's naked. Damaged as well. There's blood on her smooth young belly. Her eyes are open. Nicky puts the light in her eyes. Fixed and dilated. He moves the light onto her neck and sees bruising.

Her neck is . . . wrong.

He slips on his latex gloves, reaches in, and touches her throat under the left side of her jaw, where the muscles join. She's no warmer than the surrounding night. He holds his fingers there long enough to feel the stillness inside her.

This is a crime scene, he decides, and reaches for the

portable that he doesn't have with him. Dammit, he says to himself, and takes a breath to calm himself down, and this is when he catches a scent that reminds him of rust, and he thinks about what was on the dog's muzzle. He steps back away from the vehicle, and the rust smell gets stronger and catches in the back of his throat.

He puts the circle of light on the ground and sees a beaten-down section of long grass leading away from the Jimmy. Twenty feet it runs, into a blackness outside the dim circle of his Maglite, where it disappears into a gap between old and twisted trees. He squats down and studies the marks in the grass. Two people, maybe more. They walked away from the Jimmy in that direction.

Nicky thinks hard about his role in all of this. On the one hand, he's a cop, and this sort of thing is part of the job. On the other hand, he's seen this whole scenario before, and it was always with some opening credits scrolling down in front of it and scary music playing. He's the lone cop in this scene. Everybody knows the lone cop never makes it past the opening credits.

He sighs, gets up, and follows the track into the gap between the trees. He's now in a large clearing, circular, perhaps twenty feet wide. In the glow of the flash he can see a body lying on its back in a section of crushed and flattened grass.

Secondary crime scene, he thinks, and starts to map out all the ways he has moved around the whole sector. He's going to have to explain it to the GIC people when they get here. He moves in, puts the light on the body from six feet away.

A white male, tanned, head shaved. Young, maybe in his twenties. Very muscular, a weight lifter or a pro football player. Wearing a white—now a partly white—tank top. Nude from the waist down. Oh man, thinks Nicky. This is going to be bad.

Nicky steps in closer. The rust smell has another element here, a sewage smell, and a bitter stink of stomach acids. Someone has thrown up here and maybe lost control of their bowels as well. He puts the light on the man's torso.

Below the bloodstained white tank top, the man's belly has been opened up like a piñata, spilling multicolored fruit everywhere. Below the belly there's nothing but a tangled mass of pink and blue and shiny red tissue all the way to the man's lower thighs.

Something—that goddamn gator-dog—has been eating the man from the crotch up. Nicky moves backward, fighting his stomach. There's no way the GIC guys are going to find anything from inside Nicky Cicero anywhere in this disaster area.

He looks down at the man's face. It's a mask of bruises and blood. One eye is open wide, the other pinched shut by swollen tissue. His mouth is open and full of black blood. He looks as if he was beaten to death by someone in a bare-knuckle fight.

Nicky kneels down and looks at one outstretched hand. He lifts it, a slack meaty weight, and curls the fingers. The knuckles are raw and scraped. He fought, anyway, fought back hard, judging from the wear and tear. Whoever did this to him, that person will have some marks on him, on his knuckles and his face, his arms where he blocked incoming blows. This Nicky knows something about.

He gets to his feet again and sees the clearing in a new way. This was a stand-up fight. Bare-knuckle and toe to toe. A challenge fight? Maybe some twisted kind of contest. Through the gaps in the stand of gnarled old trees, crazy red-and-blue lights were fluttering in the blackness. They made Nicky think of tropical fish floating in a black lagoon. He turned away and walked slowly back to the cruiser.

"Echo one four to base."

"*Nicky, having a pee break?*"
"No, Gracie."
"*You sound funny, Nicky. Are you okay?*"
"No, Gracie."

THURSDAY, JUNE 22

OFFICE OF THE ASSISTANT U.S. ATTORNEY

FEDERAL BUILDING, ALBANY, NEW YORK

0950 HOURS

In the morning Jack Vermillion called his lawyer, Flannery Coleman, from his house in Rensselaer and found out in damn short order that Coleman emphatically agreed with Creek Johnson on this one, that trading an ATF bust on Earl Pike for a mercy plea on Danny Vermillion was a totally bat-shit stunt that would certainly end in tears, so of course Jack proceeded to ignore his advice as well.

Two hours later he and a grumpy and dissatisfied Flannery Coleman—a wily old boot-leather lawyer who had spent nine years with the New York DA's office before he went into private practice up in Albany—met with the special agent in charge of the Albany office of the Bureau of Alcohol, Tobacco, and Firearms, a compact black cop with white hair named Luther Campbell.

Luther Campbell was brisk and funny, seemed competent and grateful for the tip-off, but he had company with him. And this is where Jack Vermillion for the first time meets Valeriana Greco herself, the assistant U.S. attorney for that sector.

She was a machine-tooled little number in her midthirties, with great legs and a sharp face and shiny black hair cut to her jawline and held back on the left with a sterling silver gecko with two emerald eyes. Jack noticed that her eyes were the same shade of green as the gecko's eyes. She wore the usual federal power suit, a navy blue pinstripe number with a short skirt, and came equipped with a Dell Inspiron laptop and a chrome-plated cell phone the size of a hamster's dick. She was all business and drive and managerial chutzpah and was extremely successful in pissing Jack off right from the get-go.

She sat them both down in her office full of mahogany furniture and wall-to-wall plaques citing her legal accomplishments and her influential Washington friends, and waited while Jack tried twice to get his burgundy leather briefcase to stand upright on a rug deep enough to conceal a leg-hold trap. Finally he let it fall over a third time and lie there. She looked down at it with an expression of pained interest.

"Nice bag, Mr. Vermillion."

Jack looked down at the bag. It was lying on its left side, showing a sterling silver plate in a frame stitched under the handle.

JACK VERMILLION
HAPPY 50TH BIRTHDAY
FROM HIS FRIENDS AT LA GIOCONDA
JUNE 29, 1997

Jack raised his shoulders, let them fall in a very Italian gesture. "Thanks. Nice office."

"I know La Gioconda," she said.

"Do you?"

"It's in Astoria, isn't it? In Queens? On the boulevard?"

It was easy to see where this was going.

Jack decided to get there first.

"I grew up in Astoria. I have a lot of friends there. Including Frank Torinetti. If that's a problem for you, we can stop right here."

She had a small mouth, full lips like a cherub on a cathedral wall. In spite of this, her smile managed to be reptilian.

"Not at all. I was just making an observation."

Flannery Coleman broke in with a flat statement.

"What specifically is your role here, Ms. Greco?"

She obliged him with a set speech. It took eleven minutes by the Seth Thomas on the sideboard, next to her graduation picture from the Kennedy School of Government. This was *her* case, she made that clear. Ms. Greco was very interested in Jack's story. She of course applauded his loyalty to the cause of justice. Ms. Greco could of course make no promises regarding the incarceration of Daniello Vermillion, since Mr. Vermillion was being held by the state of California, but certainly there were *ameliorating* steps that could be taken as a cooperative effort between state and federal agencies, and depending upon the *outcomes* . . .

There was much more of that kind of crap, but Jack had extracted the clear impression, later supported by his lawyer, that cooperation with ATF in the matter of Earl Pike would very likely result in parallel, but not *officially* reciprocal, review of the terms of Danny's imprisonment. This would include an immediate—and this was the important part as far as Jack was concerned—transfer to a medium-security detox facility in Fresno.

"That's, like, right now, you follow?" said Jack, interrupting her aria. "Because if he goes back into gen pop where he is, he's as good as dead and our deal is off. It ends here. Right here. That's not negotiable."

"I understand. I agree. Immediate. We'll make the call today. Anything else?"

Jack had some ideas. Perhaps a real attempt to deal with Streak's addictions and his . . . He paused to think.

"Dysfunctional lifestyle?" was how Ms. Greco

phrased it, her lips shaping around the phrase like a nun blowing dust off a dildo.

However, Ms. Greco had some questions.

Luther, who had watched this extended warning label from under his white and bushy eyebrows while he toyed with a Ka-Bar letter opener and glanced occasionally at Jack, had then settled his gaze on Jack's face. Jack had the feeling there was a warning in the look. What questions? Ms. Greco seemed to coil up.

Motivations, really. She had run an NCIC check on Mr. Pike and had discovered nothing at all against him. According to reliable sources, his firm, Crisis Control Systems, had a long and respectable history of corporate consultations. His associates were, as far as her people had been able to determine, retired naval and army personnel with unblemished records. He was a registered firearms collector and was even on the board of directors of the William Cody Museum in Cody, Wyoming.

She had also contacted the Department of the Army and they had given her a glowing report on the military record of the Pike family, which apparently went back to the War for Independence and the liberation of Texas, all the way up to the career of Colonel Earl Pike himself, which began with three tours of combat duty as a G2 officer in the First Air Cavalry in Vietnam and was followed by another twenty-four years of active service in Central America, the Middle East, Colombia, Peru, and lately in Central Africa.

So here we find a successful businessman, an ex-military professional, with many valuable and influential contacts, and yet, amazingly, he is apparently willing to risk all of this to execute a patently illegal shipment of apparently problematic weaponry down the Hudson and from there on to Merida, in Mexico, all of which was entirely contrary to highly publicized ATF shipping restrictions. And he contracts the shipment to a complete stranger, although, she had to admit, a man who—she hoped Jack would forgive her—a man who did have connections in some fairly colorful parts of the city. It was therefore odd, she said, and did not conform to her eleven years of experience in these matters. And there was the risk to Black Water Transit Systems. Here she paused and her lids closed and then opened again, as if she had just received a cosmic transmission or was having some intestinal problems—the fact that Jack had *initiated* an investigation against Pike, the fact of his status as an *informant,* would that not damage his relationships with legitimate businesspeople in Albany? She felt it must. And therefore what puzzled her, what troubled her in all of this, was the *uniqueness* of the situation. It had not been her experience that ordinary citizens, powerful businessmen such as Jack, were given to *paroxysms* of civic altruism, especially in a matter where they might suffer serious damage to their corporate interests. So, she said, all sweet reason, she was left with questions.

Jack understood her meaning completely. He leaned forward and spoke forcefully, right into her personal space.

"Before I get into why, let me say that I expect to remain completely anonymous in this matter, or I go no farther with you. Can you guarantee that for me? In writing?"

Ms. Greco sent a sidelong glance over at Luther Campbell, who shrugged back at her.

"Possibly. There are disclosure problems, of course, but the nature of the source can be sealed in the indictment and known only to the judge. Our interception could be at the Red Hook Terminus, or even out at sea. Perhaps an ocean interception would be the best way to go. We'll have to work out the details . . . if we agree to this operation. But it's natural that there will be reactions and . . . consequences. So my question remains, Why do this at all?"

"Two reasons. One, it might have been a sting. Pike might have been one of your informants already. He was wearing a suit jacket on a hot day. He made his approach outside, by a parking lot, where there was an opportunity for surveillance, for taping."

"You assert that you intended to turn him down. If it *were* a sting, then, well, you were safe from it. You had behaved legally."

"But if I failed to report the attempt? If it *had* been a federal sting? Illegal guns? My shipping company operates under a federal license. Under the terms of that license, a failure to report attempts to bribe or otherwise evade state and federal regulations is grounds for a summary cancellation of my permit. That's the end of my business right there. That's reason one."

She nodded, waited, her face showing nothing.

"Two, you bastards wanted something to trade for my son. This is what I have. All I have."

"As pure as that? A father's love, then, is it?"

Jack's look was all he needed to make his point about that.

"No need to become defensive, Mr. Vermillion. We're aware that Black Water Transit has been the subject of . . . interest . . . by various federal and state investigative branches. As I said earlier, you have social connections with elements of the Italian community. You know La Gioconda is a Mafia-associated location. You make no secret of that connection. You have it on your very wonderful Hermès briefcase here. We know that Frankie Bulls is—"

"His name is Torinetti. Francis Torinetti."

"He's a friend of yours. You don't call him Frankie Bulls?"

"He doesn't call you Val the Greek."

"Fine. I stand corrected. Mr. Francis Torinetti is an old school friend, but he has nothing whatsoever to do with Black Water Transit, and all you're trying to do here is help out your troubled son. As I said in the beginning, a father's pure and simple love?"

Jack had nothing to say.

One more brief trance for Ms. Greco. Luther put the Ka-Bar down hard. She opened her eyes at the sound, smiled.

"How *admirable,* Mr. Vermillion," she drawled. "And how *rare.*" She sent Luther a wrap-this-up look and picked up her cell phone without another word to either Jack or Flannery Coleman.

Campbell got out of his chair and hustled them into the hall, offered to get them coffee.

"What's happening now?" asked Flannery.

"We'll have to discuss it. Can you give us ten minutes?"

"Five," said Flannery.

"Okay. Five. Don't let her get to you, Mr. Vermillion. She has to be a bit of a hard-nose in this line of work."

"She's a complete ball-breaker, Officer Campbell."

"Agent Campbell. Five minutes? For the sake of your kid?"

It turned out to be fifty. Jack was already at the elevator, with Flannery Coleman on his heels, when Campbell caught up with him.

"Jack. I'm sorry. Ms. Greco wanted to discuss this with her superiors. There are several levels of enforcement involved."

"Run another criminal intelligence check on Jack, you mean," said Flannery. Campbell smiled.

"Not at all. Main thing, they all said yes. We're in. It's a go."

"Disclosure?" asks Flannery. Campbell nods.

"Jack's name never comes up. If Jack can make sure the container goes on one of his boats—"

"Ships. I have two. The *Agawa Canyon* and the *Ticonderoga*. The *Agawa Canyon* is the one I have in mind."

"Okay, great. The *Agawa Canyon* ties up in Red Hook. Maybe the best thing is to take the shipment down there, we make it look like a random cargo check. Personally, I'm not happy about an interception in the open ocean. We'd have to involve the Coast Guard and the FBI, and who needs those mutts. The *attempt* to ship is enough for me. If it's what we think it is, if even some of the weapons are banned or restricted, Earl Pike's on the dock with a hook in his gills before sunrise."

"And what do you think it may be?" asked Flannery.

Luther looked acutely uncomfortable and gave his answer some thought for nearly thirty seconds. Jack felt his heartbeat climbing. What was he getting himself into?

"We have . . . some reason to believe that Crisis Control Systems . . . may . . . be involved in the illegal shipment of weapons."

Flannery's reaction was a small controlled explosion.

"I thought you said there was nothing against his firm!"

"Nothing has been proven."

"So it's all supposition, then?"

Campbell pulled out his blankest stare.

"All we can say is that CCS has connections with certain political elements in Washington that tend to favor unilateral military aid to a number of right-wing governments in Central America and perhaps even in Mexico. Their client list is not . . . accessible . . . to our agencies, but according to a conversation we had with the State

Department this morning, CCS is . . . a matter of interest to the current administration."

"Which administration is that? And what *part* of which administration? Listen, my friend, don't hand my client that sort of vague national-interest bullshit. If there's more to this than you're telling us now, if there are outcomes that damage Jack's operation, I'll make a project out of you and that Greco harpy and every federal agent in this whole damned building!"

Campbell had taken the eruption from Jack's lawyer with widening eyes. His skin was flushed and dark.

"Look, Mr. Coleman, this is the ATF. We want to get prohibited weapons off the street. Even if this Mexican shipment Jack is describing really is a private collection, if even one of the pieces is banned and he's trying to dodge that, that makes him a criminal asshole, and my job is to nail his hand to a door for even thinking about it."

Flannery's vestigial conscience bleated weakly from some distant corner of the lawyer's soul and moved him to ask about Pike's military service to his country. It got him a blunt answer from Campbell.

"With respect, fuck that. That was yesterday."

Flannery looked at Jack.

"This Pike character, Jack . . ."

"Yeah?"

"You think he'll buy the random check?"

"Forget about that," said Campbell. "What Pike buys or doesn't buy means sweet dick here. A weapons beef? The destination some military officer in a foreign nation? Hah! Personally, all that crap about Pike's business, his influential friends, cuts no ice with me. Don't try to move weapons around on my turf without a genuflection in the center aisle. I'm gonna bust his ass with a yard-wide grin. That's my job. And don't worry about what this mutt thinks. Next time we hear from him,

Chelsea Clinton will be mayor of New York. Have some faith, hah?"

"In what?" said Flannery, but Campbell was already walking.

"Forget about it," said Jack, watching him go.

"I wish you would," said Flannery, but it was way too late for that, and anyway Jack Vermillion had stopped listening to his lawyer hours ago. He wasn't even thinking how all of this might look to Frank Torinetti, who seemed to be involved in some way. Frank was a friend. He'd understand. He had a son of his own. Right now, all Jack could hear was Danny on the prison phone from Lompoc, the fear in his voice so loud you could hear it humming in the background like an overloaded circuit.

Please, Dad. Please help me.

JOINT TASK FORCE HQ

BROOKLYN

1300 HOURS

Casey Spandau was alone in the Jay Rats office that same day, holding down the duty desk at the HQ in a second-floor office suite in an out-of-the-way section of the Albee Square Mall, off Fulton Street. The rest of the unit—Detective Jimmy Rule, Sergeant Dexter Zarnas, and a white shield named Carlo Suarez—were all over at the academy on Twenty-first Street doing a surveillance seminar with the training cadre. Casey was happy to see the back of Jimmy Rule, known to the Jay Rats as Jimmy Rock. She'd spent an entire night shift in his 511 unit, and the blue-eyed rocky-faced Irish son of a bitch hadn't spoken one word to her.

They'd blown the entire six-hour shift covering a

meaningless stakeout location, sitting outside a dry-cleaning shop in Maspeth, doing a payback favor for a drug squad unit. Jimmy Rock had passed the time on his cell phone or listening to a swing station from New Jersey. He never slept and he didn't move much. He was dressed in a lovely navy-blue silk suit and matching leather loafers, and his hands were smooth and white. In the darkness of the car, when he moved his hands to turn the dial or pick up his cell phone, they looked like luminous white birds. His breath smelled of mints and his cologne was something spicy with a sandalwood undertone. He was extremely handsome, and a total prick.

Every time Casey tried to start a conversation—maybe explain why she had been transferred out of the Two Five—get the guy to see her point of view perhaps—or just to stay awake—he held up his hand, the right one, turned it so the gold detective's ring on his finger glittered in the light from a street lamp, and then put his index finger on his upper lip. She got the message.

She was new, she was black, she was here under false pretenses, ducking an undisclosed career-crippling beef that ought to have seen her on a fixer in Coney for generations yet unborn. She was therefore invisible to him, a nonperson. It was a demanding position to take, but Jimmy Rock hadn't softened up a degree all night. Casey had never before understood the power of absolute silence. Jimmy Rock used it like a skinning tool. When the replacement unit arrived, at the first skim-milk lightening of a fogged-up dawn in Maspeth, Jimmy Rock had tossed her the keys to the 511 unit and walked away to a subway station without a backward look. Watching him leave, Casey had found tears coming.

After a while, she pulled herself together and drove the unit back to the Jay Rats HQ, where she took the elevator up to the second floor. According to the brass sign on the wood-veneer-over-steel-plate front door of the Jay Rats base, the business operated inside Suite 2200 was known to the world as

BOSTON BAR INVESTMENT MANAGEMENT
NEW YORK / LONDON / HONG KONG

Casey figured the investment firm had put a lot of *somebody's* money into the place, security video cameras in the approaches and inside each of the nine separate offices in the suite, motion detectors everywhere, weight-sensitive floor pads as well, all of this connected to silent alarms running to a nearby Brinks station. Verizon had run secure data lines into the suite through shielded lead-armored piping, and the doors were reinforced with steel plates and frames.

The office of the CEO and president, at the back of the 1,700-square-foot suite, had been taken over by the boss himself, who had formed the unit three years back. It was lined in solid teak, had indigo wall-to-wall carpet, and the big picture window behind the rosewood desk had bulletproof glass, through which you got a narrow westward view of the Brooklyn Law School, the redbrick Borough Hall, the bell tower of Saint Ann's Church, and in the haze beyond them, the twin towers of the World Trade Center and most of lower Manhattan, looking like the backdrop of a Broadway play.

It was a hell of an office, she figured, and seeing it yesterday evening had convinced her that the Jay Rats unit was higher up the food chain than the CO of the Two Five had led her to believe.

Jimmy Rock, the street boss of the Jay Rats unit, had ordered a special doorplate engraved for the boss when the unit took over the Boston Bar offices. It was on the door right now, under a framed black-and-white photo of Primo Carnera, the old pug fighter, who Casey had decided really did look a bit like the boss.

DETECTIVE VINCENT G. ZARAGOSA
NYPD GOLD SHIELD 3179
"Il Padrone"

There was a note for Casey, from Zaragosa, pinned to the door:

> Casey:
> Gone to One Police. There's a bunk in the gun
> room; get some sleep. Dexie and Jimmy Rock
> and Carlo will be gone until two. You have the
> duty desk. Be on it by 1300 hours. Nothing
> much is on, so you should have a slack day.
> Welcome to the Jay Rats!
> Vince Zaragosa

Casey dropped her briefcase beside her desk and found the bunk. It was clean and neat, the sheets crisp and white, folded down in a military style. She sat down on it, inhaled the scent of gun oil and cigarette smoke, and rubbed her face with her hands. She lay down on the cot, shifted her hips twice, let out a long ragged sigh, and was asleep in seven seconds. At noon, the phone rang in the main office. She woke with a jolt of adrenaline, remembered where she was, got to her feet, staggered, and crossed the floor to her desk.

"Joint Task Force."

"Hello. This is Officer Nick Cicero. I'm with the New York State Police. Badge five-five-seven-eight-one. I need to talk to somebody at the Joint Task Force."

"This is Officer Spandau. What can I do for you?"

"Okay. I'm working on a double homicide here. We

got two dead, and the story is, we figure there was some kind of road-rage thing involved."

"How come?"

"I'm in a unit last night, on Highway Eighty-two, off the Taconic there, near Blue Stores? You know it?"

"I was born in Carthage. I've been up and down the Taconic all my life."

"I know Carthage. Up there near Fort Drum, right?"

His voice was deep, even silky. There was Italian in the accent, Casey figured, maybe Queens.

"Yeah. What can I do for you, Officer Cicero?"

"I'm sorry. I didn't get your name, Miss . . . ?"

Not Queens. Maybe Brooklyn.

"Spandau. Officer Spandau."

"Hi. I'm Nicky. They call me Nicky."

"Hi, Nicky."

"Can I get your first name?"

Christ. How old was this kid?

"It's Casey."

"Okay, Casey. I can call you Casey?"

"You seem to be."

"Okay . . . where was I?"

"You were in a unit, patrolling Highway Eighty-two in the region of Blue Stores."

"Right. I see this black Jimmy in a stand of trees. Long story short, there's two dead citizens. You need the details?"

How long had this guy been a cop? Three days?

"No. What can we do for you?"

"After CID arrived, I went back south on Eighty-two, looking for whatever I could see. About three miles from the Taconic exit for Gallatinville, I pick up broken glass in the middle of the road. Headlight glass. I bagged it."

"Why?"

"At the crime scene, the Jimmy had a brand-new scrape on the right rear tail section. We got some paint off it. Navy-blue paint."

"So you figure there was contact up the road, then a secondary confrontation where you found the Jimmy?"

"Yeah. We also have a witness, a flatbed driver, says he saw two cars, a big blue one and a black Jimmy, they were parked by the side of the road there. Says the blue car had passed him a while back, doing a flat ninety. Now he's off the road beside the black truck."

"And you have two dead at the scene?" Casey's interest was rising. "Names?" she said, fumbling for a pen and some paper.

"The female is Julia Maria Gianetto, DOB 02-14-1980. A resident of Albany. First year at SUNY there. The registered owner is Donald Albert Condotti, DOB 08-28-1978. Unemployed. Lived in Paramus. He rang some bells on NCIC. Assault, weapons, some minor drug beefs. The ME says he was a major steroid user. His liver was already bleeding, and he was what . . . twenty-two?"

"How dead were these vics?"

"Bad dead. The girl had her neck broken. She'd been . . ."

"Been what?"

"Sexually abused. It was postmortem."

"Any semen?"

"Nothing. Maybe he used a condom."

"Safe sex even for psychos, hah? And the other body?"

There was a length of silence. Casey could hear men talking and the sound of a distant elevator. The call display on her desk showed a hospital in Albany. He was probably calling from the morgue. She could see him standing in the hall outside a bright white room, with two bodies laid out under a nasty blue light. She knew whatever he was looking at had affected the cop, and it made her want to know the guy better. Most cops pretended that nothing got to them. It was tiresome. If this stuff didn't bother you, you should quit.

"There'd been some kind of stand-up fight in a clearing. The vic was a very big guy. Huge. Like I said, used steroids. A weight lifter. Whoever killed him was either much bigger or much better. I'm going with much better. Basically, the vic was beaten to death."

"With what?"

"Bare hands. Fists. Not even a boot involved."

Christ.

"It gets worse. Then he was . . . gutted."

"Gutted?"

"We figure a tree branch."

Holy Christ.

"Postmortem?"

"They think no. There's a footprint on the guy's throat. He was held down while it was happening. There was a lot of bleeding, which means he was alive for a while afterward. There had to have been a lot of noise coming from him, but so far no witnesses. It was a long way to the next house, and the people there are retired, spend all day with their TV on and the air-conditioning going."

Man, thought Casey. The guy's a bug. If it *was* a guy. Had to be. No woman could do that. At least she hoped not.

"Tell me what we can do for you, Nicky."

"Our lab guys have run the glass. It's headlight glass from a Mercedes-Benz. An older model, likely a mid-eighties saloon car known as a Six Hundred. Here's the thing. We dug glass slivers out of the male vic's shoes. Similar type of glass. We figure at the primary contact site, back down Eighty-two near the Taconic exit, there's some sort of traffic dispute, and it could be the vic kicks out the headlight on the Benz. That's why the road-rage scenario."

"It stands up. The paint do anything for you?"

"Yeah. Also from a mid-eighties Benz Six Hundred."

"Okay. You run this by DMV?"

"Yeah."

"How many?"

"In that color, DMV shows three hundred sixty-one statewide."

"And in New York City?"

Nicky paused, and Casey knew that whatever he said, it was going to mean a hell of a lot of legwork. She was right.

"Eighty-three Mercedes-Benz vehicles that fit the paint and the glass."

"And you want us to help you run the owners down? Why not go to citywide auto?"

"I did. They can't help us until next week sometime. By then this bug may be somewhere else, or . . ."

"Or he's ditched the vehicle, or had it fixed in a crooked shop, or had it shipped to Dubai in a container. Right?"

"You got it."

"Fax me the list. I'll run it by my boss."

"Can I bring it?"

"Bring it? I thought you were in patrol!"

"I've been attached to investigations for this case only."

"Somebody must like you. When can you be here?"

"Three hours. Maybe less."

"You miss Brooklyn that much?"

"How do you know I'm from Brooklyn?"

"It's in your voice. You taking a vacation?"

"No. I want this guy. I want him very bad."

"You figure he's a New York City guy?"

"I don't know. HQ has three officers doing the others. I asked for this. That's my part in this. Is that okay?"

Casey could see it. Some state cop, shiny as a new cap pistol, tagging along like your kid brother on a trike.

"Knock yourself out, Nicky."

She gave him the address of the Jay Rats HQ and told him to phone when he was close. She'd see that somebody would be around to work with him. Thinking about it, she hoped it would be her.

HEAD OFFICE

BLACK WATER TRANSIT SYSTEMS

TROY, NEW YORK

1510 HOURS

It was a little past three and now they were all sitting around in Jack's offices in Troy, waiting for a call from Earl Pike or one of his people—for an overt or predicate act, Luther Campbell had called it, and the only one doing anything active right now was the pocket-rocket assistant U.S. attorney, Valeriana Greco.

She had her head down so her thick black hair was a screen over her face, and she was clacking away on her matte-black laptop computer. So we would know she wasted no taxpayer moments, Jack supposed, or maybe she was just crazy.

She was wearing a different black suit thingy, tight short skirt and a matching jacket. She had great legs and all the sex appeal of broken glass. Now and then her tiny little cell phone would give a sprightly chirp and she'd flick it open with a practiced move and say something cryptic into the thing.

Whenever this happened, the three androids she had brought along with her from the Albany office of the

ATF would turn their heads and stare at her as if she had just materialized in the room.

He never bothered to get their names. They were just a three-round burst—each man as much like the others as the rounds in a magazine, the federal suits, the crew cuts, the military mustaches to give authority to faces completely unsmacked by reality, the pricey Glocks—what Jack liked to think of as combat Tupperware—in their shoulder rigs, the weight-lifter physiques, and the obvious belief that anyone not an actual member of the Bureau of Alcohol, Tobacco, and Firearms was either a hardened criminal or studying on it for the future. Typical feds. Jack, who had seen some things in this world, wasn't interested enough in the three of them to attempt to change their views. At twenty minutes after three, the phone rang.

Everybody froze, and now the three-round burst was staring right at Jack. Jack swiveled around in his chair and picked up the receiver. It was Earl Pike.

"Jack. How are you?"

"Good, Earl. And you?"

"Fine. I've made the arrangements."

"Okay. Let me get a pen . . . okay. Go."

"I have a container truck coming in now. The guy just called. He's outside Saratoga. Where do you want him?"

"You sure you don't want to have your driver take it straight down the Taconic to Red Hook, save you some handling costs?"

Jack was watching Greco's face while he said this. She was monitoring the call on a surveillance tap. Her pale face sharpened and her eyes glittered with anger. She shook her head so hard her hair flew out in a ring and slapped the side of her cheekbone. Pike was saying something and Jack had to ask him to repeat it.

"You got somebody else there, Jack?"

"I'm in my office. My business is still operating. What do you want me to do, close the door and hang a sheet over my window?"

"Don't get testy. No, I don't want to have my driver take the container to Red Hook himself. There's lots of routine federal and state surveillance all over the New York and Jersey waterfront. We take the load at your docks, it goes into bond there, by the time it arrives in Red Hook, nobody's going to pay any attention to it. It's simpler, and simple is always best. You follow?"

"I follow. I've got a freighter waiting at the river here. The *Agawa Canyon*. You know the address?"

"Your docks, right?"

"Right."

"I know them. When can we get the load on?"

"There's no special handling. The *Canyon*'s almost full. She leaves around six tonight. She'll be at the Red Hook Container Terminal around one in the morning. That work for you?"

"Yeah. I'd like to have someone meet her there."

"Why? The container's in customs bond by then. You can't approach it. Technically it's not in the U.S. anymore. It's going straight onto a container ship out of Baltimore."

Greco's face was a picture. Jack was looking her right in the eyes, and what was there was cold-blue fury. Two tiny red patches floated on her pale cheekbones. Jack had his hand raised. *Quiet.*

"I just want the transfer covered."

"You don't trust me?"

"I trust you. I trust in Allah too, but I tie up my camel."

"Okay. Your call. No problem. Give me the name of your driver. I'll see the yard man has dock space cleared. We'll get your container on as soon as it arrives. After that, you know where it will be. Send whoever you want to Red Hook. My guys will do whatever it takes to make your man happy. I'll see to it. Okay?"

"Works for me. Where'll you be?"

"Where do you want me? You want me there too?"

"No. Once again, why flag the shipment that way? Your guys would wonder why the hell the boss is there at two in the morning. Somebody would talk. How about you stay where I can reach you?"

"I'll be right here. At my desk. Or at home, by the phone."

"Done. We'll talk again."

Pike rang off. Greco stood up, still in a frozen rage.

"That was extremely stupid, Mr. Vermillion."

"No it wasn't, lady. I acted like any shipper would. His container is in bond—had to be for your predicate act, anyway—and there's no reason to follow it around the system. It was a reasonable response to a client. You heard him."

Greco's face was hard and cold, but she worked at a sudden chirpy smile and managed to show a lot of teeth to Jack.

"I see. Good. Very good."

"Now what?" asked Jack. "You have a tail on him? You follow him to Red Hook?"

She smiled.

"There's no tail on him. Too risky. He's too good for that. If he spotted any surveillance, he'd just ditch the whole operation. Anyway, we don't need to track him from his hotel to the terminal. All we need to nail the case is Pike's arrival at the dock, claiming the cargo. All you do, when the container comes in, you see that it's loaded. We'll have someone videotape the loading operation. For continuity, chain of evidence. When it gets down to Red Hook, we'll be waiting. We're going to take it down right there. Luther advises me that an oceanic interception is tactically questionable and would involve too many other agencies. I agree. We're going to keep this an ATF operation. Even if Pike doesn't show up, it doesn't really matter, because we still have him on the audiotape here, setting it all up, which constitutes a predicate act in furtherance. We'd like him to be there, but it's not necessary. Whatever happens, he's all ours."

"What do you want me to do?"

"You told Pike you'd be available. That's what he'll be expecting. Stay by your phone. When it's over, we'll call you."

Greco walked over to Jack's desk and put out her hand. It was cold. Perhaps it was the air-conditioning. She pumped his hand once, her green eyes hard on his face. The three-round burst stood up and looked right through him. Long after they had left, Jack felt her chill in his hand. It troubled him, made him feel that he didn't really know what was going on. And further down, buried deep but not deep enough, he felt a pang of guilt about betraying Earl Pike. Pike had done him no harm, had seemed to be a good man at the core, was even a veteran of the same stupid war. And here was Jack Vermillion, feeding him to a woman like Valeriana Greco.

Please, Dad.

No. He was into it now and would have to see the thing through to the end. If they were keeping something from him, well, that was just the way of all cops. Whatever it was, he'd find out sooner or later. Jack had that part right, anyway. It was sooner.

At seven-thirty that same evening, with a heavy rain pelting the windows outside, the concierge in the tower lobby of the United Nations Plaza Hotel looked up from her copy of *The New Yorker* and saw a white male, late twenties, his lips thin and dry-looking, standing in the at-ease position in front of her bronze desk, wearing a tan trench coat over a dark-gray wool single-breasted suit.

He was rumpled, windblown, and slightly damp. The scent coming off him was part rain-damp and part lime-scented cologne. His close-cut hair was a shiny blue-black. The suit jacket was open and she could see the dark-gray butt of a semiauto pistol in his belt. This did not surprise her, since the UN Plaza Hotel was ground zero for all sorts of federal agencies. Lean sharp-faced cops in nicely cut suits were a buck a basket around here.

The cop—he had to be a cop—smiled at her, showing her how charming and nonthreatening and cuddly he was. His eyes were the palest blue she'd ever seen, so clear and colorless they struck her as slightly inhuman. She smiled back.

"You have a guest in the hotel, Earl Pike?"

"Possibly. We have many guests. Wish I could help you, but—"

"Does he have a vehicle parked in your valet section?"

She showed him a lot more of her truly excellent teeth.

"I'd like to see your ID."

Jimmy Rock pulled out his gold shield, held it up in front of him, not showing her his ID card, keeping it hidden as well from the people strolling into and out of the green marble foyer of the hotel.

The concierge contemplated his shield for a long moment, as if it were something her cat had coughed up onto the rug.

"We don't normally—"

"Also, I need to know his room number."

"Now that's not possible, Detective."

She hit the *not* hard enough to make it ring faintly, a kind of silvery ping. Her smile was still holding. Jimmy decided that he liked her; she had sand. He gave her his best smile, the one he liked to think of as boyish, charming. It wasn't. Jimmy Rock watched her as she worked out the angles. It took her about thirty seconds.

"What is the purpose of your visit?"

"Nothing critical. We're just following up on an accident report. Mr. Pike showed up on our computers as registered in this hotel. He also owns a type of car we are interested in, in connection with a motor vehicle accident upstate. It's nothing at all serious. You mind answering my questions?"

The woman sat back in her leather armchair and thought about the question. Then she smiled and stood up.

"Wait here one moment."

She crossed the marble floor, heading for the main desk. Jimmy Rock watched her go, admiring the way she handled gravity. The foyer was decorated with thousands of tiny white pinpoint lights. Down the long glimmering hallway, a grand piano the size of a Lincoln Town Car was filling the lobby with some sort of concerto, although there was no one sitting in front of it. Maybe the ghost of George Gershwin.

Jimmy Rock lit up a cigarette and waited for the woman to get back. Three people in a crowd by the elevator were staring at him as if he'd just stuck a dead rat in his ear. He smiled and blew some smoke toward them. They huffed and glared back, and then the door to the elevator opened and they were gone. He grinned at the closing door and took another puff. Damn, it was good to be alive.

"This is a no-smoking environment," said a voice.

He looked back. The concierge was considering him. "Damn. Sorry."

She picked up a heavy crystal plate and held it in front of him. He toyed with the idea of dropping a quarter into it and decided not to. He butted the cigarette. She set the plate down.

"The manager is on the phone to our lawyer right now, Detective. I'll need a card if you have one."

Jimmy handed her one of his cards. She took the card and read it, looked up at him again, smiled, and then put it in a leather folder on her desk. She pulled one of her own cards and handed it to him. It had a linen finish and her name was in raised gold letters: MERCEDES GONSALVA.

Odd coincidence. He was here looking for a guy with a blue Mercedes-Benz, and that's this woman's first name. Maybe it was a sign they were destined to be lovers. Maybe it was a meaningless coincidence. His money was going on meaningless. Jimmy put the card in his breast pocket and patted it once. He gave her his best smile, saw the blank space on her ring finger, and considered his chances. Absolute zero, he decided.

"The man you're inquiring about is registered with us as Mr. Earl V. Pike. He's in room twenty-nine-ninety. He is one of our oldest and most valued clients. He's in his quarters now. If you wish to speak with him, I can call up and see if he'll be able to accommodate you."

"I'd rather take a look at his vehicle first. Does he have one parked in your garage?"

"Yes. He does."

"Do you know what kind it is?"

"No. The bellman would have the location."

"Okay. Please don't call Mr. Pike yet. All right?"

"I feel I should contact . . . fine, since this is a police matter, I'll leave it with you. I'd like to remind you he's a very valued client."

Jimmy Rock was already moving away. He was at the door when she called him back.

"One more thing, Detective Rule. The manager—"

"What's his name?"

"Mr. Siggerssonn."

"Siggerssonn?"

"Yes, he's Icelandic. Mr. Siggerssonn trusts there'll be no disturbances in the hotel. I can reassure him, can I?"

"What's his first name? Thor?"

"Gunnar."

"Gunnar? What is he, like, one of those *GQ* models with the cheekbones, got a jawbone you could chip a tooth on, three-day beard? Icy-blue eyes? Whoa, I'm getting all shivery here."

She was fighting it, but the laugh was winning.

"No, that doesn't quite catch him. What may I tell him?"

"Miss Gonsalva, you can tell Mr. Gunnar Siggerssonn that we were never here. This was all a dream. You follow me?"

"I do. I will. And it was. Bye."

The 511 unit was parked in a loading dock halfway up Forty-fourth Street toward Second Avenue. Casey Spandau was waiting behind the wheel. Nicky Cicero was in the backseat, wearing civilian clothes, a black leather jacket over a white tee, blue jeans, and black cowboy boots. He was wearing a Beretta nine-mill in a shoulder holster. He looked tired and rumpled. He'd been on the case since last night. Sleep was low on his list right now but climbing fast.

Jimmy Rock got into the passenger seat and spoke over the back of the seat to the state cop. He never even looked at Casey.

She said nothing.

"Okay. Pike's here. He has a car down in the valet section."

"Should we go look?" asked Nicky.

"In a minute. Run by me again why you two came up with this guy? I'm getting a bad feeling about this one. The concierge talks about him like he's Martin Luther King."

Casey started to speak and then looked straight ahead. The concept of a complete resignation from the department was developing by the minute. Nicky waited for Casey to speak and then realized she was still not talking to the gold shield. This was getting ridiculous. It was unprofessional.

His answer was short and had an edge in it.

"Okay. We had eighty-three matches on the DMV list."

"All Benz Six Hundreds?"

"Yeah. All registered in the five boroughs. We eliminated thirty-six right off because the color was listed incorrectly on the DMV files, either light blue or silver. That left us forty-seven possibles. Casey used some pull and got citywide auto to check out seventeen Mercedes-Benz Six Hundreds from Staten Island, the Bronx, and parts of Queens. They were all eliminated."

"Why?"

"Either the car was clean, no marks of an accident, or the owners were able to provide proof that the vehicle wasn't anywhere upstate last night or yesterday."

"So that leaves you thirty."

"That's right. Fourteen of them are in Manhattan. Casey and I spent the afternoon running down all of them. It was a bitch."

"And what did you get?"

"Mostly nothing. Nine of them were fleet vehicles, and they all checked out negative. Two had been sold to a dealer and were still on the lot. Citywide is still on the ones in Brooklyn."

"So you end up with how many?"

"We have five possibles in Manhattan. This Pike guy, he has one registered in Manhattan, but he lives in Annapolis."

"Why does that kick out for you?"

"Tell him, Casey."

"You tell me."

Nicky sat back, looked at the two of them.

"You know, why don't the two of you just fuck off somewhere, let *me* go talk to Earl Pike?"

Jimmy Rock started to say something. Casey cut in.

"We were wheel-spinning. I cross-referenced the possibles with credit card purchases made yesterday."

Jimmy Rock was staring at her.

"How the hell did you do that?"

"You're not the only cop in town with sources."

"And what did you get?"

At least they were talking to each other now. It improved the atmosphere slightly. Now it was merely suffocating.

"Two of the Benz owners used credit cards to buy gas in midstate New York yesterday. One purchased twenty-seven gallons at an Exxon station in Lake Placid."

"Too far north," said Jimmy Rock.

"Why?" Casey asked, her throat working, angry at his casual dismissal of her evidence.

"Just is. And the other?"

"Earl Pike. He used a Chase credit card to buy gas at a town called Castleton, just outside Albany."

"So?"

"So we called the service station," said Nicky. "The guy remembered the car."

"Why?"

"It had a broken headlight. Driver's side. The gas guy noticed it because the car was in mint condition. It looked recent."

Jimmy Rock was quiet for a long time.

"Nice," he said after a while, looking at Casey. "Very nice."

"Thank you," she said, and gave him a smile sharp enough to open a vein. "Now what?"

"Now?" said Jimmy Rock. "I'll go look at the car. You two go have a little chat with Earl V. Pike."

2217 GRANITE VALLEY PARKWAY
RENSSELAER, NEW YORK
2015 HOURS

By eight in the evening, Jack had been home for one hour and had already worked his way through two bottles of Beaujolais. It wasn't a typical thing with him. He had come in through the front door, setting his Hermès briefcase—which actually was a gift from Frank Torinetti himself—onto the front-hall table, and headed straight down to the cellar, where he snagged two bottles of Beringer. By eight-fifteen he was pacing like a man with a sore tooth through the darkened rooms of his granite-walled townhouse in Rensselaer.

In the greenhouse dining room, on a broad, polished mahogany table, a single place setting of cold cuts and cheese was sitting relatively untouched since his house-keeper had put it out for him at seven, along with a chilled bottle of sauvignon blanc.

He hadn't touched any of it personally, but the stray cat who had gradually become a fixture around the place had tucked into the breast of chicken as soon as he figured out Jack wasn't going to eat any of it. Jack had named him Smoke, because he came and went like smoke, a gray-and-white six-toed stray with yellow eyes who weighed in around twenty pounds. He had been haunting the edges of Jack's property for about two months, ragged and matted and covered with burrs. One eye was closed and puffed out, and he was limping badly, but Jack could get no closer to the animal than ten feet before the beast would flatten out and let out a high-pressure hiss like a blown tire.

It had taken Jack weeks to get him to eat from a plate on the back steps, and although the cat had gotten used to being inside, he was a long way from tame. Jack liked him because he was a cranky loner who reminded him of himself, although he had lately come to the conclusion that Smoke was about the stupidest cat in the east-ern United States. But he was company, about all Jack could stand.

Jack was listening to a soundtrack of the music from *Chinatown*. The trumpet solos followed him as he walked from room to room, along with the tinny cross talk on the marine radio set he kept in his office in the rear of the main floor, a wood-paneled den overlooking a narrow ravine where a stand of willows hid a tiny river. The marine radio system allowed him to monitor the movement of his container barges and his two freighters up and down the Hudson. The volume was on high, loud enough to carry through the main-floor rooms.

So far, all he had heard was the usual marine traffic

conversations. Now and then he could hear the familiar husky growl of Dinsdale Kerr, the captain of the *Agawa Canyon*. Kerr was one of his best people, a sixty-two-year-old salt, Scots-Irish in background, completely without humor, as steady as a tombstone.

Jack had filled his captain in on the details of an operation they were now calling Red Hook around the Albany ATF offices. Kerr had listened in silence, his flushed and weathered face closing up like a fist as he took in the details. When Jack was through, Kerr had blown out a sigh through his trim gray mustache and said only one word: "Foolishness."

Around about now, Jack was inclined to agree with the man. He had the cordless phone in the pocket of his jeans, waiting for a call from Luther Campbell as soon as the Red Hook thing was over, but he half expected to hear nothing at all from any of them. He had been pushed right out of the loop from the moment he ended his talk with Earl Pike.

All he could gather from a hurried phone conversation with Luther was that Greco was running the sting in cooperation with the ATF and the New York Port Authority Police, that the entire Red Hook Container Yard in Brooklyn had been placed under twenty-four-hour surveillance as soon as Pike had called Jack, and that the operation would begin as soon as Pike or someone representing him called at the riverside terminal to collect the container.

Greco had referred to the final stages as a "takedown," which sounded as energetic as hell. Although the woman was a mystery to him, and what he did know he didn't like, it was obvious that she was having a fine time running the show and was already figuring out how to play it to the press gallery when it was all over.

Jack was in the middle of his fourth circuit through the living room and into the dining room and on his way back to the office to stare out the window again when the cordless phone in his back pocket chirped and he jumped a foot and a half into the air. There was a bark in his voice when he keyed the talk button.

"Vermillion."

"Hey, Jack. How you doing?"

"Frank?"

"Yeah. You mind my phoning? I was thinking about you, thought I'd give you a buzz."

"I thought you were in Italy—Venice. You and Claire."

"Nah. Place is fulla tourists. What's it that Yogi Berra said? Nobody goes there no more. It's too crowded. And Tuscany looks like Penn Central. Nips and slopes with their fucking Nikons. Some dinks wrote a book about the place, now it sucks. Never go there."

Frank's voice was a whisky growl. Jack could hear music in the background, a jazzy piano number, and people talking.

"How's Claire?"

"Good . . . she's good. Great. Look, Jack. You busy?"

Jack was thinking about Creek's warning. Any contact with Frank Torinetti could screw up his deal with Galitzine Sheng and Munro. And tonight was no night to be away from the phone.

"You mean now?"

"Yeah. I mean now. I was wondering, maybe you'd come by, see the place since we done it over. We got a few people here, friends of yours. Plus Claire's got a brand-new kitchen put in."

"Again?"

"Again," he said, laughing. "So I was thinking, maybe I'd send Carmine over for you. I got a new car. A Viper. It's a pistol. Ask nice, you can drive it back here."

"Frank, this is a bad time for me. I got a thing going on."

"Give me an hour, Jack. It's been months since I seen you. Claire's been asking about you, too. Come on over. You have a drink, coupla canna-pees. Maybe a bowl of *vongole*. Then you go home."

"I'm expecting a call. It's pretty important."

"So? Forward your home number to your cell phone."

"Frank, I wish I could. . . ."

"Jack, you're coming. I already sent Carmine. He'll be there in a coupla minutes. See you inna bit, hah? You take care, *paisano*."

"Frank—"

The line was dead. Four minutes later the doorbell rang. Jack opened it. Carmine DaJulia was standing there, grinning at him, a wall-sized Calabrese *luparo* with a smooth tanned face and a bald head and cold black small-caliber eyes, wearing a gray silk Zegna suit over a purple T-shirt. Parked in Jack's circular drive was a sleek purple Viper. Under the porch light it glowed like a neon sign. The engine was still running, a muted rumbling like boulders rolling around under the ground. Carmine's smile had always reminded Jack of broken china. His teeth were too small for his head, and slightly pointed. He was smiling like that now.

"Jack, how you doing?"

"Carmine, did you dress to match the car?"

He looked down at his T-shirt, laughed.

"Yeah. I like things to be neat. How you been?"

"Good, Carmine. You want to come in?"

Carmine shook his head.

"Frank says you can drive the beast."

"Carmine, you're gonna have to tell—"

"You tell him yourself. He's feeling pretty bad tonight. He needs a lift. The chemo's kicking hell out of him. Claire's no fucking use. He sent me to get you. I gotta bring you back. You don't come, you'll hurt his feelings. You be a friend now, hah?"

Carmine was still smiling. Jack decided to keep him that way.

Pike was standing at a plate-glass window looking out across the midtown skyline at the cold-chisel roof of the Citicorp building, waiting for the doorbell to ring. The summit looked like the tip of an iceberg, and a plane of hard light shone up from the northern edge, cutting a cold white slice out of the rainy midtown sky. Pike found the building a pleasure to look at, as simple and elegant and perfectly formed to its purpose as the very best kind of weapon.

He had a glass of bourbon and soda, the weight of the heavy crystal pleasing and solid. Music was coming from the radio, a lilting fugue by Bach. He was barefoot, wearing jeans and a soft plaid shirt in tones of red and blue. The knuckles of his right hand were heavily bandaged and wrapped in a Tensor strip. He could feel the rawness under the bandages, the skin healing and tightening. He flexed his fingers and looked out the window again, this time at his own image in the window. His reflection in the plate glass was shadowed and his face hidden. The narrow angular room behind his reflection was lit by a single lamp standing next to a low green leather sofa and a pair of green leather armchairs. Through an open door, a large king-sized bed could be seen. Pike had his gear laid out on top of the emerald-green satin spread, a Star Lite night-vision scope, his Smith, and four extra magazines. A large brushed-steel case about four feet high stood in the corner of the room, next to the night table. Although it showed signs of wear, the locked case was solid and secure, and the .50-caliber sniper rifle it contained was as perfectly suited to its purpose as the Citicorp tower.

He had asked for his usual room next to the elevator, so when he heard the car gliding to a stop at his floor, he sipped once at the bourbon and then padded across the sage-colored carpet and quietly closed the door to the bedroom. A minute later the bell chimed twice, a perfect G sharp, and Pike pulled open the door.

Two obvious cops were standing in the doorway, a black female in her late twenties, well-made and fit-looking in a forest-green suit and tan leather shoes. Pike noticed her eyes and decided she had Chinese or Vietnamese blood in her background. The man with her, wearing a black leather jacket and jeans, was six feet or better and had a slightly deviated nose. Although he was good-looking in an Italian way, the tiny network of scars around his eyes suggested a fighter. So did his frame, wide at the shoulders and tapering down like a blade. Under the white tee was a shelf of pectoral muscle, and his hands were knotted, the knuckles slightly swollen from working a rhythm bag. Definitely an amateur fighter. Class him as a light heavyweight. He looked quick and nimble. There was real intelligence in his eyes. It would be interesting to try him out. One thing was clear. He was not the blue-eyed Irish cop that Mercedes Gonsalva had carefully described to him a few minutes ago. So there were three, at least, and this was obviously not a simple traffic inquiry. Both cops were reacting to Pike's build, which amused him.

He smiled and stepped back from the door.

"Officers. Come in. Can I get you a drink?"

The woman came in first, and Pike realized she was in charge. She pulled out a badge case and showed him her shield.

"I'm afraid we're on duty, Mr. Pike. I'm Officer Spandau, and this is Officer Cicero. We appreciate your taking the time to talk to us. It won't take a minute."

Pike nodded, walked away, sat down on the green leather couch, and put his arms out across the back. He sipped at his bourbon while the two cops sat down in the chairs. The woman was humming with suppressed intensity, and the man, Cicero, was working hard at a casual indifference to the hugely expensive suite and the view of the midtown skyline. Although it was raining, the clouds were shredding on the peaks and towers and the sunset out of Jersey was glittering on the westward glass. It was a magnificent scene, and Pike approved of the man's evident enjoyment.

"Hell of a view," he said to Cicero. The man grinned back and nodded.

"Center of the earth, New York," he said in a Brooklyn accent. "Mind my asking, Mr. Pike, what happened to your hand there?"

Pike held it up and turned it in the light from the lamp beside him.

"Flat tire. On the Taconic. Changed it myself, and the wrench slipped. Took off a lot of skin. Hurts like hell. Serves me right. I should have called AAA."

"When was this, sir?" asked the woman, her face blank and mildly interested.

"Yesterday."

"You were upstate yesterday?"

"Oh yes. I had a meeting in Albany. Drove up in the morning, came back late last night."

"I see. May I ask, what kind of car do you drive, Mr. Pike?"

"A big old Benz."

"A Six Hundred?"

"Yes. Wonderful old car. I keep it in mint condition. I never drive it in town. Just for runs upstate."

"What color is it?"

"Navy-blue. Tan leather interior. Are you shopping?"

"Is the car here now, Mr. Pike?"

"It's close. May I ask you why you're so interested in my car?"

"There was an MVA—a traffic accident—yesterday. One of the vehicles involved was a navy-blue Mercedes Six Hundred."

Pike allowed a few seconds of silence to tick away while he pretended to process the statement.

"I see. I take it the blue Benz you're interested in didn't stay at the scene, then? Which explains the police. Do I need a lawyer?"

"If you think you do, we have no objection," said the woman. "But it's not a serious matter right now. The driver of the car may have no idea he was involved in an accident. We're just trying to eliminate the possibilities. You show on the DMV records as being an owner of a Benz Six Hundred. So we're asking about your car. All we need to do is see it, and then we walk away. You said it was in the area?"

"Certainly is. You want to see it now?"

"If that's not a problem."

"Not at all," he said, getting to his feet and crossing the room to the bedroom door. "Let me get some shoes. I'll walk you there."

There was a gatehouse at the street entrance to Frank's house on Valley Mills, shaped like a turret, made of river rock, complete with a little gun-slit window. As Jack pulled the Viper up to the broad iron swing gates across the graveled drive, Carmine leaned out the window and called to the gatekeeper.

"Yo, Fabrizio. It's me."

A huge old man, easily six-three, in his late seventies, a face carved out of rough wooden planks, wearing a white dress shirt and baggy black trousers, shuffled out of the building, raised a hand gnarled and bent with arthritis, and showed Carmine a weary grin full of uneven yellow teeth. He leaned back into the door, fumbled a bit, fumbled some more, and on the third try managed to press a button. The iron gates ground open in a shriek of rusted metal. Carmine nodded to Jack, and he started up the long drive toward the Torinetti house. Jack turned around to look back at the old man shuffling unsteadily back into the gatehouse, looked across at Carmine.

"I know that guy, don't I?"

Carmine shrugged.

"Yeah. That was him."

"Fabrizio Senza? From Montreal? Fabrizio Senza, with the razor? They called him Il Barbieri? *That* Fabrizio?"

"Yeah. Papalia's guy. He's not doing so good."

"Christ. No kidding. I used to see him around; he'd be coming down Ditmars, dressed like a duke, big as a tree, walk like a parade square guard, trench coat over his shoulders, he's smiling and talking, he was always a gentleman, and everybody's thinking, Man, who's he here for? Is he here for me? Carmine. He's *old*."

"There's a lotta that going around. Anyway, he don't always look like that. He's been drinking. Somebody inna family died."

"Yeah? Who?"

"Nobody you know. Some kind of traffic thing. Hit and run. Messy. Hey! Watch where you driving here."

Jack looked back at the road, thinking about the old man.

"He used to be such a hard guy. Now he's a gate-keeper."

"He likes to be useful. He does errands, sees to the grounds, keeps the gate, like you say. Frank takes care of him now."

Now Jack could see the glow of lights through the trees that surrounded the property, soft amber squares shining through leaded-glass windows. Music was coming from the rear of the property, and at least thirty cars, BMWs, Cadillacs, a Rolls Corniche, were parked in the circular driveway in front of Frank's granite mansion. There were no button men hiding in the trees and no armed guards in the doorway. It was just a big suburban palace like a thousand others in the Albany area. When he got out of the Viper, Carmine stopped him by the door.

"Frank's glad you could come, Jack. He appreciates it."

"You have any idea why he needed to see me tonight?"

"Yeah."

"Why?"

Carmine shrugged, raised his arms in a gesture that strained his suit jacket and took Jack all the way back to Astoria Boulevard.

"He'll tell you. You take care now."

The double doors were opened and Frank Torinetti was standing in the light when Jack got to the top of the stairs. He stepped out onto the landing and took Jack's hand, pumped it twice, holding Jack's forearm with his left hand like a campaigning politician.

"Jeez, you're like steel, Jack. When you gonna fall apart?"

Jack looked at his friend in the archway light. Frank's heavy tan wasn't hiding the effects of his chemotherapy. The whites of his eyes were yellowed, and his deeply creased face looked as if it were melting. His grin was pulled to the left, as if he'd had a mild stroke. Frank had once been a very big man, but his prostate cancer had worn him down like a pillar of salt in a slow rain. His hair was so thin you could see the dome of his skull through it. His hand was bumpy and knotted, and the bones felt very breakable to Jack.

Frank was a year younger than Jack, a kid from his own street, a friend for forty years. He felt a rush of shame and regret.

"Frank. How are you?"

Frank showed his teeth. His breath smelled of mints and cigars and whiskey.

"Hah! I'm the walking fucking dead! I got a pecker feels like a sock a wet sand. I can't pee without pills. Last time I had a usable hard-on, I can't remember. But hey, other than that, I'm fucking great. Come in, I got a bunch of the old people here, from the block."

Frank pulled him into the main hall of the house and walked him through the Gothic rooms toward a broad sunroom. Out on the terrace, about fifty people were standing around the pool talking way too loud and listening to nobody.

Frank made a point of introducing Jack to a series of half-remembered faces and repeating their names often enough for Jack to pull out the right memory. They worked their way through the crowd until they got to the gray stone pool house at the back of the property. Frank's wife, Claire, was sitting by the pool, barefoot, in a silk blouse and a short skirt, talking to a red-haired woman in a black string bikini, when she saw Jack coming up with Frank still holding him by the arm. She got up and glided over.

"Jack . . . so good of you to come . . . this is wonderful."

She leaned forward, her unlined face as cold and hard as a diamond facet, her neck shining blue-green in the glow from the pool light, her eyes china-blue and a little too bright. She kissed him on both cheeks while she held his hands in hers. Her skin was warm and dry and she smelled of spice and scotch. She was triumphantly without a bra, and her pink silk blouse was three buttons short of decency. Jack tried not to look at her nipples and failed. She stepped back, still holding on to his hands, while Frank watched them both.

When Jack looked at him again, Frank arranged his face into a grimace that passed for a smile, and invited him to sit down beside him. Claire said something about getting drinks and moved off into the crowd, laughing and touching people as she passed. Having a hell of a time. Jack watched her working the crowd.

She was Frank's fourth wife, and seventeen years younger than he was, out of an Upper East Side family whose money had blown away in the Savings-and-Loan firestorm. Frank had saved her from a life of genteel poverty, and she dedicated the rest of her life to making him pay for it. The last time Jack had been at the house, Frank was just going into the hospital for the first of several rounds of chemotherapy. Carmine had driven Frank to the clinic. The big house was empty except for Claire, who had answered Jack's buzz through the intercom at the gatehouse. When he reached the main door, she was waiting for him with two gin-and-tonics, wearing a long gauze robe, pure white, standing in the light under the big stone archway. The door behind her was open and light was spilling out, making her glow like a Chinese lantern. Under the robe she was naked, had nothing on but a pair of silver high heels. Jack did not take this as a personal compliment. He knew her by then. If he'd been the Verizon guy, she'd have skipped the robe.

Jack had never mentioned this to Frank, but he had stayed for the drinks. Maybe Frank knew about it. Maybe not. It had only happened once, but Jack was ashamed of it almost every other day. That was the real reason he had fallen away from Frank.

They never talked about these things. Most guys wouldn't mention that they boinked an old school buddy's wife either. But it was the one thing Jack had done that he was always deeply ashamed of. And that included what he had done in the war.

Anyway, they both watched her walk away, and Jack said nothing about her, and Frank let him. They talked about the old places and the new people until the crowd began to bubble like a punch bowl full of champagne. The music was so loud it bordered on actual pain. Jack had his cell phone on and checked it every few minutes. After a while, they were alone in a corner of the playground, which was what Jack had expected. The pool crowd was getting louder and Frank's face as he gazed out at them was hard and cold-looking. He saw Jack watching him, and raised a glass of whiskey toward them.

"My good and true friends. *Salud!* That guy there, in the lime-green shirt and the Dockers, looks like Brad Pitt? He's a broker, made fifteen million last year. He's fucking Claire, I think, only I ain't bothered to check anymore. I figure, I can't do it for her, long as she don't make me look bad, what do I care? But him? How he made his money? There's this company. They're totally fucked up, on the edge of bankruptcy. Brad here talks the owners into going public. So the shares start out at fifteen bucks. The owners rake in a hundred and fifty million on the offering. Last week, shares were going at ninety-one cents on the dollar. The owners sold out long time back, they keep their money in the Isle of Man. That mutt's take was fifteen million. Around town, he's considered a sharp businessman. He's on the Albany Arts Board, golfs with the governor. Me, the fucking guinea mobster, I can't get a ticket to a Variety Club bun fight. Why? I'm unsavory. Fuck is that?"

Jack listened to this carefully. When Frank stopped, breathing hard, he waited a few seconds while they both watched the crowd getting louder. It seemed to Jack they were about twenty minutes from pushing each other into the pool and a half hour from throwing up in the flower beds along the back wall.

Frank was quiet for a while. Jack watched his chest rise and fall under the flowered shirt. His breathing was ragged and sounded in his throat like a kettle on the boil. Frank pulled at his whiskey and made a face while he worked it down his throat.

"Fucking chemo," he said, grunting. "Sick alla time, can't hold nothing down. You had that thing yet?"

"What thing?"

Frank made a gesture, shoved his hand in the air.

"That scope thing? Check you out, up the pipe there?"

"No."

"Any plans to?"

"No."

Frank smacked the tabletop and glasses flew up clattering.

"Fucking right! Worst thing I coulda done. The docs

fell all over themselves making me worse. Ask me, I coulda gone for years, I don't even know I got a prostate. Now I got more people interested in my ass than I got working on the street. Never let them do it to you, my friend. It's a fucking con."

"I won't."

"Good."

Frank gave him a sidelong look, up from under. Jack saw the old button man under the ruined face, a glitter of bared steel.

"I hear you're making a move with your pension fund."

"Yeah."

"What's Creek saying about it?"

"Creek's mostly retired."

"Not putting any heat on you, go with one firm or another?"

Jack was hearing something under the words.

"Why should he? I don't think he gives a damn."

"Creek's a busy guy these days. We see a lot of him."

"Who's we?"

"Somma my guys. Around town. The clubs. The nice cars. The broads. He's selling cars, you hear?"

Jack had not. Frank saw the blank look.

"Yeah. Classics. I'm buying a fifty-six T-bird from him. Turquoise. White roof. Gonna give it to Claire."

"Where's he getting them?"

"Auburn. The classic shows. He buys and then sells. I told you, he needs the money. Doing good at it too. He makes friends."

"Creek's a social guy."

"Yeah. He was here tonight, matter a fact."

"Creek was here?"

"Yeah . . . he dropped by with the keys to the Thunderbird. It was him said I should call you."

"Yeah? Where's he now?"

"Got a call from some broad. Had to bail. Took my check for the T-bird. Bummed a couple bottles a Perrier-Jouët from Carmine, splits in that snazzy Corvette."

"He couldn't wait?"

"Had a date. Creek's always been a guy for the broads. You know he has a name for his pecker?"

Jack did. It was Steve and the Twins. It bothered Jack that Creek was seeing Frank after telling him not to have any contact. Now he was selling classic cars to Frank's dealership. Creek was part of the company too. If Galitzine Sheng and Munro got antsy about a Mafia connection through either partner, it could blow the pension project. Creek's own words. What was with this guy?

"Creek just dropped off the keys? His own idea?"

"Nah. Carmine called him, asked him to come over. I got some concerns. About you. I wanted to ask him a couple things."

"Like what?"

"I'm just interested. I'm a friend. Also, I got business concerns. You employ a lot of my people. I hear you doing things about the pension fund. Your workers there, they're counting on you. The Teamsters are still watching. We gotta think of our people."

"I do think of them. That's why I'm making moves with the pension fund. How did you hear about it?"

"I'm sick. Not dead. How's your kid doing?"

Jack looked at Frank's face. Frank was still looking at the stars.

"Not good."

"Where's he now? Still in Lompoc?"

"For now. I have hopes."

"Jack, from the heart, I have to say something to you, you're not gonna want to hear."

"Then don't say it."

"Your kid, Danny, he stole from me."

"When?"

"When he was working at the dealership. He was skimming off the shop receipts, doing his own work after hours, used the place as a chop shop, ripping down stolen cars. Carmine tumbled, was gonna use the air hammer on his knees. That's why I had to let him go."

"You told me he was a slacker. You never said he was a thief."

"Anybody else, I'd a made a point with him. You can't let that kinda thing get done to you. People get ideas."

"I thank you for it. I really do. But what's this got to do with Black Water Transit and the pension fund?"

Frank closed his eyes, reached out a bony arm, and wrapped his fingers around Jack's forearm.

"Whatever you do, don't do nothing just for that kid. You know the line 'no good deed ever goes unpunished'? You put yourself onna line for Danny, you'll be sorry. One way or another."

"Frank, what are you hearing?"

"I hear? I hear my life pouring out of the bottle. Making that glug-glug sound, hah? You making moves for Danny, that's what I hear. Talking to people downtown. Those people, the feds, they're worse than the zips. Harvard, Yale, Brown. The tennis players. The single-malt people. Cigar-suckers. Those people got no mercy in them. Us, we stab you inna front. Them, they fuck you up the ass, they kill your cat, they take everything you ever had, and then they go for a facial and later they have a decaf latte widda twist and maybe a cinnamon biscotti. You know a guy, Earl Pike?"

"Yeah. I do."

"He say he know me?"

"He said he knew the same people. Is that true?"

"Pike's people did some things for me when we was trying to set up that hotel in Costa Rica. He knew the locals, steered me to a good lawyer down there. Me, I never met the guy personally, but Carmine did. You in some kinda business with him?"

"He's using your name."

"That's why you're in business with him?"

"It was part of the picture."

"Jack, my honor, I never told Pike he could use my name. He was talking to Carmine about his collection, and Carmine told him about my guns. I don't run Carmine anymore. Carmine said he was a stand-up guy and asked me if he could hand the guy on to you. I figured you'd do what you wanted, say yes or no."

"I know that. Frank, I need to ask you—"

Frank raised a shaking hand, palm out.

"Don't ask me nothing. I ain't a priest. What I don't know, nobody can get outta me with a hacksaw. I unnerstand we gotta do what we gotta do for our kids. My boy, Tony, he's a fucking loser, he don't know that I know he's a coke-head. The guy he buys from, he's a guy I know. I set it up, I let it happen, because I don't want him going to strangers. I let him run the dealership, now I'm sick. He's skimming the till too, the mook. Sooner or later I'm gonna wish I let him crash and burn. But you and me, we're fathers, and we got no power anymore to make the way smooth for our two boys. Family. You don't throw away family. That's an *infamita*. All we can do is say the rosary and wait for the bad news onna telephone."

Jack listened to this, his face set and hard, his chest hurting. Frank was right. There was nothing Jack could do to change Danny's destiny, but he had to ride with his son all the way to the end of the line. Creek didn't understand that, never would, because although Creek had been many things in his life, he had never been a father.

Enough of this.

"You want to talk about Pike. I'm listening."

"No. I got no stake in it either way. Guy's a business associate, not my brother. But if you're inna thing with him, my advice? Carmine's too? Do not fuck up. Be sure of your troops. And if you gonna fuck with the guy in some way, make it permanent. Leave nothing behind. Not even a chalk mark, okay?"

"Carmine know about this thing?"

A flickering sheet of white-hot agony arced right across Frank's face, bleaching it the color of exposed bone. He fumbled for some pills, dumped four into his shaking palm, and downed them with a shot of whiskey. Jack watched this with his heart stopped. In a minute Frank's face softened and the pain ebbed out of it.

"Christ . . . sorry, Jack. Comes and goes. Carmine . . . he's gotta be thinking of himself now. I ain't gonna be around, I got nobody else to hand things off to, so he knows what I'm doing. He knows about this thing with Pike. He's the one told me about it. He thinks you're crazy to fuck with Pike, but Pike's not family and you are. Can't keep nothing from Carmine anyway. Maybe not even Claire."

Jack had nothing to say to that. Frank looked at him for a while and then closed his eyes. His face looked sunken, eroded. But he was in no pain. Jack patted his forearm and sipped at a drink. They sat in silence for another few minutes, until the broker in the lime-green shirt and the tan Dockers pushed the woman in the black bikini into the pool, and then Claire Torinetti jumped into the pool in her see-through pink silk blouse, and the broker in the lime-green Polo shirt dove in after her, and then it was everybody into the pool, and Frank here totally passed out in his deck chair. Carmine came over.

"Hey, Jackie. Frank okay?"

"He's dying, Carmine."

"Yeah. He is."

"I feel bad, not seeing him for so long."

"You should. He talks about Ditmars, Astoria, the neighborhood. He coulda used you, eased the day, but you was always busy. Protecting your good name, hah? Stay away from the goombahs. Go uptown. Good for you. That's nice. You can feel bad, but it's too late for that shit, Jackie. Frank ain't getting no time back."

Maybe Carmine's smile was intended to lighten the tone, take away some of the sting. Then, probably not.

It was time for Jack to call a cab and go home.

MIDTOWN AUTO PARK

200 EAST FORTY-FIRST STREET

2115 HOURS

Pike talked amiably about the various cars he had owned, as the three of them walked down First Avenue from the United Nations Plaza Hotel. The rain was fine and cool and a wind was making the flags outside the UN building flutter and snap. The northbound traffic on First banged and clattered over iron plates covering construction on the UN underpass. Pike had put on an olive-drab Hugo Boss windbreaker and burgundy Bass Weejuns. His stride was long and he covered the ground in an easy rolling walk, making Casey hurry to keep up, speaking mainly to Nicky Cicero. He looked to Casey like a man at perfect ease. They reached Forty-first and, just to make the guy change gears, she asked him what his business had been in Albany. He stopped and looked back at her like she had just snapped into existence from another dimension. He was damn tall from where she was standing, and there was a quality in him that made her think of a python flicking a tongue in a jungle clear-ing.

"I'm a consultant. I was consulting."

Casey moved by him and kept walking.

"What do you consult about?"

"I have a firm called Crisis Control Systems. We're mostly retired military. I was army. We do corporate cri-sis management."

"Sounds sexy," said Nicky, who had observed no signs whatsoever that Earl Pike had been in any kind of physical confrontation in the last few days. And he had been checking out every patch of skin he could see. The plaid shirt was long-sleeved, so he couldn't check the guy's forearms, where he would have deflected an in-coming punch. There were no marks on his face other than what looked like a very old burn scar. Other than the bandaged right hand, the guy was unmarked and he moved like a piece of oiled machinery.

After a ten-round fight up at the gym in Albany, Nicky felt like he'd spent a week doing the spin cycle in a clothes dryer with a bag of rocks for company. If Pike had been in the kind of fight that left the other guy looking the way he did, Nicky never wanted to try him on. Earl glanced at his face to look for sarcasm and saw none.

"Sexy? Not at all, Officer. Very dull stuff. Here we are."

They walked down the slope of a darkened parking garage halfway up the block toward Second Avenue. There was a kiosk at the bottom of the ramp, lit by a hanging yellow bulb. The attendant was asleep behind the greasy glass. Pike smacked the side of the hut and it shook from the blow. Casey tried not to jump. The guy was spooky as hell and she was a little afraid of him by now. Nicky was acting as if they were buddies from PS 115. She intended to talk to him about it later, when they were alone.

Pike had taken his keys from the startled attendant and was walking over to a freight elevator. They rode up in silence. The cage ground to a halt at the fifth floor. The level was jammed with cars, packed in so tight they had to thread their way around them single file. Pike stopped in front of a spot marked 219.

"There she is," he said.

In the space was a navy-blue Mercedes-Benz 600. The paint gleamed under a double bar of fluorescent bulbs. Pike stepped back and watched as Casey and Nicky went over the vehicle.

There wasn't a mark on it. No broken headlights. No scrape on the fender. No new paint. No sign of any recent repairs. The paint was smooth and covered with wax. Other than the fact that it looked as if it had just been washed and waxed, there was nothing about the Benz to suggest it had been anywhere other than this parking spot in the last week.

Casey bent down to look at the New York license plate on the rear. The screws were dull and coated with rust. No one had touched them in years. There were no new scratches around the mounting plate. She stepped back and saw that Pike was watching her carefully. When she made eye contact, he grinned at her.

"My goodness, Officer Spandau, you look disappointed."

"Can you open the hood for us?"

Pike walked around to the driver's door, unlocked it, leaned in, and tugged on the hood latch, popping the engine cover. He moved around to the front, levered the hood up. Nicky pulled a small Maglite out of his leather jacket and leaned in over the engine block. The vehicle identification number was embossed on a plate on the side of the block. It was slightly coated with oil and road dust. He rubbed at the plate with his thumb, checked the number. It matched the VIN on the DMV records for this vehicle.

Nicky read it out to Casey, who checked it with the number on the plate showing in the left side of the dashboard. Also the same. And no signs that either plate had been tampered with in any way. This was not the car. Could not be the car.

Damn.

She moved back from the car as Pike, saying nothing, still perfectly unmoved and relaxed, closed the car up and rubbed at the fingerprints on the side of the door. He looked at the cops, standing under the light from the fluorescent bars. His eyes were deep in shadow and his face looked battered and blunt, making his soft voice and his teasing tone all the more strange.

"You two look tired. How long you been on this?"

"Thanks for your time, Mr. Pike," said Casey. "Nicky, let's go. Sorry to have bothered you."

"No problem," he said. "Happy to have been a help. You sure you can't tell me what the case was all about?"

"Just a vehicle accident, sir. That's all," said Casey.

"Must have been serious. You both seem pretty intense."

"It was a nasty one," said Nicky.

Casey sent him a look. Pike grinned again.

"Well, if I can ever do anything, you'll let me know?"

"We will," said Casey.

"I'll look forward to it, then."

"Yeah. Me too."

Casey and Nicky walked back to the cover car, Jimmy Rock's brand-new Crown Victoria, and found Jimmy Rock reading a printout of some kind. He looked up from the sheets of paper as they got back into the unit, Casey in the backseat this time and Nicky in the passenger side.

"How'd it go?" said Jimmy Rock, addressing the question to no one in particular, which Nicky took as an improvement over his previous policy of ignoring the hell out of Casey Spandau.

"His car's totally clean," she said, her voice packed with resentment, aimed equally at Pike and at Jimmy Rock.

"What'd he have downstairs here?" asked Nicky.

"Big white Lincoln Continental. Valet said he brought it in this morning."

"Anything about the Benz?"

Jimmy Rock shook his head.

"Nothing we can use. I talked to the valet parking guys. Pike did have a blue Mercedes Six Hundred in here yesterday morning. They say he took it out early in the day and never brought it back here. He's got it in a garage down on Forty-first."

"Yeah."

"Why have two cars anyway?"

Casey opened her mouth, but Nicky spoke first.

"I had a car like that Benz, I wouldn't be driving it around New York City either. I'd use a rental."

Jimmy Rock shook his head, not convinced.

"Still hinky. Why not leave his rental in the public

garage and keep his precious antique Mercedes-Benz safe in valet parking?"

Casey and Nicky watched Jimmy Rock's face.

"What are you thinking?" she asked, finally.

Jimmy Rock looked at her over his shoulder as if she had just snapped into being in the backseat.

"I'm thinking, Officer Spandau, that the guy interests me. You sure about the credit card thing, the guy in Castleton?"

"Not a hundred percent. Sometimes the posting date is different from the transaction date. The guy could have been confused."

"But he definitely saw a big man, white hair, with a blue Benz, has a busted left headlight?"

Casey nodded, keeping her doubts to herself. Jimmy Rock was heating up the car with a kind of ferocious energy. She watched him as he came up the dial and realized why he was a good cop. He was a cold-assed racist son of a bitch, but he had good instincts.

"What are you thinking?" asked Nicky, who had decided that although Pike was probably some kind of bad-ass, there was no way they had enough to lay anything on his back over this double homicide near Blue Stores. For Nicky Cicero it was back to zero. Jimmy Rock smiled, shrugged, tapped the side of his nose, reached for the radio.

"Five-one-one to five-zero-zero, K?"

"Five-one-one?"

"Vince, that you?"

"It is. Where are you?"

"UN Plaza. Where are Dexie and Carlo?"

"Having dinner down in the Battery."

"Can we get them up here?"

"Sure. What's up?"

"We're on that thing with the state cop. We may have something here. We can use another car."

"You got it. I'll call them now. How's the traffic?"

"Easing up. Can you ask them to come in fast?"

"Ten-four."

Casey had been trying to read the papers on Jimmy Rock's lap. He saw this, held the sheaf up, fanning the pages.

"Pike's phone calls. Every call he's made since he checked in two weeks back."

"How the hell did you get that?" asked Casey, impressed. Jimmy Rock indicated the woman sitting behind the concierge desk inside the tower lobby.

"Mercedes Gonsalva."

"Her name is Mercedes?"

"Yeah. Coincidence, hah? Anyway, she senses my power."

"Your power?"

"Also, I begged. Anyway, I got the sheet."

Nicky had watched this interchange, puzzled. "But his car's clean. He's not the guy."

"He mojoed the car somehow," said Casey before Jimmy Rock could speak. "He's your guy, Nicky. I feel it."

"Much as I hate to agree with Whitney Houston here, I think she's right. I think this Pike guy is your man. You tell me yourself, Nicky. How'd he strike you?"

Nicky shrugged. He wasn't about to admit the guy scared him. But Jimmy Rock had Nicky's frequency pegged.

"He's a bug, a psycho, a stone-cold killer. A cockroach. A bug, like I said. That's what I'm getting from you both."

Casey spoke up in spite of herself.

"He's not a bug. There's more to him than that. He's like a guy who used to believe in something and then got disappointed or something. He hits you as a guy who has a lot of anger, but has it all tamped down real tight. Tonight, when we showed up, it was like he was . . . enjoying the whole thing. We never rattled his cage at all."

Jimmy Rock took in the speech with a nod, said nothing to her, looked into the middle distance while he tapped a finger on the steering column. Finally he spoke to Nicky directly.

"Nicky, this is your beef. But this is my show. My advice, how about we just hang off his left shoulder for a while, see what happens? We stir up his life a little and see what floats to the top of the pond. That work for you?"

Nicky nodded, privately convinced it would be a total waste of time. If Pike was the guy, they had dick on him. If he wasn't, it would become obvious pretty soon. He'd ride it out for a while, give this cocky DT a chance to screw up, and then he'd tell him to go fuck himself.

Jimmy Rock tossed the pages into the backseat.

"You read these numbers off, Spandau. Nicky, you watch the doors there. I'll do the thinking. That's what I'm good at."

Casey had a cheek muscle working but she said nothing and reached over the front seat into the glove compartment, pulled out the NYPD crisscross directory, flicked on her mini Maglite, and went down the list one by one, reading off the results while Nicky watched the hotel doors and Jimmy Rock listened very hard to what Casey was saying.

"Here's one . . . 973-343-6000 . . . an unlisted Newark number. Called this guy around six. Ben Guardello?"

"He's a gunsmith. Benny Boom-Bang, they call him. Handgun specialist. Does porting and polishing for private clubs. Gas vents. Extensions. Sound suppressors. Pachmyr grips. Laser sights. All legit, as far as we can prove. That's very interesting. What's next?"

Casey worked her way down the page, checking each

number off and flipping through the pages of the criss-cross directory. Jimmy Rock would nod or shake his head, mostly say nothing.

They both listened to Casey read and Jimmy Rock briefly wondered if Casey had family here. Probably a pack of tight-ass phony Islamic nut bars. All the little boys strapped on those stupid bow ties. Sipped Turkish tea, listened to the Revereeno slag the Jews.

"518-664-7878. An upstate number. Called the place once, this afternoon, at twenty minutes after three. Number comes back as Black Water Transit up in Troy. Mean anything to you?"

"What were you saying there?" said Jimmy Rock.

Casey started to go back up the list.

Jimmy Rock shook his head.

"No, that Troy number. The last one."

"518-664-7878 . . . Black Water Transit Systems."

Jimmy Rock considered it for a moment, shook his head.

"Any other reference to Black Water Transit in the list?"

Casey scanned the page.

"Yeah. He called . . . no, that's a Brooklyn number."

"What is it?"

"718-555-2391 . . . but it says Black Water Transit. I see, they have a branch in Red Hook."

"What. The container docks there?"

"Yeah. He called the Red Hook location at four-seventeen today. A six-minute call. Then again . . ."

"The Red Hook number for Black Water?"

"Yeah. He called them again just before we got to his room. Does the name Black Water Transit Systems mean anything to you?"

"Doesn't ring a bell. I've never seen the name on any of our intel sheets. What else is there?"

Casey and Jimmy Rock worked their way through

the rest of the numbers. It took about a half hour, and when they were finished they were no better off. None of the numbers were crime-related or suggested anything hinky about Earl Pike or his associates. When they got to the bottom of the list, Jimmy Rock sighed.

"Okay. Nothing else to do but wait until Dexie gets here."

"And where's he?" asked Nicky.

"He'll be here," said Jimmy Rock. "He's coming. We wait."

Which they did, most of it in a strained silence, everybody thinking something different about Earl Pike. All around them midtown churned and pumped away like a neon circus wagon. Diplomats from the UN sauntered into the lobby surrounded by a phalanx of security people, floating on clouds of self-esteem. An FBI unit in a black Jimmy parked outside the hotel and the driver glared across at them for fifteen minutes. Jimmy Rock stared back for fifteen minutes and eleven seconds. A guy in a three-piece suit made out of green garbage bags pushed a shopping cart filled with running shoes eastward down the street. He was barefoot and wore his hair in two stiff yellow braids like Pippi Longstocking. The garbage-bag suit was very well cut. If he'd done it himself, he was good. A light rain came and went, salting the windows of the 511 unit with tiny glittering diamonds.

Jimmy listened to a swing station play a Voodoo Daddy CD all the way through, keeping time by drumming lightly on the steering wheel. Casey thought about calling her mother and put it off again. Nicky tried to imagine how he would have done with the guy who beat the male vic—Donald Albert Condotti—to death in that clearing. Wondered if it was Earl V. Pike. Wondered if he'd have done better against Pike. Better, he decided, finally. At least he'd have lived.

Fifteen minutes later, across the street, a white Lincoln Continental pulled up to the doors of the UN Plaza. It stopped and a hotel bellman climbed out, holding a parking stub and some keys. He handed them to a big man in an olive-drab jacket and blue jeans, who seemed to materialize out of the dark.

The man was wearing a woolen watch cap. His back was turned to the street. He got into the car and rolled up the window. It was heavily tinted, so the rising line of the window was blocking their view of the driver. Nicky, who had been watching the door of the hotel so hard his eyes were burning, leaned forward over the dash.

"That's him. That's Pike."

Now the man was in the car. It rocked as the guy gunned the engine a couple of times, then jerked as he put it in gear and started to move off, going east. As the car made a left turn and went northbound on First Avenue, Casey wrote down the marker.

"You're right, Nicky," said Jimmy Rock. "That's his car."

Seconds later they were accelerating out of the loading lane. They missed the light change at First and had to sit through the cycle. Casey asked Jimmy Rock a question. She asked it twice.

"I said, are we gonna wait for the backup?"

"When I want tactical advice from you, Spandau, I'll make a point of asking for it. Otherwise do me a favor and zip it, hah?"

Casey started to form a phrase, thought it over, said nothing. Two can play. Nicky just cranked his seat belt tight and braced himself on the front of the dashboard.

The light changed and Jimmy Rock floored it, the Crown Victoria squealing as they pulled out into First. The traffic was light now, mostly cabs and delivery vans, some limos, a few private cars. The wind had picked up, blowing faster, stirring the drifting rain and sending it in little whirlwinds and eddies into the midtown skyline. They watched as the white Lincoln cleared the crest of the hill at Fiftieth, its brake lights flickering as the driver dodged a jaywalker. Then it dropped down out of sight.

He lifted the handset off the hook and thumbed the button.

"Five-one-one to five-zero-zero, K?"

Silence . . . then a click.

"Five-zero-zero. Who's this?"

"Jimmy Rock. That you, Vince?"

"Hey, Jimmy. Che cosa?"

"Boss, we're on that thing with the state guy. We have a good suspect here and I'd like to play him for a while. We're northbound on First, need a tag, both ways. What's the tag, Spandau?"

"Robert Victor Robert eight eight eight."

Jimmy Rock repeated it into the handset. They were coming up on Fifty-first now, and the white Lincoln was about fifty yards up, moving pretty fast.

"Wait one, Jimmy. Did you get a look at his Benz?"

"Yeah. Spandau and the state guy did. It's been dry-cleaned."

"New paint?"

"No. Something else. I figure he switched registrations somehow. Can you ask citywide auto to double-check the DMV records for Pike's Mercedes-Benz? Maybe something will show up."

"I will. If he's that good, he'll have friends. You seen any countersurveillance?"

"None, Vince. He's alone. I really think we got something going here, and I don't wanna lose this mutt."

"I hear that. I'll do the marker and get back to—"

"Vince, where the hell is Dexie now? It's been twenty-five minutes since we called them in. We need them now!"

"Five-zero-nine, you on the air?"

"Five-zero-nine, we're here, boss."

Casey recognized the voice of Dexter Zarnas, the sergeant she had met very briefly when she got into the Jay Rats HQ the night before. It seemed a year ago right now.

"Dexie, this is Jimmy Rock. Where the hell you been?"

"Stuck behind a broke-down garbage truck on Lafayette. We got clear a coupla minutes ago. We're on the FDR at Thirty-fourth right now."

"Can you eighty-five us at Second and Fifty-eighth, by the upper level for the Queensboro Bridge? We're on a white Lincoln, tag number Robert Victor Robert triple eight. We'll be on five for this run. Switching now, K?"

"Switching to five, K. Done, Jimmy."

They let the Lincoln get about a half-block lead on them. The car was holding steady northbound, working through light midtown traffic. Casey was straining her eyes to follow the car. Nicky was thinking that this was a lot of energy to be putting into the wrong guy, but he was just a ride-along in New York. It wasn't his play.

Jimmy Rock flicked the frequency selector over to channel five and put the handset down. He glanced into the back at Casey.

"Spandau, how much sleep you had today?"

"None. I'm okay."

"Nicky, you on your game, kid?"

"I'm fine" was all he had to say.

The car was moving north under street lamps. Yellow light from the lamps flashed across Jimmy Rock's face as he spoke.

"Are you, Nicky? On your game?"

Nicky had been around this cop long enough to recognize a hidden agenda when he heard one.

"I said I'm on my game, Jimmy. Why?"

Jimmy Rock stopped the car on the north side of East Fifty-third, reached across Nicky, and popped open his door. Nicky looked at him hard, but Jimmy Rock held up a hand.

"You really wanna nail this perp?"

"If he's the guy, yeah."

"You were telling me his hand is all wrapped up?"

"Yeah. His right hand. Big Tensor bandage. Looked serious."

"He's out of his room, right?"

Nicky got it in an instant.

"Hell no. I toss his place now, no warrant, whatever we get does us no good at all. Kills the case. We get beefed for no-knock-no-warrant. Not happening."

"Look, kid. It's fuck-the-rules time. The Benz connection is shot to shit. You got dick. This bug, he beats the life out of your vic, then he guts him with a branch, he screws around with the female, no semen, no marks, but on the male vic, Nicky, on him he leaves his own blood. Had to have. Only thing you got, kid. Be a cop. Let the DA worry about where you got the fucking bandages. You do it right, we'll say we saw him throw the bandages in a garbage can right on the street. What's he gonna do about it, we stick together? Fuck him."

Nicky hesitated another full second.

Casey got twitchy.

"Make a decision! We're losing him. Nicky, just go!"

That settled it. Nicky bailed at a quick walk. Casey got into the passenger seat and watched his back as he went south on First. Jimmy Rock was accelerating north, paying zero attention to her.

"What if he gets caught?"

"He's state. He's JAFO. And he's not one of ours."

"What the hell is a JAFO?"

"Just another fucking observer."

"He's a cop."

"Not one of mine. And neither are you. So shut the fuck up."

Before Casey could say anything, the radio clicked and popped.

"Five-zero-zero to five-one-one, K?"

Jimmy Rock snagged the handset.

"Vince, Jimmy here."

"Yeah. We got your comeback on that tag. Registered owner is a Hertz leasing company in Jersey. No help."

"Ten-four, Vince. Thanks."

"Stay on him, Jimmy Rock. I'll be here."

"You heard that?"

"I did. Watch it. You're gonna come right up behind him."

The white Lincoln had gotten tangled up in traffic and had come to a stop at the intersection of First and Fifty-seventh. Through the tinted rear window they could see the driver's head, twisting this way and that. The light changed, and the Lincoln pulled through, made a sharp left, and came to a stop on the north side of Fifty-seventh.

Jimmy Rock cursed and drove on by, not looking at the driver. As he passed the Lincoln he picked up the handset.

"Five-one-one to five-zero-nine, K?"

"Five-zero-nine. Jimmy, this is Dexter. Where are you?"

"We're westbound on Fifty-seventh Street, at First. Our player's parked at the curb about a hundred feet west of the intersection. I had to overrun him. Where are you right now?"

"We're northbound on Sutton Place. We're turning onto Fifty-seventh right now. White Lincoln, Robert Victor Robert triple eight . . . wait one . . ."

There was a long silence during which they could hear the two cops talking softly over the open mike, the rumble of the car engine, traffic noises.

Then, *"Yes—that's him, Carlo! Jimmy, we got him here, about a half block up, on the north side."*

"Okay . . . stay on him. I'll drop back and come around. What're you driving?"

"We've got the gypsy cab. Big Bird?"

"I know it. Stay *on* that player."

"Ten-four, five-one-one. Out."

"Now what?" said Casey.

Jimmy Rock was rounding the block on Fifty-sixth and coming back east. He made the hard left again and stopped a few hundred feet back of the intersection of First and Fifty-seventh. He breathed out, sighed, and frowned across at Casey Spandau. He opened his mouth to answer, and the radio burst into life.

"Five-zero-nine to five-one-one, K?"

"Five-one-one. Go."

"Five-one-one, we're westbound on Fifty-seventh—he's pulling away—okay, we're making a right onto the upper level—he's moving out fast now. You coming?"

"We're right behind you, five-zero-nine. Let's keep off the air as much as we can, hah? He might have a scanner."

"Ten-four. Out."

"Should we run Earl Pike on NCIC?"

Jimmy Rock thought it over.

"I'd say no. Not right now. Every time we make an NCIC request, it gets flagged all over the place. I don't want a lot of feds looking at our NCIC hits and wondering if we're onto something they can steal."

The engine noise filled the car as Jimmy Rock accelerated around a wandering fruit truck. Far ahead, the gypsy cab and the white Lincoln were two red sparks in the glittering field of the bridge lights, the planes and angles, squares and rooftops of Long Island City. Six minutes later they were a hundred feet back from the lopsided and badly dented gypsy Checker with the greasy windows. A hundred feet ahead of the Checker cab, moving in and out of heavy traffic, was the white Lincoln, eastbound on the Queensboro Bridge.

To their right, as they climbed up the rise, the towers and lights of midtown were wrapped in a cloud of swirling rain. Under their tires the broken plates of the Queensboro Bridge hammered. Roosevelt Island loomed up and passed and then they were coming down a steep incline and Long Island City was all around them.

In the north there seemed to be something wrong with the Bronx. No lights showed on the bluffs and the sky looked like smoked glass. The thunderstorm hit three minutes later.

Down at the exits from the bridge, and higher up in the north, a rain squall, a huge mass of gray-black haze, rolled southward out of the Bronx, sliding across the skyline of Long Island City, blotting out the lights, and all the bridge traffic was driving down into it—into a wall of rain that reduced visibility to twenty feet.

Jimmy Rock was leaning forward in the seat, hands tight on the wheel, straining to see the cars immediately ahead. Casey was struggling to see the turn sign for Queens Boulevard and stay in touch with 509, somewhere up ahead. They listened to the cross talk from the other surveillance car. You could hear the tension over the radio. Casey picked up the mike and keyed it on.

"Five-one-one to five-zero-nine, K?"

"*Five-zero-nine.*"

"Where the hell are you?"

"*Who's that?*"

"Officer Spandau. What's your twenty?"

"*We . . . we think we're on our guy, got him up ahead maybe fifty feet, far end of a dump truck there.*

He's making . . . shit . . . sorry . . . he's making a left onto Queens Boulevard. Where are you guys?"

"Maybe a block back."

"Well, you better move up, 'cause things are getting hinky here. We gotta stay on his ass and—there he goes!"

They heard the sound of tires spinning on wet pavement, and then the roar of the cab engine.

"He's evading. I don't know if he burned us but he made a snaky move there, cut by a truck on the left side, signaling a turn onto Northern, then made a right onto . . . Van Dam! He's gone southbound toward Van Dam!"

Jimmy Rock hit the pedal, powered the car around a line of cars, and ran straight down the median strip, driving through oncoming vehicles. Casey braced herself on the seat back and tried to keep from swearing at this crazy white cop.

Two cars ended up swerving right out of their path— another rose up out of the haze like a barge out of a fog bank—Casey got a brief glance sideways as they slid by the 509 car, caught in a line of cars following a tractor-trailer—a fleeting image of the pale, blurred outline of Dexter Zarnas behind the windshield—then Jimmy had the Crown Victoria bouncing over a curb and was making a hard left onto Van Dam.

Now they were ahead of 509 and Jimmy pushed the car hard, sliding out again, fishtailing, searching the huddled blurry outlines of the cars ahead, trying to see a white Lincoln, trying to pick it out of the clutter of cars and trucks inching along in the squall. He had the car up to thirty in a clear stretch . . . forty . . . they could feel the car floating and sliding on the slippery surface . . . a car was coming up on the right . . . was it the white Lincoln?

Was it? Thirty yards . . . twenty . . . ten.

It wasn't.

"Nice play," said Casey into the following silence. "A really professional play. Golly. I'm so fucking dazzled."

Jimmy Rock had nothing to say, so he said it.

Casey felt better than she had in a long time. But the white Lincoln was still gone.

SUITE 2990

THE UNITED NATIONS PLAZA HOTEL

2200 HOURS

It took Nicky seventeen minutes to work his way through the garage and up the maintenance halls of the hotel and another ten to reach the room service elevator for the tower residences. A few people saw him, mainly Hispanic cleaners and a maintenance worker, but Nicky worked hard at looking like an immigration officer— what the Chicanos called *la migre*—and was convincing enough to be invisible. Now he was in the hall outside Pike's suite, with his blood pounding so hard in his neck it was moving his jacket collar. He exhaled and studied the electronic lock. Okay, Wonder Boy. How the hell do you get around that?

He walked back to the elevator banks and saw a house phone on a pearl-inlaid table, next to a vase of roses. He picked it up, hit the icon for maid service. A Hispanic-sounding voice answered immediately.

"This is Mr. Pike, in 2990."

"You are not in your room, Mr. Pike?"

Christ. Of course. Room phones showed the ID.

"No, I'm just at the elevator. I'm in a rush. I need an iron and a board. Can you bring me one right now? I'm going to be downstairs for about ten minutes. I'll need it when I get back."

"Of course, Mr. Pike. Someone will be right up."

Nicky put the phone down, shook his head. This was lunacy. How the hell had he gotten tangled up in this kind of cowboy crap? Then he saw the forest clearing again, and Condotti's belly opened up, and the blonde girl's eyes—Julia Maria Gianetto—twenty years old, for Christ's sake—she's staring up at the underside of a coffin lid for the rest of eternity—and he figured, what the hell. If Pike was the guy, it was worth some chances.

He paced the silent halls until he heard the elevator rising, then padded quickly to the alcove where the ice machine was running. He heard the door opening and watched as a maid in a green uniform walked down toward Suite 2990. She used a code card, opened the door, and stepped inside, leaving the door slightly open.

Nicky sprinted on his toes down the hall and looked inside the room. The maid was setting the ironing board up in the living room, next to the green leather couch. Her back was turned. He stepped lightly into the suite and moved down the hall toward the kitchen. Two minutes afterward, he heard the door closing again. His right knee was shaking and his face felt hot.

The main room was empty, the view out the windows just as impressive as it had been an hour ago. Pike's scent was in the air, some sort of cologne that reminded Nicky of margaritas. He checked his watch. He'd been in the room for sixty seconds.

Moving as fast as he could, and touching nothing with his bare hands, Nicky looked for bloody bandages in any wastebasket he could find. He used a kitchen towel to open the cupboard under the sink. Coffee grounds, orange peels, wrappers from a deli, a Nat Sherman cigarette box, empty. A match book from Parnell's.

No bloody bandages.

The bedroom was all that was left. Two minutes in. He walked across the deep emerald-green carpet and went up the landing steps to the closed bedroom door, pushed it with his left shoulder, holding his hands up like a surgeon walking into an operating room. The large room held a king-sized bed, the sheet turned down, two mints on the golden pillows. The view out the window was south along First Avenue, the street full of cars now, the rain coming down harder. It seemed to Nicky that there was a storm building across the river. He turned away from the window. The bathroom door was open. He stepped in, looked around at the huge green marble tub, the mirrored walls.

The cabinet held a few items, a can of Barbasol shave cream, a Gillette Excel razor, some spares, a tube of Colgate, a stick of English Leather deodorant, a small leather case zipped shut. He lifted it out, opened it. A manicure set. He set it back on the shelf, opened the bottle of hydrogen peroxide. Nothing unusual. The rest was standard. Listerine. Bandages. A new Tensor still in the wrapping.

Everything was lined up in a row, as if Pike were waiting for a military inspection. All of the items were so ordinary it was weird. No pill bottles, no needles, nothing with a name on it, or any kind of identifying mark. He looked down at the wastebasket beside the counter. Nothing. No bandages, not even a bloody Kleenex.

That was it. Time to get the hell out. Jimmy Rock was a nitwit and Nicky was thinking it was time to go home. He began to close the cabinet door, and then he froze. The razor. Maybe the razor.

He picked up the Excel, looked at the blade. It had been used recently. Nicky could see specks of skin and beard hair, some soap residue, and tiny ribbons and flecks of red.

Was it enough? It would have to be enough.

He popped the blade off, made a move to put the razor back, and then picked up the plastic pack of spares. Would Pike notice?

He'd have to take the chance. He put a new blade into the Excel razor head, set the razor back where he had found it, replaced the pack of spares, closed the cabinet door with his elbow, and looked around the bathroom. Nothing looked different. He had been careful to touch as little of it as possible. He checked the deep carpet and saw no shoe marks, no sign that he'd been in the bedroom at all.

As he was going back out through the bedroom, he saw a long brushed-steel case on the floor beside the bed. Five feet long, two feet wide, a foot high, it looked solid and heavy. The lock was a combination, built into the handle.

Nicky thought about it for about seven seconds, made a move toward it, and then heard an electric whine through the walls. The elevator. He was through the living room and out the door in five seconds, moving quietly, feeling his muscles tightening in his back and around his belly. As he was closing the main door he remembered. The damn ironing board. Pike would see it, want to know why it was there. As soon as he called room service he'd know something was up. The whole point of the stunt was to get in and get out without letting Pike know anything had happened.

Nicky ran back into the room, grabbed the board and the iron, and made it out the door. He crossed in front of the elevator banks just as the car stopped and the doors began to slide open. He was into the ice machine alcove by the time he heard voices in the hall. Two people, a man and a woman. He waited until the voices receded down the hall in the other direction. Then he propped the board up beside the ice machine, left the iron on the floor beside it, and got the hell out of Dodge.

Jimmy Rock and Casey worked the search area for another ten minutes, saw no sign at all of the white Lincoln. Finally they got on the radio and hooked up with the 509 unit, the gypsy cab, in an alleyway off Hunters Point Avenue.

Both cops in the 509 unit were in their late twenties: Dexter Zarnas, a sergeant and second-in-command under Jimmy Rock, a battered-looking thick-necked white guy with pocked cheeks, a shaved head, a severely dented nose, and a neatly trimmed black goatee, and Carlo Suarez, a pale-faced rookie with a wispy mustache and wide-awake eyes, who looked about seventeen. They all agreed that nobody had the slightest clue concerning the current location of the target vehicle, and then there followed a long and very painful silence. Jimmy Rock sighed and picked up the radio.

"Five-one-one to five-zero-zero, K?"

"Hey, Jimmy! What's up?"

"We lost our player somewhere southbound on Van Dam."

"I heard it. Everybody okay?"

"Yeah. Five-zero-nine's with us now."

"Okay, what's your move?"

"Two ways it could go here. One, he made us, we're burned; if so, maybe the guy goes back to the UN Plaza. I need you to put a local unit down there and see if he comes back. He'll maybe be on foot or come in a cab. I need to hear if he shows up there. Boss, you got your data online there in front of you?"

"*Yeah.*"

"Can you get us anything on Black Water Transit Systems?"

"*Why them?*"

"Pike made calls to that company today. It's the only thing that stands out. It was an Albany number, and he was up in that area yesterday. Then later he calls their branch office at the Red Hook Container Terminal. Now we're sitting in Queens, fifteen minutes from the docks in Red Hook. It's thin, but it's all we got."

"*Sure. Give it to me.*"

"518-664-7878 and 718-555-2391."

"*Okay. I'll get back to you.*"

"Thanks, Vince. K."

He put the radio down. Casey was looking at him.

"What have you got in mind?"

Jimmy Rock put a finger beside his nose.

"Listen and learn, Spandau."

A silence settled in. Casey just sat there and sucked it up. As far as she was concerned, she was in cop hell, serving an indefinite sentence for thumping out a miserable little PD named Eddie Rubinek. She was, in her own words, up to her hips in self-inflicted shit. Twenty minutes pass, and they all jump as the radio beeped.

"*Five-one-one, K?*"

"Five-one-one."

"*Jimmy, Black Water Transit is a shipping company, runs out of Troy. CEO is a guy named Vermillion. Jack Vermillion. Nothing against him on NCIC, but I found a recent hit on him. Not a beef, just a background inquiry from the assistant U.S. attorney's office in Albany. It was placed by some ATF agent named Luther Campbell. Get this. It was recent. Logged just this morning. What do you think?*"

Jimmy Rock glanced at Casey, not really seeing her.

His mind was in overdrive, that she could see. He was an intense little rat.

"The ATF was asking NCIC about Jack Vermillion?"

"Today. This morning."

"And now Earl Pike is talking to Black Water."

"And Pike is what, Detective Rule?" said Casey. Jimmy Rock glanced at her, got it at once.

"Boss, Spandau says Pike is military."

"Retired. He says."

"Retired, she says. But that goes with guns, which connects with the ATF and Black Water. I mean, if he's clean, why try to lose us? If he's that surveillance-conscious, he's got something to hide."

"We don't know he burned us, Jimmy Rock," put in Casey. "Maybe you just blew the surveillance all by yourself."

She watched with real delight as Jimmy Rock's cheek bunched up. Jimmy showed her nothing but the side of his face.

"Boss, here's what I'm thinking. He was heading down Van Dam the last time we saw him. He phoned Black Water Transit twice today. Now we lose him in the vicinity of a Black Water Transit warehouse in Brooklyn. Maybe we can zip down there to Red Hook, check out the facility, see if we can pick him up again."

"Why not just go back to the UN Plaza, wait for him to turn up? What's Nicky Cicero say?"

Casey watched Jimmy Rock's face and was delighted to see him nervous.

"Boss, the state guy's . . . not with us."

"Where is he?"

Jimmy Rock was in a hard place, between his boss and a hostile black PW who was clearly enjoying his troubles. She smiled at him.

"I left him at the hotel."

"Then why ask for a cover car to attend at the hotel? You already had a guy there."

"I put him on another thing."

They could hear the suspicion in Zaragosa's voice. There was a long silence.

"I guess we'll have to talk about that later, Jimmy."

"Yes, boss."

"Okay. Go down to Red Hook. See if you can pick up the Lincoln. Stay on him for a while, see if he does anything hinky. We got nothing else on right now, so I can spare you. But I want you all back here by midnight. That includes the New York State guy, wherever the hell he is. Spandau's been on the job for thirty-six hours straight. Tell Dexie and Carlo they can split right now if they want. I'll call you if the unit at the hotel sees anything of your subject or the Lincoln. But you and me, Jimmy Rock, we are gonna have a little chat, you follow? Ten-four, K?"

"Ten-four, boss. I follow."

THE UNITED NATIONS PLAZA HOTEL

EAST FORTY-FOURTH STREET AND FIRST AVENUE

2245 HOURS

Earl Pike arrived back at the UN Plaza Hotel about thirty minutes after Nicky had come up out of the valet parking garage and walked westbound along Forty-fourth Street. He rolled the white Lincoln up to the lobby and tossed the keys to the attendant, who jumped into it and drove it into the basement garage.

Pike's arrival back at the hotel should have kicked off a stir in the police unit Vince Zaragosa had asked Midtown South to *absolutely* be there in case Pike showed up. It did not kick up a stir. That's because the cover unit didn't *get* there for another hour. Zaragosa heard later, from the XO—the executive officer—at Midtown North, they had to pull a big 10-63 first. A 10-63 is a pee break and lunch. Pike was paying no particular attention to the street at that point either. He also had a lot on his mind, but not so much that he didn't notice the look on the concierge's face when he pushed in through the heavy glass doors.

"Mr. Pike," said Mercedes Gonsalva. "How are you?"

Her hands were folded on top of the inlaid credenza, her eyes wide and her face a porcelain mask. The cops had gotten to her. How much was a very good question. If he had the time, he'd ask her. He nodded and walked through the hall and punched the elevator button.

They had a tail on him, that was obvious. Although he had finessed the immediate problem with the Benz by getting it reworked overnight in a CCS-controlled chop shop, it wasn't enough to get them off his back. He'd confirmed that by his run out the Queensboro Bridge. They had at least two units on him, a blue Crown Vic, three inside, and a rusted yellow gypsy cab, with two more cops. He'd made the blue Crown Vic as they followed him up First. The gypsy cab had picked him up as he crossed the Queensboro Bridge. Two cars. Five people. That was a lot of serious police attention. Expensive attention. He deeply regretted the reason for their interest. It had been a stupid act of self-indulgence, a weakness. Now he would have to deal with the consequences. Starting with these cops.

They were good, but not great. They'd been relatively easy to lose in Long Island City. The rain had been a stroke of luck. But by the time he got into the elevator and felt the car accelerating into the tower, he had a lot of unanswered questions to consider. When he reached the door to his suite he looked hard at the lock and saw no signs of any entry attempt. He eased his Smith out of his belt holster and kept it low against the side of his right leg and keyed the door open, pushing it wide with his foot, watching the hinge space for someone behind the door. No one.

The apartment was empty. Untouched. He inhaled deeply. No new scents . . . wait. Yes. Something floral, something cheap. It was vaguely familiar. He recognized it from somewhere. But he couldn't place it. It had not been in his room an hour ago.

He walked through the living area and opened the bedroom doors. The room looked exactly as he had left it. The steel case with the .50-caliber sniper rifle was untouched, right where he left it. The new scent was not in here. Whoever had come in—if someone had come in—they had stayed in the living room. He walked back out to the living room and went over it carefully. He saw nothing in the deep pile rug other than his own tracks and the scuffed imprints of the two cops who had called on him earlier.

Okay, now wait. What about this?

Two deep lines, about three feet apart, impressed into the pile next to the leather couch. Parallel indentations, each about an inch wide. They were brand-new. Pike thought about them for a minute and decided they were the marks left by one of those folding ironing boards. He walked over to the phone, punched up room service.

"Room Service. How may we help you, Mr. Pike?"

"Has a maid been in my room lately?"

He listened calmly as the man asked a question in Spanish, and heard a muffled answer.

"Yes sir, Mr. Pike. You ask for an iron and a board. You wish for us to come now and pick it up?"

He made the scent then. It was the kind of roses-and-lavender scent the maid left in his bedroom when she came to turn down the sheets at night and arrange those stupid chocolate mints on his pillow.

"No. No, thanks. I forgot. Thank you."

"You're most welcome, Mr. Pike. Good night."

He searched the suite carefully then and saw no sign of the ironing board. He went out in the hall and walked the length of it. He found it in the ice machine alcove, leaning against the machine, the iron on the floor beside it. He picked the board up by the cloth ring and used a pen to lift up the iron by the handle, took them back to his room, and double-locked the door. He went into the bedroom again, opened a dresser drawer, and lifted out a small forensic field kit. He went back to the living room, where it took him less than six minutes to lift a number of separate prints off the iron and the ironing board.

He put each imprint in a separate plastic bag and marked them with a pen. Then he went back through the bedroom doors and reexamined the brushed-steel rifle case on the floor beside his bed. There wasn't a mark on it, he was certain. No smudges by the combination dial set into the handle. Pike was confident it hadn't been moved. The carpet had shoe marks, but nothing that couldn't have been made by himself or the maid turning the bed down.

Pike went into the bathroom, inhaled deeply. No scent in here other than bleach and shampoo. He popped open the cabinet and picked up the can of Barbasol shaving cream, unscrewed the base, and extracted the mini camcorder inside it. A red LED indicated that it was on. It was light-activated, so someone had opened the cabinet door after he had set the camera to ready. He flipped open the tiny LED screen in the side of the camera, and pressed rewind. The tape whirred and the numbers on the LED indicator ran backward to zero.

Pike walked back into the living room with the video

camera and sat down on the couch. He let out a long breath to calm himself. Then he pressed play. The little screen was only two inches square, but the color image was excellent. It showed a clear unwavering picture, slightly distorted by the wide-angle lens.

The cop in the black leather jacket, the one who looked like a movie star, curly black hair, the scars around his eyes, he was holding the cabinet door open, studying the interior. The pinhole lens had caught him head-on. Pike watched his face as the cop looked up and down at the items in the cabinet, picked up the manicure set, put it back on the shelf. What was his name again? Cicero. The black cop had called him what? Nicky? Yeah. Nicky Cicero.

In the tiny video image, he watched as the cop looked down at something on the floor of the bathroom— probably the wastepaper basket. Then he looked almost directly into the lens, started to close the cabinet door again, and hesitated. Cicero was staring intently at something on the shelf next to the video camera. His hand enlarged and darkened the digital screen and then withdrew, holding Pike's Gillette Excel razor. He held the blade up in the light over the cabinet, did nothing for a few seconds, looking a little conflicted, and then he extracted the blade and replaced it with a new one from the dispenser.

Pike watched as the cop carefully set the razor and the extra blades back into position, and then the door closed like a lid on a coffin and the screen went black. The drive motor shut off and the red LED on the side of the camera showed pause. Pike put the camera down and stared out the window of the hotel room at the misted skyline of New York. DNA. They had his DNA.

How could he have overlooked the razor? He never reused a blade. It was a field practice, part of the general tradecraft that had been drilled into his skull a thousand times by the training cadre at Fort Belvoir. No skin, no blood, no hair, no tissue. Not even a scent. Something— a feathery tickling sensation—made a muscle in his right cheek jerk. He felt a movement on his left temple but did not bother to look at it. He knew what it was. He had pills for that.

What he did *not* have was a good reason for all this police attention. Other than the DNA—which was disastrous—they had nothing to link him to the . . . the crime. He had to face that. There was no way to call it a business matter. No way to dress it up. He had failed to control himself, he had been weak. It was a crime that he had committed in Blue Stores. But they must have had hundreds of other Mercedes-Benz 600s to tick off the list before they came back to look at him a second time. And yet here they were, acting on nothing at all, doing a blatantly illegal and therefore totally inadmissible search of his room. Even if they did try to use the DNA against him, the New York Court of Appeals would throw the evidence off the roof onto Centre Street. It made no sense at all.

There were only two ways to explain it.

Either the cops on this case were just a pack of wild-ass NYPD cowboys looking to . . . what did they call it? Flake a case. Get evidence and then lie about the source. Just to make a collar.

Or they weren't really NYPD at all and had something else in mind. Something much more interesting than a dumb dead thug and his gutter-mouthed little whore. It had not been his experience that federal law enforcement cared very deeply about the random deaths of two obscure civilians. Everything he had seen in life was telling him that this contact was important, that a forceful response was vital to his interests. He thought about CCS, about the various contracts he and his associates were processing. Was there something in one of those sectors that would draw this kind of attention? Yes, he decided, but there had always been a great deal of federal attention directed to any project connected to CCS. None of the attention had ever turned into an illegal search. What was different? What had changed? Who was new on his horizon line?

Pike put the camera back into the case and set it down on the coffee table, next to the phone. He spent a few moments controlling his breathing and trying to ignore the spidery tickles on his cheek and up under his hairline. The Citicorp building glowed with pale white fire and he remembered seeing the same kind of pale glowing fire moving along a network of radio antennae on top of a Russian freighter as his surveillance chopper hammered through a hurricane off the Grand Banks. What was that light called?

Saint Elmo's fire. It wasn't really a fire. It was an illusion created by static electricity around the antennae. Not all that different from his hallucinatory infestation of tiny red spiders. There was a rational explanation for both experiences. He found the insight a calming one. The spidery sensation near his temple subsided slightly. He picked up the telephone and carefully dialed a number. He scratched his cheek lightly with the tips of the fingers of his left hand and studied the Tensor bandage covering the knuckles on his right hand as he listened to the phone ring. It rang five times, and then someone answered.

"Vermillion."

"Jack, how are you?"

"Earl. What can I do for you? Everything okay?"

"Where are you, Jack?"

"In my house. Watching a retard cat eat chicken legs. Why?"

"You alone, Jack?"

Pike listened hard as it took Jack a few seconds to get

his voice under tight control, and when he did speak, it was calm, contained, not overly friendly, just about the way a guy would speak when somebody he doesn't know real well calls him at his home number at eleven-thirty in the evening with a smart-ass comment.

"Yes, I'm alone. Why?"

"Everything okay up there?"

"Yeah. Where are you?"

"I'm in New York. I'm going over to the terminal later, see the *Agawa Canyon* come in. Unless you got some other advice?"

There was another silence. He heard Jack breathing.

"Pike, don't play me like this. I'm tired. You go if you want, or you skip the whole thing if you want. I'll call my captain right now, tell him to leave the container on board, he'll take it right back up here. Have your guy with the trailer pick it up, and you go find another route. Right now you're beginning to get on my nerves."

"Hey . . . relax. I'm just calling in. I said I would."

Jack didn't remember that. Maybe it was true.

"Yeah. Well, it's late. I'm tired. I got a lot on my mind."

"Yeah," said Pike. "Me, too. *Adiós, compadre.*"

Pike put the receiver down softly and considered the skyline. He was certain now that Jack Vermillion had somehow sold him out. If Vermillion was the trigger, it would explain the surveillance, the illegal search. And it meant there would be people covering the movement of his container of weapons. They had to, to establish the chain of evidence.

Which meant that there would be heavy surveillance at Red Hook too, either these cops or maybe the ATF. This was a sting, a federal sting. It had to be. If he was right, and he knew he was, then it was too late to do anything about it. He couldn't call it off, because he'd already arranged for the container to be delivered to the

Black Water Transit yards upstate. He had confirmed it on a phone call to Vermillion, a call that had to have been taped. The container had been delivered by his driver and placed straight into customs bond under his name. That was a predicate act all by itself. He was already deep into the trap. Thanks to Jack Vermillion and all these cowboy cops, his collection, the trust of his father and his father's father, was lost to him now. Gone down the federal abyss. To be melted down or sold to cronies inside the system. And it was his own damn fault. What was he going to do about it?

Five minutes later he was walking out of the valet parking garage carrying his large steel rifle case and a small black canvas sports bag. He was wearing black jeans and his olive-drab jacket and running shoes. He caught a cab at the corner of Second and was gone. Thirteen minutes and forty-two seconds later, the patrol unit that Vince Zaragosa had asked for a couple of hours back, the one that took some quality time out for a pee break, finally pulled up in front of the hotel lobby. By that time, Pike was already out of the box and nobody at all was on him in any useful way. Not the ATF, because Valeriana Greco had decided it was too risky to tail him, and not the NYPD, because they'd bungled the Pike surveillance like a squadron of circus clowns. As far as any of the officials involved were concerned, Earl V. Pike was in the wind, totally off the radar.

PART TWO

RED HOOK

It was after midnight, or close, but Jimmy Rock wasn't anywhere near giving up on waiting for Earl Pike. They were parked in a stand of trees at the western edge of Red Hook Park. The rain had stopped and a wet wind was shaking the tree branches and gusting around the 511 unit. Dexie and Carlo were going the distance with them as well, sitting inside the 509 gypsy cab, about a hundred feet away from the Red Hook Terminal, tucked into the driveway of a warehouse, windows misted over, blank as silver coins.

On the far side of Van Brunt, the hundred-foot-long concrete walls of the Red Hook Container Terminal buildings blocked out the view of the Battery and lower Manhattan, but they could still see the glow from the city; it surrounded the terminal in a yellow haze, silhouetting them. Mist swirled and coiled in a wind off upper New York Bay. The terminal was lit up like an airport runway, as forklifts and front-end loaders cleared a long quay along the river's edge. A row of trucks was lined up inside the yard, apparently waiting for the arrival of some freighter. A group of dockworkers was standing around at the tip of the key, looking like a crew ready to take a docking line, but there was no ship anywhere around. Above the din of forklift engines and the gravelly mutter of idling diesels, the cops could still hear the channel markers sounding out in the bay, a low bass note like an organ in an empty church.

Time had passed, the way it does on a stakeout, with nobody saying much of anything, especially in the 511 unit, where Casey was having a hard time just staying awake and Jimmy Rock was listening to a jazz channel on the radio and maintaining his policy of total nonfraternization with the black woman sitting beside him.

At around midnight, Nicky Cicero arrived in a gypsy cab. They asked him where the hell he had been. He told them briefly, keeping his good news for last. After he left the hotel, he had stopped into a bar to have a quiet conversation with a bourbon-and-soda, just to calm himself down, and then gone up the block to Second, where he found a patrol car from the One Seven and showed them his badge. After about an hour of dicking him around, they had finally called a sergeant in a supervisor car, who patched him through to Vince Zaragosa at the Jay Rats HQ.

Now, Vince Zaragosa wasn't interested in talking over Nicky's activities with a harness bull on the other line, so he told the supervisor to have Nicky taken out to the Red Hook location in a patrol unit. But by now the supervisor was in a snit and giving him grief about not letting him know the Jay Rats were operating in his sector, so he finally told Nicky to ditch the harness bull and grab a cab out to Red Hook, that he'd give him a chit for it later. So he did, which meant he arrived in a cab instead of coming into the area in a marked and highly visible NYPD patrol unit, which turned out to be another tiny but perfect link in the world-class law enforcement cluster-fuck that was now coming together very nicely down in Red Hook.

Anyway, Nicky was feeling pretty good about himself when he got there, and told them all about the razor blade. He held it up in the dim light from the dashboard, the little gray blade inside a plastic evidence Baggie he had borrowed from the patrol guys in the squad car. Jimmy Rock was impressed and said so, which made

Nicky feel slightly better about him. Casey had another view.

"What if he notices the blade is gone? What if we all get beefed for break-and-enter? What if somebody saw Nicky go in?"

Jimmy Rock shrugged and said nothing.

"Nobody did," said Nicky. "We got his DNA. All we have to do is go get it typed and pick him up when the results come in a week later. For that matter, Jimmy, why the hell even bother hanging around here? We know where he lives. We can scoop him anytime."

Casey agreed with him.

"He's right. Once the state guys get a DNA match, they can find Pike wherever he is and lay a charge. Our part in this investigation is over. It ended when we lost the Lincoln."

"That's not the point," said Jimmy Rock. "Vince has a patrol unit out in front of the hotel. What have we heard? We've heard dick. Ergo he's not back there. Where is he, then? He's coming here. I want to be here when he does. And I'm running this unit. Okay?"

"Why? What's the point?" asked Nicky.

"What's the name of this unit, Officer Cicero?"

"Jay Rats. Joint Task Force."

"Yeah . . . the word is *joint,* and the job description includes helping out cops from other jurisdictions. Which I'm doing. But right now it also looks like your suspect in a double homicide may be involved in a stunt of some kind on my turf, and I'm the street boss of this joint operation, and I'm not going home until I know what this mook is up to. So let's zip it for a while and enjoy the night air, hah?"

Nicky sighed, leaned back in the rear seat.

"Okay. I'll give you an hour. Then I'm going to take this . . . evidence . . . back to my detachment and get it processed. This may be your unit, Detective, but it's my case. Anybody mind if I smoke?"

"I don't give a fuck if you burst into flames," said Jimmy Rock, who was never very good at compromises. Casey watched Nicky as he pulled out a pack of Marlboros. She groaned when she saw them.

"Man. I should have known."

Nicky looked hurt.

"What?"

"Marlboros. Jesus, Nicky. You're a walking cliché."

"Thank you," he said. "I try to amuse. Want one?"

Casey worked at killing a yawn and failed. What the hell?

"Yes," she said. "I will."

"Goodness," said Jimmy Rock. "Whitney has a vice."

Casey tried to ignore him. Nicky held out a Zippo, flicked it on. Casey puffed and the car filled up with smoke. Jimmy Rock sighed and hit the power button on the passenger window; it slid down. The smoke blew out into the soft mist and drifted on the wind off the East River. The damp air smelled of salt and dead fish and motor oil. By the time the smoke reached the razor wire along the perimeter of the Red Hook Terminal, it was hardly anything at all, but the ATF sniper lying on the roof of the truck garage could still smell it.

He keyed his throat mike, spoke in a whisper.

"Able to Six Actual."

In his observation post on top of the container terminal, Luther Campbell put down his Star Lite night-vision goggles and pulled his helmet mike closer to his mouth.

"Six Actual."

"Marlboros," said the ATF man, still watching the 511 unit through the scope on his Remington bolt-action. "Now they're smoking."

Campbell grinned at the man on the roof beside him, an ATF agent named Bunny Kreuger. Kreuger was one-third of the three-round burst Jack Vermillion had last seen up at his offices in Troy. Kreuger made a war face and clicked on his headset mike.

"Able, this is Baker. That a postcoital smoke?"

The ATF sniper, an ex–Marine Corps gunnery sergeant named Farrell Garber, chuckled softly.

"No, the other guy won't leave them alone long enough."

Campbell's radio set chirped.

"People, this isn't a game. Stay on point."

Campbell groaned. He covered his mike and spoke to Kreuger.

"Jeez, where the hell is she?"

Kreuger indicated a row of darkened windows above the main loading yard.

"The shipping office. They have a toilet and a coffee machine. She's sitting behind the desk listening to opera on NPR."

"With her gear on? The little black fatigue thingy by DKNY?"

Kreuger nodded. Valeriana Greco's habit of wearing tailor-made combat fatigues on any operation, no matter how minor, was legendary inside the Albany federal offices, as was her affection for personal firearms. She wore a Glock strapped to her right thigh and had a Ka-Bar knife—a Ka-Bar, for God's sake—in a Velcro scabbard on the left side of her Kevlar vest, under a nameplate that read *Greco U.S. Attorney*.

It fit her style, that was certain. Greco was an all-around treat to watch, if you were a clinical psychologist. Her workout routine, for example, was tae bo, a kick-boxing routine she performed on a foldaway foam mat in her office. She'd call project meetings during her workouts. Six grown guys would be standing around in suits and shoulder holsters, reporting on various ongoing investigations, while this barefoot pocket rocket in black ninja pajamas sweated and punched the air and did hip spins and bounced around on the mat, shouting "yah" and "hah" at the top of her lungs while she kicked the living lungs out of an invisible enemy. It was a surreal experience, and it worried Luther Campbell that he had gotten reasonably used to it. He sighed again and keyed his mike.

"All right, people, check in."

"Delta, post four, oh-oh-thirty-three hours, go."

"Hotel, post six, oh-oh-thirty-three hours, go."

"India, post seven, oh-oh-thirty-four hours, go."

The headset crackled as one ATF agent after another logged in with his time and position. There were nine of them in various posts around the Red Hook area, all heavily armed and dressed in full-scale SWAT gear: Farrell Garber in a sniper post on the garage roof, another sniper named Zoot Conyers paired with a spotter named Lee Ford on top of the main container storage shed, three more agents run by a senior ATF man named Derry Flynn inside a trailer near the quay where the *Agawa Canyon* was going to dock, and two more ATF—both female—a rookie by the name of Antonia Washington and her field trainer, a forty-year-old hard case named Maya Bergmann, both agents out in the river, holding a position in a Zodiac.

And of course Greco herself in the office overlooking the main loading yard, which made nine and a half. Campbell could hear the high-voltage energy in her voice as she logged in with her personal code name.

"Valkyrie, oh-oh-thirty-five hours. Go."

"Valkyrie, this is Six. Have we got a comeback from any other agency on the DMV hit we did on those plates?"

As soon as the blue Crown Vic and the gypsy cab had pulled up and taken positions at the entrance to the Red Hook yards, the sniper on the roof had called in their plates. That was an hour ago. So far the DMV computer had come up with nothing at all. Neither vehicle showed an RO of any kind, just a series of numbers cross-linked to a corporate name, Boston Bar Investment Management, and an address in Brooklyn. That's all the DMV records would show for *any* NYPD unmarked car used in a surveillance operation, since even the criminals had access to plate records, but this subtle point had eluded Greco and she was clearly getting cranky about the issue. Her response was short and sharp.

"Nothing yet. If it changes, I'll let you know. Valkyrie out."

"Thanks a bunch, honey bunny," said Campbell, but not into the mike. Kreuger laughed and crawled back to the edge of the roof. From their OP he could see the two suspect cars and the sniper nearest to them, prone on the garage roof just beneath his position. Beyond that, it was block after block of storage yards and tenements and the squat towers of Red Hook housing projects. The lights of Brooklyn were blurry inside a pale mist and the low clouds over the city reflected the orange glow of the yard lights.

Kreuger liked the Mad Max postapocalypse look to the sector. He figured, you're going to have a major weapons takedown, do it in a place like this. Just like in the movies. Bunny Kreuger was a big fan of the movies and it always bothered him that real-life law enforcement work hardly ever lived up to a Bruce Willis film. He trained his night-vision binoculars on the two vehicles down below.

The gypsy cab windows were misted over, but he could just make out two male figures behind the windshield, a tough-looking guy in his mid-thirties with an outlaw biker look to him, and a younger guy, pale-skinned, who, even at a hundred yards, gave off the impression that he was nervous. The older guy was behind the wheel. His mouth was moving, but Kreuger couldn't hear what he was saying because the damned department wouldn't spring for a serious directional microwave or laser mike. Bruce Willis would have had one. Life was not fair.

He shifted his sights. In the blue Crown Victoria he could detect more movement now. Some kind of discussion seemed to be going on. He zoomed in on the driver, a thin-faced young man behind the wheel. He had twisted around in his seat and was talking to the man in the back, the one who had just arrived in a cab. Once again, no sound. Kreuger pulled back to the second-floor exterior wall where Campbell was leaning up against an exhaust fan housing.

"You think those guys down there are really connected to this operation? I'm telling you, they look like surveillance cops to me."

"There's nothing on the plates that says so. Usually when you get an undercover car and you run it on DMV or NCIC, the computer will flag your request and whatever agency is running the UC unit will come back with a warning. So far, all we got is the registered owner as Boston Bar Investments. We've already notified the Port Authority guys about this operation, and the NYPD doesn't have jurisdiction over the terminal area. So if those guys aren't Port Authority—and Port Authority says they're not—then we have to pay attention."

Kreuger shrugged.

"Why don't we just send somebody down there to ask them what the hell they're doing?"

"And if they are connected to this op, we're blown."

Campbell popped the tab on his watch cover.

"It's twelve-forty. The freighter's due in at one. Let's just hang tight and see what happens when the ship docks."

Kreuger nodded, put his head back against the vent

housing, and closed his eyes. Campbell adjusted his position, shivered a little in the damp, and counted off the minutes in his head, a Zen thing he used to calm himself down when an operation was getting weird.

At one o'clock they all heard a huge brassy wail blaring through the air, echoing off the concrete walls, tearing up the wet night air, and everybody twitched at their positions. Campbell and Kreuger stood up and looked out over the roof of the warehouse and saw a huge ship steaming around the point through Buttermilk Channel. The ship's engines throbbed in the night, a booming bass rumble you could feel inside your rib cage, and a dirty-white bow wave was cresting along her prow. Yellow running lights and the red and green of her navigation markers looked blurry in the heavy mist. Seen this close, the ship looked impossibly huge, like a *Close Encounters* mother ship gliding in out of the dark. Now they could all hear the turbulence in the water as the captain hit his bow thrusters and the big ship slowed down in the approach canal. Down in the yards, dockworkers were hopping into their tow motors and the huge overhead derrick next to the quayside began to swing in a groan of metal and hydraulics.

Campbell was reading the bow letters through his binoculars.

"The *Agawa Canyon*. Valkyrie, this is Six."

"Go ahead."

"She's coming in now."

"Start the videotape."

"Roger, out."

Campbell dug into his kit bag and pulled out a Sony video camera, which he handed to Kreuger. Kreuger flipped the screen open and duck-walked his way back to the edge of the roof, working his way around until he could get a clear line of sight. From where they were, he could videotape the entire unloading operation and, if they were lucky, the arrival of Earl Pike or—maybe—the involvement of the suspect cars down in the perimeter yard.

Down in the 511 unit, the hammering blare of the ship's horn had made them all jerk upright. Nicky checked his watch.

"Jeez. Jimmy, let's blow. It's one o'clock, for Christ's sake."

"Hey, trooper. You're just a ride-along here. This is my unit."

"This unit belongs to the NYPD, Detective," said Casey.

"Hey, zip it, Whitney."

Casey felt her blood rushing north. A burning heat spread across her face and chest. Both her hands went completely numb. Two seconds passed while she fought it, tried to keep the valves shut, and then she blew wide open.

"You keep calling me Whitney, you sadistic little shit, and I'll report your bony cracker ass to Race Relations."

"Goodness," said Jimmy Rock, "Whitney's having a hissy fit."

That comment literally knocked the breath out of her.

"That's it. That's all. I'm out of here."

She cracked the door, jerked her briefcase out of the footwell, and began to step out of the car. Jimmy Rock twisted in his seat, leveled a finger.

"Hey, you leave when I tell you, lady."

"Jimmy, stop riding the woman," said Nicky. "We're all beat."

Casey rounded on him.

"Back off, Sylvester. I need help, I'll call your mother."

Nicky looked out the side window and his face reddened slightly. Jimmy Rock sighed theatrically.

"Lady, word on you is, you need help from every-body."

"Now what the fuck does *that* mean?"

"Now what the fuck does that mean . . . *sir*."

"I don't have to 'sir' you, you Harp peckerwood."

"Whoo," said Jimmy Rock. "Was that a racial slur?"

Casey set her briefcase down on the tarmac, stepped closer, opened up the passenger door. She held it open with one hand, leaned down, and spoke in a downy-soft voice to Jimmy Rock.

"You have a problem with me, sir, why not just get out now right here, you and me, and we work it out to-gether?"

Nicky started to speak, but Jimmy Rock stopped him.

"No, no, Nicky. Let me get this straight, Officer Spandau. Define 'work it out' for me, hah? You gonna punch my lights out?"

Casey was backing away from the car now. Her face was bony, flat, and mean. The ATF sniper, Farrell Garber, saw the motion and called it in to Campbell.

"There's movement in the blue Crown Vic."

"Ten-four . . . I'll cover. Do nothing. Everyone hold your positions. This could be a diversion."

Campbell moved to the edge of the roofline again and got up into a crouch, putting the binoculars on the suspect vehicles. Farrell was right. There was definitely a fight developing down there. What the hell it all meant, he had no clue. He watched as the black woman backed up a few feet, facing the blue car. He could see her mouth working, could vaguely hear her voice over the thumping machinery in the container yard. Inside the 511 unit, Jimmy Rock slammed the steering wheel so hard it cracked.

"Christ, I hate all this I-am-woman-hear-me-whine crap. Spandau, a bulletin for you. *GI Jane* was a fucking *movie,* okay? Demi Moore couldn't fight her way out of a fog patch. There *are* no broads in real combat. Never were. Never will be. In actual life, in *my* police department, you run your mouth off to a real cop, black, white, or windowpane check, you'll get your ass handed to you in a crate. As a matter of fact, fuck this noise—"

Nicky scrambled out of the back in a hurry, as Jimmy Rock came boiling up out of the driver's side. Casey had stepped back away from the car and was now standing in a gravel patch, her briefcase beside her, her hands at her sides and her face hard, her feet apart and legs braced. Up on the roof, Campbell shifted his position and braced himself on one knee. Three subjects out of the blue car, two of them male and a female, in an argument. He glanced down at Garber, saw him in position but not holding a rifle on the subjects—okay—good—and looked back at the action down in the lot.

Jimmy Rock jogged around the front of the car and moved forward toward Casey, with his pale face white as bone and his mouth a hard slash. Nicky stepped right into him just as Dexter and Carlo came running across the street in their direction.

Farrell Garber was back on the air.

"We have movement from the gypsy cab. Two males."

"Acknowledged," said Campbell, moving his binoculars to track the gypsy cab. The two men inside were out now and running across the park toward the other vehicle. Campbell could hear them shouting something, but the din of machinery from the terminal was drowning out the words. He looked back at the blue car.

It sure *looked* like a fight. Now the third man, the guy in the black leather jacket, was out of the car too, bracing the guy in the gray suit. If this was an act, these guys deserved a Tony.

Nicky Cicero was perhaps fifty pounds and four

inches beyond Jimmy Rock's weight class, but Jimmy Rock moved him aside like he was a cardboard cutout. Nicky caught Jimmy Rock's sleeve and hissed in his ear.

"Detective Rule, you strike a subordinate, you're *over*!"

"Hey," said Casey, "let the Harp come. I won't file on him."

Dexter Zarnas and Carlo Suarez had reached them by now.

"What the hell are you clowns up to? This is a stake-out, for Chrissakes. Spandau, get back in your unit!"

"I'm not getting into any unit with that redneck pig."

Nicky turned around, stepped up in front of Casey, and leaned down into her face. "Casey. I'm calling you a cab."

"You can call me anything you like. I'm not going anywhere," said Casey.

"This is such total bullshit," said Jimmy Rock.

On the roof, Garber had to work hard to track the action. The image in his scope danced and jerked as he tried to follow the five figures. He had the crosshairs centered on Jimmy Rock's back right now, watching as the man confronted the black female.

Campbell watched Garber's body as he adjusted, and clicked on the mike.

"Farrell, have you got your sights on those people?"

"Ten-four, Six."

"Well, get them off, dammit!"

"Ten-four. But it's getting ugly down there."

Campbell was back on the radio net.

"Everybody hold your positions. Maintain your perimeter assignments. We don't know what this is, so let this play out. Do nothing. I repeat, do nothing."

Down in the yard, Jimmy Rock came in way too close to Casey and his voice was choked with anger.

"I got a message for you, lady. Don't you push me.

Don't you run your mouth at any of my guys. I don't know why you're here. I don't know what you did. I'll bet it was massive. But this I do know: If you were white—even if you were a white *broad*—you would be *anywhere* but inside one of the best detective units in the NYPD. So hear me now, and remember. You *ever* come into my face looking for a fight again, so help me God, I'll see you bounced right out of the NYPD, I don't care if Al Sharpton pops a vein at your hearing and Oprah Winfrey gives you a two-hour special. Clear? Or do you need it in big block letters?"

"Oh, we're very clear. You haven't got the balls to—"

"That's *it*," said Nicky. He reached out to pull Casey away. She chopped him hard across the forearm with her left hand. Nicky rolled smoothly with the strike, closed his right hand around her left wrist, pulled her through the motion, and popped her into an arm bar that had her standing way up on her tiptoes. Dexter Zarnas and Carlo Suarez moved in close to Jimmy Rock, ready to put him down on the ground. Dexter called out to Nicky.

"Put Spandau in the five-oh-nine unit, Nicky. Take her home. We'll take the five-one-one unit. Jimmy, let's go."

"Into the unit, Casey," Nicky said very gently. "You're going home. Now. Into the car."

Caught up in the action down below, Campbell had moved closer to the edge of the roof. One level down, Farrell Garber was sliding to the left along the corrugated iron roofing, trying to adjust his position. Over the headset, Campbell could hear the other agents reporting on the activity around the *Agawa Canyon,* which had now docked and was preparing to off-load her cargo of containers.

He turned away to look at the ship and heard Garber's voice.

"Six, what the hell is that out there by the projects?"

Campbell stood up and walked to the edge of the roof. Garber twisted and looked back at Campbell, then pointed to the east, toward a row of projects about a half mile away. Campbell raised his glasses and saw a tiny glimmering reflection on the roof of one building. He adjusted the zoom knob and the image jumped closer.

A huddled shape, perhaps a man, and a flat clear mirror light. As he centered on it, it suddenly grew brighter—there was a sudden blue-white flicker inside the dark mass—and then he heard a sound, it was close, very close, an impact sound like a fist smacking into an open palm. A terrible weakness rolled over him, a wave of nausea, as if he were about to vomit. The horizon reeled and his muscles turned to rubber. Campbell fell to his knees and then dropped forward, down on his hands now. Something hot that smelled like iron was pouring across his fingers. Black liquid pooled out over the tin roof until it reached the row of nails holding the sheet down, where it began to fill in each tiny indentation. Campbell watched this in a bubble of total silence broken only by the sound of a distant voice on a radio, faint, tinny, urgent . . . saying what? Something . . . he was too tired to listen . . . he looked at the metal sheeting underneath him and watched with detached interest as it became a field of sparkling snow and he was flying over a huge black lake and he thought how nice it would be to lie down in the snow and rest for a while.

In one detached part of his mind he had registered the fact that he'd been shot, and since there had been no following crack of a rifle shot, probably by a weapon fitted with a sound suppressor. A very big round, judging from the huge hole in his chest, punched right through his Kevlar vest. But it all seemed somehow secondhand and vaguely unimportant right now. What counted was how *weary* he was, how heavy his body felt.

He lowered himself onto the roof and rolled over and looked up at the orange clouds moving above him. They were really quite beautiful, he thought. Someone was kneeling beside him. It was Kreuger. He was speaking into a black thing that he was holding near his mouth. Campbell tried to talk, but couldn't think of anything worth saying. Now he could hear Kreuger's panicky voice.

"Incoming! All posts! Six is down! We have—"

Campbell thought he saw a sliver of hot fire shaped like a spear. It flashed in soundlessly—Campbell had intended to say something to Kreuger about the weapon out there having a silencer, but it had slipped his mind— the round struck Kreuger's flak jacket about an inch below his name tag. It was as if Kreuger's chest blew up. Kreuger toppled backward out of Campbell's line of sight. Campbell was left looking at the covering over the exhaust fan. It was about six feet away from him. He could see what looked like a three-inch-wide hole in the steel cover. There were flecks of blood and tissue spread across the housing. He considered the hole for an indefinite period and came very slowly to an important conclusion, which he felt he ought to try to explain to Kreuger.

He moved his head, looking for the man, saw a huddled shape tumbling away, and watched as Kreuger's body rolled to the edge of the roof and disappeared. Too late, he decided, and closed his eyes. It would have been useful to tell Kreuger about the hole in the fan cover, and also the thing about the silencer, but perhaps he'd get another chance. Right now he needed to close his eyes for just a minute. Although he was much warmer now, he was still very tired. All he needed was a little rest and he'd be right as—

Kreuger's body dropped fifteen feet off the upper roof and landed with a loud bang right next to Farrell Garber, who somehow managed to ignore it. Down in the lot, the argument between Jimmy Rock and Casey was taking up all their attention, and the sound of the man's fall was lost in the general machinery noise coming from the dockside. Garber was way too busy to help Kreuger—he figured the guy was either dead or dying—and he was trying very hard to control his rifle scope enough to acquire a vague target he was sure he could see next to the tiny disc of reflected light on that distant roof—he saw the light growing brighter—in that instant Garber knew exactly what he was looking at—he had seen it once before, in Kuwait—it was street-shine glinting off the forward lens of a light-intensifying Star Lite sniper scope—a professional killer's tool—he held the image steady—he realized he was whispering the words from the Rifleman's Creed—*I must shoot straighter than my enemy who is trying to kill me I must shoot him before he shoots me I will before God I swear*—in his headset he heard a woman's voice—*Baker Baker report Baker this is Valkyrie*—Farrell Garber squeezed the trigger—his Remington jumped and the butt slammed into his shoulder—he saw a blue flicker of fire in the scope image—he started a roll to the left—the incoming round punched into his body just next to his left collarbone and exited through his right thigh and turned everything in between to jelly and pulp—*until there is no enemy but peace*—Farrell Garber's last words as recorded on the ATF communications net.

Down in the parking lot, all five cops had locked up solid as soon as they heard the big cracking boom of Garber's outgoing rifle shot, and they watched as his twelve-pound Remington .308 complete with a Leupold scope clattered off the roof and fell into the yard, where it smashed through the front windshield of a tractor-trailer.

"What the *fuck* was that?" asked Dexter.

Jimmy Rock stepped back from Casey Spandau and looked across the yard. He saw something long and black sticking up from the broken window. What the hell?

"That's a rifle!" said Nicky Cicero.

They all looked up at the rooftops around them. It took about two seconds for the cops to process what was happening, and Jimmy Rock got it first.

"Cover! Take cover! Everybody down!"

He was moving as he said it, heading for the protected side of the Crown Vic. Casey and Nicky Cicero got there at the same time, weapons out, covering the roofs and windows all along the east side of the container yards. Carlo Suarez was the only one not moving. He was nailed to his spot, staring at the rifle a hundred feet away. He was trying to figure out what to do, when Dexter Zarnas reached him and jerked him nearly off his feet.

"Cover, you moron!" said Dexter, half dragging the rookie toward the Crown Victoria. In less than fifteen seconds from the fall of the rifle, all five cops were down behind the big blue sedan. Jimmy Rock was by the right front wheel, acutely aware that the only parts of a car that can actually stop a major round are the engine block and maybe the wheel rims. He put the sights of his Glock ten-mill on the roofline of the container yards. There was nothing to look at.

Nobody was visible. No one was moving.

He could hear the boom and clank of machinery noises coming from the water side of the facility, winches and the grinding of rusted metal, the roaring of hydraulics. Whatever was going on in the parking lot, it wasn't affecting the work out on the docks. If there had been rounds fired, no one would have heard the sound above the noise coming from the Red Hook Terminal.

He turned around and checked his crew. Casey Spandau was right next to him. She looked calm and was holding her piece braced on the hood of the car. Nicky was on the ground beside her, breathing hard, then Dexter Zarnas—looking flushed and pale all at once—and beyond him Carlo Suarez, kneeling by the rear wheel with his Glock in his hands, staring back at Jimmy Rock with a dazed expression, panting like a tired dog.

"Everybody okay?" asked Jimmy Rock. "Anybody see a round coming in? Anybody take a hit?"

They all shook their heads. Casey slipped back from the hood and crouched beside Jimmy Rock.

"Call it in, Detective!"

Jimmy Rock flinched, plucked his portable off his belt, keyed the citywide channel switch.

"Five-one-one to central, K?"

"Five-one-one?"

"Central, this is an NYPD detective unit. We're calling a ten-thirteen, we have a possible sniper at Red Hook Container Terminal, Van Brunt and the Gowanus. Request additional units, K."

"Ten-four, five-one-one. A ten-thirteen at Van Brunt and Gowanus. Any Seven Six units to respond to a ten-thirteen at Red Hook."

In the meantime, up on the rooftops, all the necessary mistakes were being made, many of them at the speed of light.

"Six, this is Valkyrie. Come in, Six!"

From the secondary sniper post on top of the main container yards, Lee Ford, the sniper's spotter, came on the radio snarling.

"Greco, stop calling for Six, you crazy bitch! Campbell's down. So's Kreuger. What the fuck is going on?"

"India, this is Valkyrie. So go look!"

"Roger that," said Lee Ford, and he tapped Zoot Conyers on the left shoulder. "Let's go, Zoot. Take a look-see."

"Delta, this is India. You still in position?"

Delta was an ATF man named Derry Flynn, the leader of the three ATF agents inside the trailer near the docks. Ford and Flynn were good friends and had worked together for years. Derry Flynn was a cool head, fifteen years on the job, grizzled salt-and-pepper hair in a marine cut, slope-shouldered and lanky, with a dry laconic delivery. Derry Flynn was going to live through tonight, which turned out to be a good thing for the NYPD cops later on down the road.

"Roger, India. Orders?"

"Stay in position, Delta. Hold your post. We don't know what the hell is going on. Everybody stay in position. Zoot and I will check out Six."

"Roger that, India."

"India, this is Valkyrie."

"Valkyrie, you're not tactical. Please vacate the airspace."

"India, I'm coming with—"

"Delta, this is India."

"India?"

"Delta, assign a member to safeguard Ms. Greco. See she stays out of the line of fire."

"Roger that, India."

Lee Ford and Zoot Conyers moved in a combat assault pattern across the metal rooftops of the container building, Zoot with his sniper rifle at the ready, Lee Ford covering him with his MP Five. They cleared the crest of the main building and scampered down across the forward slope until they reached the roof of the parking garage. Lee Ford found Luther Campbell lying on his back about ten feet from a fan housing, less than a yard from the edge of the roof.

As Ford knelt down to check out Luther, Zoot Conyers belly-crawled past him until he got a line of sight off the roof. He saw the two vehicles, the gypsy cab and the blue Crown Victoria. There were figures visible behind the blue sedan. He took a position and raised his rifle. Behind him, Lee Ford was speaking into his mike.

"Valkyrie, this is India. Six is hit. Major trauma. Still alive. Get us a medevac chopper now!"

"What's the frequency, India?"

"Use the fucking telephone on the desk in front of you, Greco! Call the HQ and get us air support! Now!"

"Uh, roger, India. Out."

"Zoot, what have you got?"

"India, I have five subjects acquired. They've taken cover behind the blue sedan. I have a clear head shot at one. Shall I engage?"

Lee Ford rolled his eyes. He was fifty-one, a solid old pro, in on a transfer from a detective job with the Chicago PD, and he had a good twenty years on Zoot Conyers, who was less than five years out of the Federal Law Enforcement Training Academy in Glynco, Georgia. Zoot was one of the hard-charger law enforcement fanatics Lee Ford liked to call "the hut-hut freaks."

"No, Zoot. Do not engage."

Down in the lot, Dexter Zarnas saw something moving on the roofline. He leaned over to hiss at Jimmy Rock.

"Motion, Jimmy Rock. On the roof, near the vent housing!"

"I have it. Hold fire. Nobody fires, got it? Nobody's shot at us yet. We don't know what's going on. We wait for backup."

They had all heard several patrol units from the Seven Six come back with a rolling affirmative to the 10-13. Jimmy Rock asked for an ETA from the supervisor car, Seven Frank, and was told maybe six, seven minutes.

"Roger, Seven Frank. Come in hot. We think we may have a subject on the roof of the container building here, a possible sniper. Let's scramble an air unit."

"Any officers down?"

"Nobody yet. We have taken no fire! Repeat, we have not taken any fire. Get us an air unit ASAP, K?"

"No chopper available right now, five-one-one. Only available unit is on a traffic pursuit up in the Bronx."

"It's a hot zone, Seven Frank. Tell your guys to be tactical."

"Ten-four. A hot zone. How do we know you?"

"Blue Crown Victoria. The only one with five cops hiding behind it. Will that do?"

"Ten-four, five-one-one. On the way."

He keyed off the mike and moved along the car toward Dexter Zarnas. On the roof, Zoot Conyers had him tracked as he duck-walked, centering his crosshairs on Jimmy Rock's right temple. If they'd had their badges out at this point, what was about to happen might not have happened. Later on, the survivors got to think about that a lot. Not that it did them any damn good. But they didn't. Not one of them had badge-chain out on their chests, not even Jimmy Rock, who was the road boss, and he should have known better.

Zoot shifted around to look at Lee Ford, who was now lying down on the roof beside him. Zoot's young face was slick with sweat and the whites were showing all around the edges of his brown eyes. Zoot's whisper was charged and hyper. This was his first time on a real street scenario. Everything up until now had been training. This was real. He was still young enough to think that real was better. He was going to hold that opinion for about another six minutes.

"I see weapons. The one moving has a Glock."

Lee Ford shook his head.

"It wasn't a Glock that hit Luther, Zoot. Most of his

chest is raspberry jam. The round punched right through his vest. Then it drilled a hole in a half inch of steel housing. No Glock can do that."

"Then who shot Six? And Bunny Kreuger? And Farrell? There's nobody else around, dammit! We heard nothing. It's gotta be them."

Lee Ford grabbed Zoot's shoulder harness, jerked him in very close, pointed out across the rooftops into the dark skyline.

"Look at the angle of fire. Whoever's shooting at us is way out there somewhere, on our level, on a roof. He probably has a heavy-caliber weapon, a fifty anyway, and since we heard no shot, he's got to be using a silencer. Probably also a Star Lite night scope. We're wide open to him, you follow me? We're bright green ghosts in his sniper scope. Now stay down and stay put. You fire on my command, Zoot, not before. Now shut the fuck up for a minute!"

Lee Ford was trying to recall the radio talk at the point that Luther took his round. Farrell Garber had said something about seeing something on a rooftop. Where? While he was thinking about it, they all heard the sound of sirens. Incoming, and very fast. Lee Ford looked back down into the lot. He could see the blue car and maybe a figure or two behind it. Surely they could hear the sirens too. If they were hinky, if Zoot was right and they were the ones who'd shot Kreuger and Farrell and Campbell, they'd be getting the hell out of the area. Yet there they sat. Waiting. For what?

"Christ . . . Holy Christ, Zoot, those guys are cops—"

Something disc-shaped and shining with pale light flickered in his peripheral vision. He turned to look out at the distant rooftops. The incoming round took him in the cheek at twice the speed of sound, just below the left eye. One-half second later most of what used to be Lee Ford's head was now splattered all over Zoot

Conyers. Other than the sound of a man's skull bursting apart, there had been no other noise at all. Zoot Conyers, stunned, finally found air and screamed into his mike.

"Incoming! Lee's hit! Lee's down!"

He got back a babble of cross talk as Greco and Derry Flynn and Maya Bergmann out in the Zodiac all competed for airtime. Zoot swiveled, his breath rasping dry in his throat, put his crosshairs on the blue sedan, got motion at the rear of the car, then he too saw that distant pale disk flickering, lifted his sights off the car, and zeroed in on that huddled shape a half mile away—he squeezed off a round—it boomed in the heavy night air—Jimmy Rock jumped—Zoot was working the rifle bolt—Casey saw Jimmy Rock's face white and bone-hard in the yard lights—Zoot Conyers tried to reacquire the shooter—sniper at a thousand yards, he said into his throat mike—Casey reached out to Jimmy Rock—Jimmy, she said—we have to move—where to?—we're in the open—Jimmy was looking out into the night skyline—the full beam of the parking lot lamp was on them both now—it was so bright it hurt her eyes—she felt a weapon out there, a rifle, felt them all caught like a photo in a distant lens—Dexter was shouting into his radio—Carlo Suarez looked up at the container roof and saw a rifle barrel showing on the edge—got to his feet with a hoarse yell—centered his Glock on the roofline of the Red Hook container garage—Nicky Cicero shouted at him—began to move—Zoot Conyers had the distant sniper targeted again—he was squeezing the blade of his trigger—Carlo Suarez fired his Glock at Zoot's position—the round clanged off the roof six inches from Zoot's right shoulder—Zoot flinched—his rifle fired—the booming crack rattled tin all around him—the butt jumped in his grip—his second shot went spinning wild into the orange sky—Carlo was still yelling and he fired again—Nicky reached him and dragged him to the ground—he was screaming at Carlo—*that's not where the fire is coming from*—and then the distant sniper fired one last time from his position on top of a tenement roof a thousand yards away and the round came howling in at the blue Crown Victoria—low and true and fast—and hit the dead center of the target mass with a muffled *thwack* like a sledgehammer striking a side of beef. Zoot Conyers saw the muzzle flare a half mile away, saw the huddled shape shift, melt away, and now the parking lot was filling up with NYPD patrol cars—red lights were circling—the air was full of sirens—men in blue running and over his headset Zoot heard the voice of an ATF agent—it was Delta—Derry Flynn—and Delta was saying *hold your fire everybody hold your fire that's the NYPD—repeat acknowledge repeat hold your fire those are police officers!*

Zoot Conyers shook his head, took one last look at the distant rooftop, marking the location. Then he let out a long uneven sigh, put his weapon down carefully, and got slowly to his feet. One knee was vibrating like an overtorqued guy wire. Down in the lot, at least ten different patrol cars had gathered around the blue Crown Victoria. Somebody in the tangle of police cars saw Zoot standing on the rooftop, shouted a warning, and then fifteen weapons were on him in a heartbeat and a bright white light was blinding him—he heard a voice in his earpiece—it was Derry Flynn—*hold your fire—hold your fire—Zoot—drop your sidearm for Chrissakes drop your sidearm*—Zoot had completely forgotten about the Beretta strapped to his thigh, and then from the hazy field of red and blue flashing lights and the single white glare he heard an amplified voice—male—urgent—saying *drop your weapon now repeat drop your weapon*. Zoot plucked the Beretta backhand from his holster and threw it twenty feet away, where it landed, clanged on the tin roof, bounced once, and tumbled away into a rain gutter.

Zoot put both hands in the air and held his breath, acutely aware of the guns now trained on his body. He tried to pray but could think of nothing to say. Down by the blue sedan, a cluster of figures was gathering around the far side of the vehicle, looking down at something— someone?—on the ground. He couldn't make out what. A siren blipped once and he looked up to see an EMS ambulance rolling toward the vehicle, butting through the tangle of plainclothes and uniformed cops. He was dimly aware of a large older man standing beside him now, it was the Delta agent—gray crew-cut hair and small eyes, what the hell was his name—Zoot could not remember his name—it was Derry Flynn.

Derry Flynn was holding up a badge and bellowing down at the cops—*federal agents don't fire we're federal agents*—and now there was a sudden rushing wind and the downward buffeting blast of a hovering chopper overhead. Zoot looked up and saw a Blackhawk with the letters *ATF Medevac* on the belly, and when he looked back down at the blue sedan it was surrounded by blue uniforms and the EMS truck was stopped dead beside it, the red and white strobes on its roof circling slowly.

The doors were wide open and some poor bastard on a gurney was being lifted into the back of the EMS truck and paramedics were holding a bag of intravenous fluid over the body and someone else was wrapping the figure in a red blanket and Zoot Conyers, the former hut-hut freak, came to the important realization at that precise moment that real was not always better than training, and when real life showed up in a cranky frame of mind, you were a lucky young man if you were anywhere else.

Jack had fallen asleep in the dining-room chair, in front of the cold chicken plate. When the phone rang, he jerked upright and reached for the cordless handset beside him. Smoke, the six-toed stray tom with the brainpower shortfall, sat on the dining-room table about a foot away, blinked his yellow eyes at Jack, and yawned hugely, showing Jack a pink-ribbed cavern of a mouth and four needlepoint fangs the size of railroad spikes. Jack blinked back at him and did the same. Smoke seemed unimpressed.

"Hello?"

"Mr. Vermillion, this is Valeriana Greco."

"Yes. Miss Greco. Right . . . what time is it?"

There was a pause while somebody spoke in the background. When she came back on the line, her voice was guarded, formal.

"It's three in the morning. We have a car on the way. We're going to fly you down here in a chopper."

"How did it go?"

Another whispered conversation.

"I'd rather not discuss it on the phone."

"Okay. I'll be here."

"Fine. One thing?"

"Yes?"

"I think you should have a lawyer with you, okay?"

Jack was definitely not okay. Wide awake now, but not okay.

"A lawyer . . . why do I need a lawyer?"

Her voice was fading.

"My battery's low. I'll have to break off. I just want you to have representation with you. For your own protection."

"From what?"

"The car will be there in ten minutes."

The transmission popped and shut off. Jack set the receiver down, stared at it for another full minute, and then dialed the number of Flannery Coleman. The phone rang six times and then he heard Flannery's growling voice.

"This had better be damned amusing."

"Flan, it's Jack."

"I figured it was you. What fresh hell is this?"

Jack sketched it out.

"I'll meet you at Red Hook. Say nothing to anyone until I get there. No matter what happens. Nothing. I'm leaving now."

"You can ride with us."

"No. I have calls to make. Hear me, Jack. Not a word."

Jack put the receiver back, moved toward the bathroom with his mind in overdrive and his heart pounding against his rib cage. He was halfway there when the phone rang again.

"Hello?"

"Jack. Hope I didn't wake you?"

It was Earl Pike. His voice was as soft as sleep. Jack could hear traffic in the background and someone calling out names over a public address system. There was an echoing emptiness in the background that made Jack think of an airport or a train station. Pike was breathing hard, as if he was out of breath.

"Earl, are you okay? You sound bad."

"I'm fine, Jack. I just wanted to say thank you."

"Okay. It went well?"

"Went well? Not really. It went badly. Very badly. I just wanted to say thank you for the lesson."

"Lesson?"

"You get to a certain age, no matter what you know, you tend to get sentimental. They say it happens to men our age. Women get tougher, we get weaker. I got sentimental over my family's collection. Now it's gone. I got sentimental over you, over a man I saw as a soldier, just like me. That was stupid. You straightened me out. Showed me the truth. So I'm saying thank you."

Jack felt a sudden burning sense of shame. It was true. He had sold out a man against whom he had no grievance, sent him into a federal trap, and he had done it for what? He knew it was lunacy, but it was impossible not to say something.

"Earl . . . I have a son. He's in—"

"The kid in Lompoc? I figured that out for myself. Well, Jack, I have to run. No pun intended there. You did what you thought best. Tried to be a good father. Now you get the consequences."

"Pike—"

"See you around, Jack."

The line went dead. Jack hit the call display button.

SLIPSTREAM JETWAYS
718-551-5871

He wrote the number down on a pad by the phone, sat and held it in his hands for a minute, trying to get his breathing under control. Then he stood up and began to dress. Seven minutes later a black Caprice pulled into his driveway. Jack was outside on the front stairs, waiting for it. The two men inside it stepped out as he came down the walkway. Both of them were brick-shaped and buzz-cut and looked like combat accountants in dress blue suits and white shirts. One of them showed Jack an ATF ID folder and said his name was Conroy. The other man watched Jack carefully, said nothing, and held open the back door. Jack got in and the man slammed it hard enough to rattle the empty coffee cup in a holder between the front seats. Jack saw a blue police light in the footwell and a police radio under the dashboard. Conroy got in behind the wheel, and the other man came around and sat in the back next to Jack. As they pulled away, Conroy pressed a button and the door locks snapped down.

"What's that for?" asked Jack.

"Just routine," said Conroy over his shoulder. The man sitting beside Jack leaned into the seat and unbuttoned his suit jacket so Jack could see the dull gray sheen of the Glock in his shoulder holster.

They were airborne in a black Bell Ranger thirty-four minutes later. The chopper had no markings of any kind. Conroy sat in the front with the pilot. They seemed to know each other. The man who wasn't Conroy and who had the Glock in a shoulder holster never left Jack's side all the way down to Red Hook.

They followed the Taconic southward at a thousand feet. Jack saw pinpoint lights and the blue squares of farmyards bathed in arc lamps and now and then a single car cruising on the black ribbon of the parkway. The dulled thunder of the rotors made thinking impossible. He wondered who was in that car a thousand feet below, what his life was like, where he was going. Was it maybe Flannery Coleman down there, foot to the floor, heating up his cell phone, snapping and snarling at some hapless mutt on the far end of the line?

Away in the east, the sky turned the color of skim milk, slowly changed to pale pink, and then the haze from the city stained the whole of the eastern horizon like a spill of brown water. Yonkers went by underneath them, a scattering of suburban blocks and freight yards half-hidden in third-growth forest, then the Bronx, at first wooded and rolling, and then the trees died away, replaced by block after block of redbrick and stained concrete buildings, and then a sudden greenbelt and a dropping bluff, and now there was a flat lead-gray plain of water below as they crossed over Rikers Island and Jack could see the landing strips of LaGuardia and, away to the left, the long straightaway of Astoria Boulevard, the streetlights blazing like runway markers. He found his old block in the neighborhood, by the schoolyard, and stared at it with a sense of terrible distance and loss and loneliness until it was obscured in the brown haze behind him.

Up ahead he saw the East River and Roosevelt Island and they followed the turning of the river for another mile, with the office towers of Manhattan catching fire from the first rays of the rising sun as it blazed on all the glass and steel and marble. Cars were already pouring down the East River Drive and the FDR, traffic on the Triborough was a ribbon of headlights and taillights.

Down on the river, ferries and cruisers carved thin white lines into the pebbled gray surface of the water, trailing widening vees that looked like lace torn from a veil. Away to the southeast Jack could just make out the ocean. It looked as flat and as hard as a slab of polished marble. In another minute Red Hook Terminal was under them and he could see the *Agawa Canyon* at the dock, a low-riding blue hull with a destroyer bow, her name in tall white lettering, surrounded by derricks and trucks.

People were moving across her decks, not sailors or longshoremen. Strangers, men in black uniforms. The battered tin roofs of the container warehouses were coated with fifty years of grime and a century of bird shit. The terminal grounds were full of police vehicles.

He could make out the churning red and blue of police lights. Men and women in various kinds of uniform were standing around in clusters. Two television vans were parked at the entrance gates, their satellite dishes raised on extension poles, and he could see men milling around carrying video cameras. Here and there a hot flowering of white light picked out a man or a woman talking into the cameras, holding a microphone at chest level. The Ranger hovered, the tone of the rotors altered, and the chopper began to settle down toward a cleared strip.

Inside, a ragged circle of men in black combat fatigues; he picked out one figure among the huddled mass staring up at the chopper as it settled onto the parking lot, a paler face upturned, a sharp oval of white against the mass of black uniforms.

A woman. Valeriana Greco. Waiting for Jack.

FRIDAY, JUNE 23

KINGS COUNTY HOSPITAL

BROOKLYN

0530 HOURS

The nurse walking toward him was wearing the same kind of expression on her face that Nicky remembered from the night six years ago when another nurse in another hospital wing had come out of the operating room to tell him that his mother was about to die. He noticed that her walnut-dark skin seemed to glow as she passed under the hallway's overhead lights, and the pale green of her uniform looked blue as the light moved across it and then became green again as she went forward into darkness.

People moved out of her way, the Internal Affairs

slicks in their rumpled suits and the ties loose around the neck, the tangle of blue-and-brass hats standing outside the door into the intensive care unit, the senior brass from Alcohol, Tobacco, and Firearms, separated from the city cops and detectives mainly by the cut and quality of their suits, even Pete LeTourneau, a New York State Police lieutenant, his own section boss, looking rumpled and rural in a blue sports coat over a pair of tan slacks, the snitches from One Police and Gracie Mansion, everybody around her gave her room. Nicky watched her come through, looking at her face, seeing the way she was making direct eye contact with him, and he had the thought that she was coming toward him like a priest coming down the aisle in a cathedral, trailing bad news like sandalwood incense. Nicky remembered then that the worst memory he had was triggered by a sandalwood scent, the same scent that he could smell in the dry sweep of his mother's hair when he leaned down to kiss her cheek as she lay in her coffin six years ago. The nurse reached him, stood in front of him now, looking down at him with as much compassion as she had left in her after twenty years of walking the very same walk.

"Officer Cicero. They're finished with the body. The detectives said you can go in now if you still want."

"Yes. Thanks."

She nodded, stepped back as he stood up. His left leg vibrated like a tuning fork and a muscle in his cheek pulled at his left eye. He followed her back up the hall past the other cops and the officials. As he cleared a connecting hall, he heard a clamor of voices and shouted questions coming from behind a set of steel doors.

Through the acrylic windows with the letters *Do Not Enter* stenciled on them in reverse, he could see the broad back of the chief of department of the NYPD, in his full dress blues, the white-hot glare of video lights making a blue corona around his body, see his head go from side to side as he said something to a reporter's question that Nicky could not quite make out above the staccato chatter of still cameras and the barking of the reporters and television people in the crowded passage. Then he cleared the hallway and the nurse was holding a door open for him, with the look still on her face. Nicky stopped for a moment, gathered himself, and then stepped through the doorway.

There were two people in the room, a white-faced harness cop standing at rigid attention beside the hospital bed, staring straight ahead into the infinite distance and breathing slowly, his dress blue uniform pressed to perfection, a plate of colored medals over his silver badge, a black ribbon around the silver badge, his uniform cap straight and square and hiding his eyes inside a black shadow, and on the bed next to him, a long still figure covered with a sheet.

Nicky walked over to the side of the bed. He could smell disinfectant, bleach, and something else, rust or copper or dried blood. He looked over at the uniformed cop, then looked back down at the body, at the pale-blue sheet drawn over it.

He reached out and lifted up a corner of the sheet and slowly drew it back. It weighed nothing at all and floated away from the body underneath it as if it were a light mist over a pool of water. The corpse's face was rigid, stunned-looking, a thing made out of wood and stone, the thin lips purple and tight, as if a dreadful pain were still blazing along the nerves. A mass of stained bandage covered the entire left side of the chest, hiding what Nicky knew was terrible damage. The stillness that surrounded the body seemed artificial, frozen, as if the corpse were just an image caught in a still frame, that in another second someone would touch play again and the dead thing would blink and breathe and sit up and look around again at the wide wonder of the living world. Nicky found himself waiting for that moment, holding on to this illusion for as long as he could, but in a little while he drew the sheet back up and very gently covered Jimmy Rock's face, turned to real stone now, a thing cut out of quartz and gray marble. Then he turned away and walked back out to the hall and the world of light and air and sound.

Pete LeTourneau was waiting for him by the coffee machine halfway down the hallway, holding two cups and talking to Casey Spandau. Nicky hadn't seen her since early this morning, when a couple of Internal Affairs bulls had hustled her into a black Lincoln and driven her away, followed by a second car with Dexter Zarnas and Carlo Suarez. As a state man, he was isolated, quarantined. Casey's eyes were still swollen from crying, and she looked as if somebody had tied her to a chair and then thrown the chair down a fire escape.

She was leaning against the wall, holding her ratty brown briefcase against her belly in what Nicky was beginning to think of as a kind of obsessive manner. It was a damn ugly briefcase. It didn't suit her. She was an absolute pistol, he couldn't help thinking, and even in her state of shock she glowed like polished ebony. Maybe he should buy her a briefcase that suited her more. Matte-black steel with solid gold hinges and an engraved name-plate.

Pete LeTourneau, Nicky's boss, could have been her older brother, a craggy-faced black cop with salt-and-pepper hair and slightly hooded eyes with the same Chinese cast to them. He was known around the State Police divisions as a hard man but a stand-up guy. If he was going to hand Nicky his papers, he'd do it right now. All he gave him when Nicky reached them was one of the coffees he was holding, along with a gentle smile.

"Nicky. How you doing?"

"How do I look?"

"Yeah. Stupid question. I've been talking to Officer Spandau here, Nicky. She tells me you handled yourself pretty good out there."

Nicky looked at Casey, at her puffy face and reddened eyes, her body sagging with fatigue and guilt.

"Did she? I didn't think any of us handled ourselves pretty good out there. But thanks, Casey."

Casey just nodded, looking over Nicky's shoulder at the IAD guys down the hallway. They were talking to one of the Seven Six patrolmen who had arrived just as Jimmy got shot. Casey couldn't hear what was being said, but she figured her career was about a week from being over. Pete LeTourneau let the silence run for a minute.

"Okay, Nicky . . . I've been talking with Vince Zaragosa, the CO of the JTF. You met him yet?"

"Yeah. He was on the scene at Red Hook about ten minutes after Detective Rule was killed. We had a long talk."

"Way he told it to me, he talked and you listened."

"Yeah. That's about right."

"You want to go home, then?"

Nicky looked at Casey.

She shrugged, looked at her hands.

"You pulling me off the Blue Stores thing?"

Pete LeTourneau studied Nicky's face for a time. His eyes were hard but not mean, and he seemed to be making up his mind based on whatever he could see in Nicky's face. The voices in the hall were hushed, muted, like the talk at a funeral home. The hospital smelled of dead flowers and Lysol. Nicky waited for whatever was coming.

"No. I'm not. Nobody could see this shit coming. ATF was supposed to inform Port Authority, and they did, but only after they were in position. Port Authority never told the NYPD, so there was no way any of you could have known what you were walking into. The usual jurisdictional crap. It's not your fuck-up, Nicky. Don't race to own it. You were doing well. Casey says you got some DNA off the guy. If we can match it with blood on the male vic, we can go ahead and charge him, see how it plays out. At least we'll spoil his weekend. You have that with you?"

Nicky patted the pocket of his black leather jacket, pulled out a plastic bag with a razor blade inside. Pete took the bag, held it up to the light. Tiny flecks of blood and tissue were visible on the steel.

"Yeah, this would do it. How'd you get it?"

Casey's face was motionless and Nicky thought she might be literally holding her breath. Pete LeTourneau was a fair man, a good cop, and Nicky didn't want to lie to him. But he wanted Earl Pike. He was now quite certain that Pike was the guy. Why he had done what he did at Red Hook was a mystery. For now. But Pike was the only man who had the background for that kind of work. They had to get him now, any way they could. That meant using the razor blade.

"Detective Rule and Casey had Pike under surveillance. While he was out of the hotel, I went up to his floor. There were maids working the floor. The room was being cleaned. I got the maid to bring me out his garbage. I found the razor in the bag."

Pete's eyes widened.

"You tin her?"

"No."

"Good, because you had no warrant, did you?"

"No, sir."

"So why'd she bring it out for you?"

"She wanted to be helpful."

"Yeah? That was sweet. Why'd she want to be helpful?"

"She was from Tegucigalpa. Maybe she thought I was INS."

"You say you were?"

"No. But I didn't say I wasn't."

Pete was silent for a while, working it through.

"You can swear in court this was taken directly from Earl Pike's room? No chance of confusion? Chain of evidence?"

"I watched her go in, I watched her come out."

"Will she verify that?"

"Will she have to?"

"Maybe. Is that a problem?"

"I might have scared her off. What if she blows town?"

"I don't know. Maybe we don't need her. I mean, we call her to testify, her job's toast, and if she's illegal, she's out of here. Plus one more witness is one more chance to blow the case in court. DNA collected from a garbage bag has stood up before. Courts say you don't have an expectation of privacy for hotel garbage. If you . . . let's say you simply observed the garbage being removed from the suspect's room . . . you follow? That's a true statement. I mean, it's literally true. And, being a good investigator, you saw an opportunity to collect DNA-bearing items . . . that would just be good police work. Right? No. I'd say we don't need her. *If* the DNA holds up. What happened with the Benz? Zaragosa says the car was clean."

Casey came to life at that.

"Sir, Pike's job puts him in touch with a lot of covert sources. He could have had another Benz located by a contact. Or he got it repaired by experts. At the time we had no right to put the car through a really close examination. Pike was just a guy on a list, and the DMV numbers matched. If we get some DNA support, then we can seize the Benz and tear it apart. Whatever they did, either way, it had to leave signs under the paint."

"So you're saying he found a substitute Benz? And faked the VIN number so well you couldn't spot it? Or he had his own vehicle put back in mint condition by people so good at it that a couple of trained cops couldn't spot the repairs? And he does either one of these tricky-dick stunts in just one day?"

"It's the only explanation I can think of."

"Yeah? I got one. How about maybe he's innocent?"

Nicky shook his head.

"I've met the guy, Pete. He's capable of the crime. He was in the vicinity of Blue Stores; a witness puts him in the region. He used his credit card to buy gas. His hand was bandaged. The only thing that says he's innocent is the Benz, and I think Casey's right. I think he managed to get the car cleaned up somehow. If we can match his DNA with the crime scene, we don't even *need* the damned car."

Pete looked from one to the other, his mind working.

"Okay. Okay. That works for me. Nicky, I'll take this back to Albany, get it matched right away. Any idea where Pike is now?"

"No. I haven't really looked. But we're not the only people who want to have a chat. The ATF guys figure Pike might have had something to do with the . . ."

"Total screaming fuck-up?" offered Pete.

"Total screaming fuck-up at Red Hook. The sniper was a pro, that's a fact. What, three ATF guys down, plus Detective Rule? With a sound suppressor? Christ."

"Four ATF guys. Three very dead, and a guy named Luther Campbell hanging on to life with half his chest gone. And Detective Rule, the last hit. From a thousand yards, into the haze, into strong lights, without a brace. Everybody says that only a military-trained shooter could do anything like it with a fifty-caliber rifle. And definitely a silenced weapon."

Nicky's eyes widened.

"A fifty? Jesus Christ. What was the weapon?"

"A Barrett Fifty. The army calls it an M-eighty-two-A-one."

LeTourneau lifted up a CD-ROM, held it out to Nicky.

"This is a combat weapons CD. Put it on when you get a chance, learn about this piece. There's a video. Watch it carefully. If this is what Pike's using, we got big trouble right here in River City."

Nicky took the CD, pocketed it, shrugged.

"So what the hell was going on at Red Hook?" he asked.

"I'm trying to get that out of them. This Pike, he's military?"

"Retired a full colonel, Pete. Nobody will tell me anything about his background. But Pike's the best suspect anybody has."

"So ATF, they want him too?"

"Badly."

"And if they get him first, we have zip on Blue Stores."

"That's right."

"And if the ATF gets Pike on the sniper thing, it'll be years before he answers for the NYPD guy. So we both got reasons to be interested, am I right, Officer Spandau?"

Casey shook her head and broke a long silence.

"Sir, if Pike's connected to the death of an NYPD cop, then I got to be honest with you. We'll have a conflict when we get him."

"Let the DAs work that out. We're just cops. You suspended, Officer Spandau?"

"Not yet. There'll be a shooting board, because one of our guys, Carlo Suarez, fired his weapon at an ATF agent. We have an officer killed. There'll be hell to pay. But no, Vince says I'm not suspended."

"So your JTF team is still on this?"

"I . . . think so. If Vince wanted me off, he'd have said so."

"What about the other two guys on your unit? Dexter Zarnas and Carlo Suarez? Will they help?"

"Vince busted Suarez back to patrol. But Dexter, he's ready."

"Are you? Ready? Personally?"

Casey lifted her face, hardened visibly.

"Yes. I am. I'm ready."

Pete raised his hands, shrugged, flipped the plastic bag in the air and caught it.

"Okay. Get some sleep, both of you. Then go out and find this Earl Pike asshole, bring him back wrapped in heavy chains, hah?"

"Over the saddle or in it?" asked Nicky.

"What counts here is proof, not vital signs."

"What about the ATF? Do we cooperate?"

"With the feds? Absolutely. You will cooperate with the federal agencies involved in this case as fully and as completely as they will cooperate with you. Understood?"

"Yes, sir," said Nicky. "Understood."

Flannery Coleman arrived at the Red Hook Terminal a little after seven in the morning. There was heat building out in the long dockyard section, and the ATF agents guarding the long hull of the *Agawa Canyon* looked hot and bored, their black HK rifles held at port arms across their chests, their faces blank. Jack, watching from the window of the terminal manager's office on the second floor of the main building, saw Flannery's green Volvo pull up to a checkpoint manned by a couple of Port Authority police officers.

"He's here," he said, not looking back at Valeriana Greco. She stepped away from the small group of ATF agents gathered at the far end of the room, crossed over to the window.

"Fine. Now we can get started."

"Started at what?"

Greco gave him the same flat stare that he'd been getting from everyone else in the Red Hook buildings.

"We have men down, we have questions. We're hoping you can help us with the answers."

Jack considered pushing harder, held his temper, said nothing. Four minutes later Flannery Coleman came through the office door, wearing a dark-blue single-breasted suit over a crisp white shirt, a Yale tie. He was shaved and fresh and looked as if he had just come off a week's ski vacation in Vermont, his ruddy skin glowing and his pale-green eyes bright with battle. He ignored everyone in the room but Jack, strode briskly over to his side, gave him a wink, and then turned to face Valeriana Greco.

"Before my client says or does anything, I'd like to know what the blazing hell is going on out there."

Greco smiled at him. Flannery gave her an up-and-down look and waited. She was wearing some sort of black jumpsuit with a gold star on the left breast. Her hair was pulled back in a tight ponytail and her face was red and shiny. There was a look in her eyes, a kind of mutant sexual energy, that Jack had not noticed before.

"Mr. Coleman, the situation outside is something we can address later. Right now we'd like your client to accompany us on board the *Agawa Canyon*. We have something we'd like him to see."

"Ms. Greco. I see police cars, I see federal cars, I see a crime scene van from the NYPD, I came through a cordon of press people, there's a New York One satellite truck out there, and I passed a CNN mobile unit on the way up Van Brunt. Clearly there has been an event, and I'd like to know what it was exactly, and what bearing it may have on my client's interests."

Greco shook her head.

"We're not at liberty to discuss the . . . event . . . as it's an internal matter. Part of an ongoing investigation. I admit we have sustained some injuries as a result of the unexpected intervention of a unit of the NYPD. This is a jurisdictional matter that does not immediately affect Mr. Vermillion's situation. Now, will you allow us to take your client over to the *Agawa Canyon*?"

"Is he charged with something, Ms. Greco?"

Greco licked her lips and Jack half expected her to snag a passing fly with her tongue while she was at it.

"Not at this time. And until he is, to be frank, you're not really a part of this and have no standing here. You're here as a courtesy and as a way of ensuring that this investigation in no way violates Mr. Vermillion's rights."

"And what is the status of Mr. Earl V. Pike at this time?"

Greco's face shifted through some expressions and settled on bland and blank.

"Mr. Pike is not currently in custody."

"What about his shipment? The weapons shipment?"

"It is currently under our control."

"Were there prohibited weapons in the shipment?"

"Yes. Technically. Yes, there were."

"So there will be an arrest in the matter?"

"There will be some charges, yes. When we locate him."

"So he's missing?"

"Mr. Pike is not in his hotel room at the UN Plaza Hotel. He is not in his residence in Maryland. Messages have been left and there has been no response as of this hour."

"Does he know you're looking for him?"

"We're assuming that he does. We identified ourselves."

"What you're assuming is that *if* he had a hand in whatever the hell went on here last night—and I'm inferring from your statements that you have no proof—then he's gone into hiding. It would also be reasonable to assume that if he was innocent, he'd have no reason to be reporting his whereabouts to you and may simply be neglecting his message service. The facts seem to support both interpretations."

"We are currently actively trying to locate Mr. Pike in order to question him about the circumstances that arose last night."

"But not specifically about his shipment?"

"His shipment did contain some prohibited weapons."

"But there's no warrant out for him?"

"No. Not at the moment."

"But the deal stands? For Jack's son?"

"That situation is in . . . flux."

Jack had been watching this exchange with a rapidly depleting reserve of calm detachment. The word *flux* drained the tank.

"Flux! What the hell does that mean? Dammit, Flannery. Let's just get this done," said Jack, who was losing patience with the woman, the talk, the whole damn thing.

"All right," said Flannery, "let's go."

Greco made a gesture and the ATF agents in the room seemed to come on point. Jack was aware of their air of controlled aggression and the careful attention they were paying to his movements as they all trooped down the staircase and out onto the quay where the *Agawa Canyon* was tied up. She was huge up close, as long as a city block, and her hull rose fifty feet above the quayside. It towered over them all and smelled of algae and diesel and mud. They had her cabled fore and aft and her spring lines groaned as she heaved in a low swell off the river. The gangway was guarded top and bottom and a crime scene tape with the words *Federal Agents Do Not Cross* blocked the entrance.

Greco ripped the tape away and led the way up the staircase, her boots clanging on the metal risers. It was a long walk up to the deck and a big blond kid in an ATF raid jacket was waiting at the top of the gangway with a black machine pistol slung over his shoulder. He was glaring at Jack as he boarded, but backed away and let him pass. A wind was blowing in off the river, full of the scent of dead fish and sea salt. They could see the trees on Governor's Island bending in the wind, and a ferry was butting through the big swells on her way to Staten Island. They were standing on the main freight deck, and a thirty-six-foot wall of containers rose up next to them.

"The container we're interested in is up forward. We'd like you to take a look, verify that this shipment is a part of the official *Agawa Canyon* manifest."

Flannery Coleman interrupted immediately.

"What does that mean? Jack wasn't present at the loading dock when Pike's load came in. What purpose does this serve?"

"He can verify that it is one of his containers and that the bills of lading are Black Water Transit documents. . . . Mr. Coleman . . . are you all right, sir?"

Flannery had gone pale, staggered a bit, and then sat down on a stanchion line. His lips looked blue and beads of water were bright on his forehead. He was breathing in short sharp gasps. They all stood looking down at him. Jack had a rush of anger.

"God*damn*, you stupid little bitch! What the hell are you pulling here? Flannery, come on, let's go. Flan—?"

Flannery was holding his hand up, tapping on his chest. He put a spidery finger into his pocket and drew out an asthma inhaler, puffed on it a couple of times. He started to get up, but Jack pushed him down again and kept his hand on the man's shoulder as he raked a salvo across Greco's bow.

"This man gets sick here, you get sued to hell and back, you officious little poodle! You're playing some bullshit game, have been from the start. You got something to show me, then goddammit, show me. Otherwise I'm out of here and you can—"

"We do have something to show you, Mr. Vermillion."

She turned and walked away toward a ladder that led up onto the row of container roofs. Flannery started to follow, but Jack pushed him back down once again. She scuttled up the ladder like a lizard, and Jack followed close enough to consider biting her ass on the way up.

At the top she turned and waited for him, and then stalked down the grid toward a large black container marked *Maersk Dubai* in faded white stencil.

Her boots clanged over the metal and then she was clambering back down toward the container gates. They were closed, but two armed agents stood at either side.

"This is one of your containers, Mr. Vermillion?"

"Lady, I don't own containers. I own the ship, I carry the blasted containers, or haven't you learned dick yet?"

Jack was through with this bitch, all the way through. In a minute he was simply going to throw her ass into the river.

"These are your seals, then?"

She showed him some customs seals, cut off below the lead. Jack nodded, looking at them in the glow of a Maglite held by one of the silent ATF men. She had no time for his answer.

"And these *are* your documents?"

She fluttered a sheaf of pink and green carbons under his face. Jack snatched them out of her hand and stared down at them.

"This isn't the Pike shipment. This is a shipment . . . it says transformers. Electrical stuff. Factory equipment. This stuff's from . . ." He tilted the page into the half-light. "Montreal! For Chrissake. What's this about?"

"We have the Pike load. It's over on the right—"

"Starboard."

"The *starboard* side. Thank you. And we've dealt with that issue for the moment. We're now talking about *this* container right here, and I'm asking you again if these are Black Water Transit shipping documents."

"They look like—yeah, I think they are, but—"

"And is this an inspection seal from your office?"

"What the hell are you driving at? What's *in* there?"

Greco's eyes were little bright sparks and her cheeks were flushed. She waved at one of the ATF men.

"Show the man, Marty."

The agent stepped in, jerked the long locking rods out of their channels, and dragged the heavy steel doors back. Then he turned the Maglite beam onto the dark interior of the container. Two shapes sent back the light, in glittering black and bright chrome and the velvet sheen of expensive bodywork. It took Jack a couple of beats to understand what he was looking at.

They were *cars*.

Two of them.

A black Shelby Cobra, gleaming under the flash.

And beyond that, something low and strange.

"That car back there is called a Duesenberg, Mr. Vermillion. Very rare. Made in 1934. Marty here tells me that models in that condition run around a million dollars a pop."

"Okay. This first car here, that's a Shelby Cobra. I have one just like it. I know what the damn thing is!"

"Oh? Is this your car, then? Please be careful not to touch it."

Jack kept his hands off, studied the interior, looked around the body, checked the windshield.

"No. I don't think so. It better not be. Mine's in the garage back in Rensselaer, as far as I know."

Greco inclined her head, looked sly and smug, a hard thing to do with the same face at the same time, but she managed.

"Yes. It is. We checked."

"You checked? You checked my car? How?"

"We had some people at your house. They checked."

"My garage is locked. What the hell is—"

"We'll get to that. You agree this is not your car, then?"

"I'd like to run the number. But no, it's not. There aren't more than twenty of this particular model in the world."

"These Cobras are rare, then?"

"Of course they are. I paid over a quarter million for mine."

"So the presence of these two extremely valuable collector cars—a type of car in which I gather you have shown a particular interest—is a total surprise to you? You don't know anything about them?"

"Not a damn thing!"

"Really? You never thought, goodness me, what a chance to run a shipment of cars down the river? They're going to raid my barge looking for one container. They'll never check the rest of the boat? Is that what you were thinking, Mr. Vermillion?"

"Why the hell should I lie about shipping cars? It's perfectly legal to ship cars in containers. What's this got to do with you?"

"We've run the VINs. The RCMP inform us that the black Shelby Cobra here—such a lovely car—went missing from in front of the Château Des Jardins in Quebec City two months ago. The Duesenberg belonged to a collector who was holding it for a stockbroker at Morgan Stanley in a storage yard in Montreal. Needless to say, it's not there, since it seems to be here instead."

Jack felt his chest go very tight and his face was burning.

"You saying they're hot? That they're stolen?"

"Yes," she said, smiling a vicious satisfied smile. "They're extremely hot, very stolen, and they're sitting on your barge under seals supplied by your firm and carried on your papers as transformers. All very irregular. So, as you can understand, I'm rather *curious* to hear what you have to say about all of this."

Jack stared back at her, felt his rage building.

"What I have to say? I don't know a damn thing about this!"

Greco nodded. "Fine. Maybe this will help jog your

memory. Marty, let's show Mr. Vermillion here what we found in the trunk of the Cobra."

The ATF man led them down the inside of the container, sliding along the wall, holding his Maglite on the car. He stopped at the rear end and waited for them to edge along far enough to see what he was doing. Jack was close enough to Greco to smell her perfume and her sweat. She was looking down at the top of the Cobra trunk with a ferocious intensity.

"Open it, Marty."

The agent popped the trunk. It rose up in a hiss of hydraulics. Jack stared down at the interior, at what looked like five bales wrapped in lime-green plastic. Under the glare of the flashlight they seemed luminous, radioactive, unearthly.

"What the hell is that?" he asked. "Your laundry?"

Greco had a knife attached to her flak jacket. She peeled it off, skinned it, and used it to cut a ragged slice in the side of the bale. Jack could see compact bundles of something green and black.

"What is it?" he asked. "Paper?"

"Paper. Yes, I guess you could say paper. It's currency, Mr. Vermillion. Canadian currency. Mixed denominations, mostly twenties, fifties, hundreds. At a rough estimate, close to a million dollars' worth. Anything to say about this?"

Jack was silent. What in the hell was going on?

"No?" said Greco, looking solicitous. "No comment? No snippy tone? Don't feel like calling me some more names? Would it interest you to know that much of this money has field-tested positive for amphetamine and cocaine residue? I mean, in very high numbers? Now, we know that most currency will test positive for drug residue, but not in the degree that these bills register. That means this is very likely drug-related. So we have drug-related Canadian currency in very large amounts stuffed into the trunk of a stolen Shelby Cobra, also last seen in the fabled land of moose heads and mukluks a little to the north of us, and all of this nifty-neat stuff packed into a container sealed with Black Water Transit customs seals and carried on the *Agawa Canyon,* which is owned and operated by your company. So, as I said before, I'm curious. Would you care to comment? Would you care to . . . enlighten us?"

"I've never seen this car in my life. I have no idea how it got in this container. I have no idea how the container got sealed improperly. This is a complete . . ."

"Mystery? Really?"

Jack said nothing. Something more was coming.

"Really? You've never seen this car before?"

"Never?"

"Never driven it?"

"No!"

"Never even touched it?"

"No. How could I?"

"Not even a little fondle?"

Jack refused to react any further. Although he had an idea of what was coming, when he heard the words, it still shook him.

"Then perhaps you can explain something. Because I'll admit, since you say you have never seen this car, it's a complete mystery to me, my friend, how we managed to find your fingerprints all over the car's interior."

"My what?"

"Fingerprints. Those jiggly-swirly things on the tips of your fingers? The FBI computer matched them with your Marine Corps records."

He might have done anything then, said anything, perhaps even struck her, but a soft voice spoke from the open doors of the container behind them.

"I'd not answer any more questions, Jack. If I were you."

They all looked back. Flannery was standing in the open doors, leaning on his walking stick, his gray hair flying in a wind off the river, his face stern as he returned the hot glare from Greco.

"Very naughty, young lady. The Fourth Amendment sound familiar to you? Ring any sort of bell?"

"We're simply allowing Mr. Vermillion an opportunity to explain himself."

"You had my client's permission to open one particular container, the subject of your original inquiry. By what authority did you open this container, which was in no way connected?"

Something went over her face, a ripple of indecision, which was quickly erased with a visible effort.

"We had reason to believe there might be . . . contraband."

"Reason to believe? How timely. Provided by what? The tarot? Tea leaves? A helpful clairvoyant? The entrails of a duck?"

"I am not obliged to reveal the nature of our sources at this time. For that matter, our search warrant names the *Agawa Canyon*, Mr. Coleman. We were not limited to any particular container."

"I'd like to see a copy of that warrant, Ms. Greco."

"You will. At the appropriate moment."

"I see. Very well. Are you about to charge my client this fine June morning, Ms. Greco?"

She hesitated, glanced back at Jack, and then past him at the faces of the ATF men gathered around him.

They all watched her face as she worked out the angles.

"No," she said through her teeth. "I'm not."

"And if you do decide to proceed with some sort of indictment, you'll do us the professional courtesy of allowing us to attend the federal offices in Albany at an agreed time?"

Hearing this made Jack's stomach churn, but he kept his face blank and listened to Flannery's controlled tones.

"I will. In return for Mr. Vermillion's promise not to leave the country and to remain in contact with you or your office."

"You have our assurances. And I'd like to state for the record that this is a clear and deliberate attempt on someone's part to destroy my client's reputation."

"The reputation of a known Mafia associate?"

Flannery would not be drawn in.

"And I am confident that a vigorous investigation will exonerate him and expose the conspirators, whoever they may be, Ms. Greco, and we will follow the evidence wherever the facts may lead. To whomever they implicate. Do I make myself clear?"

"Crystalline, Mr. Coleman."

"And I have your word of honor that, in the event charges may be laid against Mr. Vermillion, we will be given the opportunity to answer them in person, that he will not be dragged off the street in one of those media-circus arrests that your office has lately developed such an affection for? He'll be processed with dignity and discretion?"

"He'll be accorded every consideration he has a right to."

"No circus arrests?"

"No."

"Your word on it, Ms. Greco, one attorney to another?"

"My word on it."

Flannery handed her one of his business cards.

"All of my numbers are on that. When you've reached a decision, you'll call one of those numbers and

I will arrange to have my client appear at whatever location you name. Now we'll be leaving, Ms. Greco, and I bid you the very best of days."

"Good-bye, Mr. Coleman. Jack, we'll be seeing you."

"Tut, Ms. Greco. No threats. I have your word."

"Yes. You have my word."

"On your honor?"

Greco smiled, not nicely.

"As a gentleman?"

JAY RATS UNIT 509

EASTBOUND ON EMPIRE BOULEVARD

BROOKLYN

0830 HOURS

Nicky drove with his eyes fixed forward and both hands on the wheel and Casey was as stony silent as he was until Nicky had the big rusted gypsy cab rolling along Empire Boulevard. Then she let out a long ragged breath, thick with grief and remorse.

Nicky glanced over at her and spoke softly.

"Casey, can you tell me something?"

"Sure. I'll try."

"What's a Sylvester?"

"Nicky, I'm sorry I called you a Sylvester."

"I figured it was an insult. I just didn't know what kind. Then I figured maybe I remind you of Sylvester Stallone."

"It's what they called white boys in Vietnam."

"Yeah? Casey, I'm no math whiz, but I'm gonna bet you're too young to have served in Vietnam."

"My father . . . he was killed there. In Saigon, 1972."

"Sorry to hear it."

"So was I. He was nineteen. My mother was four months pregnant. With me."

"What was it? Combat?"

"Yeah. It was combat. But not with the Vietcong. He was an MP at Long Binh Jail, just north of Saigon. He was stabbed to death by a prisoner. A U.S. Army soldier. From someplace called Eufalia, Alabama."

"You're kidding. By one of our guys?"

She was quiet for a time.

"No. One of *your* guys."

Nicky had to work it out, but he got it.

"Oh, let me guess, a white guy?"

"Yeah. He said, 'The nigra looked like he needed a cutting, so I give him one.' The army shrinks said he had some kind of combat-related psychological disorder, gave him a Section Eight, and he spent two years in Leavenworth. Now he has three children and a speedboat and he owns a farm equipment dealership in Waycross, Georgia."

Nicky stared at her.

"Christ . . . you keeping a file on him?"

"Yes."

"Man, you are one outstanding hater."

"I do what I can," said Casey, without a smile.

"This knuckle-walker kills your dad. Hence the black thing?"

"It's not a 'black thing,' Nicky. He was killed for being a black cop in the American army, and he was only in Vietnam because he was a black *man* in America."

"Casey, a word in your shell-like ear . . . lots of white boys went to Vietnam. My uncle—"

"No *rich* white boys."

"You're gonna have to work out whether you're a racist or a communist, Casey. You can't have both. That's just greedy. You gotta choose one and stick with it."

"You wanna know how many white kids from Harvard went to Vietnam?"

"You wanna know how many black kids went to Harvard just because they were black? I'm here to tell you I sure wasn't offered a ticket to Brown, or even given a pass on the SATs, a clear victim of racist oppression on account of I'm Africa-deficient. Black-challenged. Melatonin-impaired."

"You mean 'melanin.' "

"Yeah, whatever. My point is—"

"Can we just drop it? Please?"

"Look, I know this is not the time. Only reason I'm prodding you about it is, this thing that was between you and Detective Rule . . . it's over now. Finished. But you and me, we need to get straight on it. It can't hang around. I'm white too. We have a lot to take care of."

"I know that. But your timing sucks."

"Yeah . . . you're right. I'm sorry. And was your mother okay? Did she get around it? The thing with your dad?"

"No. She's not okay. No, she didn't get around it. Can I ask you a question, Nicky?"

"Shoot."

"Do you know how I got onto the Jay Rats?"

Nicky let the question simmer for a while, trying to figure out how to deal with a lit fuse. There was heavy traffic on Washington and he had to fight through the intersection and make the turn northbound. Brooklyn was spooling up to speed and the sun was burning a hole in the haze over the eastern buildings. What the hell, tell her the truth.

"I heard something about it."

"From whom?"

"I like it when you say 'whom.' "

"Don't get clever, Nicky. Who told you?"

"Vince."

"Vince told you?"

"Yeah."

"This morning, while we were waiting for Jimmy to die?"

"Yeah. Like I said to Pete, he talked. I listened."

"Vince talked to you about me. What'd he say?"

"Basically, you were suspected of tuning up a PD name of Eddie Rubinek."

"Did you hear why I might have done that?"

"Yeah. Vince told me you guys had busted your butts on the street making a kidnap-rape case. Then this Rubinek toad-sucker works some kind of Fourth Amendment mojo with a judge down on Centre Street and the perps walked, and then you might have taken a moment to chastise the fellow. A bit."

"Vince said that?"

"Said what? 'Toad-sucker' or 'chastise'?"

Casey laughed. It was short and sharp, but it was a laugh.

"So?" said Nicky.

"So what?"

"So . . . did you?"

"It was the Shawana Coryell case. You know it?"

"I caught it on the news. It was everywhere. It was lousy. Forgetting it is the problem there, Casey."

"Yeah . . . what would *you* have done?"

"Me?" said Nicky. "I would not have gotten caught."

"I didn't get caught."

"You're here, aren't you?"

"Oh yes . . . I'm here. The CO of the Two Five used to be Vince's partner. He figured I needed some 'guidance' and that Vince Zaragosa was the man to do it."

"Jimmy was right, you know. Most cops in your

situation, the force would hang that cop out to spin, let the crows pick his eyes out like little green grapes. But here you are."

"You have a problem with that?"

"No more than you. And you definitely do. What got to you about Jimmy Rock is, you think he may be— might have been—right, you think you got the job with the Jay Rats because you're black."

"But I didn't, Nicky. I really didn't."

"No, you got it because you're *connected,* you had a rabbi. The CO at the Two Five. He went the distance for you. Nobody gets anywhere in any police department without a friend up the scale. Maybe it's not fair, but what is?"

"Connected, maybe. But I never asked for a break because I was black. I never asked my boss at the Two Five. I pull my time."

"What's the difference? Connected or connected black, you took a break when it came to you. Other guys, not connected or not black, maybe they would have taken the hit. You ducked it. Good for you. I've ducked a few myself. That's the game. That's what makes America great. The fix isn't always in, but sometimes when you really need it, you can get it."

"That's a damn cynical point of view."

"Thank you. My favorite prayer? Please God, give me what I want, not what I deserve. You know Jimmy Rock's backstory?"

"No. And, with respect, yes he's dead, but I still, God help me, I really don't give a shit either way. Detective Rule was a mean-minded sadistic little prick. It takes more than a bullet to fix that."

"Oh my, you're a tough little black girl, hah? Know the world, don't you? Hard rain gonna fall, is that it? Want some good advice?"

"I'll listen. I'll let you know if it's good."

"Ask Vince."

"No."

"Make peace with this thing, Casey. Vince can help you. We had a long talk about . . . a lot of things. Talk to Vince."

"No."

"Suit yourself. Here we are."

They'd pulled up outside Casey's apartment block on Temple Court, across from Prospect Park. The little dead-end street was deserted and the rows of old trucks and cars under the bare trees looked tired and shabby, livestock in a pen.

Nicky had been up for twenty-four hours straight, the last eight of which had been shattering. If he'd been on his game, he'd have seen the shape of a man sitting in one of the parked cars, maybe even made him. But he didn't. However, Earl V. Pike made him.

Nicky was studying the east wall of Casey's apartment. Most of the windows in the brownstone building were shuttered against the rising heat, and air conditioners studded the exterior walls, humming and rattling and dripping water down the bricks. It was a dumpy little residence, soaked in the acid bath of chronic poverty. Nicky could see the outline of a woman in one of the lower windows.

She was watching the cab as they sat there, the engine idling. There was a red spark in her hand and a line of smoke curling up from it. It was hard to make out any facial details through the grimy window. Nicky saw Casey's wary glance up to that window as he turned the car off.

"That your place up there?" he asked.

"Yeah."

"So somebody's waiting, hah?"

Casey's face registered a couple of changes and finished with blank and empty.

"Oh yeah. Life's an endless cycle of song."

She said it with an air of resignation, with a ripple of anger and resentment. Nicky watched her and his face softened around the eyes.

"Look, Casey . . . I was gonna wait on this."

"On what?"

"You mind taking a little run with me?"

"What? Now?"

"Yeah. It won't take long."

"Where to?"

"Peekskill."

"Peekskill! What the hell for?"

"Vince asked me to take you to Peekskill."

"Vince? When?"

"During our . . . talk."

"The one where you listened and he talked?"

"Yeah."

Casey looked back up at the window, at the smoking figure leaning on the windowsill, her face hidden by the sun lying on the dust and the grease that coated the window. She rubbed her face with both hands, shut her eyes, spoke after a long silence.

"Nicky, you realize that the last time I had any sleep was two lousy hours on the army cot at the office over in the Albee Mall, and that it was you calling on the phone that woke me up?"

"Yeah."

"And that was . . . Christ, twenty hours ago? And everything that has happened since . . . The past forty-eight hours have been a flat-out nightmare. The very . . . almost the very worst time in my life."

"Yeah."

"This is something Vince thinks I need to do?"

"Yeah."

"Do you?"

"Yeah."

"Is it about Jimmy Rock?"

"Yeah."

"Am I going to enjoy it?"

"No."

HEAD OFFICE

BLACK WATER TRANSIT SYSTEMS

TROY, NEW YORK

1100 HOURS

Valeriana Greco lied. She held off for exactly three hours and then sent the whole ATF team to arrest Jack Vermillion at the corporate offices of Black Water Transit Systems. They arrived in vans and unmarked Caprices, boiled up the staircase in a pack, terrified the staffers, bulled through his secretary, stood Jack up, pushed him over his own desk, and cuffed him way too hard. Then they frog-marched him down the front stairs in front of his staff and past all of the dockhands gathered in the big yard.

Greco was waiting for him inside a crowd of ATF agents, standing next to a big white van with *United States Marshals* painted on the side in huge scarlet letters.

There was a Live Eye satellite truck from Albany there, and about fifteen reporters milling around with video cameras and flashes. Apparently somebody had called them with an anonymous tip—a powerful local businessman was about to be arrested by the ATF on charges of smuggling weapons and running a stolen car ring. He was also implicated in the deaths of three ATF agents and the wounding of a fourth, as well as the death of a New York City police detective. The tip included vague references to "connections with shadowy figures in organized crime."

Out in the yard, a brace of bull-necked ATF men

snarled at him as they pushed Jack into the van and slammed the doors on him. The last thing he saw as they jolted away into the street was Valeriana Greco right in the middle of a large circle of avid reporters.

There were bright white lights on her, and everybody was listening to what she had to say. Jack could see the glow coming off her and feel her heat. She was right dead center at the beating heart of law enforcement and was looking very good. Then the van accelerated and he lurched forward on the metal bench inside the lockdown section and the chains around his wrists snapped him up short, pain carved a white-hot trench up his spine, the trees began to slide by, the truck gained speed, and he was looking at the world through a grid of metal wire. It was a strain to focus beyond the wire, so after a while he gave that up and just focused on the grid itself and let his mind go blank. The truck itself stank of sweat and urine and stale coffee and the two guards up front ignored him completely all the way to the federal lockup downtown.

By the time they rolled down the long driveway to the portcullis that sealed off the prisoners' section, the bruises on his wrists had changed from bright pink to deep purple and the pain had settled down into a dull throbbing ache that he could, with a concentrated effort, almost manage to ignore.

The guards changed that situation for the worse when they dragged him out of the transport van by his wrist shackles thirty seconds later, forced him to bend over and step across the connecting chain between them, pulled him back upright with a jerk, twisted his arms up behind his back so hard he felt his sinews cracking, and then frog-marched him up a flight of slick concrete stairs under a bank of blue-white fluorescent lights. He fell twice on the way up the stairs, tripping over his ankle chains, which they seemed to enjoy.

While Jack Vermillion was being processed at the Albany holding cells, Nicky Cicero and Casey Spandau were walking down a darkened hallway on the third floor of the east wing of the Sisters of Providence Palliative Care Clinic in Peekskill, New York. They were following a nun in a gray habit that flowed out around her like gauze curtains blowing in a wind from the sea.

Her slippers made a whispering sound on the terrazzo flooring. She moved in and out of the circles of light coming from the ceiling fixtures, and Casey Spandau, her mind weighed down with grief and a dreadful fear of what might be coming, concentrated on the way the light changed across the nun's narrow shoulders and the way it rippled along the material of her habit.

As they passed by open rooms, she could see sleeping forms of patients in dimly lit rooms, hooked to machines and connected to monitors. Now and then there'd be a parent or a relative at the bedside, a pale face floating in the half-light, staring upward, counting ceiling tiles and heartbeats.

Nicky was carrying a new Beanie Baby named Halo. He'd stopped at a mall in the suburbs of Peekskill and bought it without much in the way of explanation to Casey, other than to say it was for a relative of Jimmy Rock's.

"What relative?" Casey had asked, but Nicky shook his head gently and refused to say anything else. Halo was a white angel bear and had a silver ring floating above her head.

They reached the door to the room where Jimmy Rock's "relative" was staying. The nun, whose name was Sister Mary Angelus, turned at the door. Light glimmered on her narrow gold-framed glasses. Her wimple was very tight across her forehead and her face seemed almost an animated mask. Her skin looked as soft as whipped cream, and she had a faint scent of sandalwood.

"She has been sleeping very well, Officer Cicero. She has some bedsores, but we've been taking care of them. They can't be helped, you know. We try to ease them."

"I know, Sister," said Nicky. "Don't worry."

"Will either of you want some tea?"

"No thanks."

"Then I'll be down the hall. If you need me, you just press that little button by the bedside table. I'm informed that Mr. Rule has passed away?"

"Yes," said Nicky.

"That's very sad. Was it sudden? I wasn't aware he was ill."

"It was very sudden," said Nicky. "No one was expecting it."

Sister Mary Angelus studied their faces. The light on her face made two reflective pools out of the lenses of her glasses. Her mouth was thin and her lips very pale.

"He was a police officer?"

"Yes. He was."

"Was his death related to that?"

"Yes."

"We heard of a confrontation in New York City last night. Four men were killed. One man gravely wounded. Terrible. Such a terrible time. So much grief in one family. So much violence. So much sorrow and loss. Mr. Rule was a good man."

"Makes you wonder where God was in all of it," said Casey. Sister Mary Angelus looked at her calmly.

"God is with all of us. But He does not create evil. Evil is in the world. Do not imagine that evil things come upon us because God allows it or wishes it. That makes the world a very dark place. You must not allow your hatred of evil things to make you hateful."

"Yes. Of course," said Casey, an age-old reflex of obedience suddenly surfacing, to her own surprise.

Sister Mary Angelus smiled at her, turned, and floated away down the hall. Casey put out a hand and stopped Nicky as he reached for the doorknob. Nicky waited, feeling cruel and more than a little ashamed.

"Nicky, what's this supposed to do for me?"

"Vince wanted you to meet this person."

"Why you? Why do you have to be the one to show me?"

"Why me? I don't know. I'm here. The guy has his ways."

"Do you know who's in there?"

"Yes."

"Have you ever been here before?"

"No. Vince . . . filled me in."

"This is a palliative care center. That means a place for dying people to get comfort. Is the person in there dying?"

"They don't know."

"Nicky, this is just plain mean."

"Yeah. It is. You don't have to go inside."

"Are you?"

"Yeah. I think I am."

Casey found her eyes were filling up and her chest was hurting.

"Okay. Goddammit. Okay. I'm ready."

Nicky paused, steadied his breathing, and made himself calm. Then he turned and went into the room, and Casey followed him.

A small child lay on the hospital bed, bathed in an amber glow from a light clipped to the headboard, the pale-yellow sheets pulled up to her shoulders. She was on her right side and seemed to be curled up around a pillow. She was tiny, her limbs thin, the skin over them like parchment. A tracery of blue veins pulsed under the skin at her temple.

Her eyes were closed and her mouth slightly open. Her blonde hair was clipped short and brushed back from her face. A breathing tube projected from her throat, and the machine in the corner huffed and wheezed in a slow cadenced cycle. Above the bed, a monitor showed five glowing green lines pulsing on a black scale. Her right hand was open and underneath it was a Beanie Baby.

Casey stepped around Nicky and stood by the bed, looking down at the sleeping child. She glanced around the room. It was filled with Beanie Babies. And flowers, and games, and a Spice Girls poster, and a South Park poster. She looked at Nicky.

"She's his daughter?"

"Yes. Her name is Morgan."

"She's in a coma." It wasn't a question.

"Yes. Vince said Jimmy Rock came up here all the time. He was trying to guess what his little girl would be like if she was walking and talking. He figured she'd be into Beanie Babies."

"How old is she?"

"Six."

"What happened to her?"

"She'd been playing in a schoolyard at Pope Pius the Tenth, up in White Plains. A six-pack of juveniles stoned on glue lit up the schoolyard with a stolen tool. Just for a jolt. A thirty-two-caliber round caught her in the back of the head. On the jungle gym. She was three years old. Apparently Jimmy Rock's wife saw it all happen. Couldn't handle it. She split on both of them a year later. Living in Oregon now. Refuses all contact. The shooters were caught. The oldest was fifteen."

"The shooters. They were all black, am I right?"

"Oh yeah. Actually, it was an all-black cast. Just a coincidence, but it made things worse for Jimmy Rock. According to Vince, I mean the way he told it to me, a black female PD cited fetal alcohol syndrome and crack-baby syndrome and early childhood abuse and even black rage in front of a black female judge in youth court, and the court-appointed social worker—also black—did a home environment study and she agreed with the PD and the PD talked to the ADA—also black—the little shits took a plea for involuntary manslaughter and pulled their time at a work farm up in the Adirondacks, where they learned valuable life skills like how to make cedar-shake birdhouses and how to tell your deciduous trees from your coniferous. Most of them were back on the street in a year."

"I see."

"Vince said one was already a daddy. One was already dead."

"And that's why Rule hates—why he hated—all black people?"

"Short answer would be yes."

There was nothing to say to that. Casey stood and watched the breathing tube where it entered the little girl's throat; it was misted and droplets of clear water ran down the inside of the tube. The machine pumped and whirred and chuffed and the five green lines on the monitor blipped in a steady rhythm. Casey knelt down at the side of the bed and leaned in close to the child. She smelled of soap and Nivea cream and Penaten lotion. Nicky came over and handed her the Beanie Baby named Halo, and she replaced the Beanie Baby under her hand with the new one.

"Her name is Halo," she said in a whisper. "She's a bear."

She watched her face the way a fisherman watches a

pool of water, alert to a ripple or a flicker of movement. After a while Casey's right knee began to tremble, so she sat down on the chair and leaned on the edge of the bed, and after a long time the light changed in the room and Casey and Nicky looked up at the window, at the sun beginning a long slow slide into the western skyline, far past the midway point of a long and terrible day, and Morgan Rule knew none of it. Nicky touched Casey's shoulder.

"Come on, Casey. It's almost two. Time to go."

Casey stood up shakily, ran the tips of her fingers over the child's face, and walked out of the room behind Nicky Cicero, closing the door softly behind her, although she knew that no sound on this earth was going to wake that little girl. On the way back down the hall, Casey put a hand on Nicky's arm and stopped him by the exit doors.

"Who's responsible for her now?"

"Vince says the Detectives' Endowment people will cover all her costs. And Jimmy Rock was insured."

"I know. But who will . . . take care of her?"

Nicky shook his head. "The nuns, I guess."

"They going to look for her mother?"

"They called her. She hung up on them."

"What was I supposed to learn from this, Nicky?"

"Jesus, Casey. I don't know. What did you learn?"

"I guess I learned why Jimmy Rock was such a good hater."

"Yeah. He was. So you and he had a lot in common, then."

Casey pushed through the exit doors without looking back. When they got outside, it was as if somebody had left the oven door open. They walked in the narrow shadow of the rambling Victorian pile until they reached the parking lot. Nicky had parked the 509 unit under a stand of willows at the far end of the lot. They could see the shattered glass around the driver's window from fifty feet away. It lay all around the left side of the car, glittering in the hard light of a match-head sun.

"Oh Christ," said Nicky, breaking into a run. Casey followed, her hand on the service Glock she wore on her belt under her suit jacket. As she came forward she studied every car in the lot. The ones without tinted windows looked empty. The others, it was impossible to say. Nicky was at the driver's door now. He slammed the roof and the gypsy cab bounced on its springs. A section of glass broke loose and dropped to the ground at his feet.

"God*damn*! Goddamnit!"

"Very helpful, Nicky. What's missing?"

They checked out the inside of the cab. It had been effectively rifled by someone in a hurry. The glovebox lid had been jimmied open, the storage box on the floor cracked and looted. Bits of paper and shards of broken plastic littered the interior. Broken glass lay all over the front seat. Casey popped open the rear door.

"Oh hell," she said. Nicky stepped up behind her.

"What?"

"My briefcase. I left it in the backseat. It's gone."

"Great. What was in it?"

"My life. Oh God. My whole fucking life."

"In your briefcase? Why?"

"Nicky, I don't even have a desk yet. I brought it with me from the Two Five. There was no safe place to leave it."

He considered the wreckage awhile longer and then turned to walk back toward the hospital.

"Where are you going?"

"To get a broom and call a cop."

He was almost to the entrance when he turned back to look at Casey and saw her sliding down the side of the car, folding. He came back at a run and knelt down beside her. She had her face buried in her arms. He touched her shoulder. She flinched.

"Can you just fuck off, Nicky? Please?"

Nicky sat back on his heels and watched her cry for another five minutes. People walked past them and whispered, but when Nicky made eye contact, they left. He reached out and put a hand on her shoulder again, and she let him keep it there. After a time she moved her left hand and placed it on top of his. Her skin was hot and she smelled of cigarettes. He fumbled in his pocket, found a Kleenex, held it out to her. She raised her head, studied it. The tears that ran down her cheeks made two shining paths and the skin underneath looked like polished wood.

"Where's that been?" she asked him.

But she took it anyway.

FEDERAL HOLDING CELLS
ALBANY COURTS
1430 HOURS

Three hours after his arrest, while the rest of the city of Albany was getting itself well into the business afternoon and talking around the water cooler about the big bust over in Troy, how some kind of Mafia kingpin got himself busted for running stolen cars, Jack Vermillion, beltless, shoeless, minus his watch and his Marine Corps ring, got collected from a cell in the basement of the Albany federal buildings by a guard large enough to have his own climate.

Jack was then forced to waddle, chained and cuffed, down a long hallway stinking of urine, clanging and clattering of steel and tin, boiling with heat and voices, until they reached a doorway—solid steel with a thick glass window reinforced with chicken wire—and burst through it into a small windowless room with smeared and pitted dark-green walls, lit by a lamp hanging inside a steel cage.

The guard shoved him into a wooden chair that had been bolted to the floor beside a heavy wooden desk—also bolted—and locked his ankle chains to a ring set in the concrete floor.

He had spoken no more than seven words to Jack during the whole process, and left without a kiss. Jack was then left to consider his situation for an indefinite period, a time he passed by studying the gang tags and obscenities carved into the wooden tabletop.

Among the other insights, such as the numbers and prices and sexual appetites of assorted bail bondsmen and public defenders, Jack found out that all white people were "fuk-ass honki dugs," that all federal law enforcement officers were "sukking anamal shetpimpuls," that an individual named "Lobo" was prepared to do almost anything in return for "hot nasty stick," and that the governor of New York was cordially invited to perform a physically challenging sex act upon somebody whose name, scratched in blunt capitals, was Khan Mohammed Jah.

Jack's introductory course in jailhouse graffiti was eventually terminated when the door clanged open and the same guard bulled into the room, followed hard by Flannery Coleman, still in his crisp blue suit and Yale tie. Jack, whose sense of smell had been sharpened by his stay in the federal cells downstairs, picked up on Flannery's fresh bay rum splash and it pushed him over the edge.

"Where the bloody hell have you been? I called your office as soon as I got through booking. That was . . ." Jack checked his watch and realized it had been taken from him, which didn't help matters. "I have no fucking idea when it was—hours—days—it was twelve-thirty. That's two hours ago! Where the *hell* have you—"

"Jack, I apologize. I had a voir dire with Brunelle and—damn, the sneaky little bitch assured me that she wouldn't be laying any charges—that if she did, she'd let us know first!"

"Just get me out *now,* Flannery. This place—"

Jack stopped short as he registered the sudden flush of something mealy-looking under Flannery's polished hide.

"Look, Jack, you're going to have to get a grip here. I've just come from the U.S. attorney's office. Greco's been busy as hell."

"Busy doing what?"

Flannery leaned in close, crossed his hands on the table.

"You've been charged under the RICO laws. Racketeering-influenced and corrupt organizations. You know what they are?"

"I run a shipping company, remember. We get watched."

"Yes, of course. Well, basically, they allow her a great deal of latitude in the scope and direction of her investigation. And she's using it very well, I have to say."

"I'm glad you like her style. Just give me the worst of it."

Flannery studied his hands and drew a breath. Jack didn't like the color of his skin and the thin sheen of moisture on his forehead.

"Okay . . . you've heard of the asset seizure laws? If the state can persuade a federal judge that some or all of your assets are the proceeds of organized crime—that's where RICO comes in—then the judge will allow the U.S. attorney's office to seize control of those assets until a determination can be made as to what part—if any—can be linked to criminal activities."

"I know all this."

"Greco is going for the seizure of Black Water Transit Systems, the warehouses, the ships, the trucks, the rolling stock, the dock facilities. The bank accounts. The whole package."

Jack felt blood leaving all his outpost stations. His belly churned and then slowed.

"Christ. Will she win?"

"The drug-tainted money was very damning, Jack. The short answer is, if she gets the seizure order, they stop you from using your resources to defend yourself—pay lawyers, pay for a lot of delaying motions, drag the case out for years—or flee the country. She—the feds—control your money, your entire business. Greco thinks she can ride your case all the way to Washington."

"I've been a solid businessman, I've paid taxes. I've never—"

"For God's sake, Jack. Look around. This is federal justice. They don't give a rat's ass about you personally. They think you're dirty, they always have, because of your friendships. They see what they want to see. Greco is sure she can convince a jury you're corrupt. You go down. You lose. She wins. If you get ruined in the process, too bad. You're just a speed bump in Greco's career path."

There wasn't too much to say in response to that. Flannery left Jack with his thoughts for about thirty seconds and then spoke softly.

"I'm going to have to ask you a difficult question."

"Ask it."

"Is there anything you can tell me about that container?"

Jack sat back, rubbed his face, looked at Flannery over the tips of his fingers, and then shook his head slowly.

"Man, how high can this shit stack? Flannery, I have

no idea in the world how those cars got on my ship. I have nothing to tell you about anything. I'm being set up. It's as simple as that."

Flannery nodded.

"Okay. Any thoughts on who might be doing this to you?"

"None. Not a damn one—what about Pike?"

"This goes way beyond Pike. Up until this Wednesday you had never met the man. This is something deeper. If you're being set up, this thing took planning. Weeks of it. Your fingerprints inside that Cobra, for example. How could that have happened?"

"I don't know. I guess somebody could have switched cars on me. Gotten my prints in the stolen one, then changed cars again. That would be . . . that might be it."

"Wouldn't you know if it was a different car?"

"Jesus . . . you'd think so. Maybe. I don't know. I don't keep a lot of personal stuff in it. I like it to be clean, so I guess you could probably slip it by me for long enough to get my prints in it. I mean, who thinks about stuff like that? I've had a lot on my mind. This shit with Danny. The pension fund thing with Galitzine Sheng."

"Has the car ever been out of your hands?"

"The Cobra?"

"Yes."

"Sure. Lots of times. Every time I park it somewhere. I use valet parking. It could have been switched on me at any one of a hundred different times. I have it tuned. The engine is cranky. You have to look after the timing. And I had it detailed just this week."

"Okay. There's a place to start. By whom?"

"By . . ."

Flannery's eyes narrowed as he watched Jack's face.

"By whom?"

"Hudson Valley Fine Cars."

"That's Frank's dealership."

"Yes, but Frank wouldn't . . . he's a friend, Flannery."

"Does Frank have any reason to be angry with you?"

"No."

"Nothing you're holding back here? This is your life they're fucking with, Jack."

"Frank and I are friends. Old friends. It wasn't him."

The old lawyer gave him a long look.

"You know Creek's been dealing in classic cars."

Jack's face went tight.

"I know."

"You know he's selling them to Tony Torinetti? Frank's kid?"

"Yeah. He sold Frank a turquoise T-bird, for Claire. So what? Creek didn't set me up. He wouldn't. Even if he wanted to, he's getting hurt by this bust, just as bad as I am. He's a full partner in Black Water Transit. They take me down, they take him down, too."

"Jack, a guy like you, a loner, only a friend is going to get close enough to set you up. You don't have any idea at all?"

"Christ. None. And definitely not Creek. Look, when do I get bail? When do I get out of here? I get out, I can make some moves. We can figure this thing out, one way or another. But I want out of this hole right now."

Flannery had been studying his hands while Jack was talking. Now he looked at him hard and straight.

"I have bad news, then. There'll be an arraignment before a federal judge. But I'm informed it will be pro forma. The word has come down from DC. You'll get no bail. You'll stay in custody."

"Why? On what grounds?"

"Risk of flight. Also, Greco says there's a security element."

"Security? For whom?"

"They're treating this like a mob thing. Greco has

convinced DC that you can be turned, that you're the tip of a huge conspiracy. Money laundering. Drugs. Weapons. She says they let you out on bail, you'll be . . . a target."

"Fuck, Flannery. What a farce. The word is *whacked*. This bitch needs to get out more. She's seen too many Tarantino films."

"She thinks she can use you to nail Frank Torinetti."

"Frank's a car dealer, Flannery. If he's into anything else, I sure as hell don't know anything about it! I told her that."

"I hear that, Jack. But she's making a strong case. And your prints in that Cobra, the cash, all of it looks pretty damning. This thing took work, planning. Somebody's making a project out of you."

"Thanks for the bulletin. Maybe it was that bitch herself."

"That bitch, and you're going to have to try not to call her that in court, had no access to your private life, no way to switch your Cobra, no way to get that far inside your head. And she reeks of self-righteous zeal. She knows in her heart that you're guilty. She has that look. I've seen it before. If you're being set up, it's being done by somebody inside, a friend. That's flat. Deal with it."

Jack leaned back in the wooden chair, rubbed his face. Flannery studied him under the hard planes of white light from the bulb in the iron cage. Coleman's face was as hard as Jack's. When Jack looked at him again, he saw something in there that he had never seen before. He saw suspicion.

"Flan. Answer me straight. Do you think I'm guilty?"

"Jack, if you were guilty, I mean actually guilty, of any of these charges, and you were to tell me—to admit to me—then it would make my job very difficult. The canon of ethics allows me to do whatever I need to do for my client, but if I were to be in possession of clear and inculpatory statements . . . as an officer of the court, it would . . . limit the scope of our defensive strategy."

"Don't blow smoke at me. I asked you straight out."

"Fine . . . I believe that you are being set up, yes. That you have been set up. I cannot say with absolute certainty that you are without . . . culpability . . . in some areas of your business operations. I dislike having to say it, but you pressed me."

"You really think Black Water Transit is bent? That I'm bent?"

"I'll admit that I—that we all—found it unusual that your troubles with the Teamsters last year seemed to dissipate so easily. They're not noted for their willingness to accept compromises."

"Hoffa's dead. The Teamsters aren't mobbed up anymore. I took a hard line with them, and my workers backed me. I made my people a better offer. That's what the pension fund thing was all about. They chose me over the union. That was all it took. It was a union probe, nothing more. Where's Creek?"

"You can't see anyone until after your arraignment."

"Fuck that. I need him here. Where is he now?"

"He's sitting outside Greco's office. He's exceedingly angry. She's refused to see him. He says he won't leave until she does."

"Christ. He's not armed, is he?"

"I doubt it. They have metal detectors in the entrance halls. Good God, Jack, you're not serious?"

"I want to see Creek. I want to see him now."

"Jack, I don't recommend—"

"Now, Flannery. Make it happen. It's the only move I have."

"I'll try." He stood up, began to gather his papers.

"One thing?"

Flannery stopped, waited.

"What . . . what happens next? To me?"

"Well . . . I'm told they'll be transferring you tonight. To Allenwood Prison. In central Pennsylvania. For your safety."

Jack's stomach burned and he felt the room lurching to the left. He thought he might pass out. In his throat, his carotid was surging. He could hear the hissing of blood in his ears. His chest was locked up tight. He saw Flannery's wary expression, swallowed hard.

"Fine. Okay. Allenwood. Get Creek down here."

HENRY HUDSON PARKWAY SOUTHBOUND
YONKERS, NEW YORK
1450 HOURS

It had taken a female Peekskill cop named Moira Stokovich, who looked about fourteen, over an hour to take down all the details of the break-in on their unit in a careful childish script, and when she had finished she told them a bit smugly the chances of getting back their papers were less than zero and really, as police officers, they should try to be more careful about the security of their vehicles.

Nicky had thanked Stokovich very nicely with his jaw muscles bunched up and his teeth hurting and he signed the report while Casey sat in the passenger seat inside the gypsy cab with her head back and her eyes closed, talking on her cell phone. It was almost three o'clock before they got back onto the Tarrytown road.

"Who were you talking to?" asked Nicky.

"Vince."

"Yeah. How'd he take it?"

"Oh, he was impressed. Thrilled."

Casey's voice was flat, the message plain. Nicky was

quiet for a while, fighting the traffic. In the distance they could see the midtown towers burning like red-hot iron bars in the dirty sunlight. When they pulled onto the Henry Hudson in Yonkers, he risked another question.

"What do you figure, Casey? Who did it?"

"Christ. Some crack-head. Kids. I don't know."

"What was in that briefcase?"

"Nothing. Case files. Reports. My Rolodex stuff. Contacts."

"You said it was your whole fucking life."

Casey's face was hard and flat and she seemed to freeze up.

"I was upset. You and that prick Zaragosa had just sandbagged me. How the fuck did you think I was going to handle it? You guys made me feel like shit."

"Did Vince say anything about Morgan?"

"Yeah."

"Care to share it with me?"

"No. And don't any of you be stomping around in my head anymore. I'm too tired for any more of this pop psych crap. Okay?"

She put her head up against the window and closed her eyes and had nothing more to say until they reached Casey's apartment block on Temple Court in Brooklyn. Across the road the sun was slanting sideways through the trees of Prospect Park and the dusty air was glowing yellow and gold. Nicky pulled up outside the entrance and touched Casey's shoulder.

"Casey. We're here."

Casey's eyes opened. She blinked a couple of times, sat up, shook out a cramp in her shoulder.

"Thanks, Nicky. See you in the morning."

"Okay. What's next?"

"Vince says we should start with Pike."

"Rocket science. Where is he?"

"Vince says the ATF has been in touch with Pike's

office in Maryland. CCS tells them Pike is on a business trip. Won't say where. Told the ATF he'd taken a private charter flight out of LaGuardia around midnight last night. Outfit called Slipstream Jetways. Left on one of their Lears."

"And that gives him no time to be the shooter at Red Hook and then make LaGuardia. Neat. Where's he supposed to have gone?"

"ATF asked for the flight plan. There wasn't one. You don't have to file one if the flight is private. CCS asked the ATF if there was a warrant on Pike."

"And . . . ?"

"ATF said no. CCS said good-bye. Then some macho ATF muscle-head leaned on this poor female behind the desk, threatened her, made her cry, according to Vince. Called her a stupid . . . I hate the word. Starts with a *c* and ends with *t*."

"Cat? Coot? Coronet?"

"Don't be clever, Nicky. You don't have the tools. When Vince got involved, the ATF told Vince this was a federal matter. Vince told them that Pike was wanted in connection with the death of an NYPD detective. They said they'd keep him informed, they were the lead agency, and he should keep out of their way."

"What did Vince say?"

"He told them to . . . you're Italian, right?"

"Last time I checked."

"What does something man-jah va fa-gool something mean?"

"Let's say it's an eating disorder. Then what?"

"So then Vince talks to Slipstream himself, asks the clerk very nicely, and the woman is happy to tell him the plane went to Harrisburg."

"So?"

"So he sent Dexter Zarnas to Harrisburg this morning.

He's going to talk to the airport people there, see if he can confirm that Pike was on the plane when it landed."

"The ATF will be all over Harrisburg."

"Vince doesn't care. He told Dexter to do whatever he had to."

"What about us?"

"There's an internal shooting inquiry at One Police. Ten o'clock sharp. You're picking me up here tomorrow morning."

"In what? This piece of shit?"

"No. Motor pool has a Caprice for us. You're taking this unit in to them. They'll give you the keys. Where you staying?"

"I have a room at the Thunderbird. In Yonkers. What's Vince doing in all of this?"

"Planning Jimmy Rock's funeral. It'll be a big one. Saint John the Divine. Dress blues all around. We have to be there."

"When is it?"

"Monday. June twenty-sixth. Two o'clock."

"Okay. Well, if that's it, then I'm going to bed."

"Good idea."

Casey climbed out of the car, started to walk down the path, and then stopped halfway to the door. She turned and came back to the car, leaned down into the window. Her look was harder in some way. She studied Nicky for a moment.

"Nicky, have you got a minute?"

"Sure."

"Come up for a bit? There's somebody I want you to meet."

"Me? Meet who?"

"You'll see. Come on."

"Casey, I'm dead beat."

"So was I, but that didn't stop you from dragging me

all the way up to Peekskill and feeding me through a bark chipper."

"Is this about Jimmy Rock?"

"No. It's about me."

"Am I going to enjoy this?"

"Not if I work it right."

"Jesus, Casey . . ."

She held his eyes and it was clear she wasn't going away. Nicky let out a sigh, nodded once, got out of the cab, made a move to lock it, and remembered the shattered side window. He put the keys in his pocket and followed her into the building. There was an elevator at the far end of a long wood-paneled hallway that smelled of Lysol and bleach and stale cigarette smoke. Casey dragged the mesh gates open and stepped inside. Nicky followed inside and the cab sagged on its cables. Casey said nothing, punched the number-five button.

They rode up in silence. The cab creaked and groaned and rattled. Nicky looked for the safety permit and saw a blank frame with a gang tag scratched in the old glass. At the fifth floor he followed Casey down a long narrow hallway lit by bare bulbs toward a door at the end. Casey stopped, waited for him to catch up.

She unlocked the door and opened it. Nicky's first sensation was the powerful smell of marijuana being smoked. When Casey looked at his face, waiting for a comment, he said nothing at all.

The apartment was large, done in a forties style, with plaster arches between the rooms, trimmed in gumwood and oak. The furniture was rounded and massive, a huge dark-green leather couch, two armchairs also in green leather, polished hardwood floors, a boarded-up fireplace with a painted art deco screen, an inlaid sideboard with a stereo, low table lamps in some sort of white stone with stained-glass shades in tones of amber, rose, and emerald-green. Music was playing, a big-band sound.

Nicky recognized Glenn Miller's "In the Mood." The light from the setting sun filled the room with a hazy yellow glow. Someone was lying on the couch, a woman. She stirred as Casey came into the room, sat upright on the couch, wrapping a pink satin robe around her body. Cigarette smoke rose up into the yellow light, snaking and twisting in the dead air. She covered her eyes against the shaft of sideways sunlight and peered at them both.

"Casey, is that you?"

"It's me. I've got someone from the office."

The woman stood up, swayed a little. She was white, so white she looked to be made of candle wax, very thin and gray-haired, her skin dry and her face deeply fissured, as if marked by continuous pain. She looked at Nicky and then back to Casey. When she spoke, her voice was soft, husky, and accusing.

"Casey. I've been calling. I've been sick. The television said there were shootings. Policemen were killed. I called your boss. He said you were okay, but he wouldn't put me through to you."

"I know. I'm okay. I'm sorry. They wouldn't let me call you until the scene had been released. This is Nicky Cicero."

The older woman rose to her feet and walked toward Nicky. She was working on a tentative smile, but there was something very wrong with her. She put out her hand and came in close. Her pupils were huge in dark-brown eyes, her cheeks thick with uneven powder, her mascara blurred and indistinct. That she had once been beautiful was there in her bones and in her carriage, which was still erect and poised, but it was layered and hidden by the slackness and dullness in her eyes. When she spoke, her low husky voice was slurred, as if she'd had a stroke, which was what Nicky first thought—she had reached him by now, after a difficult navigation over ten feet of hardwood flooring—she put out her hand like a countess waiting for a kiss on the ring and gave him a smile that was borderline grotesque.

"Hello," she said, "I'm happy to meet you."

Nicky was hit by a cloud of scent—something spicy, and an overlay of stale marijuana smoke. He put out a hand to take hers.

She stumbled into him and he caught her. She reeked of beer and brandy. Her gray hair was like straw and it scratched at his cheek as she fell against him. He caught her shoulders and pushed her upright—her bones were like wires—and she gave him an awful leer, heavy with ruined sexual promise.

"Sorry, Nicky . . . my God, he's *gorgeous* . . . Nicky . . . you're gorgeous . . . isn't he, Casey . . ."

Nicky smiled at her and glanced over at Casey. Casey's eyes were shining. She looked scalded. Nicky waited for an introduction that didn't seem to be coming.

"Casey . . . ?"

When she finally spoke, her voice was dry and low.

"Nicky. I'd like you to meet Elena Spandau."

Nicky looked back down at the older woman, and then he saw the bones, the slightly Oriental eyes.

"Miss Spandau, pleased to meet you."

"And I you," she said, wavering like a flame in a breeze. She tried for a curtsey and wobbled. "But it's Mrs. Spandau. . . ."

Casey cut in.

"Nicky, this is my mother."

Jack's arraignment was held under a press ban, all reporters barred from the hearing, in a broom-closet courtroom down a dead-end hallway on the third-floor annex of the old federal courthouse. It went just the way Flannery said it would. Jack stood upright and steady in his shackles, wearing the same clothes he'd been arrested in that morning, blue jeans and cowboy boots and a white T-shirt under a blue blazer, his face set and hard, listening while Valeriana Greco read a list of RICO charges in a voice ringing with outraged virtue and a sleepy-eyed judge in a mud-brown business suit held his sagging face up with one liver-spotted hand, watching Jack through his half-closed lids, his spindly fingers drumming a little paradiddle on the desktop pad.

Flannery had Jack plead not guilty to each charge as it was read off, and then asked the judge for a release on own recognizance. Greco popped up like a duck in a shooting gallery and quacked on feverishly about Risk of Flight and Security Concerns and Ongoing Investigations—Jack got a master-class lesson in the fine art of speaking in capitals—while Flannery humphed and brooded and the sleepy-eyed judge nodded away at Greco as if his neck had been presnapped especially for the occasion. Which was true. The fix was already in. She reached her aria, peaked on a high note about the Majesty of the Law, and in the pounding silence that followed, Jack found his ears were ringing. The judge blinked twice, sat up straight, reached for the gavel, raised it high, paused as if he were waiting for a suicidal cockroach to scuttle into position, and brought it down hard, a practiced snapping crack that sounded like a pistol shot.

Bang.

Bail denied.

Bang.

Prisoner to be transported this day.

Bang.

It's Miller time.

Bang bang.

Greco made meaningful eye contact with Jack and offered him a vicious victory leer that made Jack think of a poxed-up nun in fishnet stockings singing a Weimar drinking song in a basement bar in Munich. Flannery gripped Jack's shoulder hard as the guards led him away, narrowed his eyes to signify his rock-ribbed resolve to fight them on the beaches and fight them in the streets, and barked fiery promises at his back, until the big steel door slammed shut between them.

Jack was taken back to the same interview room and rebolted to the wooden chair. The steel door slammed shut with a dull boom that shook the floorboards. He heard their boots in the hall, and a muffled joke, and some low rolling laughter. Then he was alone.

Time floated in the still air of the tiny windowless room, stirred by nothing but Jack's slow and steady breathing. The chair back prodded his ribs and kidneys as if it had a personal grudge. His legs went to sleep after thirty minutes and he followed soon afterward.

The prison transport came for Jack an hour later, at eight-thirty that evening, a steel-plated white van with squared-off angles, two windows in either side made of thick green glass. It emptied itself of two U.S. marshals, who boomed into the holding room, woke Jack up with the slamming of the door, and then he was blinking up at a man and a woman, the male black, in his early thirties, with a double row of burned-in tribal scars across both cheeks. His eyes were as black as an oil slick and shiny with contempt. The woman was a frowzy trailer-park blonde, a face marked up by bad genes and beer, with wide-spaced brown eyes and a round ruddy face. Both of them were short, beefy, and packed with muscle, both wearing suit pants and white shirts under Kevlar flak jackets, heavy combat boots, thick black equipment belts hung with cuff cases, radios, pepper spray, and matte-gray Glock pistols.

The woman showed Jack her ID, introduced herself as Deputy United States Marshal Sharon Callahan. Her voice was husky, and she smelled of a very recent cigarette. Her air was official and bored, but the first thing she did was take the ankle chains off Jack and undo the chain that held him to the wooden chair. When Jack stood up, he almost collapsed, but Callahan held him up, her fingers on his upper arm as solid as angle iron, with a grip he felt right to his bone.

"Sweet Jesus, cowboy. How long have these assholes had you trussed up like this?"

Jack straightened up, hiding the sharp pain in his lower back.

"I don't know. What time is it?"

"They took your watch, hah? Was it a nice one, cowboy?"

"My name is Jack Vermillion. It was a Rolex."

"Too bad. Guards around here are worse than gypsies. You sure you aren't a cowboy? Got that big white longhorn mustache. Pair of Dan Post boots there. Wear your hair all combed back. Got the look in your eyes. You look just like Heck Thomas. You know who Heck Thomas was?"

"No. I don't."

"Famous lawman. A life-taker. I own his Winchester carbine. Paid eleven thousand dollars for it. Bought it at a gun show in Cheyenne. Damn, look at this. It's twenty minutes to nine. Buster and I gotta get you on the truck. We got a long run ahead of us."

"I was supposed to be seeing a friend. Before I left. I've been waiting for . . ." He did the math and realized he'd fallen asleep in the interview room and the bastards had just left him there, chained to a ring in the floor. "I've been here for hours. His name is Raleigh Johnson."

"Hours. Hear that, Buster?"

Buster's face in no way registered anything more complicated than a broadband low-level threat that came off him like the hissing heat off a steam-pipe radiator. He reminded Jack of a buffalo bull calf, a bad one. Jack held Buster's eyes for much longer than he had to and saw Buster's eyes begin to flicker. It was like blowing on hot coals. Face him directly in any way, he'd go off like a Roman candle. Callahan saw the silent exchange of mutual dislike and laughed.

"Now now. Play nice, fellas. Jack, they feed you?"

"No. Nothing."

"Damn. Sadistic little shits, aren't they? We'll get you something once we're clear of the city. Can you walk?"

"Raleigh Johnson. Can you get in touch with him?"

"If you're talking about a big old blond buck who looks like he used to play football, he's sitting on a bench out in the hallway for as long as we been here, anyway. You supposed to talk to him?"

Jack managed to keep his tone civil, but he felt like drop-kicking the woman through the open doorway behind her.

"Yes. I am. He's my business partner."

"You been arraigned, right?"

"Yeah. I have been well and truly arraigned."

"We'll see what we can do. Come on now."

They rearranged his shackles, left the leg irons on the floor behind him, Jack now cuffed only at the wrists to a steel chain that ran around his waist. They went down the long hallway toward the steel-barred exit gate. Beyond it, in the portcullis area, Jack could see a white van parked under a blue-white yard light, no markings of any kind on it. It was big and blocky and looked like an armored car.

Callahan tapped Buster on the shoulder, nodded toward the door marked *Visitors,* and walked Jack down the hallway to the gate. There was a bench there, beside a Coke machine and some guard lockers. A turnkey inside a glass booth was leaning back in a big stuffed chair and watching a black-and-white television. *Law & Order,* as it turned out, one of Jack's favorite shows up until recently. Being dragged up a flight of concrete stairs by a couple of bad-tempered prison guards jerking on your wrist shackles tends to fog up your clarity about concepts like law and order. Callahan sat him down on the bench and stepped back, studying him, her arms folded across her flak jacket, her hip cocked.

"You the one they popped for the gunfight over at Red Hook?"

"No."

"No? They told me you were all over that!"

"They told you wrong."

"You look the part. A gunfighter. Ever been in a gunfight?"

"Yes."

"Yeah? Where?"

"Vietnam."

"In that, were you? What was it like? The gunfight."

"Unpleasant. I don't recommend them."

"Maybe. I guess you'd know. We'll have to see. I joined the marshals because I always wanted to be a famous gunfighter, and they got me stuck in prisoner transport. Been at it for eleven years. Never fired a shot in anger. Hate my job. Hate my partner too. Buster has no bounce at all. He's from Nigeria, used to be in the police there. His real name is In-gwu-mee something. I can't pronounce it, so I call him Buster. He has a bad eye. Mean. You seen it too, I know you did. God only knows what evil things he's done back there in Nigeria. But now he's a U.S. marshal, because we seem to need more black U.S. marshals. I don't know why. You need to pee, Mr. Vermillion?"

Jack did, but he was damned if he was going to let her help him. Or some Nigerian psycho named Buster. She read his expression.

"Oh hell, don't you worry. I got no mandate to assist you in pecker deployment, Mr. Vermillion. And Buster would take it as a personal insult, we ask him. Like to slice it right off and eat it raw. There's a washroom right in there. You go on in. Have a good long one. There's no way out but back this way."

Jack stood up, let her undo his wrist shackles, and was about to go into the washroom when he heard a shout from down the hall. He turned and saw Creek Johnson striding down the hallway, his face white as bone, his eyes fixed, Buster following hard. He reached Jack and pulled him into an embrace, but Callahan and Buster stepped in and jerked him back.

"You got ten minutes, Mr. Vermillion," said Callahan. "You, sir, we said no physical contact. We search all our prisoners before we put them in the van, remember. Thoroughly."

Creek stood rigid, waiting for the guards to back away. Jack saw that Creek's eyes were wet and his face looked haggard.

"Jack, what the hell they doing to you?"

"You talk to Flannery?"

Creek waved that away. "That son of a bitch! I think he thinks you're guilty. He's sniffing around a goddamn plea bargain!"

"There'll be no plea bargain. I haven't done a damn thing."

"Jack, they're taking over Black Water. The whole package. Including the accounts. Going to try, anyway. What should I do?"

"You get down to the offices right after you leave here. You got the keys? Computer codes? The entry cards, all of it?"

"Yeah. Greco hasn't got her order yet. I still have it all."

"Then you get up there and you take over Black Water."

"Take it over?"

"That's right. You're my partner. You and I started this thing. You have a legal right. You haven't been charged with anything?"

"No. Not a thing. They're laying this all on you."

"Fine. Then you get in there and you run the damn thing. Business as usual. You call Dave Fontenot, you call all of our clients one by bloody one, you tell them whatever they need to hear, answer every question, then you go down to the loading docks, you call everybody together, tell them we are by God still in business and nothing changes. Get the trucks out, get the boats moving, get the day going. Just like always."

Creek was staring at him, his face going through changes. When Jack finished, his face was harder, his eyes dry.

"What do I say about . . . all this shit?"

"Tell them we've been set up, that I'll beat the charges. Tell them the truth. Be short but be straight. Don't let them think we're worried. Take the high ground all the way."

"Yes. Damn. The high ground. You're right. What happens to you? Where they taking you?"

Jack filled him in, the "protective custody" stunt, the night run to Allenwood Prison in central Pennsylvania.

"Where the hell is that?"

"Somewhere near Harrisburg. They call it Club Fed."

"Okay. I'll be there the first of the week."

"No. No, you can't leave the Black Water offices. You bunk there, in my office. The whole weekend. There's a bathroom, and a daybed in the closet. You live there. If you're physically on the site, if you're acting as CEO, then I don't think they can seize the whole operation out from under you. Not unless they indict you too, and they haven't, right?"

"Not yet. What about Martin Glazer, those people at Galitzine Sheng and Munro? The pension fund?"

"Call Glazer. See what he says. My call is, you won't get through. But try. That shows due diligence. If you do get through, then it's business as usual. But I doubt you will. It's hard to make big moves when the CEO's in prison."

"Man, they're really fucking with us, aren't they? The pension fund is a promise to our own people. This could bring the Teamsters back at us. They're killing us."

"Well, let them try. We'll beat this. Something else. I need you to talk to our good friend."

Creek's eyes widened and then he recovered.

"I hear you. The whole thing?"

"Yes. Somebody's fucking with us, and I don't think Flannery has the balls to find out who. Tell him the whole story."

"Okay. I can talk to Carmine. . . . Jack, I . . ."

Creek's eyes looked empty. Jack had never seen him like this.

"Hey, Creek, don't go all touchy-feely on me, okay?"

"It's not that. Jack, there's some things that went on. . . ."

"What things?"

Creek hesitated, looked away.

"Creek, did you have anything to do with getting a Cobra? Is that it? I know you're into cars. You can tell me."

Creek's face went white, then red.

"What the *fuck* are you saying? Jesus, I never—"

Callahan heard Creek's angry tone, stepped up.

"That's it, Mr. Johnson. Time to leave."

Creek sent her a sideways glare, looked back at Jack.

"Look, if they get their seizure order, you're gonna be out of cash. I can help you. I got some put aside. Separate. I can back you."

"Creek, this could get very expensive."

"We're . . . partners. I can fix this. . . . I can help."

Silence came down again. Callahan took Jack's arm and Buster stepped in close, separating Creek, edging him back.

"Time to go, cowboy," she said, locking on his chains.

The portcullis gate was heavy and when it opened it made a sound like an anchor chain running crazily over a huge steel bow and dropping away into cold deep water. Jack never looked back, but he felt Creek's eyes on him all the way to the van sitting white and cold under the hard blue light. He reached the van, his shadow before him, and saw the black outline of a big man with chains hanging from him, and the hard blue light made the bright stainless-steel chains glitter. When they slammed the door shut on him, the van rocked and the portcullis walls echoed with the force of it.

Callahan was behind the wheel as the box van cruised up the ramp and out through the portcullis gate. The federal yard was lit by cold blue street lamps and cut into hard black shadows. The street was empty as they pulled out of the yard. Buster lit himself a Kool, made it a ceremony, leaned down to hunt for a radio station, and didn't notice the big white Lincoln, windows tinted black, that was idling in a cross lane, waiting for them. Pike gave them a full city block before he moved out into the street and followed them south toward the highway. He was tired now, and hungry, but there was no time for rest. Payback first.

He'd broken off from the city cops after Peekskill and headed north when he heard that they were arraigning Jack the same day. He knew they'd be taking him to a federal pen, and he needed to be there when they left. He put on a Duke Ellington CD and settled into the soft black leather, shifted his body to ease the old familiar pain of the five round scars across his belly.

A Robert Frost line ran through his head. *For I have promises to keep. And miles to go before I sleep.* He said it to himself a few times as he trailed the big white van, until it seemed to blend in with the lazy grace of Duke Ellington's big brass section. Once they reached the interstate, he dropped back. They were going south and west. That probably meant Allenwood Prison. If they reached it.

TEMPLE COURT APARTMENTS

PROSPECT PARK

1930 HOURS

Nicky was lying on Casey's bed in her apartment at Temple Court, trying not to listen to the shouting and screaming going on out in the living room. Casey had a desktop PC on her dresser table. Nicky found the CD-ROM that Pete LeTourneau had given him, the one with the combat weapons data file. He pushed it into the CD slot and hit enter. The screen flickered and flashed and showed him a search slot. Nicky typed in *M82A1,* hit search. In a few seconds he got the words, and he got the picture.

The weapon was huge, brutal, and undeniably heavy. The M82A1 was a .50-caliber military sniper rifle. A big, blocky, and brutal-looking killing machine. There was a body of text along with the picture of a massive bolt-action rifle. It read like a rave review.

> The Barrett Model 82A1: a fifty-caliber sniper rifle that is capable of delivering a huge round at three times the speed of sound over distances of up to two miles. Almost five feet in length, superbly machined in blue steel, it weighs close to thirty pounds. It carries a heavy sniper barrel, fluted and ported, with a flared flash suppresser and bull-nosed muzzle-brake to divert the staggering propellant gasses of the huge fifty-caliber rounds. Under the barrel, just at the end of the fore-stock, there is a folding metal bipod made of flanged and drilled steel. The semi-auto receiver is angular, muscular, precision-cut as if by a German watch-maker, the right-hand cocking lever down-curved, the pistol-grip with smooth mahogany fittings set perfectly under the cheek-piece, the trigger long and slightly recurved to fit the trigger finger. The rear stock is tubular steel with an angular steel butt, padded with synthetic neoprene over hard rubber. A carrying handle is fitted just before the leading edge of the scope, angled sideways to clear the line of sight. An eleven-round detachable box magazine snaps in under the receiver block. There is a standard Leupold sniper scope fitted to the receiver mounts, but an optional Star Lite night-vision model is available, reinforced and re-engineered to withstand the massive recoil force of the weapon. Although it is as big as a barracuda and a thousand times more lethal, it rides very well in the hands, is finely balanced and easy to control. Everything

fits, the ergonomics are superbly engineered, and the entire
weapon is a masterpiece of the gunsmith's art.

There was a tab on the page that said *See video?*

Oh God . . . why not?

Nicky clicked on the tab, and a video clip began to
run on his computer screen, with a bad sound track attached. A laconic male with a Texas accent on the voice-
over reported that the video was made during the Gulf
War. It showed a unit of U.S. Army Rangers that had
penetrated the Iraqi forward lines at some nameless location in the endless Iraqi desert. The picture was grainy
and the camera often seemed handheld, so the image
was sometimes a little shaky.

The unit had set up the Barrett on a cleft of rock at
the eastern edge of a dry wash with a long view down a
barren rocky valley toward a thin black highway that
may have been the road to Baghdad. The camera took a
position to the right and rear of the fire team, four men
in desert camo, whose faces were never shown. The
camera had a Telephoto lens and must have been, at that
stage, tripod-mounted or braced on a rock, because it
zoomed smoothly in on a small black dot moving slowly
across the desert, perhaps a mile away. The air rippled
and danced like a waterfall and the vehicle—an Iraqi
staff car, judging from the flags on the hood—seemed to
be rolling over a thin sheet of glass, probably a heat mi-
rage.

There was a long silence broken only by the mur-
muring rustle of wind over a microphone. The camera
stayed on the staff car. Then someone off-camera said,
"Range eighteen hundred meters," and gave a series of
numbers that Nicky recognized as windage corrections
and temperature data.

Then the sniper said, "I have him, sir."

Another short silence. A dry wind rustling.

Then a single word.

"Engage."

The force of the muzzle blast rocked the camera. Even on film the sound was massive, a brutal slamming explosion. The camera steadied and then regained the long image. Far away in the hazy distance, the Iraqi staff car seemed to shudder, and Nicky saw a thin puff of silvery powder jet outward from the far side of the vehicle. It may have been window glass shattering. Inside that silvery puff, darker objects, shapeless, flew from inside the car.

The vehicle immediately lurched sideways, rudderless, and sank its front wheels into a sand drift. The driver's door popped open and a tiny stick figure in dirty tan with some kind of scarlet flashes on the uniform collar began to stumble away to the south.

Another word from the sniper.

"I have him."

And the answer.

"Engage."

Another huge cracking boom that rolled away across the desert. The stick figure seemed to straighten and lurch sidelong. Something thick and solid separated from the body of the stick figure and flew several yards farther into the desert, and the stick figure fell facedown into the dirt. There was a profound and unique stillness. The wind ruffled and rumbled across the open mike. Finally someone off-camera said, "Okay. That's a wrap."

The image froze while the Texas voice-over continued. It sounded to Nicky like a sergeant speaking to a roomful of trainees.

"That, Mouseketeers, was the Barrett M-eighty-two-A-one sniper rifle, firing the Browning point-five-zero caliber round. You saw two confirmed kills at eighteen hundred meters.

Down a slope. In a crosswind. The projectile delivered by this weapon can penetrate an armored car, bring down a Hind attack chopper, and vaporize the skull bone of a Brahma bull at three miles. When an Iraqi column reached that staff car, they thought the colonel inside it had his head bitten clean off by a lion. The inside of the staff car was like a slaughterhouse floor. The driver on the ground had nothing between his neck and his tiny rag-head pecker but pink mist and hungry scorpions. This weapon is the very hammer of Thor. Hear me, ground-pounders, and pray to the god of battle that you never—ever—come under this hammer."

Needless to say, this video clip ruined Nicky's evening. This is what had killed Jimmy Rock, and those poor ATF men. That could have killed him, too. He was still brooding on it when Casey knocked on the door and came in, sat down on the bed beside him.

"You not asleep, Nicky?"

"Nope. You want your room back?"

"Not yet. You can stay here if you want. She acts up, I may have to sleep with her. She needs to be watched sometimes when she's stressed out. She'll leave in the middle of the night, try to buy drugs. Came home once in a patrol unit. God, I'm so tired, Nicky."

"Is she asleep now?" he asked, his voice a whisper.

"Yes. She is. Finally."

She held up a cigarette, and Nicky lit it, and watched Casey inhale, and said nothing. Through the window of Casey's bedroom the light was changing, turning from a pale pearl to a rich deep black.

Nicky sighed, adjusted the pillow under his head, and stared up at the ceiling. She had offered him her room, made it clear it was the bed only. Weary to his core, facing a long run through traffic back to Yonkers, he had been too tired to argue with her. She had walked away into the living room to deal with her mother, leaving Nicky too depressed to sleep after watching the CD about the Barrett Fifty.

He had spent the last few minutes wondering about her room. Casey must have spent days sticking literally thousands of tiny golden stars, the kind they used to give kids in school, all across a deep matte-finish, navy-blue paint. He figured that when the bedside candles were lit, the whole ceiling would look like a night sky full of glimmering golden stars. Thinking about it, he had decided to light them all. He was glad he did.

It was a very sentimental effect, very feminine, and it puzzled Nicky how a woman as hard-nosed as Casey Spandau could have a bedroom like this. On the other hand, he thought the effect was outstanding, so he had decided to say nothing, just in case she took it as an insult and immediately painted it over. Casey blew out a cloud of smoke, bent over, and retrieved a glass of wine from the floor beside her. She sipped the wine, smiled at nothing in particular.

"Okay . . . the black thing. When I was a kid, because of my mom being white, well, we couldn't live in a white neighborhood, because she was a white woman with a black kid, we couldn't live in a black neighborhood for the same reason. So I guess I spent my time in the middle. In 'nobody's town,' I used to call it. You grow up seeing both races from the outside. Since you're on the outside, whatever's going on inside looks normal, how things should be."

"I follow," said Nicky. "I grew up a guinea wop, the street was so tight we were like a family, in and out of everybody's place all the time. Same food, same music, the Church."

"Yeah . . . so when I went to school and I found out I was black as far as the school system was concerned, I had to go to the colored high school in Carthage—"

"Was the town really called Carthage?"

Casey smiled at that.

"Yeah. Well, it was a burned-out town all right. There is a river there, comes down out of the Adirondacks, wide and deep and fast, and the water so dark and cold it looks black. Once I watched a dog try to get out of the current, and it was still trying when it hit the sluice gates down by the bridge. Carthage, my hometown."

"Anyway, you were saying?"

"About the schools . . . they were rat traps. Worn out, peeling paint, no books, no supplies . . ."

"Yeah, like in New York. Explain me something, Casey. If you're half white, how come the black power stuff all the time?"

Casey clouded over completely.

"You ever wonder, Nicky, why black blood is so fucking potent that even one drop in your history means you're a nigger? And while you're at it, explain to me why it is that if you have a *white* mother, even your black friends think you're an Oreo, and you can't be happy in either race?"

Nicky kept his mouth shut, which was a smart move. He reached out, took her hand in his. She let him. He touched her cheek. He felt a deep shaking tremor run through her. She reached for another cigarette, lit it with short hard motions, and kept her body half turned away. Nicky was silent. He was looking up at the starfield above them. The candle flames flickered and the ceiling shimmered with soft golden sparks. It was possibly the silliest and certainly the most beautiful thing he'd ever seen.

"Casey, is it all about these gold stars?"

"What do you mean?"

"Gold stars, like you get at school. Are you doing this for your mom so you can get a gold star? From her, I mean?"

"I never thought about it. But thanks anyway, Oprah."

"I sound like Oprah? Thank you. I think."

"Nicky, Oprah Winfrey is a forty-watt bulb. She shines, but she's dim. People are drowning in shit, she throws them a little wicker basket of positive affirmation. I once heard her refer to a bunch of Crip thugs in South Central as 'sad little boys crying bullets.' I mean, give me a break. My mother's a doper and I'm her keeper. That's reality."

"Well, you gotta do something about it."

"Yeah? Like what?"

"I don't know. But something. You need to do something that's good for you, not just your mother, or the city, or the goddamn NYPD. Something just for you."

Casey turned to look down at him.

"Really? What did you have in mind?"

SATURDAY, JUNE 24
HIGHWAY 11 WESTBOUND
EASTERN PENNSYLVANIA
0430 HOURS

Sometime during that night-long run down to Allenwood Prison, they began to track the Susquehanna River. Jack could get glimpses of its wide flat reach as they flew through the hilly countryside, the rippling surface of the big river gilded with tiny yellow flames under the light of a yellow moon, the river water half seen through spiderweb gray tangles of scrub brush and spindly trees. Here and there along the course of the river he could see the outlines of low islands in its stream, where the river would boil and bubble around their shores, making the yellow moonlight that glinted off it spark and flare in the darkness that seemed to lie in the deeper valleys and ravines.

Against the screen of stars, he could make out the rounded hump-backed shapes of conical hills as uniform and regular as if they were man-made, looking like great mounds of coal or the tailings of a huge open-seam mine. Along the far shore of the river there were necklaces and chains of cold white and green and violet lights shaped into grids and rectangles and towers and arcs, and inside one of these constructions he'd seen a tall steel tower with a plume of fire at its tip, burning bloody-red and cobalt-blue and sulfur-yellow, fluttering crazily, plucked and flaring in a smoking wind.

Between the narrow winding track of the highway and the riverbanks there was a rail line. Now and then, as they drove through the countryside, a freight train would keep pace with them. Jack could see the spray of red sparks coming off the brake pads as the train slowed its descent down a valley slope or chuffed into a siding, picking up speed again as it cleared a ridge. It slowly pulled away from them, and faintly through the greasy windows of the van he heard the steady drumming of steel wheels on the tracks.

Then there'd be an explosion of town lights as they raced through some run-down village and Jack could see by the pale-yellow glow of the street lamps the boarded-up facades of wooden row houses with sagging porches and peeling paint, the hulks of rusted cars parked under low tumbledown shelters.

Here and there in the tiny front yards was a brightly painted swing set or a pair of shabby lawn chairs, and once as they flew past, Jack got a brief but oddly memorable glimpse through a bay window into a front room where a fat old man in a white T-shirt sat on a stuffed chair and stared intently into the flickering glow of a hidden television, all of this lit by a single overhead bulb.

Then the scene was behind them and they were back in the country again, the road ahead a tunnel of spidery gray trees caught inside the hard white cones of the headlamps. In the sudden dark, he had nothing to look at but the pale glint of his handcuffs and the greenish light that came up from the dashboard and outlined the shapes of the guards through the grid of the steel cage that held him.

Callahan drove and played country music on a Nashville station while Buster, in the shotgun seat, chain-smoked menthol Kools the entire run. Jack could see the red spark of the cigarette as Buster turned to speak to Callahan, see the tip flare as he drew on it, and when he exhaled the green light made the smoke luminous, and sometimes Buster would look up into a convex prisoner-view mirror over his seat and stare directly at Jack, never speaking—you don't speak to meat—his scarred-up face greenish and alien in the glow of the control panel, his eyes dead spaces. The smoke of the cigarette would drift backward through the wire grid and fill up the inside of the cage so that for months afterward, whenever he smelled a certain kind of menthol cigarette smoke, he would see that same blurred tunnel of tangled gray trees and the black ribbon of the two-lane blacktop in the headlamp glare and the weird green light that glowed through the drifting smoke inside the van. When a sun the color of a rose-pink lightbulb climbed high enough in the sky to turn the trees and the grassy hillsides from gray to pale purple, Callahan saw a Denny's sign near a mile marker and turned around in her seat to look at Jack slumped on the prisoner's bench, his head resting on the window glass.

"Hey there, Heck. You ever have that nature call?"

It hadn't occurred to Jack, in his exhaustion, that he

did need a washroom, but when he remembered, it suddenly became a priority.

"No. But I sure as hell need one now."

Callahan laughed, looked back at the road.

"A Denny's. Couple miles up. Me and Buster, we always stop here. You can get a good breakfast. I love the Grand Slam. We'll stop, get us some coffee, get you drained and cleaned up. Can't have you showing up for your very first day in prison looking like we dragged you backward through a bramble. Makes a poor impression."

Buster grunted, reached up, tapped the rearview, and looked across at Callahan, who checked the mirror and narrowed her brown eyes, tightened her lips up.

"Hey, cowboy. You know anybody in a blue Benz?"

Jack twisted around in his shackles, craned to look out the rear window panels. There was a large navy-blue Mercedes-Benz following them, perhaps a quarter mile back. As he watched it, it seemed to be gaining on them, its blue-white headlamps on high. The glow from the beams lit up the inside of the van and Jack squinted against the glare.

"Yes," he said. "I do."

Callahan jumped at that, and Buster turned to glower at him.

"Who is it?"

"I don't know who this is. But the guy who got me into this shit drives a blue Mercedes-Benz that looks a lot like this one here."

"Well, Buster first noticed him way back there, outside of Nanticoke. He's been laying back a mile or so ever since."

Although Jack found it hard to believe that Earl Pike would be hunting a U.S. marshals van, he found his breath coming short, and Callahan picked up on his reaction.

"Not a friend, I take it," said Callahan.

"No. Not a friend. He's a dangerous son of a bitch."

"Well, he's coming up fast now the light's getting better."

The big Benz was clearly accelerating to overtake them. The headlamp glare filled the interior of the truck. Callahan reached down and pulled something out of a slide drawer, and when she straightened she was holding a large Glock pistol. Buster now had a short-barreled shotgun in his hands and was glaring into the mirror, watching the oncoming car as it moved out to pass. Jack tried to see who was driving the car, but the light from the lamps was too strong. The Benz came alongside, and Jack turned to watch it pass. White plates. He couldn't make out the state or the numbers. The plates were coated with mud and road dust. The windows were heavily tinted. He heard the sound of a big engine winding out. Buster tracked the passing car and held the shotgun tight. It blew by the van without slowing, cut back into the lane in front of them, and moved away fast, finally disappearing around a curve of two-lane blacktop.

Callahan tapped Buster's shotgun lightly.

"You got that musket right in my face, Buster."

Buster lowered the shotgun, settled back in the seat.

"Guess it was nothing, hah, cowboy? Unless you recognized the driver? I couldn't see anybody myself. Windows were too dark."

"Neither could I. But I don't think Pike's Benz had tinted windows. I can't remember. Did you get the plates?"

"Maybe New York. I got three of the numbers."

She picked up the microphone.

"Marshals four five, radio?"

The radio hissed and popped and settled into a low white noise, like water rushing over sand. Callahan looked at the conical hills all around them, the rocky ravines and gullies, shook her head.

"No reception. Damn hills. Happens all the time. Here comes the Denny's. We'll use the pay phones."

The Denny's was on the outskirts of a little town called Beach Haven, a mill town right on the banks of the Susquehanna River. There was a strip mall with a Laundromat, a package liquor store, a NAPA auto parts shop, all closed down and steel-grated in the early predawn light. The Denny's was lit up and looked empty. There were two cars parked in the lot, a Geo and an old Dakota pickup with a sagging left rear shock. There was no big blue Benz.

Callahan parked the truck right by the entrance, climbed out, and walked around to the rear doors. When the doors opened, the inrush of fresh air made Jack's heart jump, made him feel some pale hint of what it was going to be like to be a prisoner, to never have a chance to breathe fresh air or see sunlight that isn't crosshatched with razor wire and steel grates. The blue-white bolt of anger that sizzled through his skull right after that left him shaken and silent. The injustice—the sheer insanity of the thing—burned in his gut like bad vodka. As he stepped down onto the dew-coated pavement he looked directly into Buster's cold eyes, narrowed at him down the sights of the shotgun, his finger inside the trigger guard.

Jack saw fear and hatred there and a wild hope that Jack would do something—anything—that would make it okay to kill him. They walked on either side of him as he went up the stone stairs and walked through the open door of the restaurant.

A young black girl in a Denny's uniform was reading a copy of *USA Today,* sitting in a booth at the front. Her brown eyes showed white as she saw Jack in his chains, the bleak and angry look in his eyes. Callahan lifted a hand.

"Relax there, Annie. It's just us. This isn't Jack the Ripper either. Get us some breakfast, and coffee. Black?"

The girl named Annie jumped up, nodding, and trotted over to the counter, began to pour out three cups of coffee. Callahan gave Buster a warning look and sat Jack down in the booth opposite her. Buster sat beside Jack, close enough for Jack to smell his skin, a dry-grass-and-cigarettes scent. Heat was coming off Buster in spite of the air-conditioning, and his cheeks looked damp. In the rising light Callahan looked tired and old, her puffy skin seamed and dry.

"Stop studying on me, cowboy. Nobody looks good this hour of the morning. What'll it be?"

Jack ordered a Grand Slam, and so did Callahan. Buster made a face at the bacon pictured in the menu, and ordered dry toast, a glass of iced tea, and a bowl of barley soup, his Nigerian accent heavy and his voice much higher than Jack expected. They ate in total silence, and then Callahan pushed her plate back with a sigh, reached for the Kools, saw Jack's face.

"Damn, cowboy. You were supposed to pee. Buster, take the lad in and see he gets his business done. I'll go phone in that Benz."

"I do not touch men," said Buster, his face hard.

"Neither do I," said Callahan. "Here's the keys. Unlock him, stand outside the toilet. Jack's a good lad, right, Jack?"

Jack had nothing to say. Buster got out of the booth and stepped back as Jack came out after him. He nodded at the rear of the restaurant and moved away to let Jack walk in front of him. The waitress stared at them as they passed and Jack winked at her. Annie looked away as if struck, picked up her *USA Today*.

Buster stopped Jack at the door to the men's washroom, said one word, "Stay"—as if Jack were a dog—and went inside the washroom. Jack stood alone in the hall and watched through an open delivery door as the sunshine crawled up the side of a hill and trucks geared down on the low grade leading into the town. It occurred to him that the open door was a trap, that Buster would like nothing better than the chance to pump a load of double-aught buck into the spine of a man running. Or maybe it was just an open door. A fresh wind fluttered along his cheek and stirred his hair. He felt his blood rising, and a heat spread along his chest and belly. There were cars parked across a grassy field, two small sedans and a big white Lincoln. If he could reach that . . . then what? Die? Go to Bolivia? Find out who was doing this to him? Maybe stay free long enough to beat him to death?

Jack, wavering between flight and fear, watched as the sunlight reached the top of the grassy hill and lit up a stand of golden aspen at the crest. The door to the women's washroom opened and Earl Pike stepped out, holding a semiauto Smith and Wesson.

Jack looked right into Pike's eyes as Pike lifted the pistol. Pike's eyes were sleepy and held a kind of shining calm. He looked as if he were about to administer a sacrament. Jack's voice was gone, and his breathing too, and all he could hear was the sound of blood rushing in his neck. Pike smiled at Jack, moved the pistol, and shot Buster twice in the side of the head as he came back out the door of the men's room. The sound in the narrow hallway was massive, booming. Buster's brains hit the floral-pattern wallpaper and fanned across it, a spray of bloody-pink jelly with bits of skull floating like fragments of eggshell. Buster reeled, slammed off the wall, and went down like a tree falling.

Pike grinned again, turned, put a hand up against

Jack's chest, and pushed him aside as Sharon Callahan came pounding down the main aisle of the restaurant and through the doorway, where she skidded to a stop, her Glock out and ready, her eyes huge, moving the muzzle back and forth between Pike and Jack.

"Drop your weapons! Now!" she bellowed, her voice racketing around the narrow space. Her eyes flickered downward, saw the mess on the floor, and came back up again, by which time Pike had shot her three times, once in the throat and twice in her left cheek.

"Jesus," breathed Jack, looking at Callahan's eyes.

She blinked, reeled, tried to raise the Glock again. Pike stepped in close, took it out of her hands gently, tossed it to Jack, who caught it by the barrel with one cuffed hand, awkwardly, trying to bring it around and grip it properly. His motions were panicked and jerky. He knew he was getting the next bullet. Pike reached over, put a hand on the weapon, held Jack by the wrist, and spoke to Callahan, who was now sliding to her knees, her back against the floral wallpaper, black throat blood bubbling over her flak jacket and two small clean holes drilled into the papery dry skin of her softly rounded cheeks.

"Never look away," he said. "That's what killed you."

The look in her eyes was bleak and sad. Her stunned animal gaze shifted to Jack. There was a kind of supplication there, and a rebuke. She tried to say something to Jack, but only blood came out of her mouth, and Jack felt he owed it to her not to look away. They both heard the front door slamming and the sound of footsteps clattering down the front stairs. Pike turned to Jack, his hand still on Jack's wrist, covering Callahan's Glock.

"Got to run, Jack."

He stepped backward quickly and reached the open door.

"Suggest you do the same," he said, and then he was gone. Jack watched him running, saw him cross the field of grass and get into the white Lincoln, heard the sound of a car engine, saw the Lincoln moving off, and then there was a slow fade to absolute quiet.

He looked down at Callahan. Her eyes were fixed on the middle distance, a place only the dead can see. Buster lay facedown on the fake-Persian wall-to-wall carpet, his skull broken open like a gourd. He had fouled himself in his death, and the raw sewage smell filled the hallway, a choking obscene stench. Jack bent down, took Callahan's keys off her belt, unlocked his shackles, snatched the van keys, threw up violently, and ran like hell.

SATURDAY, JUNE 24

TEMPLE COURT

PROSPECT PARK

0800 HOURS

Nicky was standing in front of the plate-glass window of Casey's apartment in Temple Court, looking out at the yard and watching a group of kids play football in the yellow grass. The trees were leafed out now, the thin branches bright green against the blue sky. He was listening to the sound of Casey's voice through the closed door of her mother's room. Behind him there was a stereo system on a blond wooden bench. He stepped over to it and hit play and the CD he'd been listening to began again, a group called Squirrel Nut Zippers, doing "The Ghost of Stephen Foster," a bizarre swing number that began with what sounded like Luciano Pavarotti being fed through a wire-pulling machine. Slowly. It was loud enough to drown out the sound of a confrontation that Nicky didn't want to hear.

Nicky sat himself down on the big green leather sofa, which hissed air and wrapped itself around him and breathed a rich leather scent all over him. And also Casey's perfume. And the smell of grass. He waited, listening to the CD, and watched a patch of morning sun crawl across the polished hardwood floor. Ten minutes passed, and then silence, perhaps a faint sound of someone crying.

In another minute Casey came out of the room and closed the door. She was wearing black jeans and high boots and a tight black T-shirt and her hair was pulled back into a ponytail; Nicky thought she looked like a Beretta pistol, right down to the bright red nails, which were just like the red safety tabs on a Beretta.

It wasn't that Nicky was kinky about pistols, but she had that polished hard-cut look that reminded him of one. Her face was guarded and defensive when she crossed the room and stood in front of him. He looked up at her, at the dead-flat expression in her Chinese eyes. She had been crying, that was obvious. He lifted a pack of Davidoff cigars and raised an eyebrow.

She plucked one, still standing, and lit it with a match from a tray on the coffee table. She pulled on it, inhaled, and stared down at him through the smoke, her arms held across her chest.

"How is she? Sleeping again? You gave her something?"

She looked away and then nodded once.

"This is probably none of my business. . . ."

"Got it in one, Nicky."

"Casey . . . it's not like she's got the plague."

"What would you know about it?"

Nicky leaned back into the couch, crossed his legs

and put a hand on one ankle, blew out some smoke at her.

"Casey, I didn't want to know anything about it. Now we have to deal with the fact that I do. I'm either in your life or I'm not. Your mother's an alcoholic. And an addict."

Casey was quiet for a long time. Nicky watched the play of emotions crossing her face, had the idea that maybe he was being too rough on her. Casey finally spoke in a low throaty whisper.

"She's been a drunk for years. Ever since I was a kid, ever since my father got killed, maybe. And the pills. I hold the pills for her. I never leave those in the house, because she'd overdose. When I come home she's drunk, or well on the way, or sleeping it off on the couch. I hunt down all the bottles, every time, but she buys more. She hides it in vinegar bottles, plastic jugs, anything she can find. When she's drunk, she gets real social and makes passes at anyone she finds attractive. That's just before she turns mean. When she's hung over—which is hardly ever, because you have to *stop* drinking to get a hangover—she's like a wandering corpse. Last night, my fault. I wasn't home and she was hurting. . . ."

"Hurting? For what?"

"I give her Valium, sometimes Elavil."

"How do *you* get Elavil?"

"You ever hear of double-doctoring?"

"Holy Christ, Casey—that's a crime! Don't tell me—"

"Do I keep the drugs with me? Yes, I keep the drugs with me . . . at least I used to. They were in my briefcase. Why do you think I was so worked up about losing the fucking thing? It was full of prescription medicine, all of it double-doctored. Xanax. Ritalin. Antabuse. Valium. Percodan. All the shit she needs to keep her under control. Also every letter I've ever written. Doctor's names.

A letter from Bellevue. Detox intake forms. I was keeping a file."

"And you kept that in your briefcase?"

"Where the hell else? At home? At the office? In my hat?"

"Well, you better hope whatever junkie asshole who stole it opens it up and parties himself to death. Jesus, Casey. What if that little dork cop in Peekskill—what's her name—Moira Stokovich—what if Officer Moira finds the briefcase and opens it? She's a smug little bitch. She'll fry your whole life!"

"Golly, I'm glad I confided in you. I feel so much better now. Avoid the caring professions, Nicky. You don't have the knack."

"No, I'm a cop, and I'll bet your mother's a damn expensive problem. How much has she stolen from you or from your friends?"

"Not that much. I . . . I give her all she wants. She has no need to go on the street for pills. Nicky, if there were real treatment programs . . . but there aren't—alcoholism is not a crime."

"And you really double-doctor?"

"Like you said. I'm a cop. I know how."

"Oh, peachy. Fucking peachy. And one day you'll be doing that—and some doctor will tumble—and you'll get popped in a bust and there you go. Listen to the huge flushing sound. And when you're in the slammer, what happens to her?"

"It's all I can do."

"How did this start?"

"It's a very long story."

"Okay, let's save it, then. What are you going to do now?"

"Go on. What else can I do?"

"Casey, she's killing your life. And maybe you're

killing hers. The pills . . . at least you have to stop that part."

"The pills are the only way I can keep her under control. If she doesn't have Valium or Elavil and it's just the booze . . . and she likes to go visiting . . . the neighbors have brought her back drunk and half-dressed. With the pills, I know I can go to work and nothing really bad will happen. Besides, I won't *get* caught."

"Casey, if that Peekskill cop finds that case, you just did."

She locked up, then walked away and started to pace.

Nicky got up off the couch and walked over to her. He put an arm around her shoulders and she let her head rest against his chest. He could feel her body vibrating. They'd spent last night together, in her bed, and this morning everything was very different, and although he was happy about the change and maybe already in love with her a little, what he knew about her now was dangerous for a cop to know. *Forget what she's going to do,* he thought. *What am I going to do?* The phone rang. Casey stepped away from Nicky and walked to the bookshelf, picked up the receiver.

"Casey? This is Dexter Zarnas. Vince said you'd be home."

"Dexter . . . what's happening?"

"Nicky Cicero there?"

"Yes. He just got here."

"Good. I'm in Harrisburg. At the airport. I talked to the desk people at Slipstream. ATF has already been all over them, and they swear they don't know dick about Earl Pike landing in Harrisburg. I believe them. I think the charter thing was just a diversion."

"Now what?"

"Now you get yourself out here and help me."

"Why? If Pike's not there—"

"I think he is. You catch the news this morning?"

"No. Not yet."

"That Vermillion guy, the one the ATF popped?"

"Yeah?"

"He escaped. Supposed to have killed two guards. The feds are ripping up the state looking for him. Thing is, I don't buy it."

"You think Pike helped him?"

"It's a theory. Vermillion was a business guy. Taking out two U.S. marshals isn't one of the things they teach you at Harvard Business School. At least I hope not. I could use the help, okay?"

"Okay. We'll get a car out of—"

"Too slow. Vince has a flight voucher filed at La-Guardia. Get the next regional flight to Harrisburg. Any carrier. I'll pick you up at the airport. You've got my cell number. Call me as soon as you get a flight time. Bring your gear. You follow me? And plan to stay."

"Both of us? What about the shooting board? What about Jimmy Rock's funeral?"

"On for Monday afternoon. The department's handling all of it. And Vince is handling them. Things are happening. Now go pack."

SATURDAY, JUNE 24

HAZLETON MILLS WAL-MART

HAZLETON, PENNSYLVANIA

0930 HOURS

When Jack pushed through the glass doors of the Wal-Mart, the first thing he saw was a bank of video surveillance cameras and a black-and-white monitor hanging from a steel brace over his head. In the grainy backlit image, bleached by the sun pouring in through the glass wall behind him, he saw a big man in a white tee and jeans, saw him standing still while a swirling stream of shoppers eddied and coiled around him, saw the man staring back down at him. The video surveillance suddenly made his situation very clear.

He forced himself forward, joined the walking dead milling around in the aisles, and worked his way through the store until he reached the hardware section, where he picked up a five-gallon can of dark-green marine enamel paint and a set of horsehair brushes. As far as he could tell, no one had looked at him sideways. He hefted the can and the brushes and headed back toward the cash registers. On the way he passed the electronics department and stopped to watch the CNN headline news. Stopped dead-short.

The sound was turned down on the huge Sony screen, but the image of Valeriana Greco in a press conference, standing in front of a podium with the seal of the Department of Justice and taking questions from a roomful of reporters, was hard to resist. No one else was paying attention, so he stepped up and found the volume button, notched it up a few bars. Greco looked like a woman on fire, her face a white-hot mask, her voice controlled and forceful. Somebody had propped the mike too close to her face, and Greco pushed it lower with her left hand, getting it out of the camera line. She was wearing a black jumpsuit with her name on the chest, *Greco,* above a gold star and the words *Detectives/U.S. Attorneys.* Her black hair was brushed and shining like a crow's wing, held back with a thin gold bar. She looked like the kind of stiletto that Fabergé would have made if Fabergé had decided to make a stiletto. The camera jumped to show a man standing in the back row far left, looking at the notes in his hands.

"Ms. Greco, do you expect to arrest Mr. Vermillion anytime soon? Do you have any idea where he might be at this moment?"

Greco was nodding before he finished. When she spoke, she made direct eye contact with the camera. Jack had to admit, she had star power. The camera loved her.

"Yes, we have deployed assets all over the state. We have the assistance of the Pennsylvania State Police as well as members of the ATF and of course the U.S. marshals fugitive pursuit team. We expect an arrest at any time. He can't hide from justice."

Another question, from a tweedy geek in the second row.

"Can you tell us anything about the fugitive?"

"I can. As you know, his name is Jack Vermillion. He was being transported to Allenwood under a U.S. marshals escort. Apparently he was able to overcome one of his guards and take the man's weapon."

"We understand the guards are dead?"

"Yes. Both of them. He shot them both. In cold blood. We have a witness to the shootings. She was working at the restaurant when the transport arrived. She saw the whole thing."

"Can we talk to her?"

"No. She's in protective custody."

"Do you have any idea where the shooter went?"

Greco shook her head, again looked right into the camera.

"No. But we know he's traveling in a white van. If anyone out there sees a large white box van with government plates, Echo nine Bravo four one five, we ask that you call nine-one-one and tell the police immediately. This suspect is armed and dangerous. Do not approach him. We cannot stress that too much."

"Can you tell us what Vermillion was charged with?"

"I can. Mr. Vermillion has been implicated in a cross-border drug and weapons smuggling syndicate. He's been indicted under the RICO laws of this country, and I have petitioned a federal court judge to grant the government control of his assets under the federal forfeiture laws. That request has been granted this morning."

Somebody in the middle wanted to know why she was doing that. Did it not seem a bit draconian? Greco frowned at the question.

"The purpose of the forfeiture law is to prevent accused felons who are involved in organized crime to use the proceeds of their criminal operations to delay the progress of justice. To allow Mr. Vermillion to continue to draw on the assets of a multimillion-dollar corporation would severely hamper the administration of justice."

"But doesn't the Justice Department have unlimited resources?"

"That's not the point. As we've seen in some recent criminal cases—I'm thinking of the JonBenet Ramsey case here, not to mention Mr. Simpson—money can be used to create barriers in the path of a thorough investigation. Should Mr. Vermillion be exonerated, he will of course regain control of whatever remains of his assets and resources. But he cannot use them to defer justice."

"Have you already seized the companies he controls?"

"That process is ongoing. A business associate of Mr. Vermillion has . . . attempted to obstruct the process. That issue is being dealt with in the courts today. I expect a resolution very soon. And that, I'm afraid, is all the time I have today."

She shook her hair out, glanced to her left, nodded once.

"I would like to stress, however, one final matter. The Justice Department has authorized a reward of one hundred thousand dollars for information leading to the capture of this felon. One hundred thousand. And no further questions. That's all I can say at this time."

The image jumped and now Jack was looking at the intake photo the ATF had taken when they brought him into the holding cells at Albany, full face and profile, with the numbers plate, a black board with little stick-on white letters. *Vermillion, Jack. Alcohol, Tobacco, and Firearms. 1377620.*

It was a bad moment for him, standing in the middle of a Wal-Mart in the middle of middle America and seeing his haggard face staring out at him from the huge screen. He looked angry. He looked dangerous. He looked like a dead man. And he was worth a hundred thousand. Maybe he should turn himself in and claim the reward. He could use the money.

Jack hit the off button, walked away from the screen, bumped into a blocky young kid with a green Penn State jacket on, the kid with his head down, fondling some sort of CD player. The kid looked up at Jack, made a pug-nosed brute face, but Jack was already by him. One thing anyway, it looked like Creek Johnson was holed up in the Alamo and making a fight of it.

Good for him. Jack hoped he was having fun.

He pushed his way to the cash counter and paid $38.63 for the paint and the brushes, which left him a little less than $90, all he had found in Buster's black equipment bag under the passenger seat of the van. He also had Buster's Visa card in his back pocket and Sharon Callahan's service Glock stuffed into the top of his cowboy boot, where it was chafing the hell out of his calf muscle and banging into his shin bone every time he took a step. What the hell he intended to do with either of them was beyond him right now.

The cashier was an elderly woman whose hair looked like cotton candy. Jack could see the shiny dome of her skull under the wispy hair. She had age spots on her cheeks and a huge smiley face on her blue vest, which sported a badge with the name *Ida May* and the title

Sales Associate. She gave him his change and showed him a set of dentures that had been around since the Truman years and needed a lot of repair work. Her hand was shaking as she counted out the coins and Jack wondered if she'd recognized him. Her pale-blue eyes looked watery and she had a slight cataract in the left eye. Under her huge glasses, her eyes looked wide and wet and as raw as egg yolks. Although he tried to track her shaking hands, she managed to spill several coins onto the floor. Jack was bending down to retrieve them when he felt someone bumping past him, the impact pushing him into the side of the cashier station.

He recovered, looked up, and saw the same thick-bodied young man wearing black jeans and a baggy nylon sports jacket, emerald green, with *Penn State* in white across the back. The boy was leaving at a brisk walk, not even looking back. Jack, already wrapped way too tight, snarled at the boy's back.

"Excuse me, asshole."

The boy stopped as if hooked, spun around. He had a bright red face, bumpy and unformed, small blue eyes spaced wide apart, a wispy blond goatee, and of course he wore his ball cap backward like every other brain-dead suburban mutt in every other brain-dead suburban hellhole just like Hazleton. He had on a pair of running shoes big enough to float to Cuba on, floppy sides and laces hanging.

"The fuck you say, faggot?"

Jack stood up, remembered his actual situation. This was no time to be picking a fight with some of the local pond scum. Jack smiled, shook his head, turned back to the elderly cashier, who was staring at the boy with a look of absolute terror. The kid stepped in so close to Jack that he could smell the kid's sour-milk breath.

Jack looked at him, made eye contact, tried in the

silent exchange to make him understand that a fight between them could go either way, but that Jack didn't really want one right now. It sounds complicated, but guys learn this kind of stuff very early. The kid got it in one and seemed happy to interpret it as a win for slacker mall rats everywhere. He puffed up at Jack some more, the effect spoiled a bit because Jack had four inches on him.

"Just watch the fucking mouth, faggot. Next time—"

"Yeah, thanks. I will. You have a nice day, now."

Jack turned a shoulder on the kid and smiled at the cashier.

"Sorry for my language, ma'am."

The woman was watching the boy, who stood at Jack's right shoulder for another ten seconds and then turned and walked off, trailing a cheap plastic chain of hip-hop slang behind him. When he got through the doors she breathed out through thin papery lips.

"Goodness. My. What a temper."

"Yes," said Jack. "I'm sorry about that."

"Oh never mind," she said. "I know Jason from around. He's always been a bad one. You held your temper pretty good there."

"Thanks," he said.

"You're welcome, son. You have a nice day."

You too, he thought. And enjoy your golden years as a Wal-Mart sales associate, Ida May.

The truck was in a three-story parking garage called Ticknor's Auto Park, about six blocks away down a four-lane street lined with shopping malls and fast-food restaurants, bleaching white under the summer sun, unmarked by a single growing thing. The parking garage had been under construction, half-built, but the site was deserted when he drove the truck inside. It was as good a place as any to try to do what he had to do.

He walked all the way back to the lot with the fifty-pound can of paint tearing at his shoulder muscles and saw two police cars cruising past him, a Hazleton police car and a Pennsylvania State Police Jeep Cherokee with a roof rack and a shotgun showing in the rear window. The female cop in the Stetson and the aviators never looked his way. The sun was bitter hot on his shoulders and the back of his neck. By the time he reached the car park and walked up the long deserted ramp, he was dripping with sweat and starving.

The truck was on the top floor. The level was unfinished, white with concrete dust, and littered with metal shards. Discarded scaffolding and sections of rusted pipe littered the upper levels. No one was anywhere around. He stopped at the top of the ramp and listened with every nerve ending he had, but heard only the roar of traffic on the street and the pounding of his own heart. He set the can down, used a can opener he'd found in the glove compartment of the transport van to pop the lid. The opener had an enamel crest on it, a sunset against a big saguaro cactus, and the words *Big Sky Country* in a circle around the picture. He tried not to think about the look in Sharon Callahan's eyes as she was dying in the hallway of that Denny's. The opener was clearly hers. She had wanted to be in a gunfight and she got her wish and it killed her, as wishes sometimes do.

He closed his mind on the picture with a hard-locking snap and dipped a brush into the thick shiny green paint. The first stroke across the van left a streaky band of white showing under the dark-green paint. The second pass covered it completely. He kept at it and tried not to think about what he was going to do next because, frankly, he had no damned idea. None at all.

The next flight out of LaGuardia turned out to be an Appalachian Air shuttle that got Nicky and Casey to Harrisburg at one o'clock in the afternoon. Dexter Zarnas had met them at Capital City Airport in Jay Rats unit number 552, a black Lincoln Town Car with heavily tinted windows and a dashboard full of computer gear and electronics. It was Vince Zaragosa's best police unit and letting Dexter take it all the way to Pennsylvania was a hard thing for the boss to do. Casey spotted Dexter in the middle of the airport concourse as they came up the arrivals ramp, a slab-sided hulk sitting at the bar drinking a bottle of Heineken, wearing black jeans and boots, a black T-shirt under a gray sports coat, his shaved skull shining under the airport fluorescent lights, his black goatee carefully trimmed. He looked like a corporate biker.

Dexter drained the Heineken as they walked up, nodded once, and they were doing a steady eighty miles an hour on Interstate 81 a few minutes later. Casey waited until they were out of the main traffic press and then asked Dexter where they were going.

"I been trying to meet with the ATF ever since I got here. They were already at Slipstream when I got there. This bitch—sorry, Casey—but this bitch running the show, name of Greco, total stonewall."

"I saw her on CNN before we left," said Casey. "She was up there where Vermillion got away. At Beach Haven. She likes the camera, I think. They were talking about a press conference."

"Anyway, I'm leaving—I'm pissed—and this ATF guy takes me aside, Derry Flynn. He was there at Red Hook. He's not happy with this Greco broad. Gave me his cell phone number. When they heard about the shooting up in Beach Haven, he called me, told me what was happening. He doesn't think Vermillion did that all on his own either. From what he saw of Vermillion, he figures the guy's pretty tame, just a business geek. He thinks Pike was the shooter. But he can't get this Greco woman to pull her teeth out of Vermillion long enough to consider a different scenario."

"We're going to Beach Haven, then?"

"Yeah. If Pike was in on that, somebody would have seen him around. Anybody confirms it, we know we're on the right track. I never met the guy, but from what I hear, he'd stand out."

"I've met him," said Casey. "He'd stand out."

TICKNOR'S AUTO PARK

HAZLETON, PENNSYLVANIA

1330 HOURS

Jack was about halfway through with the passenger side of the van, sweat running down his face and his eyes stinging, when he heard footsteps, shoes grating on the sandy concrete behind him. He set the brush down on the can lid, stood up, and turned to watch as three teenage boys reached the top of the parking ramp and came out onto the deserted level. He recognized the kid with the Penn State jacket right away, and then he saw what was in his hands, a section of rusted rebar about three feet long.

His two associates were also in the usual gangbanger togs, Hilfiger jeans hanging low showing plaid boxer tops, big sweatshirts, one kid wearing a shiny Knicks jacket, the other a black sweatshirt with a picture of a bullet-skulled wrestler and the words *Austin 3:16*. Both kids were also holding sections of steel rod.

The one on Jack's left, in the Knicks jacket, was pale white, a dark-haired kid with huge brown eyes—almost feminine—and the mandatory variation on the goatee theme that seems to have caught on with the young and the pointless all across America. The other kid was large, over six-four, and had to weigh in at three hundred pounds. This kid had a big bovine face unmarked by any kind of internal life, dull brown eyes, and a slack hanging mouth. He was nodding his head to nothing at all, a robot movement, mindless as a twitch. Penn State hefted the rebar, stepped forward into the parking area, and the other two—Jack was already thinking of them as Knicks Jacket and Tank Boy—shuffled forward behind him.

Jack shifted his footing and remembered that he had taken the Glock out of his boottop. It was now sitting in the glove compartment of the van. It would take some doing to get at it, and he doubted he'd have that much time. Thinking about it almost lightened his mood; he'd never been a guy who liked weapons or who took comfort from having one around. The Glock banging up his shin bone was just six pounds of useless steel, so he'd set it aside while he went to work on the van. Big mistake, it seems.

Penn State got to within ten feet of Jack and stopped. Knicks Jacket and Tank Boy spread out to the left and right, both of them breathing short sharp gasps through their mouths, Tank Boy still nodding in time to something only he could hear.

"Hello, faggot," said Penn State.

"Hello yourself," said Jack, smiling. The sun was shining at an oblique angle through the grid-work bars of the parking garage, painting the floor with hard black shadows and hot white bars. The dusty air looked like it was filled with fire. The place smelled of concrete and wet wood and rusted metal. Every footfall echoed, every word slammed off the walls. Jack knew there was no one else around. Hell, what was he going to do? Call 911?

"We seen your picture there, faggot. On the TV."

Jack shook his head sadly.

"You know, I really hate that word."

"What? Faggot?"

"Yeah. That word. I really, really hate that word. Okay, you want to call me something so I can understand how mean you assholes are. But why *faggot*? I mean, it's so damn boring. Why not . . . *fuck-head*? Or *puke*? Or *scum-sack*? I don't get this whole *faggot* thing with you kids. Unless, you know, you're overcompensating."

Jack's tone of sweet reason had them off balance, and they took a few seconds to try to figure out what Jack was up to. Since that called for actual working brain cells, they had to give up on it.

"Hey. Fuck you, faggot. There's cops all over the place want to know where you are. And you right here."

"I have a quarter. Why don't you go call one?"

Penn State shook his head slowly, grinning hugely.

"Oh no. Not yet. We gonna fuck you up good. Then we gonna turn in what's left, collect large. Then we par-tay, dude."

"Stop talking, man. Let's just do it!" said Knicks Jacket.

Tank Boy just nodded more energetically and made a kind of low rumbling noise that might have been a laugh or simply an inadequate breakfast. Jack sighed for the nation, for the quality of criminal assholes we now have to settle for in this great country. He thought of Frank Torinetti, of Carmine DaJulia, old Fabrizio Senza the killer barber, all the boys of Astoria. Thugs in his day wore Burberry trench coats, custom-made silk suits, Mara ties, Mauri slippers, had gold rings and loved Verdi, cried like girls at *Carmen*, drank Barolo, loved hugely, hated brightly, forgave easily, forgot nothing. And look at these sorry mutts we have here. Heartbreaking.

Jack stepped away, got his back up against the wall of the transport van. Having fun yet, you miserable son of a bitch? Down in his belly, he felt a spurt of acid, cold and yet burning. The skin across his shoulders went numb and his chest was tight and hot. Penn State looked like he was trying to find the right moment for a rush. Jack's vision was going a little rosy around the edges and his heart was hammering inside his rib cage. He was going to die right here. It was insane. Come through three years in Vietnam and get beaten to death by three mall rats in a suburban parking lot. And all of it because he was trying to help his kid get out of Lompoc. It was just too much.

Penn State yipped out a sort of yowling cry and rushed at Jack, who kicked the five-gallon can of paint over into his path, the oily green flood catching Penn State's floppy rubber runners—Penn State slipped—slammed hard to the floor on his back—the iron bar tumbled loose—Jack stepped in and snatched it up—Knicks Jacket was on him now—Jack ducked one wild swing, felt a thrumming rush as the rebar went past his left temple—Knicks Jacket put way too much in the swing and he stumbled off to Jack's right—now Tank Boy was coming in—Jack caught Tank Boy's downward blow on the bar—it drove Jack down to a knee—Tank Boy raised his bar again and Jack managed a sideways blow at Tank Boy's braced knee—he connected and saw the joint snapping—Tank Boy's howl was pure animal pain—Penn State was slithering backward in the spreading pool of paint—trying to get to his feet—Knicks Jacket had recovered his balance—swung the rebar again—Jack parried it on his bar—damn, this was just like the pugil-stick exercise they taught you at Lejeune—dropped the end—rammed the butt hard into the boy's face—Knicks Jacket went backward into the green paint pool and when he hit hard in the center of it his head bounced once with a cracking sound—Tank Boy was holding his ruined knee and hopping to his left—his bloated cheeks dull as candle wax and his forehead bright red with agony—Jack stepped in—braced both feet—set himself—swung the rebar at Tank Boy's head—felt the brute snap-shock of the blow all the way to his shoulders—Jack was turning away before Tank Boy was all the way down—Penn State had reached the edge of the paint pool and he was scrabbling for a grip, his sneakers making feathery green skid marks on the gray concrete, his hands wet and shiny green—Jack tossed the rebar—heard it bounce and go clanging away—popped the van door and picked up the Glock—his boots slipping as he crossed the enamel—Penn State turned around—saw Jack's face—the pistol in his right hand—Jack with his war face on—Penn State got to his knees—got to his feet—tried to run—fell facedown on the concrete floor. Jack reached him in three long strides, put the muzzle hard up against the back of the kid's head.

"Please, mister . . ."

Jack's fear and his anger were twinned wires, one blue and one red, burning through the inside of his skull. He could smell Buster's Kools and had a fleeting image of the fat man in his undershirt Jack had seen on his way to prison, watching TV in a shabby small-town room, and then Claire Torinetti standing in the doorway of her husband's house with the light shining through her robe. Penn State was crawling forward, leaving a green trail—*please mister please*.

Hell, thought Jack, watching him, he was only a child. The kid has his whole life in front of him. Think what he would do with it.

"Hey kid."

"Yes sir?" His voice was thin and high.

"Suddenly things went terribly wrong, didn't they? How are you handling this? Is it a disappointment? Are you finding it necessary to rethink your position?"

"Please . . . what are you gonna do?"

"Well . . . what would *you* do? Say we trade places, I'm down there, you up here with the gun. What would you do then?"

"Man . . . I'd let you go. I swear it. I never meant for anybody to get bad hurt. I just wanted the money. Please."

"You know, kid, I have to say, I don't find your answer persuasive. I think you're not being candid with me. You promise never to call anybody a faggot again?"

"I do, sir. I swear, sir. Please, sir—just let—"

"On your honor? Blood of the Holy Virgin?"

Jack figured Penn State had no idea who the Virgin Mary was or what her blood had to do with his life. At that point, the kid began to babble and the squeaky rasp of his voice, high, whining, pleading, was painful to hear. Jack shifted his position, thought about it, then he squeezed the trigger, the pistol boomed in his hand, Penn State's skull bounced once. A neat round black hole had appeared in the back of his head, the skin peeling back from the muzzle blast, bits of pink bone showing, and a sudden pool of bright blue blood—reddening as the air touched it—came oiling out from under the boy's face and spread across the stony floor. All Jack could hear was his own breathing—short sharp gasps. He watched his hand moving downward—the skin on the back of it stained with green paint—watched from deep inside his own skull as he moved the weapon—and put two more carefully considered rounds in the center of the kid's spine, right between the shoulder blades, precisely between *Penn* and *State*. Each time the pistol went off, the parking garage rang like a big iron bell. Each time a round punched into the kid, the band of fear clamped around Jack's chest seemed to ease up a little more. After the third shot Jack's ears were buzzing and his hearing had gone. He was inside a cone of silence. He was calm. The fear was gone. It was like he had sailed out of a tropical storm and into a sunlit lagoon lined with palm trees and white sand.

He stood up, stepped away from the body, and pulled in a long ragged breath. The air was rich, layered with strong smells: gunpowder, spilled paint, blood, dust. His breath in his lungs was like a strong wind in tall grass, hissing and rolling. His mouth was parched. He looked down again. My goodness, Penn State was a mess. Just look at you. Jack shook his head, sighed deeply again, rolled the tension out of his neck and shoulders, walked back over to where Knicks Jacket was lying spread-eagled in the paint pool, a thin sheet of blood running from his broken nose, staining his teeth red.

The kid must have heard—or felt—him walk over, because he opened his eyes, blinked twice, as Jack leaned down over him. What do I do with you? he wondered, pressed the pistol into the kid's forehead, and shot him twice just above the place where his thick eyebrows knitted together. The holes were tiny and black but the force of the muzzle blast ripped the pink skin open all around them in a ragged shape that reminded Jack of a starfish. He found Tank Boy lying on his side in the center of a small lake of green paint and his own blood, his eyes wide open, staring at a point on the floor about ten feet away. Blood was running down his face from a terrible crushed-in wound over his left temple. The blood had not mixed with the green paint—oil and water, Jack realized—but had threaded a complex channel through it so it looked like a bright red river against a flat green forest. Jack thought of the Amazon at a fiery red sunset and liked the image very much. He found it . . . painterly. He had always liked watercolors. Maybe he should try his hand someday. After things settled down. He could use a hobby. Jack squatted beside the kid, looked into his eyes, saw the pupils narrowing.

"Hey there, tiger. Still with us? How you doing?"

Tank Boy's lips moved. He was staring up at Jack, eyes huge now. He was trying to speak. His left arm was caught under his body, his hand projecting out from under him, blue-white, tubular as sausage meat, veined pink on the palm. Breath from his mouth made a tiny ripple of waves on the slick surface of the paint. They moved out and settled into a delicate fan of shining green curves. Jack reached out, gently patted the kid on his shoulder, feeling the landslide of thick muscle, and the rubbery flesh over it, put the Glock up against the kid's cheek, listened as Tank Boy's breath started to rasp out in puffy little gasps, pressed the muzzle in tight, braced his arm, turned his face slightly to the right, but not so far that he wasn't still making good eye contact with the kid, and fired twice.

He sat back on his heels, studied the effect, and decided that firing into the soft fleshy tissue of a man's cheek produced a much different pattern than firing into a thin layer of skin stretched over the skull. For one thing, there was the interplay with the molars. You didn't get that with a skull shot.

He had to go back to the Wal-Mart and buy another

can of paint, but since he had discovered $976 dollars in grubby bills rolled up in an inside pocket of the dead boy's Knicks jacket along with a plastic bag stuffed full of rock cocaine, he decided to treat himself to some new T-shirts, three black, two white, along with a new pair of jeans, a summer-weight jacket, a pair of olive green slacks and also new Top-Siders, and some necessary toiletries. He remembered to get some groceries and a tool set and some turpentine and a handheld CB radio and a cheap cell phone that came with a prepaid calling card. There were many excellent bargains at Wal-Mart and Jack was gratified to see how far his hard-earned money could take him in such a fine store. America was truly a wonderful country. On the way out he walked through the crowded parking lot and used his brand-new multi-tool with the screwdriver head to pop the plate off a garbage truck he found parked behind the store. The big orange truck was covered with dust and looked like it might stay there for a long while before anyone noticed a missing plate. Although it was a long way back to the parking garage and he had a lot to carry, he enjoyed the walk very much and found the weather very pleasant. He did see a few cop cars, but he felt quite invisible walking along the four-lane road in the company of so many fellow shoppers out and about on this lovely June day.

It took him another hour, but he finally managed to put a complete and convincing coat of green paint on the van. It was slow work, but he wanted it to look just right. Now and then he'd step back and see how it was going, and once he asked the boys what they thought of his work, but they just lay there and showed no interest in anything he was doing. Typical teens, he decided. Ignore them.

It was late afternoon by the time he screwed the borrowed plate onto the transport van and tossed the government tags through the window and into a Dumpster next to a section of plaster tailings. They landed with a clatter and slid sideways under a nail-studded section of particleboard. He threw his jeans and the stained white tee down a fifty-foot-deep construction tube and dropped his boots in after them. He regretted having to throw away the boots, but he figured Dan Post was still making them. Jack then used the turpentine to clean himself up as much as possible, changed into the olive-drab slacks, and put on a black T-shirt and his new Top-Siders—no socks, thank you—splashed on some Eau Sauvage—very lime and quite refreshing—climbed into the van, fired it up, and rolled slowly down the exit ramp and far away from Penn State and his little dead friends.

Out in the busy traffic he found an FM station that played soft jazz, turned it up high enough to hear it through the ringing in his ears. Small-arms fire in a tight space did that to your ears. The van had a police radio too, and Jack clicked the selector switch through several channels until the LED display read *Info State City*. He heard a dispatcher discussing a car theft out at someplace called Laurel Run and a state trooper logging on to respond. So far nothing about him. Jack set the volume low, opened a cold bottle of spring water, and drank half of it at one go. Buster had left a package of Kools in a shelf under the dash. Jack took one out, lit it up, and rolled the window down. The day was cooler now, and the leafy suburban avenues he was soon driving through were fragrant with the smell of cut grass and flowers and backyard barbecues.

He took a two-lane blacktop numbered 309 north out of Hazleton and hit Interstate 80 a half hour later. Interstate 80 goes west through Chicago and Omaha and Cheyenne all the way to Sacramento, and it goes east to the George Washington Bridge and New York City. West was the famous sundown road, and perhaps Mexico beyond it. East was back into the shit and maybe find out who put him there. With a little luck, maybe kill him before the ATF got to him. After that . . . well, forget that. There was no after.

Jack went east.

PART THREE

HOME IS THE HUNTER . . .

Nicky was sound asleep in the backseat and Casey's mind was on her mother when Dexter's cell phone started to beep. Dexter fished it out of his pocket, thumbed the send button.

"Zarnas."

"Sergeant Zarnas?"

"Yeah. Who's this?"

"This is Derry Flynn. With the ATF. I said I'd call?"

"I remember. What's up?"

"What's your twenty?"

"About a mile out of Delano on Eighty-one."

"You anywhere near a mobile display terminal?"

"Got an MDT right in front of me."

"Hazleton."

"Hazleton? What about—"

The line was dead. Dexter put the cell phone down, looked across at Casey Spandau.

"Log us onto NCIC, Casey? See if there are any hits with the word *Hazleton* in them."

"Proper name? A person?"

"I don't know. All the guy said was Hazleton."

Nicky, awake now, leaned forward.

"The map shows a town called Hazleton. It's right on Highway Eighty-one, maybe thirty miles north of here."

"Okay. Try that, Casey."

Casey punched in her access code and the computer screen flashed on, a string of luminous numbers and letters showing various law enforcement databases.

EPIC MIRAC NADDIS
NESPIN / WSIN / MAGLOCEN /
RMIN / MOCIC / ROCIC
VICAP INTERPOL FINEST CATCH CPIC NCIC 2000

Casey tabbed over to NCIC 2000, hit enter, found a search bar, and typed in *Hazleton*. The LCD screen flickered and a paragraph in yellow letters scrolled across the bright blue screen:

NCIC DATA FILE INCIDENT EXTRACT
HAZLETON PA

Hazleton PD report triple homicide gang-related three male victims location Ticknor Auto Park 11356 Appalachian Way beaten with iron bars and shot with nine-millimeter pistol close range. Witness describes possible white male answers description Vermillion, Jack, fugitive, notify USMS or ATF advise if contact. Investigation ongoing. ATF notification attending at scene ETA 1830 hours.

Casey read the extract out loud.

"Okay," said Dexter. "That's gotta be it."

"Who logged this on NCIC?" asked Nicky. "Usually these reports are a day late. What's the reporting code say?"

Casey checked the bottom of the screen.

"DOJ logged it. I mean, it was logged on a DOJ machine."

"Your guy Flynn?" Nicky asked Dexter.

"I guess so. Sit back, Nicky. We're gonna fly."

Dexter hit the grill flashers and floored the unit, accelerated around a slow-moving Greyhound, and powered into a long straightaway. Big blue mountains crowded the northern horizon line. The countryside was green and rolling. The heat was strong enough to make it seem that pools of water covered the highway in the shimmering distance. Casey turned the cooling up. The car settled into the passing lane at 120 and they blew by a stream of cars.

Six minutes later they were on the outskirts of Hazleton. Four minutes after that, they pulled up in front of Ticknor's Auto Park.

"I guess this is it," said Nicky.

"No shit," said Casey.

The three-floor garage building was almost completely surrounded by official vehicles, including Hazleton PD cars and two Jeep Cherokees with Pennsylvania State Police logos on the doors, a tan Caprice, three EMS trucks with their strobes pulsing, and about fifty cops holding back a crowd of citizens massed in front of a crime-scene-tape barrier. Dexter blipped the siren twice and a startled female state trooper who had been holding up a hand to stop their car stepped around to the window, took off her Stetson, and leaned down to look into the car. She was ruddy and young and had the bluest eyes Nicky had ever seen and a bronze tan. Her voice was flat and nasal and held a midwestern snap. Her ID read *Salt*.

"Who're you? Jesus or the ATF?"

Dexter showed them his gold sergeant's shield.

"Neither. NYPD. Where's the ATF team?"

"Not here yet. They're coming in on a chopper. Supposed to be here any minute. We're just holding the crime scene. Who the hell're we, right? What's the NYPD doing all the way out here?"

"Chasing a man. We think this is connected. Can we go in?"

She shrugged, stood up, keyed her portable.

"Captain Billy, this is Pepper, down at the ramp. I got three NYPD here, long way from home. They wanna come up."

They heard a garbled burst of static and talk, but Pepper seemed to understand it. She keyed the radio off and stepped back.

"You go ahead. Park it on the second floor and walk up. The third floor's the crime scene. Captain Billy's the whip hand up there. Looks like a bald cranky parrot. You'll know him when you see him. Am I ever gonna know what this is all about?"

Dexter laughed.

"Your name really Pepper Salt?"

"No. It's Sandy."

"Sandy? Sandy Salt? Not really?"

"Yeah. My father's an idiot. So of course they call me Pepper. It's what passes for smarts around here. Your name really Dexter?"

"Yeah. They call me Lefty."

"Very funny. Dexter. Sinister. Right. Left. I get it. You make sure I find out what's going on, hah? They never tell me anything."

"I'll see you do."

They rolled up the entrance ramp and past a barricade of uniformed cops who watched as they went by with frowning faces and their hands on their service Smiths. Casey got most of their attention. She figured there weren't very many black female detectives in the State Police and said so. Nicky, a state cop himself, knew better but kept his mouth shut. They parked the Lincoln on the second level and walked up the dusty concrete ramp to the third floor. The sun was low in the sky and soft yellow shafts of light streamed in through the grillwork. The air smelled of dust and turpentine. And something worse.

A short man in a black three-piece suit, a white shirt with a high stiff collar, a narrow red tie, and thick black brogues was waiting for them at the top of the ramp, legs apart, braced, silhouetted against the setting sun.

He had a corona of frizzy white hair and thin gray metal glasses. His face was leathery and his mouth a hard line, his eyes little nailheads, his handshake a sharp snap-and-release, his skin dry and rough.

"I'm Captain Billy Frick. Pepper says you're NYPD? What the hell you three doing here?"

Dexter, who had the rank, did the talking.

"Captain Frick, we're looking for a man, escaped from a marshals van this morning. We have—"

"Vermillion. Jack. I know the pecker-head."

"The NCIC hit said a witness made an ID?"

"Ida May."

"What?"

Captain Frick turned and walked away, stopped short, looked back. "I said Ida May. Ida May Barbaree. She works at the Wal-Mart down the road. Come take a look at this mess. No consideration. Private property too."

They followed Captain Frick's wiry little frame as he strut-walked across the parking area like a rooster with a blister until they reached a section at the rear, cordoned off, guarded by three uniformed state troopers and a Hazleton cop. All four cops straightened up as Frick came boot-thumping across the floor.

"All right, boys. We got the NY-damned-PD here for a goggle. Go ahead, you three. Enjoy."

He stepped away, and they walked up to the yellow crime scene ribbon, stopped there. Three bodies lay inside the ribbon, stiffened in death, blood pooling in dry green paint. The smell of sewage and turpentine was stifling. The heat still in the day wasn't helping. The wounds were massive, the scene a butcher's nightmare.

"Holy Mother of God," said Nicky.

"Don't blaspheme, boy," said Frick. "We ID'd them. One in the Penn State jacket is Jason Bulger. Useless little shit, got a juvie sheet longer than my . . . sorry, ma'am.

Big kid there, on his side, skull whacked in and the big hole where his face used to be, he's Ratko Krukovac. Another waste of space. Looks better now. And the sorry-looking bastard with the surprised expression on his face is Dylan Currie, who is, as we like to say, known to the police. A drug-dealing asshole. He got two in the forehead and it has improved him greatly."

Frick stopped to light up a short nasty-looking cigar and push his hat backward. He spat out a shred of tobacco and chuckled.

"All three got serious whup-ass before they got their nine-millimeter therapy. Guess they picked a fight with the wrong guy this time. Only a dumb little shit like Jason Bulger would be stupid enough to take a piece of rebar to a gunfight."

Dexter looked at Casey, whose face was gray with shock.

"Christ. Jack Vermillion wouldn't do this," he said.

"Heck he wouldn't," said Frick. "Ask Ida May Barbaree."

There was a sudden massive roaring howl that settled into a steady thundering beat. Dust flew in the grating and whirled across the floor. Frick went straight up into the air, bellowing in solid brass.

"God*damn* those people. Henry!"

One of the state troopers jerked upright again.

"Get down there, see if that's those fools from the ATF. If they're landing on the roof here, you have my permission to shoot them all. Now scat!"

Henry scatted. Dexter tried to stay on topic while the chopper noise buffeted and slammed the air and the dust clouds choked them all. In less than thirty seconds they were lost in a cloud of drifting dust. Frick was a ghostly figure in front of them.

"There goes the crime scene," he said. "Damned idiots."

Frick kicked at a paint can nearby.

"Two of these was bought at the Wal-Mart down the road. Any damn fool could see they was a clue. I went over there myself, talked to the people. Ida May Barbaree sold this paint to a guy, answers the description of your Jack Vermillion pecker-head. Ida May says he had words with Jason Bulger over there. Way I figure it, Bulger followed the man back here, brought some friends to help, maybe looking for that reward money, and they got more than they was expecting."

They heard the sounds of angry voices echoing in the ramp and the shuffle-stamp of boots. Henry, the state trooper, reappeared at the top of the ramp with five people hard on his heels, a slender black-haired woman in a black jumpsuit in the lead, four ATF men in field gear shuffling up in her wake. Casey recognized Valeriana Greco from the CNN news brief that morning. Dexter Zarnas was busy trying not to recognize Derry Flynn, a slope-shouldered gray-haired man with deep creases around his brown eyes, a blunt harness-bull face, standing apart from Greco and watching her in action. She came right up to Frick, ignoring the three people standing beside him.

"Captain Frick, Greco, U.S. attorney. Who are these people?"

"Lady," said Frick, "don't you come sharp with me in front of my own troopers. I told you damn idiots not to come swooping in here on your whirlybird. Look what you done to my crime scene."

Greco looked as if he'd slapped her, but she came right back at him, her voice raspy, her face bright with battle.

"Captain Frick, this is a federal investigation. This is not your crime scene. This is my crime scene. I can take control of any jurisdiction I damn well please. I am doing that now. Any interference in a federal investigation will result in strong disciplinary action. Do I make myself clear, Captain?"

Nicky, Dexter, and Casey, who had gained some insight into the captain, braced themselves. They were not disappointed.

"Henry!"

His bark made them all jump. Henry scrambled around the fringe and came up to stand beside Frick.

"Henry, you're my witness. Young woman, until the governor of this great state advises me that I am no longer in charge of this investigation—which, I take no pleasure in advising you, miss, is how the statute actually reads in Pennsylvania—I will conduct this investigation as I see fit. Now you and your whirlybird pals have scattered my crime scene to the four winds, and although we are recent acquaintances, miss, I find you a most abrupt and unpleasant person and Henry here— stand up straight, Henry!—is going to assist you as you all delocate my area of operations. Now."

Greco looked from one face to another and Casey expected her to go off like a pipe bomb. But she just froze solid, turned on a heel, and walked away. Three of the ATF escort shuffled their feet, looked at each other, and then followed her down the ramp. Derry Flynn stayed behind and a huge grin spread across his grizzled face.

"Captain Frick, I've been waiting for days for someone to do that. It was a pleasure to watch."

Frick didn't bend.

"Why are you still here?"

Dexter spoke up for Flynn.

"Captain, Agent Flynn here is a good man. We're sorry for the . . . jurisdictional disputes. This is your crime scene. Can we just get a little information from you?"

"You can tell me what the devil all this is about."

Dexter nodded to Casey, who sketched out the background of the investigation, the Red Hook shootings, their suspicions about Earl Pike, their belief that Jack Vermillion couldn't be responsible for this level of violence. Frick took it all in but he was shaking his little round skull before Casey finished speaking.

"Don't know this Pike fellow. But it was Vermillion did this. Got him on a video. He walks into the Wal-Mart big as life, stops and looks up at the camera like he was admiring himself. Had them print me a still. See for yourself."

Frick extracted a rumpled sheet from an inside pocket, unfolded it, smoothed it out on his chest, handed it to Nicky. The image was black-and-white but clear, a big rangy man in jeans and boots, a white T-shirt, big cowboy mustache, long hair combed right back. His face in the photo was hard, worn-down, and bleak, his eyes hidden in darkness. He looked dangerous as hell. Nicky handed the shot to Dexter, who stared at it.

"This still doesn't prove that Vermillion did . . . this."

Frick tapped the picture. "See them boots?"

"Yeah."

"Nice pair of tan boots."

"Yes."

"Found them at the bottom of a construction tube. Right over there. Even got the same stitching."

"But . . ."

"Son, you're a cop. You got to follow where the trail goes."

Dexter shook his head.

"Even that doesn't . . ."

Frick shook his head sadly, walked over to a plastic storage box, popped the lid, lifted out a big plastic bag with a pair of tan leather boots inside. He brought it back over to Dexter.

"What's that on these boots, son?"

"Green paint."

"Yep. And . . . ?"

"And blood."

"And blood. That nail it down a bit, son?"

"Yes sir," said Dexter. "It does."

SATURDAY, JUNE 24

BLUE MOUNTAINS BAR AND GRILL

SAINT JOHN'S, PENNSYLVANIA

2145 HOURS

They got away from Hazleton about an hour later, after Dexter had stopped to talk with Pepper the state trooper, keeping a promise to fill her in. He was glad he had; she turned out to be Captain Billy's niece. Then they drove north on 81 until they reached the intersection of Interstate 80.

Casey stopped at the entrance to the Ramada to call her mother. Nicky and Dexter went into the bar. Derry Flynn was waiting for them, alone. They filed into the booth and sat back. Derry Flynn was shaking his head slowly before they got settled.

"Damn, you two are a sorry-looking lot. *Que pasa?*"

"I blew it," said Dexter. "I called this whole thing wrong."

Derry Flynn raised a hand, got the waitress over, ordered something called a bucket o' brewskies. It took two waitresses to haul it to the table. Nicky slapped a brand-new box of Marlboros on the table and fumbled for a lighter. Casey came into the bar as they were cracking open the first cold bottles. She peeled the pack and slipped one out, waited while Nicky lit hers and then his own, and Dexter watched this ceremony with a yellow glitter of flame in his deep brown eyes. He grinned at Casey, shook his finger.

"Casey, you fraternizing with this horrid little trooper?"

Casey, to her surprise, managed a blush.

Nicky looked a bit puffed out and then he laughed too.

"Casey's slumming. It amuses her. How's your mom, Casey?"

"She's okay. Somebody called her just now, asking for me."

"Yeah? Who?"

"A guy. Deep voice. She didn't get a name. She said he sounded sexy. He asked where I was."

"She tell him?"

"Yeah. She's . . . a little under the weather, Nicky."

Nicky understood that. It worried him.

"You have call display?"

"Yeah. She can't work it. Don't worry. Probably a bill collector. I'll check the call list when I get home. Forget about it. Agent Flynn, nice to see you. Thanks for coming."

Nicky looked at her face. She was worried. He could see that. Very worried. He opened his mouth to say something to her, but she shook her head and gave him a not-now look. He shut up. Derry Flynn took a long swallow, set the glass down hard.

"What is it you people wanted, anyway? I thought you were all fired up about Earl Pike. Why the interest in Jack Vermillion?"

"They're connected," said Nicky, and told Flynn the basic story, all the way from the double homicide at Blue Stores through the Red Hook disaster. Earl Pike was the link, the consistent thread throughout the case. And Pike led straight to Jack Vermillion. You couldn't separate them. Flynn listened with his eyes on the tabletop. When Nicky wrapped it up, he studied them, clearly making a decision.

"You know anything about Earl Pike?"

"We know about CCS," said Casey. "And we've met him."

"Have you? Well, then. You can see he's a handful. I got my theory about what's going on here, but I can't get Greco to pay any attention. She's got Vermillion on the brain. What did you people make of that mess back in Hazleton?"

Dexter's face darkened slightly.

Nicky answered for him.

"We were working on the theory that Jack Vermillion wasn't a hard guy. That he was basically straight. We were wrong."

Flynn nodded.

"Captain Frick made the wounds as nine-mills, right? And we figure Vermillion is carrying Deputy Callahan's piece. That was a Glock nine-mill. So yeah, I figure he did the thing. But killing three scum-sacks isn't the same as shooting two guards in cold blood."

"You figure the captain was right? About the reward?"

"Why else would they tangle with him?"

Casey shook her head.

"We all looked at the bodies. Each one of them was already down. The fight was over. He didn't just kill those kids. He executed them. If he could do that, he could do anything. I think Greco's right about him. If it quacks like a duck, it's a duck, right?"

Flynn didn't buy it.

"Do you people know anything about Vermillion? About the case against him?"

Dexter shook his head.

"Not much. Our target here is Pike. We know this Greco number, she's been on TV, she's painting a picture of a bent guy with Mafia connections, running stolen cars, drug money. Now also a stone killer. I'd say that makes him a bad guy."

"It's not as simple as that," said Flynn.

"Never is," said Nicky. "Fill us in, then."

Derry Flynn sketched out the basic case against Vermillion, the Red Hook connection, the transfer deal for Danny Vermillion, the link with Earl Pike, what had been found in the container, the stolen cars, the cocaine-tainted cash. The three NYPD cops listened quietly, but nothing they heard outweighed what they had seen back in that garage. When Flynn had wrapped it up, Dexter spoke for all of them.

"A guy who could do what we just saw could do anything."

Flynn didn't back down.

"I'm just not convinced Vermillion's as dirty as Greco wants him to be. There's no proof that his transport company is mob-connected. He grew up with some mob guys. So what? He had a good reputation in Albany, fought hard for his workers, treated them right. Even the Teamsters couldn't break his shop floor. Now everything he had is gone, snapped up by Greco under the RICO laws. People have limits. You take a basically solid guy, businessman, do him like Greco's doing him, sooner or later he's gonna get cranky. Okay, *cranky* is not the word. This guy's life has just been ripped up, everything he ever had taken away. Maybe he deserves it. The stuff we found is hard to explain. But a murderer? I don't know about those guards. I talked to the witness up there. She didn't actually see Vermillion shooting anyone. She heard two shots, real close together, then the female guard comes out of a phone booth, goes pounding back to the washrooms. She hears the guard screaming, 'Drop your weapons.' Get it? Like she was talking to two people. Then three more shots. Then she hears a man say something like 'Never look away.' "

"So Vermillion was saying something to the guard. After he shot her. That's what the waitress heard. Vermillion's voice."

"No. She took Vermillion's order, a Grand Slam breakfast. She says this voice was softer, deeper, and had a sort of a western drawl to it. Vermillion's voice is real New York. He grew up in Queens."

"This is a very good witness," said Dexter.

"Oh yes. Smart kid, Annie. She wants to be a criminologist."

"Pike has a western drawl," said Nicky.

"So I'm told. Also, the rounds we got out of the guards, none of them was from a Glock, and that's all the guards were carrying. They were killed with a big Smith. Whose Smith? Not Vermillion's. He's a prisoner, and the marshals would have shaken him down thoroughly. So who brought the Smith? Earl Pike owns three, according to the register. Greco doesn't like that information one bit. She says it's all guesswork. Something else. Somebody threw up all over the shooting scene. We figure it was Vermillion. Try to imagine a kind of Grand Slam in reverse. Better yet, don't. But it tells me that, whatever happened there, it got to him. Got to him so much he vomited. That's not what you call cold-blooded. If Jack Vermillion's a killer, then he's a hot-blooded killer. About the van, I wouldn't worry too much. Let's just say we're on it. He'll turn up."

"You're on it?" said Nicky. "How?"

"I just mean we have assets, resources. We'll find him."

"Something I don't get," said Casey. "Pike's the best bet for the shooter at Red Hook. But Greco's been all over Vermillion, and I don't see you people doing much about finding Earl Pike. Why?"

"One thing, there's not even a warrant out for him. Vermillion gives us the original heads-up on Pike. We do the sting at Red Hook, you were there. What's the word?"

"Fubar," said Casey.

Derry nodded in appreciation.

"Exactly. Fucked up beyond all recognition. Everybody got shot to shit. Smoke clears, I lost good friends. Lee Ford. Luther Campbell's hanging on by a thread. Farrell Garber, one of our snipers. Bunny Kreuger. So we crack open Pike's box. What do we find? Antique weapons, Winchesters, Sharps, a lot of swords, flags, medals, militaria, that kind of thing. All of it connected to his family in some way. Went back two hundred years. Most of it was nothing we'd care about, but there were some pieces, full-auto stuff, M-sixteens, a couple Garands, some M-fourteens—Vietnam-era—a Stoner, an M-sixty—also full auto, takes a seven-point-six-two round—they had them in Vietnam too—and all this stuff, it's now banned under the Brady laws. So there's a lot of technical violations, but seeing as how Pike's a decorated soldier, connected all over DC, known inside the Beltway, the usual course would be to work out a fine, let him off with a reprimand. No headlines in that for La Greco, see?"

"Would he get anything back?"

"No. It's all marked for destruction. Of course, some of our guys will get a chance to pick through it. It's a perk, sort of. We call it 'extracted from source for training purposes.' The rest will get sold off or sent to the crusher. Proceeds will go to DOJ revenue."

"So still no warrant?"

Derry shook his head.

"What have we got? Sure, I like him for the shooting at Red Hook, but I have zero proof. We found the sniper location. Not a single shell casing, no boot marks, no used cigarettes, no candy wrappers. Some abrasions on a railing that looked like bipod marks. Since nobody heard anything, we figure the weapon was sound-suppressed. In short, we have dick on the guy. He's too sharp."

"We have something," said Casey. "We have DNA."

"How the hell did you do that?" asked Flynn, his eyes wide.

Nicky explained the injury on Pike's hand, the connection to the double homicide in Blue Stores. Flynn liked it very much.

"Okay. I like this. Have you heard from the lab?"

"Yeah," said Nicky. "I talked with my LT an hour ago. They got a match on fourteen indicators off the male vic at Blue Stores, Donald Condotti. Nothing on Julia Gianetto. But Pike's toast."

"Well, I feel better. If we can't make him on the Red Hook thing, then you guys can fry him for the double homicides. Force a statement, maybe. Will the DNA stand up? How'd you get it?"

Nicky looked at his hands. Dexter took some beer. Flynn got the point. Casey had been thinking about the Red Hook incident.

"What made you search the rest of the ship?" asked Casey.

Flynn gave her a careful look, then tapped the side of his nose.

"Got a phone call."

"A snitch?"

"Yep."

"Who?"

"Don't know. Greco knows. Won't say."

"So Greco shifts her sights?" asked Casey.

"Maybe. I know her first target was Frank Torinetti, and Vermillion's a known associate. I think she's running a snitch inside Black Water Transit. Somebody who knows how the outfit runs."

"This the guy who made the call about the other container?"

"Could be. Like I said, I'm not in the loop. Know

what they call her around the office? The Pirate Queen. She's the undisputed champ when it comes to asset seizures in upstate New York. Last six years, since she's been the assistant United States attorney in Albany, she's generated over seven million dollars in forfeiture funds. She's a gold mine for the feds. And this is the biggest case she's ever had. Black Water Transit is worth millions. And all that money goes right into her operating funds, so she gets to run even bigger cases. She's already been promoted to New York City."

"Why pick on Vermillion in the first place?" asked Casey.

"Like I said, his Mafia buddy, Frank Torinetti. Jack grew up with the guy, still sees him. And the Teamsters never hassled him. Vermillion has an Italian name. Therefore he's corrupt. We see what we want to see."

"Vermillion's a French name, actually," put in Casey.

The other cops blinked at her, then went on talking. Nicky winked at her. She smiled back. *Men.*

"Torinetti owns Hudson Valley Fine Cars," said Nicky. "Porsches, Ferraris, Corvettes, classic cars. I go there all the time. Look in the windows and cry."

"Me, too. Anyway, Greco runs Vermillion through the machine, and now she's got a ruling, gives her control of his company."

"What's she going to do with it?"

Derry Flynn shrugged.

"She's going to sell it off. Like I said, the Pirate Queen."

"Kind of like the spoils of war," said Dexter. "We do that too. That Lincoln out there, we got that from our own seizure program. It used to belong to a Russian importer, got popped for money laundering. Our department makes a bundle out of seizures too. Who's Greco selling Vermillion's outfit to?"

"No idea. Greco's pretty tight on things like that. I'm just a street guy. They don't tell me much and right now she hates me."

"Because we showed up in Hazleton?" said Casey.

"Yeah. She saw the NCIC log, nailed me for it. That's okay. I'm going home. I got friends to bury."

There was a long silence after that. In a while Dexter lifted his glass. They raised their beers, drank deep.

"What's Pike after in all of this?" asked Casey.

"Vengeance. I figure Pike's returning the favor. I think he's fucking with Vermillion for ratting him out on his gun collection."

"Why not just kill him when he had the chance, back there at Beach Haven? He had a piece, he had the guy right in front of him?"

"Christ, who knows? Maybe he enjoys watching Vermillion scamper around. Cat-and-mouse thing. Pike's cold enough."

Dexter drained his glass, poured them all another round.

"If Pike is making a project out of Vermillion, then the smartest thing Vermillion can do is come in from the cold. Out there, Pike on his case, he's gonna last as long as a butterfly's fart."

Nicky broke up at that. Nicky was also getting a little smashed.

"A butterfly's *fart*? How long is that? Have you looked into it? Dexter, you can't go around citing etymological data without some sort of scientific proof. Chaos would ensue."

Dexter gave Nicky a look of sorrowful rebuke.

"Nicky, you should have stayed in school. Etymology is the study of words. Entomology is the study of bugs."

"So what's the study of bug words?"

"Bugs don't have words. They communicate with their antlers."

"Antennas, Dexter," said Casey. "Bugs have antennas. Not antlers. Moose have antlers."

"It's 'antenn-*eye*,' not 'antenn-*ah*,'" said Dexter primly. "And it's the plural form. It's from the Latin, which you should know, being an educated woman, as I am pleased to observe, and anyway, everybody knows moose have horns, not antlers."

"*Cars* have horns," said Nicky. "You ever see a car with antlers? Hah? Answer me that."

"As a matter of fact, I have," put in Derry Flynn. "It was on an old Cadillac I saw once in Denver. Guy had stuck antlers right on the hood. Big old deer antlers. I have also seen cars with antennae. I believe we've got one or two in the ATF."

There was a silence while they pondered the implications.

"Bucks," said Casey after a time, looking very smug.

"What?" They all looked at her.

"Bucks have antlers. Does don't have anything. They're the ladies. In your world of the deers, it's the *bucks* that have the antlers. This has been my experience."

"Bucks," agreed Nicky. "She's right. I love this woman."

Dexter remained unconvinced and said so.

"You're being . . . obtuse," she said. Nicky approved.

"I believe he is, my dove. You're obtuse, Dexter. It's not your fault. You can't help it. You're management. By the way, for the record? Butterflies can't fart. It's anatomically impossible."

"Yeah?" said Dexter. "How would *you* know?"

Nicky extracted a Marlboro, lit up, and gazed off into the distance with a look of deep and profound sadness.

"You weren't there, man. You had to be there."

"Where?"

Nicky rubbed at his eyes with his knuckles, faked a racking sob, clutched at Casey's hand.

"The Nam."

Dexter blinked at him.

"Nicky, you're thirty. You were a baby when the war ended."

"You're right. I was drafted. Right out of kindergarten. My whole class went, except for little Donnie Nubbins. His mother wouldn't give him a note. Osh-Kosh made combat jumpers for all of us, with teddy bears all over. Plus matching backpacks. We sang the *Sesame Street* song on our way up to the front. God. We were so innocent. We got cut to ribbons at Phu Bai. NVA regulars. It was hell. I was the only one who made it back. I've been holding it in for so long. Maybe now, with the love of a good woman, the healing can begin."

Nicky held out his hand, palm up. Casey put a Kleenex into it, which Nicky thought was a nice touch. Dexter's cell phone beeped. He picked it up, said his name, and listened to the voice at the other end for about three minutes. The others watched him.

"Well, butter my butt and call me toasted."

"What?" said Casey. "Who was it?"

"Our esteemed leader, Detective Vince Zaragosa. Guess who's just come in from the cold?"

"Jack Vermillion?" said Derry Flynn.

"Nope," said Dexter. "You do not get a new car. Vanna, throw this man out into the street. Anybody else?"

"Holy Christ," said Casey.

"No. But an interesting choice."

"I meant Earl Pike," she said.

"That's cheating," said Dexter. "But yes."

Two hours out of Hazleton his hearing began to improve and the shock began to subside; the zoned-out calm, the euphoria, the crazy confidence he was feeling, it all dried up and blew away. He had executed three people. It didn't matter that they were penny-a-pack street thugs who could only make the world a better place by decomposing in a drainage ditch. What happened back there was murder. Up until that moment, he had been an innocent man fighting to get his life back. Now he had no life to get back. There was no way around that, no way out from under it. Another five hours of racing along back roads and hiding under bridges and scuttling around villages in western New Jersey like a big green cockroach, and Jack was just beginning to realize the dimensions of the stone wall he had smacked into. He'd been monitoring the van's police radio. Every half hour he heard the same bulletin, a taped alert:

> *"Units of state and local police are asked to continue watch for a white United States marshals prisoner transport van plates unknown direction of travel unknown suspect vehicle being driven by escaped federal prisoner Vermillion, Jack—wanted in connection with the death of two deputy marshals shot during an escape at Beach Haven, Pennsylvania, oh-four-thirty hours yesterday morning. Suspect description male white fifty-three years height*

*six-two weight one-ninety-five hair white worn
long and brushed back white mustache
description clothing possible olive pants black
T-shirt deck shoes suspect armed and dangerous
if located approach with extreme caution repeat
armed and dangerous approach with extreme
caution suspect vehicle last seen Hazleton,
Pennsylvania, at seventeen-thirty hours
yesterday afternoon. If located notify nearest
ATF office immediately or post on NCIC
through MAGLOCEN and duty desk.
Originating agency ATF Albany NY."*

There you go. A description of the van he was in, what
he looked like, with the warning that he was armed
and considered dangerous. He'd have abandoned the
van miles back, except for two things. They never mentioned a direction of travel, and they were still describing the vehicle as a white van with government plates.
Which meant his lunatic stunt, the paint job, the stolen
plate off the garbage truck, was still working. God
knows why. Jack would have described this as a lucky
break if the phrase hadn't made him choke every time
he tried. Whatever was going on in his life, and he meant
to find out in the next few hours, good luck wasn't a
factor.

He was listening to a late-night DJ play a Sinatra
song—"Summer Wind," by Johnny Mercer—the traffic
roaring all around him as he rolled eastbound through
the lights and the noise and the eastern New Jersey landscape, full of towns and suburban sprawl. Here was
Paterson coming up now, all the buildings lit up, the
glow from downtown, the highways busy even at this
hour, trucks and the vans and the cabs, all the familiar
names that came up bright electric green out of the
dark—a few miles back he'd passed Highway 287 and a

sign that said *Albany 163* and *Troy 170*—he could be home in three hours—in his own bed by sunrise—here was Elizabeth, where he'd gone for a kid's birthday party with Frank, Frank's father driving them in a huge old pink Packard that smelled of cigars—Teaneck—he had an uncle there who had been gassed at Inchon—Union City—bought his first truck from a yard in Union City—Palisades Park—made out with a big blonde girl there three years before joining the Marines—can't recall her name—she had one blue eye and one green eye—Paramus—used to go through there on the way to picnics at Mount Nebo—his father driving the delivery van he used for his flower shop—his mother knitting in the passenger seat—Hoboken—where Sinatra was born—and all the New York names—Van Cortland—Mosholu—Yonkers—Riverdale—the Bronx—Harlem—Long Island City. And Astoria, and his own block.

A few miles on and he could just make out the strutwork of the George Washington Bridge, a glimmer of it through the huge green darkness in between the city lights, and up ahead, just around the curve or seen through the trees that filled the rolling countryside, the huge skywide glow that lit up the low clouds floating over it—the lights of New York City. He was back on his home ground.

Now what? One thing was keeping Jack together. Get back home, find out who the people were—the man, the woman, whoever—who had taken his life apart, for fun or money or revenge—and, maybe, prove to anybody who still cared that he was . . . what? *Innocent* didn't fit anymore. Let's say not totally guilty. If he could do that, then whatever else happened to him, he wasn't going to end up in the county morgue as another dumb-dead-and-indicted dork on a stainless-steel tray with a paper toe tag on his right foot with a little haiku epitaph that read:

VERMILLION, J.
DOA

The air inside the marshals' big van was smoky, the green glow of the dashboard lighting Jack's face in the rearview mirror, making black holes of his eyes, his cheeks pale green. He was doing a steady sixty in the middle lane, trailing a big yellow Freightliner hauling fifty-foot sections of rebar—Jack figured this was just God still jerking him around for kicks—and he had the CB radio set tuned to nineteen, listening to the truckers talk their road talk.

Jack had done the long-haul jobs himself in the early years of Black Water Transit, and in this black hour of the night he bitterly envied them the wide-open doorways of their lives, the way they took in the whole country when they talked, Oklahoma City, Fresno, Seattle, Chicago, Memphis, Kansas City, they'd been everywhere, and they were always going to be everywhere, and once in the distant past he had known the things they knew about, the quirky little road facts like you got better mileage going east on I-90 than you did going west because I-90 was downhill all the way from Bozeman to Chicago, but going west you were better off on 80 because 80 took the low road through the Wasatch in western Wyoming, with the Grand Tetons off your right shoulder, and you could get all the way to Salt Lake City on half the gas that it took to get you through Lookout Pass up on the Idaho border, but on 80 westbound you didn't get to take the long slow climb up I-90 out of the Columbia Basin west of the Saddle Mountains and see the cone of Mount Rainier across fifty miles of high desert, the setting sun coloring the glaciers on its crest as red as lava, and the glittering plume of snow crystals that fluttered from the highest peak as the mountain cut into the jet stream at fifteen thousand feet, the Kilimanjaro of the far western plains.

Hours from now, these Freightliners and Kenworths and Macks would be far away from here, rolling westbound up the curving of the earth under a wide night sky scattered with cold stars and the western horizon an arc of pale green fire, but Jack would still be pushing this hijacked prison van toward the bitter dead end of his pointless little road, because he had killed three kids for no reason he could explain or even really understand, other than at the time when he squeezed that trigger, inside that cold blue airless silent bubble, what he had really been looking at was the back of his own son's head, at Danny's skull, and it had felt so *damned* sweet to do it. It was entirely possible that he'd shot those three kids because they reminded him of Danny, that he might have been killing his own child. Why? For getting him into this disaster in the first place with that pathetic, desperate phone call from the prison clinic in Lompoc.

And he had even enjoyed shooting those kids. It had felt just damn fine at the time, which was the usual problem with that kind of thing. But in his heart he also knew that, given the same chance, he would have tried to help Danny all over again. Danny was his son, and that's what fathers do. It's the way things are, the way they have to be, if any kid anywhere is ever going to find his way back home, find forgiveness and redemption. He hadn't really been killing Danny when he shot those three little thugs. He'd been killing his fear, his sense of being helpless and afraid.

Well, it was done now, and nothing could be taken back or made whole ever again, and his time was running out. He had one thing left to do. In other words, who to kill? Who had put him here? That was the question. It was a big question.

Flannery? Could Flannery do this? Life had taught Jack that almost everybody could talk themselves into almost anything provided the circumstances were brutal enough. People betrayed for love, for money, for revenge. Usually for money. Did Flannery need money? Flannery knew enough about Jack's business to set him up. But Flannery had argued against the deal with Pike.

So had Creek, for that matter. Did Creek do this to him? Could Creek do it? Much as he loved the man, this thing had far too much in the way of organizational skill to it. Creek couldn't organize a fall off a porch swing without a book of instructions and three assistants. But Creek needed the money. Creek always needed money, and Frank had told him that Creek was into Carmine and his people.

Carmine? Carmine had a big attitude in place about Jack. But he loved Frank, and Frank loved Jack, and if Frank ever heard that Carmine had done anything to hurt Jack, it would take Carmine a week to die and another week for the cleaners to mop up the mess. Besides that, Carmine wore his anger right out there in front. If somebody from Astoria wanted to take you down, the first thing he did was convince you that you were his best buddy. Get you relaxed, get you confident. Then do it, do it while you still had that dumb happy grin on your face. Not Carmine, then. Somebody else in Frank's organization. His kid? Claire? Would Claire do this?

Maybe. Not maybe. Definitely. It was just her style. But she'd need help, and there was nobody in Frank's outfit who would make a move without Frank's okay, especially a move that involved Frank's wife. Again, the week to die and the bloodstains on the rug.

Pike, then?

Pike had the skill groups. Had the motivation. But he had lost the only thing he seemed to care about in that

ATF takedown, his weapons collection. Why let that happen? Unless the weapons were just a front for something else.

Greco, the hotshot U.S. attorney. She had made out like a bandit here, collected a massive seizure, had her name all over CNN, a case she could ride all the way to DC. And she had the contacts, the access to dirty cash, the organization. It was paranoid, maybe, but it was also possible. Here he was, on the run in a stolen U.S. marshals van, he'd crossed two states and so far no one was on his back. Was he lucky or just stupid enough to fall for it? Greco could make that happen. But why?

Why let him run loose? What advantage was there for her? She already had him by the throat, had him on the way to prison, his company assets frozen. Pike was not part of her plans, of that he could be damn certain, so Jack's escape was a surprise to Greco. Had to be. Pike's intervention at the Denny's was the X factor, something she could never have planned for.

Yet here he was, still on the run and still no sign of a tail, of any kind of surveillance. None of this made any sense. There was only one way to work this out. Play it out. But his money was on Greco now. She was the main one.

It had to be her or someone in her organization.

When he reached the George Washington Bridge he worked out the odds that the ATF could pick up his cell phone transmissions and decided he had no choice. He'd have to take the chance. He used the Wal-Mart prepaid cellular phone to call Creek Johnson's private cell phone number. It rang three times.

"Hello."

"Creek."

"Jackson! For Chrissakes! Where the hell are—never mind."

"I'm okay. Are you alone?"

"Not for long. They've got U.S. marshals in the parking lot."

"Where are you?"

"Where would I be? I'm in your office. I got the wagons circled. I called everybody, like you said. But things don't look good. Flannery called. Greco's got a court order to have me taken out by force. She's got her order and she's selling Black Water."

"To who?"

"Whom, Jackson. Whom do you think? The seal-heads we met with at the Frontenac Hotel last Wednesday. Martin Glazer, the two bum boys, Bern and Kuhlman, from Galitzine Sheng and Munro. They tabled an offer this morning. Flannery says it's a done deal. Glazer meets with Greco at her Water Street offices next Monday morning at ten. The escrow takes effect immediately. Soon as you're convicted, or killed, Glazer gets the whole package."

"Christ. Can't Flannery do something?"

"He's not trying real hard. Story on you is you're a dead man if the ATF guys see you. And everybody around Albany thinks you're guilty. Now that you're running, they just see it as proof. Not a judge in the region thinks Greco's anything but Joan of fucking Arc."

"What's the price?"

"Oh, you'll love this. Twenty million for the whole package."

"That's insane. The physical plant alone is worth twice that. The *Agawa Canyon* is worth nine million at the dockside. She's throwing the company away."

"Yeah. But she gets twenty million in seized assets for her department, which bumps up her score in Washington, and Marty Glazer and his seal-heads get a two-hundred-million-dollar company for twenty million. A fire sale. Everybody wins but us. She's even managed to have my share of the assets frozen—get this—pending an IRS review of my finances. She's gutting us both like trout."

"What's happening right now?"

"I'm about to be arrested for obstruction. They're sending sheriffs in to have me . . . *extracted* was the word. Like a tooth."

Jack was silent for a long time. He could hear Creek's heavy breathing and music playing in the background.

"Okay. Creek, you did what you could do. Don't hang in there to get cuffed and slapped around. I need you on the outside."

"Jack . . . on the news. They're saying you killed those two marshals. The ones I met. The woman, that black guy."

"I didn't kill those guards. Earl Pike did."

"Pike! Holy shit. Why?"

"For fun. For payback. Keep your cell on, okay?"

"I will, Jackson. What are you gonna do?"

"I'm going to find out who did this to me."

"And then what?"

"I don't know."

"Okay . . . right. Jackson, I talked to Carmine. He said if you got to call, use his cell number. It's clear for now."

"Can I trust Frank?"

"Can you trust Frank? I think so. But I wouldn't bet on much in the way of help from him. He's dying, and Carmine's not real big on you. He figures you ignore Frank until you need him. Now you're bringing in major heat, and Frank gets caught doing it, he's gonna die in prison. You're nothing to him. Carmine only cares about Frank."

"Yeah. He made that real clear last week."

"Money. Do you need money?"

"I have money. Creek?"

"Yeah?"

"Thanks, Creek. For backing me. For everything."

"Don't thank me, Jackson."

"You tried to warn me. I wish to God I'd listened to you."

"Well . . . I'm no fucking hero here, Jackson."

"No. Just a good friend. If I don't get through this . . ."

"I don't want to hear that shit. I got my cell on. Now go."

Jack clicked off and drove in silence for another mile. Then he dialed the cell number Creek had given him. It rang several times and then the line picked up.

"Hello?"

"Carmine?"

"Jackie. What the fuck you want?"

"Is Frank there?"

"He's asleep. I ain't waking him for you."

Jack heard a voice in the background, a woman's voice. Claire Torinetti's voice, and then the phone made a rustling sound and Claire was on the line.

"Jack, it's Claire. Where are you?"

"I can't tell you that. Is Frank there?"

"Frank had a spell just now. If he gets any worse, we're taking him to the hospital. Jackie, he's so sick."

"I know, Claire. I'm sorry."

"Carmine's worried about Frank helping you."

"I don't blame him. I just need some advice. I don't want to come live there. I need to talk to Carmine."

"Carmine, Jack wants to . . . what?"

Jack heard a muffled exchange, and Claire came back.

"Carmine says he won't talk on the phone. If you want, he'll meet . . . no, he'll send somebody."

"Who?"

"Somebody you know."

"Somebody I know . . . who?"

More hoarse whispering, then she was back.

"He says probably Fabrizio."

"Christ. Fabrizio Senza? The drunk gatekeeper?"

That pushed Claire over the top.

"Jesus Christ, Jack! Who the fuck you want? De Niro? Pacino? We're sending who we can. You got another plan?"

"Where to?"

"Carmine says . . . you remember where you and Frank used to go dig for clams, cook hot dogs?"

"Yeah. I do."

"Go there. Wait."

"Claire, can I trust Carmine?"

Another long breathing silence.

"I think so. Just be there, Jack. I have to go."

And the line was dead. He drove a mile in silence, thinking about his options. He didn't have any. After a while he saw the sign for Jerome Avenue southbound, which would take him to the Major Deegan, which connected with the Bruckner Expressway and led to the Triborough Bridge, which emptied itself into the blocks and parks and streets of Astoria, and finally right onto Astoria Boulevard itself. If he was going home to Astoria, this was his road. If he wasn't going home, he was going to have to trust Carmine.

He passed the Jerome exit at fifty miles an hour and stayed on the Cross Bronx all the way to the Hutchinson River Parkway. From there, he went south through Flushing and Kew Gardens and Jamaica and from there he saw the signs for the Shore Parkway, and that took him to Flatbush Avenue and the toll bridge across Rockaway Inlet.

By four in the morning he was parked in an alleyway between two apartment blocks just off Breezy Point Boulevard, the booming sea in front of him and the rundown tenements of Far Rockaway all around him, the sun cutting a razor-thin red slice out of the blue-black on the far horizon. The air was sharp and stinging. Jack rolled down the windows and let the sea wind flow through the truck. He leaned his head back in the seat, closed his eyes, and listened to the wind rushing and the waves boiling and crashing onto the sand. After a long while he slept.

SUNDAY, JUNE 25

JAY RATS UNIT 552

EASTBOUND I-80

0430 HOURS

The NYPD was going back home. Casey was at the wheel of the black Lincoln, running on cigarettes and black coffee and watching the interstate rolling toward her inside a long white tunnel, rolling up the same road that Jack Vermillion had taken only two hours before them. Nicky was staring out at the oncoming traffic in silence, the headlights playing across his face. Now and then Casey would look over and think about how strong his face was, hard-cut like white marble, and how much she liked to look at it. Yet he was a white man and she hated white men, had always hated white men.

Maybe she didn't hate all white men.

Maybe just the white women.

Or perhaps just the one white woman actually in her life.

Nicky had found an FM radio station and was listening to something the announcer had called the duet from *Lakmé*. Casey had heard the music before, but this was the first time she'd felt the sadness and the beauty of it. This was making her afraid that she was in love with

Nicky Cicero, a situation she had no time for and no desire for. Like that was going to make any difference.

Dexter Zarnas was sound asleep in the backseat, a green plaid blanket pulled up over his chest, his feet propped up against the side window. They were a few miles out of Paterson and heading for Yonkers, heading for the Thunderbird to drop Nicky off, when the MDT—the mobile display terminal—flickered and a line of glowing yellow letters began to roll across the screen, a statewide alert. It was the print version of the same tape-recorded bulletin they had been hearing every half hour since they had left the Blue Mountains Bar and Grill just after midnight.

> *Units of state and local police are asked to continue watch for a white United States marshals prisoner transport van plates unknown direction of travel unknown suspect vehicle being driven by escaped federal prisoner Vermillion, Jack—wanted in connection with the death of two deputy marshals shot during an escape at Beach Haven Pennsylvania 0430 hours yesterday morning. Suspect description male white fifty-three years height six-two weight one-ninety-five hair white worn long and brushed back white mustache description clothing possible olive pants black T-shirt deck shoes suspect armed and dangerous if located approach with extreme caution repeat armed and dangerous approach with extreme caution suspect vehicle last seen Hazleton Pennsylvania at 1730 hours yesterday afternoon. If located notify nearest ATF office immediately or post on NCIC through MAGLOCEN and duty desk. Originating agency ATF Albany NY.*

"Still looking for him," said Nicky.

"Yeah. Think he's gone to ground somewhere?"

"No idea. I were him, I'd ditch that van."

"Then what? He's got ground to cover."

"What do you figure he's going to do?"

Casey glanced over at Nicky, looked back at the road.

"You look beat."

"I am."

"So's he."

"Vermillion?"

"Yeah. He's exhausted. People run one of two ways. They run anywhere, like bugs avoiding the light. Or they run somewhere. I've been thinking about this guy, and I think he's been set up."

"By whom?"

"No idea. But if I had been set up, if I were being played the way I think this guy has been played, I'd run somewhere. Not just anywhere. I'd go straight at the people I thought were fucking with me, and I'd start nailing body parts to a door until somebody talked. Three dead assholes in Hazleton would be happy to tell you he's a guy you can't fuck with and walk away. I think our boy Jack's going home angry."

Nicky was quiet for a long time, and Casey thought he might have fallen asleep. As they flew by the lights of Paterson and the glow of the city appeared above the eastern hills, Nicky spoke again.

"I think you're right. And it explains something else."

"What?"

"How many times have we heard that bulletin?"

"Every half hour."

"All the way from the Pennsylvania state line."

"Yep."

"Pick up anything weird about it?"

Casey laughed.

"Yes. The white van part."

Nicky smiled.

"Yeah. They're still calling it a *white* marshals van. They gotta know damn well that Vermillion painted it green. Something else?"

"Yeah?"

"I think Derry Flynn was playing us. He was getting as much as he was giving. And he was holding something back. You see this switch here, beside the display screen? Know what that is?"

Casey gave him a look. It was a standard item for elite units.

"Of course I do. A global positioning system transponder."

"Yeah."

"So . . . ?"

Nicky raised his eyebrows, waited.

Casey got it right away.

"Dammit! I remember you asked him how come he was so confident about finding Vermillion. He said they had 'resources.' So there's a GPS transponder on the marshals van. Which means they know exactly where he is right now. They've been tracking him in that chopper. And the ATF bulletin is just a screen in case he's picking it up too, on the radio in the marshals van, and if he is, he's thinking they don't know about the van being green."

"Which means he feels safe in it, so he stays with it."

"But Nicky, he's a killer. If they were running a surveillance op on him when he killed those kids in Hazleton, they're legally culpable. If the word got out that the van had a GPS transponder, the fallout from the lawsuits would make the sunsets glorious all over the world. They'd have to be crazy. Greco, her I'd buy, but Derry Flynn didn't strike me as crazy."

"Not if they didn't really think he killed the guards. The fact that they were killed with a Smith points away from Vermillion. And they don't give a rat's ass about the three little pigs he canceled back in Hazleton. They figure nobody's ever going to know about the GPS thing, which means nobody has to know they could have stopped the Hazleton shootings. They had him on a long leash, and things went totally bat shit, but now I'll bet they're up close and personal, with a sniper ready to drill him a third eye at the first flash of green."

They were both quiet for a time. The big car purred and rocked through the turning curves and New York filled up the skyline.

"So Greco's playing him out. She knows he's angry. She's seen for herself that he's dangerous. She's letting him run."

"And they stay right with him in that chopper."

"Yeah."

"To see who he goes after," said Casey. "Does that mean that Greco thinks he's innocent? A guilty guy would just split for Belize."

"I don't think so. I think she thinks he's Italian, and all us guinea goombahs are crazy for revenge, right? So she's standing back to watch him swing a wrecking ball through his friends and family. Then she comes in to kick ass, take names, and corner all the credit."

"Derry said that somebody had called in a tip. That means somebody inside Vermillion's company. Or family."

"That's right. Greco may even know who it was. So she sits back and watches Vermillion go hunt for a snitch to kill."

"Yeah. And while he's out hunting for a snitch to kill?"

"Earl Pike is doing exactly the same thing? I don't think so, Nicky. We talked about that. If Pike was there when Vermillion escaped, why not just kill the guy then? Save himself a lot of work?"

"I can think of a good reason. Other than the cat-and-mouse thing that Flynn was talking about. Think about it."

Casey was silent for a long while. *Lakmé* was getting a bit hysterical in the third act, so Nicky found a jazz station and settled back to let Casey work it through.

"Okay," she said finally. "I see it."

"Yeah?"

"Pike's after more than Jack Vermillion."

"Maybe. But what?"

"Jack on the loose means the ATF out looking for him. They're distracted. Looking elsewhere. In the meantime, Pike's working out a way to get back the only thing that really counts with him."

"His weapons? The collection? That's a theory. But . . . ?"

Casey flashed a sidelong look at Nicky.

"I think I know what's bothering you."

"Yeah? Enlighten me."

"Pike came in on his own."

"Yeah. But he doesn't know what we have on him. The DNA. So I guess he figures he can finesse the Red Hook thing somehow, beat the ATF charges, then he's home free. I ought to feel good."

"And you don't?"

"No. Actually, I feel worried as hell."

"Because Pike knows something we don't?"

"Yes," said Nicky, looking out at the highway. "I think so."

"Yeah," said Casey. "So do I."

Rain drumming on the roof of the marshals van woke Jack out of a dream about black helicopters. He'd been dreaming that he heard a chopper hovering somewhere close, but the sound was elusive, fading and rising, as if it were coming from between the buildings, the direction impossible to guess. The chopper sound changed into the sound of rain on the roof and he sat up, rubbed his face, looked out at the water. Although the clouds were broken and sunshine glittered on the rollers from time to time, the farther sea was blurred with rain and seemed plated with iron, a kind of hammered plain that resembled fish scales. Surfers were rising and falling on the slow rollers, backs hunched over, wet hair hanging down, riding on stubby boards, now and then sliding down the glassy green face of a slow-moving beach break. Jack idly prayed for a big fin in the water, but didn't expect to get one, God being too busy fucking him over to pay attention to the lesser creatures of the sea.

The ocean sounded like a sheet of tin that somebody was rattling. Thunder was out there somewhere, he could hear it in the distance, like enemy artillery. Low clouds heavy with unspilled rain lay across the horizon line, looking like a fence running along the edge of the world. And now Jack could see a single figure trudging along the waterline in the hazy distance.

"Okay, here we go," Jack said, talking to himself, watching as a man came down the shoreline, old and slightly bent, but big, powerful, heavy in the chest and shoulders, wearing a gray plastic raincoat over a dark brown suit, thick black leather shoes. Now and then he'd put a cigarette up to his face and puff at it and shreds of smoke would fly away from him like white birds let out of a cage.

Jack popped the door of the van, stepped out into the warm wind and the feathery rain. He reached back inside and took one of the uniform jackets hanging on a hook, shiny dark brown with a big gold star on the right breast, slipped it on, and walked out onto the beach. The old man saw him, stopped and waited. The beach was long and wide and empty and the whole place had an end-of-the-earth look. The old man was facing out to sea, watching the surfers.

"Hey there," Jack said, coming up slow on his right side. "Mr. Senza. Thank you for coming."

The man did not turn or speak. Fabrizio Senza was a big man, over six-two. Up close like this, Jack could smell his cigarette smoke in the wind off the sea, and a scent coming off him like garlic and wet wool. His hollowed-out cheeks were heavily tanned, dark as hardwood planks, covered with spiky gray hairs, and his trimmed white mustache was large and stained with tobacco. His deep eyes were surrounded by lines and rays of seamed skin, as if he'd been freeze-dried. His shirt had once been white and expensive and his thin black tie was pulled in tight.

"Mr. Senza," he said again, and reached out to touch the man's shoulder. Senza moved it just enough to avoid the contact.

"I know you," he said, still not looking at him. "Little Jackie Vermillion. Used to see you on Ditmars. Your momma was a wonderful woman, lovely like a cypress. Your pop I knew as a man you could talk to. Had the flower truck, I think? Big blue one with the yellow letters. I don't remember so good anymore. Frank says they're both dead now. Everybody's dying these days.

Where's your buddy, what's his name, stupid name? Like a ditch, only smaller?"

"Creek. Creek Johnson."

"Yeah. The party boy. I seen him at Frank's all the time. Booze, women. Always with the Vegas line, always the bookies and the bets and the booze. Not a serious guy. Frank says you're a serious guy. That's why I come. Carmine says to say hello. Hello from Carmine. Will ya look at those mutts out there? What is that, spend all your day out on the board, waiting for a wave to ride? Why ain't they working?"

Jack watched the surfers, waited.

"Okay," the old man said. "Open up your jacket there."

He turned around to face Jack. Four hundred yards away, on the roof of a shabby apartment block called the Sea Heaven Towers, two ATF agents huddled next to the seaward wall of the roof and struggled to keep their gear dry. One was Derry Flynn, wearing a rain slicker over black jeans and a black tee, combat boots, the other a female in full rain gear, late forties, thick around the middle, with a wide Slovak face and small bright black eyes, skin powdery and coarse, by the name of Maya Bergmann, one of the agents who had been there at Red Hook and survived.

"Who is it?" she asked Derry. Derry had his eye up to the scope of a video camera fitted with a directional microwave mike. Maya was handling the Nagra recorder.

"I don't . . . okay, dammit! It's Fabrizio Senza."

"That's Torinetti's gardener, for God's sake."

"Maybe now. Back in the seventies he was a button man for Johnny Papalia, ran the family business in Montreal and Toronto. They called him the Barber because he liked to use a straight razor on guys who pissed him off. He'd take an hour if he had one."

Maya Bergmann peered over the roof at the distant figures standing together on the shoreline.

"So tell me Vermillion's not connected."

"I don't know," said Derry. "When the law itself starts to fuck you over, who you gonna call? Amnesty International? The UN?"

"You still soft on this hapless mutt, Derry?"

"Quiet," he said. "I'm trying to follow this."

The old man stepped in close to Jack and frisked him expertly. Jack had left the Glock in the van, knowing that a pistol would do him no good with Fabrizio Senza and maybe a lot of damage. The old man even raised Jack's cuffs to see if he was trailing antenna wire. A gull shrieked into the thin gray sky and wheeled away over the water. Jack watched it go, keeping very still. Then the man stepped back, shrugged, and let his hands fall to his sides.

"You may be clean. I dunno. Could have some guys taping all this from a truck up there. Got a guy on the roof. Forget it. Who cares? Frank says to check you out. Me, I got no game going. What do I care, you wanna tape me anyway? Frank's a worrier. Lotta things have changed since I was a player."

"You got that right," said Jack. "Last time I had a guy feel me up like that, I was twenty years old and the guy was the doctor at Camp Lejeune."

"I'm being careful. Frank said be careful. Frank says to me, go down there, talk to him. I'm here. Fine. I do what I'm told. I'm a fucking errand boy now. But I know you supposed to be inna slam, and here you are walking around inna jacket widda nice gold star. Why, I don't know. Maybe now you got a federal leash on you, you working against Frank."

"I'm not the only guy standing here," said Jack. "This is Far Rockaway. They know you all over here.

How'd it be, Jerry Vale comes back to Queens and nobody knows him?"

"Nobody *would* know him," said the man, baring his sharp yellow teeth. "It'd be 'Jerry Vale? Who the fuck is Jerry Vale?' "

The man closed his eyes and pulled in a breath, let it go slowly out. Jack saw that his eyes were sunk into dark pouches and rimmed in red. He remembered Fabrizio being drunk that night at Frank's, and Carmine saying something about a dead child.

"Carmine said you lost somebody. A relative?"

The old man rocked as if buffeted by a wind off the sea, his craggy face hardening. He looked at Jack as if Jack had struck him.

"You don't mind, we don't speak of her. I don't like to think about it. Nothing can be done. Let's stick to the business."

"I'm sorry. I apologize. I saw you at Frank's last week, I thought you were in Sicily. Everybody said you had gone home."

"Hah. Where you think a guy like me is gonna go? I went up to the north for a while, shit, Milan's just like Pittsburgh, fulla Swiss and Krauts, and the weather's worse than here. I'm old, I need sunshine. I got some friends in Taormina, nice view of Etna in the morning, sun's on it from out of the Aegean Sea there."

"I know it," said Jack, smiling at the memory. "My father was from Catania. I was back there just last year. Why'd you leave a beautiful place like that?"

"You hear things. Even *il papa* was shooting off his Polack mouth about our business. Crazy old prick. Why we let some Polack get the job instead of one of our own, that's all screwed up there, hah? Old ways are changing. People start acting funny around you, stop talking when you come in the room. I figured I should go."

"For your health, Zio?" said Jack, asking politely,

but maybe teasing a little. Fabrizio Senza had been caught up in the federal RICO actions of the late seventies, busted for tax evasion. He pulled his time and never testified about anything. But the Mafia didn't like to take chances. Nothing personal, but we need you to be dead now, *paisano*. The old man didn't smile back and seemed to have decided to stop talking for a while.

"So . . . how long you been back, then?"

Another long silence. The gull came back from the sea with something dead hanging from its beak. Other gulls appeared out of nowhere and tried to take it away. They cawed and screeched in the voices of schoolyard children, and then the whole flock soared away inland and the silence came back down.

Eventually the man spoke.

"I dunno . . . six years, maybe. What's it to you? You was gonna rat me out to the press, you'da showed up with the New York One truck. So, what is it? You in a jam. What do you want from Frank?"

"You know I have some trouble. With the feds?"

"The feds," growled the old man, suddenly angry. "Forget about it. Those mutts couldn't throw a cluster-fuck in a steambath."

Stung, Jack's temper flared.

"With respect, Zio, they did a job on you."

The old man blew out his cheeks and went for another cigarette. His hands were bumpy and knotted like lumps of oak burl. A wedding ring, thin and pitted and bent, was almost buried in the arthritis that had swollen around his knuckles and in his fingers.

"*Stati di grazi, io.* I said nothing, ratted out nobody. Took my time and ate it cold in solitary. Still the Papalia family sent a guy after me, a *pezzo novante* nigger with a shank. I cut his *pezzo* off and flushed it downa crapper, him lying there on the floor, bleeding and squealing, beggin' me don't do it. Hah! I'm supposed to worry about the guys running things now? Alla old-timers, the serious men, they're gone. Big Paulie was the last of the good ones, and that fashion model had him whacked. Now what? The Jews, the Russkies, the blacks? I saw that, I figured, *salud,* there goes the neighborhood. And I was right too. That mook Gravano calls himself Sammy the Bull—nobody else ever called him that—I hear he has a book out. Alla 'bout the hard guys he personally whacked. What is that? My day, you *did* things, you didn't *talk* about it. I'm gonna hide out from a bunch of celebrity mutts like that? From TV stars? Let them come find me. I am in my *stagione morta* and I am not afraid. What am I now? Fucking gate boy. Frank's dying. Everything is different now. Enough of this. I'm getting wet here. You talk to me, your situation, what Frank's supposed to do about it."

The old man fell silent, waited for Jack's answer. There was an air about him of livestock, of animal calm. Jack nodded once, cupped his hands in front of his mouth and blew into them, rubbing them.

"Here it comes," said Derry Flynn, up on the roof of the Sea Heaven Towers. Maya Bergmann shivered in the wind and pulled her collar up against the dripping rain.

Jack looked out to sea, thinking about Fabrizio's question. What was Frank supposed to do? What was fair to expect?

"You know Frank's dealership?"

"Yeah. Little toy cars for little toy boys."

"Who runs it now?"

"Whaddya mean? Frank runs it."

"I mean the day-to-day, now Frank is sick."

"Frank isn't sick, Jackie. Frank is dying. His kid runs it. Tony. The blowfish, the coke boy."

"Okay. Tony runs the day-to-day, but it's still Frank's shop. Would Frank know if something hinky was going on in the detailing area? Where they clean up the cars for people?"

"I don't know. Why would he? I been there. It's a big shop. Whaddya mean by hinky?"

"I had a car in there last Wednesday. A black Shelby Cobra. It was in for detailing. It's a rare car. Only twenty in the world. I got busted for trying to ship a stolen one down the Hudson. The feds got a tip, they cracked the container. Found the Cobra, also found a trunk full of drug money from Canada. My prints were all over the car, inside and out. Somebody switched the cars on me. Set me up."

"Canada? What? You mean like Montreal?"

"Yeah. Like Montreal. Why?"

Fabrizio was silent. He turned and looked at the rows and blocks of wooden houses, the shabby apartment towers that studded the flat sweep of the island. The wind whipped at his coat collar and his thin white hair fluttered against his shiny scalp. His eyes were squinted almost shut and his mouth was a thin hard line. He looked at Jack and then turned to face the ocean. The surfers were sliding down a wall of green water. The sun was breaking through and shafts of light were shimmering through the clouds. A surfer arced through a patch of sunlight, his wet suit shining with yellow fire.

"Jackie, you need to watch these kids," said Fabrizio.

"Why?"

"You turn around now, kid. Watch these mooks."

They both turned to face the sea. Senza pulled out a little notebook, scratched out some words, held it up so Jack could see it.

YOU GOT A TAIL
YOU GOT CAMERAS ON YOU RIGHT NOW
YOU GOT MIKES ON YOU
SHUT UP

Jack read the note. He wasted no time trying to convince himself that Senza was wrong. It made sense. It was the only thing that did. He hadn't been running at all. He'd been let loose, see where he goes. Now he was bringing the trouble all the way back home.

Up on the roof, Flynn and Bergmann were getting nervous.

"Okay. Now they've turned away. I can't get anything but the damn wave noise."

Maya adjusted a dial.

"That better?"

"No. It just makes the hissing louder."

He looked through the telephoto lens. He saw the two men standing side by side, looking out at some kids surfing. Out on the horizon, the sunlight was a wavering screen of shining silk curtains.

"What are they doing?" asked Bergmann.

"I don't know. Dammit. I can't get anything."

Down on the shore, Jack was watching Senza write on his notepaper. Senza's hand was knotted and he wrote with effort.

SAY SOMETHING TO END THIS
GET IN THE TRUCK
GO TO CONEY AND TAKE THE GOWANUS
WAIT FOR A CALL ON YOUR CELL PHONE

Jack read the words, nodded once. He started to walk away, but Senza put out a hand, stopped him.

"Hey, Jackie, you know Montreal? You ever been there?"

"No. Not in a long time."

"Good food. Great broads. I just come back from there."

Jack said nothing. He watched Fabrizio's hands.

"Yeah, I know a guy, goes alla time. Always back and forth. This time he takes me. He needs a driver. For the cars. You follow?"

Jack waited. The wind ruffled the tops of the waves, making the white tips glitter in the sun like shark's teeth. Fabrizio was writing one last word. The pen moved across the lined page like the needle on a cardiograph, shaky and spiking, the old man's fingers knotted as tree roots, the little blue plastic pen tiny in his hand.

CREEK

SUNDAY, JUNE 25

U.S. ATTORNEY'S OFFICE

WATER STREET

LOWER MANHATTAN

1200 HOURS

Earl Pike came into the U.S. attorney's office alone. Valeriana Greco was waiting for him, along with several agents of the ATF. Derry Flynn and Maya Bergmann were still on the Jack Vermillion surveillance. Pike walked into the spacious mahogany-paneled office wearing a navy-blue pinstripe suit by Armani over a sapphire-blue shirt and a sky-blue silk tie held in place with a gold pin through the collar points. He wore shiny black brogues and had a ring on the third finger of his right hand with the insignia of West Point in raised enamel on the bright yellow gold. Greco watched him move across the thick Persian rug from behind a desk the size of Kansas. She was wearing a gray suit and a black silk blouse. Behind her on the wall was a massive carved wooden crest, the eagle of the Department of

Justice. A wide window opened onto a view of Water Street, the Brooklyn Bridge, and the East River. The other agents, all male, all packed with muscle, all young and angry and wired to the teeth, stirred and tensed as Pike reached the desk and put out a hand. Greco, smiling sweetly, shook it.

"Thank you for coming in, Mr. Pike. We've been looking forward to seeing you. Please have a chair. Ben, can you run and get us some fresh coffee? Will coffee be all right, or would you like tea?"

"Coffee would be wonderful, Ms. Greco."

She nodded at a young man with black curly hair, who jogged out of the room and was back in seconds with a silver tray and a full sterling coffee service. Greco poured out two cups, handed one to Earl Pike, who took it with a gracious comment and sat back, erect in the heavy damask chair, the coffee cup balanced on one knee. Greco took her place and there was a generator hum of power and silence as she leaned forward over the desk.

"You're sure you don't want a lawyer present?"

"Am I about to be charged?"

"You're aware of the interception of your shipment?"

"I am. My colleagues at CCS were very diligent. I got the word last night and flew straight in."

"Flew? From where?"

"Sioux Falls. I've been out there on a job."

"Sioux Falls? Really? There's no record on any major carrier that indicates you were a passenger on any domestic flight in the last three days. Last Friday night there was an indication that you were on a private jet out of LaGuardia. You are said to have left at midnight. And you are said to have gone to Harrisburg and not Sioux Falls. The time frame is rather important, since, as you are no doubt aware, there was a confrontation at Red Hook that same night during which several of my people were taken down by a very skilled sniper. The weapon used was a Barrett Fifty. You know this weapon?"

"Of course. I'm fully checked out on the M-eighty-two-A-one. So are thousands of other ex-army shooters. I read about Red Hook. Terrible thing. I've been under fire myself. Such a senseless tragedy."

"Well, you'd know about such things. We understand from your army records that you yourself are a fully qualified military sniper, that you spent several years doing just that kind of thing for the Special Operations forces in places like Guatemala, Ecuador, the Middle East, the Gulf War. You earned a Bronze Star for what you did in some place called Co Roc, although the record isn't complete."

"No, it isn't. Never will be. But I wasn't at Red Hook. Sorry."

"But then we have this discrepancy. As I have pointed out, the clerk at LaGuardia said you had taken a midnight flight to Harrisburg. Not Sioux Falls. This presents us with a conundrum."

"And I think I can resolve it for you."

"Really? I'm so pleased for you. This is so exciting for us."

"I took a Lear to Harrisburg, South Dakota. Not Harrisburg, Pennsylvania."

There was a long, stunned silence.

Greco showed her teeth.

"You're being clever, Mr. Pike. I don't recommend it."

"Really? You should try it yourself. For example, when one of your agents here pushes a female clerk around at the Slipstream desk at LaGuardia, makes a lot of ugly threats, and generally acts like a Gestapo thug, and the wretched clerk tells your agent where the plane went—under duress—and the answer is Harrisburg and nothing more, then the *clever* thing to do would be for that young ATF agent to determine which Harrisburg the girl was talking about."

"The clerk said Harrisburg, Pennsylvania, Mr. Pike."

"I think not. The video camera at the Slipstream flight desk caught the whole incident. The tape is at my lawyer's office. The clerk simply said Harrisburg. Your agent then smacked the desktop with his fist, said, 'Was that so hard?' and as he stalked out of the office the audio recorded his last words. They were 'stupid cunt.' "

"This agent had just lost three men to a sniper. I think we can cut the man a little slack. And we looked into Slipstream Jetways, Mr. Pike. The owner is a man named D'Arcy Pruitt. Mr. Pruitt is also a full partner at Crisis Control Systems. This seems convenient, to say the least."

"D'Arcy Pruitt is an old friend from the army. And a business partner. Why the hell wouldn't I use his charter service?"

"And this work you claim you were doing in South Dakota. I take it you were working alone?"

"No. I had two men with me."

"From CCS, I take it?"

"Yes."

"And they'll verify your presence in South Dakota, will they?"

"If you ask them. Please do."

"You can count on it. And when we crack them open, they'll be charged and indicted right next to you."

"Lady, the brutal fact is I really was in Harrisburg and I have people who'll back me on that. I'm sorry about your agents. From what I can gather, this Vermillion person is some sort of Mafia figure. You want to look for your sniper, start with them. They're all over the shipping business. Maybe you stumbled in on something and got your guys killed for it. You forgot to ask which Harrisburg. You got fixated on the wrong man. You have several flunkies here. Be a leader. Burn one and move on."

Greco could not restrain herself from sending a death ray at one of the ATF men, who received it with a stony face.

She then recovered, smiled thinly at Pike.

"And the purpose of your trip?"

Pike shook his head.

"Can't tell you. Client confidence."

"But you were unable to respond to our calls?"

"I didn't get them. Harrisburg is right on the Iowa border. It's quite rural. There's no cell phone service in that region. I was pretty involved. My client is a large landholder in that area. We were trying to be discreet. Now I would like to ask you a question, Ms. Greco."

"Certainly."

"What is the status of my collection right now?"

"Kiss it good-bye, Mr. Pike. It has been seized."

"Has it been destroyed?"

"Not yet. But it will be. You broke the law, Mr. Pike."

"I do not admit that I broke the law."

"You attempted to ship prohibited weapons. That's a felony. Weapons specifically banned under federal legislation of 1994."

"I can—and will—make the argument that those weapons constituted part of a collection with great historical value and therefore were exempt from that statute."

"There's no record of your making such an application for this collection. You attempted to move illegal weapons out of the country and sell them to a foreign national. A military officer in Mexico."

"I filed an application for exemption with the ATF

last year. I have been waiting patiently for a decision ever since. In the meantime I had every reason to believe that my collection had not been rendered illegal since, according to articles of the firearms act, a collection for which an exemption application has been filed cannot be the subject of a seizure operation until the application has been adjudicated."

"You claim you made this application . . . when?"

Pike handed her a sheet of triplicate paper.

"Here's my receipt. There's the date."

She plucked it out of his hand, tossed it to one of the ATF people, who left the room in a hurry.

"We'll confirm that. I still maintain that an attempt to ship weapons—illegal or not—without a complete disclosure to the ATF is a serious criminal offense."

"Yes, I fully agree. You are absolutely correct."

"You do? We are?"

"Without a shadow of doubt. I gather you have already arrested the man. And then I understand you let him get away. Unfortunately, after he killed two guards, I hear."

"You're talking about Jack Vermillion?"

"I am. He was the shipper of record. The disclosure responsibility lies with him. I informed him of the contents of that container, and I assumed that he would make all the proper filings. That's his business, isn't it? That's what Black Water Transit does."

Greco's makeup was being sorely tested by this.

"You colluded with Mr. Vermillion to disguise—"

"I colluded? You have surveillance tapes? Recordings? The usual grainy telephoto shots you people love to take?"

"We have the testimony of—"

"My word against his. And his word, I understand, is the word of a dealer in stolen cars, a money-laundering criminal. A Mafia-connected criminal. You said as much yourself. I watched your press conference in a roadhouse yesterday. You were quite persuasive. And this is the witness you'll bring to court to testify against me?"

Greco's makeup failed at this point. A sheen of moisture had appeared on her porcelain upper lip. The door opened up and an ATF agent jogged back in with a printout, which he placed on the desk in front of Greco. He backed away quickly while Greco read the sheet.

"Bad news, Ms. Greco?"

"It seems you did file an application to have your collection granted a historical exemption. At least the record suggests it."

"The record suggests? It's in your own computer."

"The process is . . . these records may have been altered. I—"

"Okay. Now I'm faking records inside the ATF database. You're sounding a little desperate, lady. I think that's all the time I have to waste with you people right now, Ms. Greco. Is there anything more? Shall I be off? Shall I . . . tarry?"

Pike's smile was blade-thin, his tone full of contempt.

"Tarry?" said Greco. "No. You needn't . . . tarry."

Pike got up, brushed the creases of his trousers, straightened his suit jacket, and stood a moment, looking around the room.

"This is your office, Ms. Greco? Very impressive. I thought you were based in Albany, in the federal courts up there."

"No. I've been . . . transferred. I'm now on staff in New York."

Pike gave her a direct look, his eyes remote and cold.

"Really. A promotion? Very nice. What a wonderful view."

"Thank you. You can go. But this matter is far from over, Mr. Pike. We'll be talking to your friends at CCS. I'll ask you not to leave the state."

"I wouldn't dream of it. I'll be nearby, Ms. Greco. You may depend upon it. In the meantime, please take good care of my collection. I know I can trust you to keep it safe. I expect it to be returned to me very shortly. I want you to know, however, that should any clerk in your office allow a single item to be damaged, or lost, or 'extracted from source for training purposes' . . . if the collection is in any way interfered with, I am going to view such an event as a deliberate act on your part—an act of cold malice—and I will hold you responsible. Professionally. Personally."

"Oooh, not a lawsuit," she said. "I'm all aquiver. Take your best shot, Mr. Pike. We'll see each other again."

Pike smiled broadly at that.

"My best shot? Very droll. You all have a great day."

GOWANUS EXPRESSWAY WESTBOUND
BROOKLYN
1215 HOURS

Derry Flynn and Maya Bergmann were airborne again in the black ATF chopper, Flynn at the controls, Bergmann watching the big green van as it rolled westbound along the Gowanus, part of a slow-moving stream of trucks and cabs and vans. The sun had broken through the cloud cover and the glare off the traffic a thousand feet below was hurting her eyes. Flynn was keeping an eye out for other aircraft and following the gray concrete ribbon of the parkway about a mile back from the van.

They had two cars laying ~~~ third vehicle, a Verizon truck, ~~~ Flynn was keeping the units advise ~~~ tored the progress of the green van. ~~~ the towers of lower Manhattan floated ~~~ and the East River was the color of spilled ~~~ thunder of the chopper's blades was givin~~~ ya a headache.

"Why don't we just scoop this prick?" she said, fighting to keep the binoculars trained on the target.

"He's already met with one of Torinetti's people. Just like we figured. He'll do it again. Now he's moving. See that collection of buildings up there, where the Brooklyn-Battery Tunnel starts? That's Red Hook. This all started there. Maybe he's going back. Let's just hang back and see what he's up to, okay?"

The stream of traffic on the Gowanus was thickening as it approached the jam around the tunnel entrance. As they watched, the green van slowed and edged toward an exit ramp.

"Okay, units. He's taking the BQE. I think he's going to Red Hook Container Terminal. Everybody stay clear. Don't get burned. We have the transponder, so we're covered."

Now the van was within a few yards of the exit ramp onto the Brooklyn-Queens Expressway. For a Sunday morning, the traffic was brutal, a river of cars and trucks, bumper to bumper and stop-and-go. The first weekend of the summer, and the town was already choking on tourism. They could see the Verizon truck a few cars behind the van. Flynn pressed his transmit button.

"Delta, you're too close."

"*Baker, I don't want to lose him. The traffic's piling up here.*"

"I know. Remember, we're on him too."

"*Ten-four, Baker.*"

van had come to a full stop now, and cars
ing up behind it. A section of road opened up in
of the van.

"He's thinking it over," said Maya.

"Yeah. Be ready."

The van moved out, passed by the turnoff to the
BQE, and stayed on the Gowanus.

"Okay, all units, cancel Red Hook. Target is taking
the Brooklyn-Battery. Delta, move back. Charlie and
Alpha, come up on him. He goes down the tunnel, you
lose us, so stay close. We're gonna pick him up when he
comes out the other end."

"*Ten-four, Baker, Charlie out.*"

"*This is Delta, affirmative. Pulling back.*"

"*Alpha moving up. Ten-four.*"

"I don't like tunnels," said Maya, leaning back in the
passenger seat and rubbing her face. "Shit happens in
tunnels."

"We have three units on him and a transponder in
the vehicle. Even if we lose visual, we have him on the
GPS. Take a red one."

The chopper gained altitude as Flynn increased the
collective. They watched as the green van inched up to
the tollbooth and stopped.

"*Alpha here. He's paying the toll. It's him. I got a visual.*"

"Roger that, Alpha."

"There he goes," said Maya. "I wish the hell we had
a cell phone trace on him. Why don't we?"

"Maya, a Blackbird trace costs thousands of dollars.
We already have a GPS transponder in the truck."

"I got a bad feeling, Derry."

"Well, lighten up, Maya. Okay?"

The green van moved away from the tollbooth and
disappeared into the twin black squares of the tunnel entrance. They hovered as the Alpha unit, a white Lumina,

moved up to the toll plaza and stopped. The other two units, the Verizon truck and a green Ford Windstar, were visible in the line several cars back. It was a choke point, but they still had the transponder signal, although it was fainter now and fading even more as the van moved under the river and the concrete tunnel interfered with the signal.

"Baker, this is Alpha. We got a problem."

"Alpha, this is Baker. What is it?"

"They're not letting any more cars in right now."

"Why?"

"Wait one . . ."

"I told you," said Maya.

"Baker, they say they got an MVA in the tunnel. Stalled vehicle."

"I told you," said Maya again.

"So tin the guy and go!"

"They got the barrier down. They say nobody's going in until the jam is cleared up here. They say I can shove the tin up my ass."

"Alpha, go in on foot. Go now!"

"Roger that!"

They watched from five hundred feet as the two ATF agents jumped out of the Lumina and jogged down into the tunnel. Both men had their weapons out.

"Cowboys," snorted Maya.

"Delta and Charlie, you copy this?"

"Ten-four, Baker."

"Delta, you assist Alpha on foot. Charlie, hold your position. We're going to the Battery and cover that exit. People, move it!"

"Roger that, Baker."

Flynn increased the collective and pushed the cyclic forward and the chopper rose up in a hammering wind and soared out across the East River. The trees of Governor's Island were swaying in a wind off the Verrazano

Narrows and boats were cutting white lacy patterns in the blue-gray plain of the upper bay. Flynn brought the chopper in low around the bottom arc of the Battery, took it up to five hundred feet, flared out, and hovered over the exit ramps where they came up out of the greenbelt of Battery Park.

"What if he takes the FDR tunnel?"

"We'll see him. We'll follow him. You're in a real negative frame of mind today, Maya."

Several minutes passed with Flynn fighting the controls, the chopper rocking in the crosswinds off the bay and the Venturi effect of the tall buildings all around them. He was listening for the transponder signal. There it was. It was growing stronger. Thirty seconds later they both watched as the green van popped out of the tunnel and rolled up along Greenwich.

"Okay, units. This is Baker. I have him. He's on Greenwich . . . he's turning right onto Rector . . . he's going to Broadway. Okay, he's stopped in traffic at Broadway and Rector. I have the transponder signal. He's five by five. Copy?"

"This is Charlie. Delta and Alpha are still in the tunnel. I can't raise them. Do I hold here?"

"You have no choice. I'll stay with the van. You hold and wait for Delta and Alpha. Copy?"

"Ten-four, Baker."

"Derry, that van's not moving," said Maya.

Flynn looked down at the van. It was stopped in the middle of Rector. Traffic was building up behind it.

"What's he doing?" asked Maya.

"I don't know."

"I got a bad feeling, Derry. Go down."

"This is Wall Street. Look at these buildings. I can't go down. The currents are nasty. I'll wreck the chopper. Kill people."

"Something's wrong. He's not moving at all."

Now the traffic behind the green van was stopped up completely. People were getting out of their vehicles. Flynn saw a police car with *NYPD B 1* on the roof roll up the sidewalk and approach the vehicle.

"Maya, get the citywide for the NYPD! Warn them."

Two police officers were getting out of the patrol car and walking toward the side doors of the green van.

"Central, this is an air unit of the ATF. We're at Broadway and Rector. Your patrol unit Boy One is approaching a green van. Suspect inside is armed and dangerous."

"Identify yourself."

"This is Special Agent Maya Bergmann of the ATF. You better get on to your patrol unit now!"

"One Boy, K?"

One of the two police officers stopped. Then the other one. They were less than ten feet from the door of the truck. Flynn and Bergmann watched as he keyed his shoulder mike. Then they heard his voice.

"One Boy, Central."

"One Boy, we have an air unit of the ATF on scene."

The cop looked up. They saw his white face in the crowd and the blue blur of his jacket.

"I see them, Central."

Maya cut into the transmission.

"Officer, this is Special Agent Maya Bergmann of the ATF. The green van you're approaching is under our surveillance. Suspect is armed and dangerous. Do not approach the suspect. Repeat, do not approach. This is a federal operation. Do not contact the suspect."

"Do not contact? He's sitting in the fucking traffic, Agent Bergmann. People are gonna lynch him. I gotta approach."

"Do you have visual contact?"

"I do. Guy's sitting right in the driver's seat. Wearing a marshals jacket with a gold star. Grinning at me."

The police officer had his gun out now and his partner had moved into a hostile-contact position at the left of the van. Both guns were trained on the doors of the green van. Crowds of people had gathered. The operation was blown.

"What the hell," said Flynn. "Let them take him."

"Out?"

"No. Into custody. This is getting too hairy."

"One Boy, this is the ATF."

"Not now, ATF. One Boy, this is Central. Report status."

"Report status, Central. Ten-four. Wait one."

Flynn moved the chopper in as low as he could manage, threading it down between the glass towers of Wall Street. The trees and the grasses of Battery Park were flattened and silvery-looking and the dust of the streets was coming up in clouds. The two NYPD officers approached the side doors of the vehicle with their guns out. There was a rush at the driver's door, the cop ripped it open, stuck his weapon inside. The other cop came through the passenger door at the same time. The van rocked, and then the first cop reemerged, dragging a white-haired man in a brown marshals jacket.

The man was thrown to the ground and cuffed. The crowd around the scene looked to be either cheering the cops on or booing them. With New Yorkers, it could go either way. The cop making the arrest got off the suspect and keyed his mike.

"Central, get us a detox unit. We got a street person here."

Maya Bergmann cut in.

"One Boy, this is the air unit. Say again?"

The cop looked up at them, holding his cap on tight.

"This the mutt you looking for, ATF?"

"We can't ID him from here."

"Well, I can. His name is Trendy Freddy. He lives

in the Brooklyn-Battery Tunnel. He's pissed as a newt. Also he stinks."

"You know the suspect?"

"I do. He's always coming up outta the Brooklyn-Battery. Everybody knows him around here. He has a roost in one of the maintenance rooms. He says some guy in the tunnel just stopped the van next to his bunkie, tossed him the keys, and got into another car. What's that, Freddy?"

They watched as the cop leaned down to speak with the man on the ground. He straightened up again and looked up at them.

"He says it was a very nice car. A blue one. He hopes that helps you out. Also, he wants to take the van to Florida. He always wanted to go to Florida. So, whaddya say, ATF? Can he keep the van?"

"Can he describe the man who gave him the keys?"

"Lady, Freddy can't describe his thumbs. Looks to us like you been had. Freddy says the guy got into a blue car. So go look for it. Now please get that chopper the hell out of my face."

WATER STREET AT PECK

LOWER MANHATTAN

1300 HOURS

Casey and Nicky were sitting in a navy-blue Caprice, waiting for Earl Pike to come out of the U.S. attorney's office on Water Street, Casey still in the black jeans, boots, and black tee she'd been wearing the day before, Nicky in a two-piece blue suit, white shirt, plaid tie. Dexter, also dressed for work, was standing six, on foot, a half-block down, in case Pike bolted. They could see him reading a paper and watching the girls go by.

A hot wind was whipping up scraps of paper and trash and sending it in little whirlpools through the tiny alleys of lower Manhattan. Casey looked up. It was like being parked at the bottom of the Grand Canyon. The tightly packed stone and steel buildings pressing in all around them, the narrow lanes, the offices barely far enough apart to move a car, the bumpy cobblestone streets, thousands of Sunday tourists jammed into one square mile.

Casey had the police radio on and tuned in to the Manhattan frequencies. They'd heard the entire exchange between the First Precinct patrolman and Maya Bergmann in the ATF chopper. Nicky had even rolled the window down to see if he could hear the chopper over by Battery Park, but the city was a waterfall of white noise. He could perhaps dimly hear—or rather feel—the faint drumbeat of a helicopter above the muted roar and booming rush of the city.

"Okay, what'd you make of that?"

Casey was watching the door to the building as if the answer to all of life's questions were going to materialize in the glass. She answered Nicky without looking away.

"I'd say Jack Vermillion didn't do that alone."

"Brilliant. You should be a cop."

"I've considered it."

"Neat stunt, hah?"

"Yeah. Thrilling. The guy's a genius. Where the hell is Pike?"

"How long you think he'll be?"

"If they don't bust him right there?"

"Casey, they're not gonna bust him. He'll be out."

"I hope so—"

Casey's pager bonged twice. She took it off her belt.

"Switch to five, Nicky. Vince is calling us."

"Okay."

He set the radio selector switch to channel five and Casey picked up the handset.

"Five-one-one, K?"

"Casey, that you?"

"Boss."

"What's your twenty?"

"We're in the unit, parked at Water and Peck."

"Pike come down yet?"

"Negative, boss."

"Okay. Dexter ready on the street?"

"Yes, boss. We have him on visual. He's ready."

"I just heard from the ATF. He's walking. They can't break his alibi. They can't hold him. He'll be down on the street any minute now. They're not going to put a tail on him because I told them you're gonna scoop him as soon as he shows. Don't blow this. You nail him as soon as he comes out. You want any backup? We can have a patrol unit from the Fifth to assist."

"He's not Godzilla. There are three of us."

"Okay. Oh yeah. Peekskill PD called. About your briefcase? A PW named Moira Stokovich?"

Casey's fingers tightened around the radio but she kept her voice calm. She tried to keep her eyes on the door across the street but her vision was blurred and the blood was pounding in her throat.

"Great. That's super. What'd she say?"

"Since it was a cop's briefcase got stolen, they decided to do some footwork on it. They canvassed the whole area around the hospital. Even put up notices describing it. It was brown, steel-reinforced, had a PBA sticker on it. Right? The ugly sucker you brought with you from the Two Five?"

"Yes. That's the one."

"Stokovich says a guy comes into their duty desk this morning early. Says he saw the flyer on a pole. Turns out

he owns a Mail Boxes Etc. about a block from the hospital. He says a citizen came in with it about two o'clock on Friday afternoon, paid cash to have it packaged and held for delivery. Sounds pretty dicey. That's why she called me."

"Did Stokovich go there, get the package?"

"No. That's why I'm calling you. Wasn't it at your place?"

"My house?"

"Yeah. I figure the citizen opened your case, looked inside. You must have had something there with your home address on it. Apartment Five-B. Temple Court. Prospect Park. That right?"

"Yeah. That's right. My home address. Okay."

"You haven't got it yet?"

"No. Why?"

"You should. The citizen called Mail Boxes back last night, around nine o'clock, while you were out in Pennsylvania. Asked them to send it right away. Immediately. Which they did. The courier driver picked it up at nine-fifteen last night. Peekskill is only forty miles from your door. It should have been there when you got home."

Water Street wheeled and Casey's throat went tight and her mouth dried up. Dexter had dropped them both off at the Thunderbird in Yonkers and taken the Lincoln in to the Jay Rats garage at Albee Square. She had called her mother from Nicky's hotel room. Her mother hadn't said anything about a courier delivery.

"I . . . Mom didn't . . . she was asleep when I got home."

"Well, she signed for it. The driver got her signature. Elena Spandau. Right on the waybill. You didn't see it in the hall?"

"No. But she might have put it in a closet or something."

"Stokovich wants to hear back from us. Should I call her?"

"Call her?"

"Yeah. Stokovich is getting a description of this active little Boy Scout from the Mail Boxes guy."

"Right. I have her card. I'll call her when we're through here."

"Ten-four, Casey. Call me as soon as you have Pike in the car. And Casey, be real careful around him. All of you."

"We will, Vince. Ten-four."

Casey looked as if she was about to pass out. Nicky reached out and held her by the shoulder.

"Casey, you want to take the unit? I'll get a patrol unit from the Fifth to back us up here. Dexter and I can do this without you."

"No. Do you have a cell with you?"

"Yeah. Here."

Casey took the phone and dialed her home number. She was still watching the glass door, but her heart was in another place. The line rang once. Twice. Three times. Earl Pike walked out onto Water Street, stopped to look for a cab. Dexter came on point, pushed himself away from the wall, opened his suit jacket. The line was still ringing. Four. Five. Nicky was out of the Caprice now, and Casey followed him, still holding the cell phone. Six. Seven. Eight. Pike saw them all coming. He tensed and looked as if he was about to run, then stopped. Nicky had his badge out and his suit jacket open, his right hand on the butt of his service piece. Nine rings. Ten rings. Pike was smiling at them. Eleven rings. No one was answering the phone. Twelve rings. Dexter was calling out to Pike now.

Casey hit the off button and came after them.

She had her own piece out and down by her leg. Nicky was ten feet in front of her, everything in his body radiating tension. Pike looked calm, even a little amused, his arms raised slightly, his palms up. Dexter was five feet away and coming in fast. Casey tried to focus but her head was spinning and all she could think about was what her mother was doing right this minute.

"Earl Pike," said Nicky in a carrying voice, loud enough to make people in the street stop and turn. Nicky and Dexter reached Pike at the same time, stepped hard into the man, and shoved him up against the stone wall of the building so hard he bounced off once. Dexter stepped back and held out his Smith while Nicky did a quick frisk, leaning in close to Pike and growling in his ear.

"Earl Pike, you're under arrest for the murders of Julia Maria Gianetto and Donald Albert Condotti on the night of June twenty-first, in the vicinity of Blue Stores. You have the right to remain silent."

Nicky had his cuffs out now, Dexter and Casey standing a little away, both of them watching Pike's hands.

"You have the right to an attorney. If you cannot afford an attorney, one will be appointed for you."

Pike was cuffed up, hands behind his back, and Nicky was turning him toward the Caprice. Dexter was holding the backseat door open. People were staring at them up and down the street. Pike offered no resistance at all. Nicky held him by the cuff chain and Dexter had a grip on Pike's upper biceps.

Pike smiled at Casey as he reached the rear door.

"Officer Spandau. You're very black today."

Nicky shoved him hard. Pike staggered into the side of the car and recovered, twisted around, and spoke directly into Nicky's face.

"We'll have to go a round, you and I. See how you do."

Nicky put his hand on Pike's blue shirt, shoved him

backward and into the car. He leaned down, pushed Pike's legs free of the door.

"Your fight career just ended, hammerhead."

Nicky slammed the door so hard the car rocked and the echo banged around the narrow street, slamming from wall to wall and then fading into the general rushing noise of New York. Dexter and Casey looked at each other. It was over. They had Pike.

"Damn," said Dexter. "That felt so good."

Nicky tried to smile but couldn't find one. It took them another three hours to get Pike through Central Booking and into an interview room. Casey called her mother every chance she could, but she was part of the arresting team and her reports had to be typed and filed right on the spot. If she left before the process was complete, Pike's lawyers could make mileage out of her absence later. She had to stay.

Pike sat in the chair in the interview room with his arms folded across his chest and a polite but disinterested smile on his face. Through the window he could see Casey on the cell phone, her face tight and drained. He imagined her listening to the line ringing and ringing and ringing. He imagined how unpleasant it would be. He watched then as the two male cops stood together in the hallway, Nicky Cicero and the biker-looking cop named Dexter Zarnas. He could not hear what they were talking about, but he could speculate, and the possibilities amused him very much.

Pike's guess was a good one.

Out in the hall, Nicky was talking about Casey Spandau.

"Dexter, Casey needs to do something. Can you and I run this mutt on our own?"

"She's part of the package. She knows this mutt. I'd like her to do the talking. I think she knows how to get under his skin."

"Dexter, Casey has a . . . domestic thing. She needs to go home. I mean, she really needs to go home. Now."

Dexter knew nothing about Casey's home life, but he could tell from the intensity in Nicky's voice that whatever it was, it was bad.

"What is it, Nicky?"

"Dexter, she can't say. It's personal."

Dexter glanced across the hall to where Casey was standing, holding a cell phone, looking down at the wooden flooring.

"She got her paperwork in?"

"All done. Me too."

Dexter thought it over, watching Casey.

"Hey, she wants to miss the party, be my guest."

He called her over, spoke to her briefly out of Nicky's hearing. Casey looked over at Nicky once and then back to Dexter. Then she came over to Nicky and kissed his cheek.

"Thank you, Nicky."

"Hey, get going. Call me when you get home?"

"I promise."

She left at a fast walk. By the time she reached the front door she was running. She got a cab at the corner of Canal and was on the Manhattan Bridge a minute later. She had made three more calls by then and could not draw a steady breath. The phone rang and the phone kept ringing. She thought about calling an EMS truck. They could be there in minutes. It was going to take her at least an hour in this damned Sunday traffic. And what would they find there? If they got there first, what would they see? A cop's briefcase packed with double-doctored drugs? An overdosed mother? A dead overdosed mother? How could she ever explain it? There would be no way. None. So Casey never made that call.

Fabrizio Senza took every back road and byway in the state and all the way north Jack lay in the backseat and watched the treeline blurring past the windows and thought about what was going to happen. Senza was listening to a big-band station, the music turned up loud because he was slightly deaf, and chain-smoking menthol cigarettes that reminded Jack of Buster and Deputy Callahan and how she had looked at Jack as she died.

Just outside of a little town called East Chatham, close to the Massachusetts state line, the news came on. Jack listened to it for any sign that he was being pursued, but other than a short statement from a Special Agent Derry Flynn of the ATF that the hunt for escaped killer Jack Vermillion was ongoing and an arrest was expected soon, the news was mostly concerned with baseball and the race for the mayor's position in New York City. It closed with a wrap-up of police beat stories from around the state, which began with this item.

> *"And from New York City, the AP is reporting that an arrest has been made in what New York State troopers have been calling the Road Rage Murders. Detectives with the joint task force of the NYPD, along with officers from the State Police CID, today arrested ex–army officer Earl V. Pike as he was leaving the offices of Assistant United States Attorney Valeriana Greco on Water Street. Pike was allegedly connected to the deaths of two young people in a wooded area near Blue Stores last Wednesday after an*

*intensive investigation by law enforcement
officials. Officials will not release any
information at this time, but sources close to
the case are saying that DNA evidence collected
at the scene led directly to the arrest. Pike is a
full partner in Crisis Control Services, a
Maryland-based consulting firm made up of
retired military officers. He is now being held in
Manhattan pending an arraignment scheduled
for tomorrow at the Albany courthouse. In
other news, authorities are still searching for
survivors in the deep waters off—"*

Senza shut the radio off and drove in absolute silence for
at least ten more miles. Jack tried to make sense of what
he had just heard, and failed miserably. He vaguely re-
called hearing a news report about some sort of road
rage killings in the upstate area, but that was shortly before his life got ripped apart and he had other things to
worry about. The Pike connection confused him.

He considered asking Senza what he made out of it,
but the silence coming from the front seat was a blank
wall, and Jack decided to say nothing. Senza had spoken
very little on the trip up and not at all after the newscast.
It was clear to Jack that the old man had a lot on his
mind. They had talked very little about Creek, mainly
because Jack found the idea too damn depressing to
think about. Creek was half his life, the only true thing
in it, other than the business. They'd known each other
for almost forty years.

But the pieces fit. There was even a Canadian connection. Back when they'd had their steaks on the roof of
his condo, Creek had mentioned a student he had met,
some sexy number, a lit major. The deconstructionist.
Yes. She was from McGill. Jack was pretty sure that
McGill was the name of a university up in Montreal.

And Frank had told him about the cars, the turquoise '56 T-bird he was buying for Claire. Flannery too. It was all right in front of him. But why? Nobody could tell him why. What reason could Creek have? All Jack knew was that he'd ask him that very question. In person. And soon. When he had Creek's answer, he'd know what to do about him. He tried for a breath and felt the pain.

Jack knew what the feeling in his chest was, the tightness and the cold. It was a kind of heartbreak. Senza seemed caught between loyalty to Frank and his suspicions about Jack and Creek, and the closer they got to home the more it looked like loyalty was winning. Jack had asked the old man several times to tell him where they were going, but all he did was grunt and keep driving. Jack could feel the big gray Glock digging into his ribs. He had loaded the magazine with the last of Sharon Callahan's nine-mill rounds, seventeen in the box, one chambered up and ready to go. He took whatever comfort he could get out of that. About where they were going, he found out a few miles later, when they pulled into the same park in Kinderhook where he had met Earl Pike the week before, Riveredge Park, right on the Hudson. Senza parked the Crown Victoria under a stand of willows and turned around in the seat to look down at Jack.

"We're here. I want you to stay inna car for a bit."

"Okay. What's happening?"

"We're waiting."

"For whom?"

"I asked for some help."

"From Frank?"

"Yeah, Frank. Who the fuck else? The Blessed Virgin?"

"What's he going to do? Is he going to go get Creek?"

"We'll find out when he gets here. Inna meantime, stay put and shut up. I gotta go take a leak."

The big car rocked on its springs as Senza opened the door and got out. The scent of riverside mud and trees and wildflowers poured into the car on a cool breeze and washed over Jack's face. He inhaled and tried to relax. All he could see while he was lying on his back like this were the branches of the willows above him. They moved in the wind from the river and showed their silver undersides and Jack remembered the last time he had looked at willows like that, only a few days ago, when he was watching them through the leaded-glass windows of the Frontenac Hotel, Creek sitting beside him, and thinking about the amberjack schools swimming in the South China Sea. The sound of the wind in the willow leaves was a feathery hiss. The sky showed through the flickering waves of willow leaves, a deepening blue with a gold-green tint in the west as the sun moved down into the afternoon sky.

He passed several minutes in this way and got his heart rate down to almost normal for the first time in several days, and then he heard three clear gunshots, one light, two heavy. Jack rolled sideways out of the Crown Victoria and landed in a tumble on the stones of the river's edge. He had the Glock out now and the weight of it in his right hand was solid and reassuring. He was under the willows and the waving leaves made it hard to see what was out there. He moved as quietly as he could until he reached the big leathery trunk of the nearest willow. He got his back up against it. He sat up far enough to look out into the park.

The park was deserted as far as he could see, the only vehicle in it the Crown Victoria. The lot ran parallel to the big river for about a hundred yards, and the park itself for a quarter mile. The banks of the river were lined with willows, but the area closer to the road was rolling grass dotted with picnic benches. Beyond the grass, the two-lane highway that led into Kinderhook baked in the sidelong sun. Thin purple shadows stretched across the deep green lawn. The river sound was rushing and deep, and the wind stirring the willows made a similar rushing sound, but not as deep and not as steady. Jack could see the surface of the Hudson from his position, not more than ten yards away through the willows. It was broad and brown and flat, with little roiling eddies that spun up in white froth. The sunlight lying on the river looked like little yellow flames. He moved to his left slightly.

A round slammed into the trunk right by his head, sending slivers into his temple. They stung like bees. He crashed away through the long grass, heading for the river. Then he heard the sound of the shot, a cracking boom that rattled around in the trees and then died away under the hissing of the wind and the rush of the river. He reached the bank and pulled himself in behind a huge tangle of willow roots. It was impossible to tell where the sound of the shot had come from, but the round had struck the trunk from the downriver direction. Who was shooting at him? The police? Senza? Pike?

Creek?

Certainly not Pike. He wouldn't have missed. Not Senza. Senza could have killed him anytime in the last two hours. It had to be Creek. Creek would have missed. He had never been a great shot, not even in the war. Jack shifted his position again. He raised his head and scanned the park. There was a cluster of sumac and a little knoll of apple trees about fifty yards away. Whoever was shooting at him was using a big pistol, from the sound of the shot, so fifty yards was about the effective range. The apple trees were leafy and full, and the shadows underneath them were blue-black. Inside the blue shadow was a darker shape, rounded, hunched over, moving slightly through the shadow. Jack froze and watched the shape. It moved again, and Jack saw a blue-white flowering—he jerked away—the round smacked into the root tangle—the booming crack racketed in the air—Jack slipped and fell into the river—the current was frighteningly fast—he clutched at the root cluster with his left hand—felt the branches tearing at his skin—his shoes were pulled off and gone—the water was icy cold and stank of mud and dead wood—he caught at the root cluster again—the slick wet bark peeled off in his hand and he was taken out by the rushing water—it was like being coat-hooked by a freight train—the current was immensely strong—Jack held onto the Glock as the banks went blurring by him—he saw a stony little outcrop coming up at him—Jack hit it hard—felt something pop in his chest—the breath slammed out of him—the current dragged at him—but he held on. The pain inside his chest was razor-thin and chilly and every time he took a breath it cut him somewhere deep inside.

He ignored it, burrowed up onto the riverbank. A shadow moved across the edge of the bank over his head, a black flicker in the standing weeds and the long grass. He was very still. The shadow passed to his right, going upriver. Jack pulled himself carefully out of the water. After three hard kicks he was able to get his head level with the edge of the grass line. He saw a big man in a gray suit moving carefully up the shallow rise, moving in the direction of the root tangle where Jack had gone into the river. He had a large stainless-steel pistol in his right hand. It was Carmine DaJulia.

Jack lifted the Glock, rested it on an outcrop of grassy earth, and aimed at the broad stretch of shiny gray silk over Carmine's ribs, just beneath his right underarm. Drops of water were running down Jack's face and into his eyes and it was hard to breathe. Every breath hurt and made the sights of the Glock shake. Carmine was less than twenty feet away, looking upriver, moving in a low crouch. All his attention was up the river. That was a mistake, thought Jack, who knew something about these things. He pulled the trigger.

The pistol jumped in his hand, jerking his arm, which sent a jagged bolt of pain through his chest. The round plucked at Carmine's coat, thudded into his thigh bone, splashing a red rose on the shiny gray silk. Carmine, turning, cursing, lifted the Colt—fired it at Jack—the round punched a clod of dirt into the air above his head—he was slipping down the bank—caught himself—he saw Carmine coming toward the bank now—his broken-china teeth showing yellow against the tan skin—Jack lifted the Glock again—heard a voice calling—Carmine jerked around—Fabrizio Senza was standing in the clear a yard to the right of the apple-tree knoll—blood was running from his face and glistening on his shirt—Carmine twisted and aimed the Colt at Senza—and Jack fired again, and Carmine went backward and down and lay still, one arm stretched out and limp, the Colt lying in the green grass a foot from his hand.

Jack pulled himself up the riverbank, stood up shakily, and walked over to where Carmine was lying. He could see Carmine's big belly going up and down like a bellows. Jack was barefoot and the grass felt warm and dry against his skin. He reached Carmine and stood over him, looking down.

Carmine's blunt face was flushed red, his mouth gulping air like a hooked fish, his chest rising and falling. He had wet himself and a dark stain colored his crotch. Blood coated his right leg now, shiny and red, and ran down into the green grass, and Jack had a sudden replay of Tank Boy on his side in a wide flat green lake with thin red lines running through it. There was a second bloody wound in Carmine's belly, low and to the left.

Carmine shifted, looked up at Jack.

"Fuck you, Jack," said Carmine, and closed his eyes.

Fabrizio Senza, breathing fast and shallow, moving slowly, reached them, bent down, and picked up the steel Colt lying next to Carmine. Jack saw a black hole in the man's left cheek, blood running in snakes down the leathery skin. His eyes were black, half shut against the pain in his skull. He lifted the Colt and pointed it at Carmine's face. Carmine turned his face a little away and Jack could see he was holding his breath, ready for the shot to punch through him. Jack stepped over, put his hand out and placed it on Senza's arm, pushed the arm gently down. Senza looked at him in confusion, his lips set and thin, his chest heaving.

"I need him," said Jack.

TEMPLE COURT
PROSPECT PARK
1630 HOURS

The cab was still rolling to a stop in front of Casey's apartment building when Casey threw a twenty into the slot and stepped out. She tried to walk down the concrete path but failed. She was doing a fast trot by the time she hit the glass doors. She still had the cell phone in her hand. It was hot to the touch. She'd called her home number every five minutes during the hour and a half that it took the driver to work his way across the bridge and through the Sunday traffic to Prospect Park. The sound of the line ringing over and over again was still echoing in her mind.

The elevator clanged shut and groaned upward, taking a year to pass a single floor. Casey banged on the doors as they opened, pushed at the edge, and squeezed her way into the hallway. The hall smelled of cooking and she heard the crowd noise of a ball game coming through one of the heavy wooden doors. She ran all the way down to her door, keys out. She had to try three times, but she got the door open and stepped into the apartment. It was silent.

"Mom? You here?"

Nothing.

She walked into the main room. The sun was pouring in through the casement windows and lay like spilled honey on the polished hardwood flooring. The green leather couch was empty, a dark blue blanket bundled up in the corner. The television was on, showing a CNN channel, but the sound had been muted. The wooden coffee table was littered with drink glasses, pill bottles, the ashtray overflowing, and the smell of marijuana and menthol cigarettes floated in the hazy air. The stereo was on and soft swing music was playing. The door to her mother's room was closed.

"Mom! It's Casey."

Silence.

Casey crossed the floor. The door to her mother's room was slightly open. She saw a corner of her mother's bed, unmade, and some clothes tossed on the carpet. She pushed the door open.

The bed had been slept in. Casey touched the sheets. Cold. And damp, as if her mother had been sweating. The table beside the bed was a mess, coated with spilled red wine. The door to her mother's bathroom was half open and the light was on. Casey moved toward it. Reached it. Her hand, as she held it out, looked elongated and disconnected. The bathroom was empty. Two minutes later, after a search that grew increasingly frantic, Casey found her mother.

She was lying on Casey's bed, under the deep blue ceiling covered with thousands of glittering gold stars. A city made out of candles was burning on the bedside table, although the sun was shining in through the white cotton drapes. Her mother was lying on her back, in a yellow silk nightgown, her hands folded across her breast. Casey's briefcase was on the floor beside her bed. It had been opened, and the contents were scattered across Casey's sea-green carpet, pill bottles opened, letters and papers everywhere. Casey came over to the bed and looked down at her mother's face. It was blue-white, creased and sunken, her cheekbones sharp, her eyes closed, her forehead shining. She leaned down to touch her mother's throat.

Her mother's eyes opened.

"Casey."

"Mom."

"I was so worried. What time is it?"

"A little after four. Sunday. You found my briefcase?"

"Yes. It came last night. I opened it. I'm sorry."

"I was calling you. Just now. Didn't you hear me?"

"I think I did. I may have. I was looking at your stars."

"For Christ's sake, Mom. I thought—"

"You thought I was stoned. Or dead."

"Yes. What else would I think?"

"I took some pills. I took a lot of them. I had myself quite a party last night. But I also read your letters. All the letters. To the doctors. To the detox people. The apologies. The excuses. I read everything in your brief-case. I read about those awful people who kidnapped the little girl last week. Shawana Coryell. I read the court papers, the one where that judge with the lovely name? Euphonia? She let those three men go free. After what they did? How terrible. Your whole life is in that briefcase, Casey. It's not much of a life, is it? You do nothing but fight. You have nothing else."

"Mom . . ."

She lifted a thin yellow hand and placed it on Casey's

cheek. Her fingers were cold and her hand shook a little.
Her eyes were wet.

"I've made your young life a hell, Casey."

"No. Yes. Perhaps. I've been trying to help you."

"I know. Are you through trying to help me?"

Casey's eyes were burning, her throat pounding. Her
mother waited for whatever answer was coming. Casey
shook her head.

"No, Mom. I'm not."

"Then I'd like to start."

"Start what?"

"Start trying. Do you think we can do that?"

"We can try."

Casey even managed to believe her for quite a long
while.

1600 VALLEY MILLS

RENSSELAER, NEW YORK

1800 HOURS

Carmine had said nothing to either of them during the
entire trip, sitting in the back of Senza's blue Crown
Victoria and staring at the back of Senza's huge dented
skull as if he could drill a hole into it to match the one
he had put in Senza's left cheek. Jack was in the passenger
seat, holding the Glock casually, and smelling Carmine's
blood in the air-conditioned interior. It smelled of chlo-
rine and rust. The blood had run quickly at first, but had
slowed to a thin red ribbon by the time they pulled into
Frank's driveway in Rensselaer. Frank had been waiting
in the shadows under the trees beyond the wrought-iron
gates. Creek Johnson was nowhere around. Nor was
Frank's wife, Claire. Frank Torinetti's garage was big

enough to hold five cars. Once they had the doors down, it was as dark inside as if it were midnight. The garage was solid brick and stone, as cool as a cave. They had to move the Cord and the split-window coupe and Claire's turquoise T-bird to make room for the wooden chair that Frank had carried out from the gatehouse. Jack moved the cars out of the way while Fabrizio Senza stood over Carmine DaJulia.

Frank Torinetti leaned his back against the redbrick wall. He was dressed in pale pink satin pajamas under an emerald-green robe. His ankles showed blue-white and bumpy with purple veins above the burgundy leather slippers. Under the single hard light his face was shiny and wet, his skin sagging like melted wax, his deep-set eyes glittering with a yellow light. He was smoking a cigarette and watching Fabrizio Senza as the old man draped sheets of plastic over the nearby cars. Then Senza lifted Carmine DaJulia up off the floor beside the chair as if he were a plaster model, sat him down into it, and pushed him upright.

Carmine's face was stone, his breathing slow and steady. They had taken off his pale-gray silk suit jacket and his shirt. His hands were behind him, cuffed with black plastic cable ties. Others bound him to the rails of the heavy wooden chair. His heavily muscled body looked whale-white under the light, his big belly smooth and round, a blood-soaked bandage pasted onto it over his lower left side, held in place with a section of his torn shirt.

The blood had dried into a brown mass, but every time Carmine exhaled, a thin ribbon of fresh blood would pulse out from under the bandage and run down into the waistband of his suit pants. Enough of it had run down over his belly to soak the entire front of his slacks. Just above the wound near his right knee there was a leather belt—his own belt, black crocodile with a

buckle made of lapis lazuli and a gold C on the crest—
cinched in tight, bunching the fabric up around the tourni-
quet, and under the fabric his leg was swollen and tubular,
straining against the material. He had one shoe off and
one shoe gone, lost somewhere during the long careful
journey back from Riveredge Park. After a few minutes,
during which no one spoke and Carmine's breathing grew
less steady, Frank stepped away from the wall and stood
in front of Carmine. Jack leaned against Claire's Thunderbird, saying nothing.

Carmine lifted his head and looked back at Frank,
his expression blank. Frank nodded over Carmine's head
and Fabrizio Senza stepped into the circle of light. The
bandage on his cheek was fresh, but a huge blue-black
bruise had spread across the side of his face, and tears
were seeping from his left eye and running down into
the bandage. Jack studied Fabrizio, looking for pain, but
the man's face might have been cut from a slab of wood.

"Show him," said Frank.

Fabrizio Senza reached into his rumpled and bloody
suit coat and extracted a long cedarwood box. He
leaned down to show Carmine the box and popped the
silver catch that held the lid. The lid was spring-loaded.
It snapped open to reveal a dark-blue satin interior.
Lying in the little satin coffin was a straight razor, glittering steel and silver filigree, with a long curved handle
made of bone.

Carmine's breathing became less regular. Senza
straightened up, took the razor out of the case, set the
case down on the plastic sheeting covering the fender of
a dark green Bugatti, and walked around to the back of
Carmine's chair. Carmine tried to follow his movement
but could not bring his head around. The muscles of
his neck and shoulders were too thick. His eyes strained
in their sockets until the whites showed, giving him a

wild-horse look, but it was no use. Senza was behind him now and close enough for Carmine to hear the man breathing and smell his dried blood.

Carmine looked back up at Frank.

"Frank, this isn't right."

"No? Why?"

"This was between me and Jackie."

"You and Jackie?"

"Yeah. I mean, it was you or him."

"Me or him?"

"Yeah. I was . . . I was taking care of you. Frankie, you know I been backing you up. You been sick, you got no energy. Somebody had to look out for us. All I was doing—"

"Are the feds watching this house?"

"How the fuck would I know?"

"Are they?"

Carmine hesitated and then shook his head.

"No."

"Why?"

"They don't know Jackie was coming this way. After Fabrizio called, I told them they was going south. Jersey. They broke off."

"You wanted them off, right? So you could kill Jack?"

"It wasn't about Jack. He was bringing the feds in on you. Whining and begging. Alla this time, Jack's too fucking good to hang out with people like us. He gets into trouble, all of a sudden we're family. I done it for you, Frank. He's gone, the feds can't get to you. All I been doing in this is keeping them off you."

"You put the feds on Jack in the first place."

"It wasn't that simple."

"You talking to the feds, hah? About me?"

Carmine shook his head.

"No. That's not how it went."

Frank shook his head, glanced over Carmine's shaved

skull. Carmine followed the look and tensed up so hard the sinews in his neck popped out like cables. Senza did nothing, only waited. From where Jack was standing, he could see all three men, arranged in a tight group, Senza half in shadow, Carmine upright in the chair under the light, bathed in the kind of glow you expect to see around angels, and Frank, his weight on one foot, body held up by nerves and anger, but calm, calm in a way Jack had never seen him before.

It was Frank's business calm, he decided. This was how Frank looked when he was involved in his business. He wasn't Jack's old childhood buddy anymore. He was a grown man and most of his life had been spent doing things that Jack had never wanted to believe he would ever be capable of doing. Things like this. Frank's voice was low and soft, his anger damped down but present.

"Fabrizio knows what each one a them spinal bones does. He's like a doctor. He can cut you so your arms don't work, or your legs and your arms, or just cut you so your pecker don't work, or you can't breathe, or you can't move only you can still feel everything."

"I know . . . Jesus, Frank, I know."

"So don't embarrass me like this. I ain't having any fun here."

"I know. Jeez, Frank—we're friends. This wasn't about you."

"You got busted. For something. The Canadian shit?"

Carmine was silent for perhaps another thirty seconds. Jack waited and wished with all his heart that he had never come back from the war. Senza shifted his weight, his shoes grated on the concrete floor. Carmine jumped as if they had wired him to a socket.

"Fabrizio," he said, "come out from behind me, hah?"

Senza said nothing. Frank reached out and lifted Carmine's chin so the light was full on his face and he could see the man's eyes.

"Carmine. You gotta explain this. We can't walk away from here without knowing what the deal is. I don't wanna hurt you. But I can't let this thing get away from me. On my mother, Carmine, I'm gonna let Fabrizio do whatever it takes, and you know, at the end of it, you gonna tell me everything. This ain't the movies, Carmine. You gonna be in bad pain. You never gonna be a walking man again, you gonna piss in a diaper, live the rest of your life on your back, breathing through a tube in your throat. We go back all the way to Ditmars, Carmine. I don't want this. Please, be a friend here."

"I was being a friend! I gave them Jackie. I coulda given them you! But I covered you. Now I'm inna chair here, and that cocksucker over there is laughing at us both."

Frank lifted a hand, touched Carmine's cheek.

"Listen to me. This is about you and me. Inna beginning. What did they pop you for? Drugs?"

"Okay . . . it was the cars. And the money."

Jack pushed himself off the car, spoke to Frank.

"Ask him about Creek."

Carmine sent Jack a look of hundred-proof hatred.

"Creek's a fucking mope, a tool. I used him. He's bringing in cars from Auburn, I put him on to a seller in Canada. Creek goes up there, buys a couple, maybe once or twice a month. Sometimes he takes Fabrizio for the company or to drive one back with him. I ask him, can I get in on this? The mook says yes. He don't know shit."

Jack wanted to believe him but could not.

"Why did you want in on his deals, then?"

"Hey, he's a mutt. I packed the trunks with dope, with shit, and he never tumbled. That dumb bastard, he drives up to the customs stop at Wolf Island, up there by Cape Vincent, they could have sniffer dogs, whatever, he never thinks of that. But they don't, and he goes back and forth, him and Fabrizio, just an old wop and a cowboy numb-nuts. The customs guys never gave him a look, just wanted to feel up those old classic cars. I used them. I used Creek, I mean. Not you, Fabrizio. Not you, I swear. I would never have let—"

"What were you bringing in?" asked Frank, his voice soft.

"I been doing some stuff for the Canadians. Moving cash mainly. For the bikers. The Mohawks. Frank, I needed the money. You ain't active now. People are making their own moves. New people. You ain't paying any attention. I know you're sick, but jeez, Frank, you got fucking responsibilities."

"I know I got a wife."

Carmine flinched.

"Claire's got nothing to do with this."

"She didn't know?"

"She . . . knew I was protecting you."

"You and Claire close, then?"

"Frank, she's . . . worried. About the future."

"So you the future for Claire, hah?"

"No. It wasn't like that."

"Yeah? Tell me what it was like. I'm lying in bed at night, you mutts think I'm stoned, I'm gone. I watch you and her. You doing it right in front of me. I watched, Carmine. Don't tell me you both doing all this for me. You got busted, then. How? Did Creek find out? Rat you out?"

Carmine pulled his lips back, showed his teeth.

"Creek rats me out, he'd be a greasy smear on my heel."

"How, then? How'd you get nailed?"

"The Canadians, the fucking horse cops. Whaddya call them?"

"The RCMP?"

"Yeah. They had a fink in the Mohawks. He rats me out. The Canadians hand me over to the feds."

"The feds? This Greco broad?"

"Yeah. I mean, she's the main one. Once I got busted, the FBI handed me over to the U.S. attorney. Make a deal. That was her."

"How long?"

"Shit . . . six, seven months."

"Who's the target?"

"It was gonna be you. I had to give her something. I don't give her something, my deal's off. She figured Jackie here was dirty already. She was primed up. So I give her what she wanted. I give her a guy, big shipping company, lots of assets, told her he was all mobbed up, connected, a made guy. She went for it like a snake at a chicken."

"This Pike guy. He a part of this?"

"Pike. Shit, no. The guy's a fucking loose cannon."

"How'd he get into it, then?"

"He come to me about his guns. I figured, hey, this is fucking icing on the cake. I already had the Cobra primed up. Jackie takes the gun thing on, all I need to do is find out when it's going down the river, and I make sure the Cobra's on board same day. Then I call Greco and ba-bing, they got Jackie for guns too. It was a walk-in off the street. It was too good to pass up. Then Jackie goes all civic and rats Pike out. Man, that rocked us all. Greco almost shit when she got the call. Then she figured it didn't matter. They had Jackie either way. But it was beautiful all the way around. They get Jackie here, and they get Pike too. Bonus, two for one."

"How'd you do Jack?"

"Jackie brings his Cobra in. I got another. Guy I put Creek on to, in Montreal, he knew where to get one just like Jackie's."

"Did Creek help you? Get the Cobra?" asked Jack.

"No. I couldn't trust him for that. Why? He saying I did?"

"I haven't asked him. Yet," said Jack.

"Well, he ain't been no fucking friend, Jackie. You think he's such a big buddy? Fuck that noise. Ever ask him where he gets his money? He paid me a hundred thousand on the vig just a month back. You see him, ask him where that came from."

"No. Not my business."

"No? You dumb prick. You so fucking stupid, you drove that fucking Cobra for two whole days, didn't even know it wasn't yours. It was a walk. Setting you up was a fucking pleasure."

Jack kept his mouth shut. Frank walked away to the workbench and poured himself a glass of red wine, another for Jack. He placed each glass carefully on a wooden tray with the words *Lake Placid* painted in a forties arc of bright fall colors. Jack thought he looked like a priest, working at the low wooden bench under the dim light. Frank walked over with the tray held out before him, his face moving from light to shadow and back into the light again as he reached them. Jack looked in Frank's eyes and saw pain, loss, and death there, and also the kid he used to be, the boy's face under the ruined mask of sagging skin. Frank touched his glass to Jack's glass.

"*Salud,*" said Frank.

"Now what?" asked Jack.

"Up to you."

Jack looked over his shoulder at Carmine. Carmine was staring at them both. Behind him Fabrizio Senza stood in the half shadow, staring down at the back of Carmine's head, the blade in his right hand shimmering like a little silver flame.

"You got your cell phone with you?"

Frank pulled it out of the pocket in his bathrobe.

"Give it to Carmine."

"Carmine?"

"Yeah. He's gonna make a call."

"I'm calling nobody, you fuck," said Carmine. Nobody looked at him. Carmine was over. Frank raised his right eyebrow.

"So who?"

"Pike," said Jack.

Frank was quiet for a while.

"You think that's safe?"

"No," said Jack.

"Then why?"

"I owe him."

"Owe him for what?"

"Carmine's not the only rat in the room, Frank."

OFFICE OF THE DISTRICT ATTORNEY FOR MANHATTAN
CENTRE STREET
1900 HOURS

Nicky Cicero and Dexter Zarnas had spent two hours sitting in the outer offices of the district attorneys assigned to cross-jurisdictional cases in New York State, waiting to see which way a three-way tug-of-war was going to snap loose. Inside the glass-walled offices, the two cops could see at least seven different lawyers representing three different agencies, the United States attorney's office, the state DA, and two ADAs for the city of New York. Pete LeTourneau was in there as well, along with some senior police officials from the NYPD and even a lawyer representing the District of Columbia. The argument was loud and angry and right now it looked as if everybody but the state lawyers was winning.

Dexter was leaning back in the wooden chair with his feet propped up on a trash can and sipping at a cup of black coffee. Nicky was sitting opposite him, stretched out on a slatted wood bench, his hands folded behind his head. He was . . . conflicted.

Casey had called him a little after five, just as they were getting Pike processed and into a state-federal lockup in the basement of Central Booking. Nicky listened to her story with a great sense of relief—the briefcase was back in her hands and Casey's mother hadn't OD'd. But the stuff about her mother's change of heart, Nicky found that less than convincing. He'd heard that kind of thing many times before, and it always ended up in a Friday night jail cell, a crowded ER on Saturday, or the city morgue on a rainy Monday. The call had ended with Casey telling him she'd try to call him at home—at his hotel room in Yonkers—later this evening. No, she wasn't coming back in today. She figured he and Dexter could handle the rest of the Pike arraignment. If they needed a statement, she'd be on the job tomorrow. She and her mother had a lot to talk about. Good-bye, Nicky, was what he heard. What he was still hearing.

"Whaddya thinking, Nicky?"

Nicky looked over at Dexter.

"What?"

"You look like somebody buggered your cat."

"I don't have a cat."

"Buggered your hamster, then."

"These are mental pictures I do not need to have, Dexter. How long are these weasels going to bat this thing around?"

"They're lawyers. We could die here."

"Who'll win, you think?"

"You will. The only thing the rest of the jurisdictions have on Pike is suspicion. Until the ATF finds that Barrett Fifty and links it to Pike or gets somebody at Crisis Control Systems to rat Pike out, they got nothing going. The witness at Beach Haven never saw Pike there, and so far they haven't come up with the Smith that Pike is supposed to have used on those two guards. This guy's a hired killer, Nicky. A professional assassin. That's what he did in the army, it's what he's doing now. And CCS is protecting him."

"Why? Why would his firm go the distance, take a chance on an obstruction charge or accessory after?"

"I figure Pike has as much on them as they have on him. These guys work the gray areas between the CIA and the FBI. Companies like Executive Outcomes, Military Professionals, the rest, they work for private companies or third-world governments in places where due process is a midnight wake-up, a free ride in a white van, and a bullet in the back of the head. Pike's probably insane, but he's not crazy. He had all the angles figured before he went after any of these guys. He had his route in and his route out and what he'd say later all planned, right down to the distance between Red Hook and LaGuardia. Compared to him, these federal mutts are Teletubbies."

"Then how'd we get him?"

"We didn't. He came in."

"Yeah," said Nicky. "That's what I was thinking about."

"Me too, kid. Oops, here we go."

One of the suits was walking toward the glass door, one of the women representing the state and the Criminal Investigation Division of the State Police, a blonde-haired beauty with wide cheekbones and a big sport-model frame tucked into a two-piece silk suit in emerald-green. She put her hand out as she came toward Nicky and Dexter, who were on their feet by then.

"How are you, Officers? You must be Officer Cicero, and you're Sergeant Zarnas of the NYPD. I'm Bridget McCarthy, the ADA for New York State. I'd like to congratulate you on bringing in Mr. Pike. As you can see, he's quite the wanted man."

"You're welcome," said Dexter. McCarthy beamed at them both and turned away, began to walk down the long terrazzo hallway toward the door. Halfway there she stopped, looked back.

"Well, boys? Let's go."

"Where we going?" asked Dexter.

"To chambers, of course. The Pike defense has asked for a hearing, and we're going to give them one."

"What kind of a hearing?" asked Nicky.

McCarthy smiled at him over her shoulder.

"A short one, I hope."

She led them out of the building and out across the deserted parks and sidewalks of Centre Street until they got to the courts. She jogged up the steps and pushed through the brass-bound doors, waved to a couple of guards on her way through the metal detector—Dexter and Nicky at a jog right behind her—and up a curve of marble stairs to a long hallway lined with offices. She stopped in front of a large wooden door with gold lettering:

JUDGE GLORIA BETHUNE
CHAMBERS

"Here we are, boys. You can come in, but sit quiet. This is for lawyers and other grown-ups. Whatever you think, say nothing."

She knocked on the door and opened it. The room was small and lined with law books and framed artworks in heavy gilded wood. There was a worn Persian carpet in front of a battered mahogany desk, and four chairs on the carpet. One of the chairs was filled with a small elderly black man in a three-piece navy-blue suit and shiny black shoes. He was tiny, wrinkled, and his salt-and-pepper hair was mostly salt. His eyes were crinkled up in a permanent squint and were surrounded with smile lines. He looked like a cheerful man, in general, who had something particularly pleasing planned for later.

The woman behind the desk, leaning back in her tattered leather wing chair and puffing on a cigarette, was a lean-faced black woman in her fifties, a serious knockout, with fine snow-white hair brushed back from her strong face and held in place with a red ribbon at the back of her neck. Her eyes were soft and calm, and she had an air around her that some judges have, of having seen it all at least three times and been shocked only once. She rose as Bridget McCarthy came over with her hand out.

"Ms. McCarthy, how nice to see you. I think you know S. Walter Kendall."

"I do, of course. I was in Professor Kendall's moot court at Yale several times. I don't suppose you remember me?"

"Oh but I do," said Kendall, rising unsteadily out of his chair and extending a firm but bony hand. "And these two young men?"

McCarthy introduced Nicky and Dexter and got them arranged around the desk. As she sat down beside Professor Kendall, she sent Nicky and Dexter one warning look and then settled in. The judge leaned forward, crossed her arms, and nodded to Professor Kendall.

"I think we can begin if you wish, Professor Kendall."

"Thanks. I know we're all tired, and I do want to express my own appreciation, and that of my client, for the favor of this unusual Sunday evening hearing."

"I was available. I am intrigued," said Judge Bethune.

"Intrigued?" put in Bridget McCarthy. "Why intrigued?"

Kendall laughed softly and gave them all a benevolent look over his thin gold-framed glasses.

"I'll explain. Now, for the benefit of these young officers who have chosen to be present, I'll just skip all the legalese and say, in the plainest possible terms, that one of the bulwarks of freedom is the Fourth Amendment right to freedom from unreasonable search or seizure. I think this is a principle upon which we may all concur. I also want to point out, off the record, that I deeply regret having to make this argument in the case of our Mr. Pike, who is an individual with whom I share very little in the way of ethics and beliefs. Personally, I'd like to see the brute chained to a wall and stoned. But I must make it. The canon of ethics compels me."

"And your argument?" asked Judge Bethune.

"The foundation of the state's case against Mr. Pike is the DNA evidence found upon the body, is it not?"

"Not the foundation," said McCarthy. "We have also seized Mr. Pike's Mercedes-Benz and are subjecting it to a very close forensic analysis, which has proved, I might say, very fruitful."

Kendall showed her a gnome's rueful smile.

"Perhaps, but according to Elstad and other rulings with which I will not burden you, since you are quite aware of them, whatever you find that can be shown to have been what we call the fruits of a poisoned tree cannot be offered to the court."

McCarthy was getting jumpy. Nicky was having a hard time staying in his seat. Every instinct he had was on full alert.

"Everyone here understands Elstad and the Fourth Amendment. We're all professionals. Perhaps Professor Kendall can be more specific?"

"I'd be delighted. As I understand the chain of evidence, the DNA that seems to implicate Mr. Pike came from a razor blade extracted from Mr. Pike's hotel room at the United Nations Plaza Hotel on Forty-fourth Street. Correct me if I misstate the facts."

"No. That's right."

"DNA, it is stated in the information filed by your office, that was legally and properly collected by our handsome young policeman over here. DNA that was a product of a fortuitously cooperative maid at the UN Plaza Hotel, who was no doubt beguiled by Officer Cicero's striking good looks and irresistible charm."

McCarthy nodded, looking at Nicky and raising an eyebrow. Kendall grinned at Nicky and then winked at him.

"Yes, I thought I recognized him."

"Recognized him?" said McCarthy. "Have you met?"

"Not personally, no. Although I am delighted to make his acquaintance today, I admit that I know the young man only by his memorable work on the silver screen."

It wasn't hard for Nicky to see what was coming at him. What was hard was to get out of the way. He swallowed with difficulty and hoped for a miracle. He didn't get it. Professor Kendall was rooting around in a baggy leather satchel on his knees. He fumbled around in the interior and lifted out a small Sony camcorder.

McCarthy jumped in.

"Your Honor, if my colleague has evidence he wishes to introduce, this is not the venue—"

"Your Honor, this is not evidence. Not evidence in this case, at any rate. Let's call this an exculpatory demonstration."

"This was why I said I was intrigued," said Judge Bethune, smiling at Bridget McCarthy. "Go ahead, Walter. Get on with it. You've dragged this performance out long enough."

Kendall placed the camcorder on the desk where they could all see it. He reached out, popped open the tiny LCD screen, and carefully pressed a button. The screen lit up with the word *play* and a date/time marker. The screen stayed black for about ten seconds, and then burst into light. Nicky watched as his own face appeared on the screen, huge, distorted by the camera lens, but very recognizable. He looked at McCarthy, who was staring at the screen as if she had found a freshly severed finger in her Cobb salad.

"Oh jeez," said Dexter in a hoarse whisper.

The video ran for less than forty seconds. In it they could clearly see Nicky's face, his fingers looming large as tree trunks in the foreshortened image, picking his way through the contents of Earl Pike's medicine cabinet until he settled on the razor blade.

"I draw your attention to that," said Kendall.

The video image showed Nicky considering the blade, holding it up to the light over the cabinet, and then plucking the blade off the handle, replacing it with a new one, and then putting the razor back in position on the shelf. He reached out for the door then, and blackness came down on the image. The tiny recorder showed the word *end* and then shut off. The silence in the room was fairly complete, other than the rustle of the old man's breathing and the sound of a guard walking the halls and whistling the theme from *Dr. Zhivago*. Finally McCarthy got to her feet.

"Your Honor, I think I need to consult with my superiors."

"Of course," said Judge Bethune, inclining her Sphinx-like head.

"I couldn't agree more," said Professor Kendall.

"Thank you," McCarthy said, and walked out of the room. The two police officers followed behind, Dexter closing the door after him as softly as he could manage. Judge Bethune could not hear all of the conversation that took place immediately outside her door. The best way to characterize it would be to call it vigorous. Earl Pike was back on the street two hours later.

He looked untouched and calm in his navy-blue Armani as if he had never been arrested at all. The night was cool, the sky still streaked with the sunset streaming out from the Jersey flatlands. He walked a few blocks north along Centre Street, past the tangled alleyways of Chinatown, along Broome to Mott, where he stopped in at Il Grand Ticino and had a quiet meal of angel-hair pasta and some mussels in a white wine reduction, along with a very nice Soave. Halfway through the meal, his cell phone rang. It was Carmine DaJulia. Carmine sounded tired. Carmine had a tip for him. He knew where Jack Vermillion was going to be later tonight. Did Pike want to know?

Pike did. He listened to Carmine DaJulia in silence for about three minutes, then he said thanks, said get some rest, Carmine, you sound terrible, said good-bye, Carmine, put the phone away, signaled for his bill, paid it in cash, and left.

He came back out into the bustle and the sounds and scents of Little Italy and caught a gypsy cab at the corner of Kenmare and the Bowery. He was back at the UN Plaza Hotel before the night had come fully down over midtown. Nicky Cicero was waiting for him in the lobby. He got up and faced him in the middle of the hall.

"Officer Cicero. More official business?"

"You made an offer. I accept."

"An offer?"

"Yeah. You said we should go a couple rounds together."

Pike felt something feathery tickling his skull. Nicky's face was pale and bony, his eyes hunted-looking. Pike thought about the boy he had beaten to death in that clearing and what had come of it.

"Kid, you couldn't take me on your best day."

"This isn't my best day. Maybe I'll win. So let's go."

Pike felt the tiny columns marching under the skin of

his temples. He managed to avoid looking at his reflection in the mirrored glass walls beside them. Nicky was waiting, his heart hammering, his ears filled with a hissing sound, blood moving. In the thick muscles of his neck, an artery was pulsing. Pike watched it throb for a time, deciding.

"You're a brave man, Nicky. I'll give you that. In the unlikely event that you actually managed to hurt me, and even if I killed you, you'd still have my blood on you. My blood means my DNA. Legally obtained. Ready for court. I think I won't oblige you this evening."

Nicky watched him all the way to the elevator. Pike never looked back. Nicky walked out onto Forty-fourth and caught a cab to Yonkers. He called Casey from his room. They talked for an hour. Then he went to bed and, after some time spent watching the ruby-red numbers on the bedside clock change from 1:30 to 1:31 to 1:32, he fell asleep. In a dream, he saw the faces of Julia Gianetto and Donald Condotti. They were rotting in death. Nicky tried to wake up but he could not move his arms or breathe or cry out. After an eternity, he woke himself with a hoarse scream. He sat up in bed, shaking, chilled, sick. Milky-blue moonlight lay on the bed, cut into slices by the window blinds. The noise from the street was a dull and continuous roar. The red numbers on the clock beside the bed blinked at him. The time was 1:39.

MONDAY, JUNE 26

RED HOOK CONTAINER TERMINAL

VAN BRUNT AND GOWANUS

0300 HOURS

Earl Pike had his back up against a second-story ledge on the roof of the parking garage, the Barrett Fifty cradled across his knees, his gloved hands resting on the rifle. He had a fine view across the river. A low ceiling of gauzy cloud and fog had settled down over Manhattan and the buildings glowed inside the haze as though the city were burning. On the East River the city lights wavered and shimmered. The yard lights were on at the Red Hook Terminal, but since it was Sunday night—early Monday morning—the quays were empty and the warehouses and yards deserted, silent. The guardhouse was dark, the gates open. Razor wire sparkled along the wire fencing, electric-blue under the arc lights that lit up the compound. A black Shelby Cobra was idling inside the cone of yellow light coming down from a lamppost near the main warehouse, its windows tinted black, the sound of its engine a throaty rumble, and the car rocked rhythmically on its springs, taking the weight of the big camshaft turning inside the engine. Pike had been waiting for it. It had arrived, as Carmine had predicted, a few minutes ago, but so far the windows had remained closed and no one had gotten out of the car. Fine. Pike was a patient man. Sooner or later the other cars would arrive, maybe Greco herself, and then the man inside the car was going to have to get out of it, and then Pike would kill him, and perhaps the woman too, and this thing would end.

He shifted the Barrett again and ran a hand down the angular steel flank, savoring the balance and weight of the thing. Down in the big yard the Cobra rocked and rumbled under the yellow light, the canvas roof misted over with dew. It was a beautiful car, and Pike was going to see that no harm came to it. It was a relic of the days—the years—when America knew how to make things like that, and it was as important in its way as his family's own collection, part of the nation's heritage, and as worthy of protection.

He moved again, his belly muscles tugging at the fish-hook scars in his gut. Something feathery was moving across his cheek and he had a momentary flash of fear, but when he put his hand up to his cheek he found a small black spider there. He plucked it off his face and held it in his hand, watching the creature scuttle around in his palm. It was real. It was not a hallucination. Some spiders were real. The spiders in that Ecuadorian latrine had been very real.

Every night and every day for seven weeks he had lived with them, in their thousands, in their columns and phalanxes and battalions. And the guards, of course, who would come in now and then to entertain themselves with the prisoner. When the leftists had finally traded him back to the U.S. Army in return for the release of six politicals, he had been quite insane and had gone back to Bethesda in a Blackhawk without being able to speak at all. But he was recovered now and at peace. He tipped the little black spider out over the edge of the roof, leaning forward to do it, and as he did so a man dropped to the roof next to him and shoved a pistol up against the side of his head. Pike tensed, felt the cold steel on his skull, and froze.

"Hello, Earl," said Jack. "Let go of the Barrett."

"It will fall," said Pike, holding himself very still under the muzzle of the gun. "I don't want it damaged."

"It won't be," said Jack, and then he slammed Pike across the side of the head with the Glock. Pike reeled back and let go of the Barrett. Jack caught it by the stock and pulled it in, turned it on Pike. Pike shifted and recovered, blood running down the side of his temple. He looked into the muzzle of the Barrett and then back up at Jack Vermillion. Jack was smiling at him.

"Carmine says hello."

Pike nodded, his face blank.

"Who's in the car?"

"Creek Johnson."

"Brave man. How did you know I wouldn't just take the Cobra apart with the Fifty?"

"I figured you'd want to see the look on my face. And maybe you'd wait for Greco."

"How'd you know where I'd be?"

"I was in the room when Carmine called you."

"Carmine working for you now?"

"Carmine's working for himself. He has a lot on his mind."

"I see. Good for you. You got me. I'm dazzled. Now what?"

Jack lifted the muzzle of the Barrett, hefted it.

"This the piece you used on the feds?"

"Perhaps."

"I'm keeping it."

"You are? For the government, I guess."

"Depends."

"Really? On what?"

"I set you up. I regret it. Now I let you walk away."

Pike was silent for almost a minute. A barge sounded out on the river, the huge black shape gliding down toward the bay, a black island against the golden lights moving on the surface of the river, the wake boiling like molten lava behind it. Neither man moved.

"What is this, Jack? Penitence? Forgiveness?"

"No. Atonement."

"Atonement? Usually the victim determines the atonement."

"Not just for you. I did some things, other things I regret. I'm going to have to pay for them. I'm probably going to jail."

"Those three boys in Hazleton?"

"I don't have to explain it to you."

"I doubt you could explain that to anyone."

"Blood gets blood, Pike. This thing between us is over."

"It's over when I say it's over. My collection is still gone. My family's heritage. I'll never see it again. Thanks to you."

"It's over. I'm saying it. I want your word. As a soldier."

Pike looked out over the river. The city was disappearing behind a veil of golden haze. He breathed and the scars in his belly tugged at him. He felt a delicate tickle in his cheek and idly rubbed at it. Jack waited, his finger inside the trigger guard, the trigger blade cold under his finger, the weapon heavy in his hands.

"I could move now," said Pike. "I may be quick enough."

"Maybe. Your choice. It's not what I want."

Pike looked at Jack's face. He believed the man.

"All right, Jack. I see you're awake now. Between us, it ends."

"Your word? Your word on it?"

"Yes. My word."

MONDAY, JUNE 26

OFFICES OF THE UNITED STATES ATTORNEY

WATER AND PECK STREETS

LOWER MANHATTAN

1015 HOURS

Valeriana Greco had dressed for this encounter with particular care, since she had scheduled a press briefing immediately afterward, to be held in the conference rooms nearby, in time for the news media to make all the afternoon deadlines. She was perfection today in a Donna Karan suit of raw silk the precise color of the waters off the Cayman Islands, a luminous teal-blue that enhanced the tones of her black hair and her tiny opal earrings.

Her pumps were Prada and perfectly matched the suit. The desk was cleared and gleaming, decorated only with an antique pen-and-ink set from Lalique. The conference rooms in the Water Street building were very impressive, lined in teak and decorated with full-color portraits of the more illustrious members of the United States attorney's office. The huge room featured a set of antique French doors that opened up onto a terrace with a view of the Brooklyn Bridge and a section of the East River. She felt it would be a suitable backdrop for her. At precisely fifteen minutes after the hour one of the assistants in attendance stepped to her open door—Greco had her head down so that her shining bell of black hair could fall across her face as she pretended to be reading a document.

"Mr. Glazer is here, Ms. Greco."

"Show him in," said Greco.

Martin Glazer came into the room, crisp and brisk and every inch the Wall Street prince in a hand-stitched dark-gray single-breasted suit and shining black wing tips. He was accompanied by his assistants, Kuhlman and Bern, both shining brightly in excellent suits, their little goatees trimmed, their decorative gold-rimmed glasses glittering in the sunlight that was streaming in through Greco's east-facing windows, which also featured a panoramic view of the East River and the bridge.

Glazer carried nothing, but his assistants struggled under the burden of matching black leather briefcases bulging with critical documents. Glazer moved across the Aubusson without making a sound and offered a soft pink hand to Greco, who took it and shook it and released it in a firm and manly way.

"Good of you to come, Mr. Glazer."

"Please, call me Martin."

"Martin."

She didn't offer the reciprocal familiarity, which

Glazer noticed and decided to ignore. He settled into one of the three chairs arranged in a careful symmetry in front of Greco's desk, and crossed his legs at the ankles, sitting up straight in the antique rail-back, feeling it move underneath him and being careful not to let it creak in an undignified manner. Greco sat back down behind her desk and tabled a sheaf of papers, the first of which was a blue-bound folder bearing the crest of the Department of Justice.

"These are the preliminary papers that have been filed. You understand that this process is a complex one, and the purpose of today's meeting is merely to establish an agreement in principle regarding the management of the assets of Black Water Transit et alia, the holdings of which have come under the control of the federal government. The funds to be transferred today will be held in an escrow account until such time as the final resolution of Mr. Vermillion's prosecution can be . . ."

"Resolved?" offered Glazer.

"Yes. So we'll begin with the reading of these papers into the record. After which we'll have the agreement in principle notarized and then it will come back to us to be . . . yes, Margaret?"

Her assistant had come back into the room and was now hovering in the doorway, looking less than happy.

"Ms. Greco . . . may I have a word?"

"Now's not the time, Margaret. Whatever it is . . ."

Her voice trailed off as Jack Vermillion came into the room, followed by Flannery Coleman. They were both dressed for legal combat, the full suit-tie-perfect-shirt-and-shoes-like-bathtubs ensemble that makes all the difference on Wall Street. The look on her face was something Jack enjoyed very much, a scalded and cracking mask, like an overboiled egg. Glazer, seeing the look on her face, turned in his chair and let out a tiny peeping bleat. Kuhlman and Bern got up with determined looks on their faces and started to move toward Jack Vermillion. Coleman stepped forward and held up a hand.

"Ms. Greco, please forgive this intrusion, but my client and I feel we can resolve many of the difficulties before us by a simple exchange of information. May we sit?"

Greco had already buzzed for help. Four ATF agents bundled into the room through a side door and arranged themselves in the attack position in front of Greco's desk. They were all young and hard-looking in shirts and slacks with pistols in their belts. They looked like a team of security enforcers from Brooks Brothers. Flannery smiled at them. They scowled back at him.

"Your indulgence, gentlemen. Neither of us is armed, and Mr. Vermillion is here to go willingly into custody. All we ask is a few minutes of discussion before the process, Ms. Greco. As a courtesy? I know you to be a reasonable person."

Greco hesitated and then sat back down.

"Fine, Mr. Coleman. It would have been appropriate to provide some prior notice. As you can see, we're in the middle of a meeting here."

Glazer was still goggling at Jack Vermillion. Jack smiled at him and moved over to a sideboard. He put his weight on it carefully, crossed his arms over his chest, and nodded to Flannery.

"Thank you. Thank you all. I do hope these gentlemen from the ATF will stay in the room. I'm sure we all feel safer with their presence. Perhaps one of you fellows could find me a chair. I'm a little tired. We've been working all night."

"Working at what, Mr. Coleman?"

"Call me Flan, Val."

"At what?" she said with a snap.

"At uncovering a rather distressing conspiracy against an innocent man, a conspiracy that, it pains me to say, Val, might have been uncovered by your office if you had cared to apply some of the principles of justice so eloquently stated in the motto on that crest behind your desk. *Qui pro domina justitia sequitur*. Do you know what those words mean, Val?"

"Of course I do. 'Where the power of justice leads.' "

"Roughly translated, yes. You catch the gist, at least. You're familiar with a man named Carmine DaJulia, then?"

Greco did not move at all. Her stillness became obvious to her after it had become obvious to everyone else in the room.

"I am."

"Yes. I understand he has been the chief informant in this case against Jack Vermillion. Is that right?"

"This information is classified, Mr. Coleman. There are security considerations. The safety of our confidential informants is critical to the operations of the Justice Department."

"Of course. Well, perhaps we can hasten the proceedings here. . . . Please don't leave, Mr. Glazer."

Glazer had gotten out of his chair and was moving toward the door. Kuhlman and Bern stood rooted in place.

"I wonder if the gentlemen from the ATF here might persuade Mr. Glazer and his associates to linger awhile?"

Glazer paled as two of the ATF agents moved a little closer to him and fixed him with an unblinking stare.

"This is ridiculous."

"God, don't blubber, Marty," said Jack. "Why do they always blubber? Just shut up, okay?"

Flannery gave Jack a hard look.

"These proceedings are a serious matter, Jack. I know you've been under a great deal of strain. But there's no need to be abusive."

Jack smiled back at him and recrossed his arms.

"Now, we've been in the process of obtaining an affidavit from this CI of yours, Carmine DaJulia"—Flannery pronounced it badly, as if he were describing a type of skin disease—"and I have brought along some copies of it for . . . goodness, I think we have enough for everyone. Excuse me, young fellow, could you . . . ?"

He was holding ten thick typewritten documents bound in sky-blue, with the logo of his law office on the covers. He was asking for help from one of the ATF agents, who hesitated and then took the papers and handed them to Greco, to Glazer, to the rest of the ATF men. Flannery ignored Kuhlman and Bern. Jack had to admire the old bastard. He had turned the ATF men into court clerks and he was the presiding judge. He had taken over the room. It was the kind of thing they couldn't teach you at Harvard Law. You had to go to Yale.

"Good, thank you. Now, let me give you a précis of the contents of this affidavit, which, as you can see, has been fully witnessed and notarized and which was freely given by Mr. DaJulia without coercion or duress of any kind. If you wish, I have videotapes of the discovery interview in the car."

Greco was scanning the pages with an expert eye. As she read it, her face was going through some color changes.

"Let's cut to the chase here . . . Flan," she said, packing it with as much ironic detachment as she could muster. Jack figured she was already trying to work out how this could be twisted to make her look good. She was a contender, no doubt of it. Flannery raised his eyebrows in a mock show of concern.

"Cut to the chase? Goodness, Val. Isn't that what you've been doing all this week? Chasing this poor man all over the Eastern Seaboard? Still, if you insist. Mr. DaJulia conveys the information in this affidavit that it was he who planted the stolen vehicles in the container you found on the *Agawa Canyon* and that it was he who was the source for the cocaine-tainted currency you found."

"Why the hell would DaJulia do that? What possible benefit could there be in it?"

"You were putting a great deal of pressure on Mr. DaJulia, my dear. You wanted information. You wanted a score. Frank Torinetti was at the top of your list. DaJulia gave you something else. Somebody you were quite happy to destroy. Jack Vermillion."

"DaJulia gave us information that implicated your client. Nothing we did was outside the canons—"

"I'm not blaming you for being misled by an informant. I'm blaming you for missing a much more interesting issue. You played DaJulia, and he played you. Of the two, DaJulia was the better tactician. You underestimated him, but he had you pegged."

"This is absurd. Get to the point."

"I'd be delighted. Mr. DaJulia confirms that he was approached by our Mr. Glazer here a few weeks ago, who explained in some detail to him exactly how it was possible to implicate Mr. Vermillion in drug trafficking and money laundering. Apparently he knew something of Mr. DaJulia's reputation through mutual friends in the . . . leisure industry. He also outlined the workings of the RICO laws and the process by which a man's property might be forfeit under certain carefully defined legal circumstances. Mr. Glazer's firm had already begun a thorough investigation of Black Water Transit under the guise of offering to do a pension fund reorganization, and they had concluded that Mr. Vermillion's association with certain individuals who are thought to have connections with the Cosa Nostra provided the perfect background for such an . . . escapade. You do admit that most law enforcement professionals in the Albany area were privately convinced that Jack Vermillion was—I love this phrase—mobbed up. I admit to some suspicions myself. So the stain, if you will, was already on the man. All that was required was an ambitious—and gullible—prosecutor, one who had already made a name for herself through a series of extremely aggressive actions against a wide range of businessmen and -women over the last six years. You are known, I am told, around these very offices as the Pirate Queen."

"This is fucking absurd."

"Not really, Val. It's all here. Read it, my dear, and weep."

"Are you trying to suggest malice here, Mr. Coleman? Because malice is—"

"Hardly malice, Val. I'm suggesting stupidity. Stupidity, pure bull-headed blind-minded stupidity. It causes much more grief in the world than malice. You have to accept this, my dear, if you're ever going to succeed in Washington. DaJulia's little game is croquet compared to the games that go on down by the Potomac."

Greco had nothing to say for a few seconds.

"What about Earl Pike? How does your client explain him?"

"My client doesn't explain him. He's your problem. You were already running an operation against my client. You were operating on information provided by Mr. DaJulia. I presume the timing of the . . . bust . . . was up to Mr. DaJulia?"

"He . . . told us that he knew when Mr. Vermillion intended to move these vehicles. He said he'd let us know how and when."

"So he was in control of that?"

"Yes. In effect."

"So when Mr. Pike contacted him in connection with a weapons shipment, DaJulia, who knew something of the man, decided to put him in touch with Jack. It could go either way then. Jack could refuse to ship the container. Or he could agree. If he agreed, DaJulia had someone in Red Hook who could tell him when Pike's shipment was going. He saw to it that the one you were expecting would go the same day, on the same ship. A weapons shipment would only sweeten the case against Jack."

"But Vermillion came into our offices. He informed on Pike himself. What did DaJulia expect that to accomplish?"

"He didn't expect it at all. When Jack informed on Pike, it came as a complete shock to everyone. All of his friends counseled him against it. As did I. Quite vigorously. It shocked you, I suspect. I wonder why you didn't reconsider your view of the man."

"I . . . we suspected some sort of diversion. Besides, we were already committed. The thing was in play."

"In play? My God, woman."

"Where is Mr. DaJulia now?"

"In a hospital in Albany. Under a police guard."

"In a hospital? If this affidavit was the result of any kind of torture, it's meaningless. Totally worthless."

"I think Mr. DaJulia will confirm the essentials of this matter. All that is required of your office is to take up the matter and investigate the allegations in a calm and professional manner. As the crest says, where justice leads—that is your job, isn't it? I suspect you'll be able to find sufficient corroborative evidence in Mr. Glazer's background to make a good case for criminal conspiracy. For example, we've found out that Mr. Glazer has been the principal liaison officer in three other federally mandated seizure operations. I've included the reports with the DaJulia affidavit. Buying businesses at a bargain rate through federal forfeiture operations seems to be a specialty of the house at Galitzine Sheng and Munro. If you can't make a case with this sort of help, my dear, you should consider an alternative career."

Glazer popped a gasket at that point.

"I'm not standing around to listen to this bullshit. You have no right to detain us. I do not have to stand here and be libeled."

"Slandered," said Greco. "Libeled is written."

Flannery shook his head.

"Don't know. We have put all this in print. You could make a case for it being libel *and* slander."

"Whatever," said Glazer. "We're going."

He hesitated and then started for the door. Kuhlman and Bern stayed where they were. He turned to look at them.

"Let's go."

"You really intend to charge him?" said Kuhlman. "Because if you do, I want a deal. I'm not going down the chute for this prick."

"Andy!"

"Nor am I," said Bern. Glazer looked ill.

"You can go, Mr. Glazer. May I suggest a lawyer?" said Greco. "We'll be in touch. Let him go, Ben. Mr. Kuhlman, Mr. Bern, you two can stay. I'll speak with you both later. I'd like to clear this room. Mr. Coleman, I'd like a word. Privately."

"Delighted," said Flannery. "May Jack leave?"

"Jack Vermillion is still in a great deal of trouble. He slaughtered two guards in Beach Haven and he executed three children in Pennsylvania. Or does he deny that as well?"

"Really, Val, you're quite the bull terrier, aren't you? I would think the unfortunate confrontation at Hazleton would be a topic of some . . . delicacy . . . around your office, since at the time it happened you had a GPS transponder on the marshals van. It could be argued—

and will be, if you push it—that you are legally culpable for the deaths that ensued. God knows what the fallout would be."

Two small roses of bright color appeared on Greco's cheekbones at the same time that her forehead grew slightly more pale. Flannery Coleman took advantage of the pause to turn around and favor Jack with an evil smile.

"Jack, why don't you go have a smoke?"

"I'd like to stay."

"Oh God, Jack, what Ms. Greco and I have to do here is something only lawyers should have to witness. Dear lad, please go."

Jack went.

MONDAY, JUNE 26

SUITE 2990

THE UNITED NATIONS PLAZA HOTEL

2200 HOURS

The sun had gone down in glory behind the towers and pillars of Manhattan, turning the sky a brilliant fiery amber shot through with streaks of shell-pink and sea-green. The lights had come on all over Manhattan and Earl Pike had sat in jeans and a soft plaid shirt and savored every golden moment of it in the living room of his suite with a CD of African drums playing softly. The insistent rhythms of the drums seemed to catch something of the spirit of the place. He had been to many cities in the world, and he had seen many terrible and wonderful things, but nothing to lift the heart and ease the soul like a sunset in New York. He looked at his glass of wine and moved the crystal, swirling the liquid around the sides of the glass. He inhaled the scent of it, oak and black cherry. He needed another and walked barefoot across the thick emerald-green carpet to pour one from a bottle standing on the rosewood sideboard. It had been a good day. One of his best.

He had been particularly moved by the television coverage of the police funeral held today at Saint John the Divine, the massed blue ranks in solemn files, the wind that stirred the snapping flags, the melancholy beauty of the Last Post played by a trumpeter who knew what he was about. The scene had touched him deeply as a military man, and he remembered the many, the too many, times he had stood at stiff attention on some windswept hillside, or in a jungle clearing, or on the flat plains of the Middle East with a chain of low saw-toothed mountains in the blue distance and watched through tears as another soldier was placed into the care of the earth, the great receiver, the last certain refuge from a violent world.

He had looked for a familiar face, the black police-woman and the club fighter, Nicky Cicero, but there were too many for that. It didn't matter. He had played his role in a greater mystery, and he knew that in some way he had taken part in the sacrifice of a brave man. He had not hated many of the men he had killed in all these years, and least of all the policemen he had killed in the last few days. They were men and women in the service of a corrupt empire, but he himself had lived and—in a way—died in the same service. All dead soldiers are brothers, he had thought, and even the enemy is purified by dying on the field of battle. When the piper had played "Amazing Grace" in the whistling silence of the graveyard in Brooklyn as the policeman's coffin was being lowered into the open grave, Pike had felt the terrible beauty of the moment as much as any man or woman there. It was a searing feeling, and it did not pass for several hours, not until he saw the newscast at six. It confirmed all his beliefs about the political system in America. And it was amusing as hell.

Jack Vermillion had come in from the cold—that was the way the Channel Seven anchor had put it—and as the details of Jack's return were described—the plea bargain, the acceptance of two years in prison—he'd serve six months at best—in return for a reduced charge of involuntary manslaughter in the case of three dead boys in Hazleton, and the return of his assets under a sealed agreement with the United States attorney's office—all of these gambits confirmed Pike's belief that there was no real honor in the justice system, only the cynical calculus of a predatory state and the struggle of the individual to preserve some measure of dignity inside what was in reality a prison that stretched from sea to shining sea.

Pike knew that Jack would be testifying in some secret room, that his eyewitness account of the murders of those two guards formed a part of his deal with Greco, but Jack's accusation was that of a confessed killer and would never find a respectful hearing with any jury in the country. Jack Vermillion had the stain now, and unless he broke his promise and used the Barrett, nothing he said about Earl Pike would ever stand up against Pike's long and honorable service to his nation. As far as the Barrett was concerned, Pike was prepared to take the risk.

Not that Vermillion had given him much choice. He had Vermillion's word, and for some reason he was inclined to believe him. The man was a soldier, and the soldier in the man wanted to atone, and Pike was satisfied that his regret had been genuine. The proof of that was the fact that the ATF had not come storming through his door hours ago. Jack had kept his part of the bargain, so Pike would keep his. It was over between them.

His collection, so far, was still in the hands of the government. It might be that it was gone forever. He had to accept that possibility, and he would hope for the understanding of his ancestors. But perhaps, if he was determined, he might win it back someday in the future. He was confident that he had frightened the Greco woman enough to ensure that she would keep it intact and protected as long as he was free. He had seen that in her eyes on Sunday morning.

She was afraid of him, and that meant she was not as stupid as she seemed. No one at the ATF would be "extracting" any of it. It would be in a vault until he reclaimed it, or until he was dead. Either way, he had punished them for the injustice of their system. It was enough that some other soldier in another place might not have his own weapons, his hard-won symbols of honorable battle, seized on a flimsy pretext to further the career plans of an ambitious psychopath.

The phone rang then. It was Mercedes Gonsalva.

"Two police officers are on their way up, Mr. Pike."

"With what agency?"

"The NYPD, Mr. Pike. A man and a woman."

Pike thanked her, got up, and walked to the window to look out on the city skyline. Not the ATF, anyway. And he had disposed of the NYPD before. He was calm. He had expected this. The chime sounded twice and he padded across the carpet to open the door.

"Officer Spandau. Officer Cicero. How can I help you?"

Casey held up a color photo. It was a picture of Earl Pike standing in front of a service desk. He had his head down, but the shot was clearly him. He was holding a battered brown briefcase in his hands. A logo on the wall read MAIL BOXES ETC. There was a time-date marker in the lower right corner.

FRIDAY 23 JUNE 1415

Pike studied the picture and worked on his breathing.

"Fascinating. What am I to make of this?"

Casey's voice was even, but anger was making her throat hurt.

"You've told the ATF that you were in South Dakota on Friday. That you left around midnight. Just before the death of Detective James Rule and three ATF agents at the Red Hook Container Terminal. And yet here we have a picture of you standing at a Mail Boxes depot in Peekskill, New York, at a quarter after two on the afternoon of Friday last. The briefcase you're holding there was stolen from an NYPD vehicle about two hours before. This looks like a problem for you, Mr. Pike."

"In what sense? I don't accept that this grainy little snapshot is a picture of me. I've never seen that case before, and on Friday afternoon I was in South Dakota with two associates."

"They may be altering that testimony, Mr. Pike. Your friends will only go so far for you. The ATF is talking to them now. They have a copy of this shot too."

"This is harassment, lady."

"I hope so. That's the effect we were going for. Right now you're coming with us. To the precinct. You can explain in the car how we got it all wrong. We going to have to cuff you?"

Pike smiled.

"I don't want to get shot for straightening my tie."

Nicky stepped in with the cuffs.

Pike offered no resistance.

"Am I charged?"

"Not yet."

"But I'm cuffed?"

"It just makes us feel better, okay?"

They were walking him toward the elevator. Pike smiled at Casey when they reached the doors.

"You're a tenacious little bitch, aren't you? By the way, how's your mother?"

"You have the right to shut the fuck up," said Casey.

They rode down in the green-mirrored elevator, Nicky on one side and Casey on the other. Something lyrical and classical was playing on the speakers. The elevator stopped at the lobby level and the doors opened. An old man in a black suit and a dirty white shirt was standing there, holding a stainless-steel revolver. He had a bloody bandage taped to his left cheek. In a detached way, in the seconds he had left, Pike recognized a Colt Python. The man held the door, leveled the pistol at them all. No one moved. Nicky and Casey stared at the man. He looked at Pike and spoke only to him.

"Julia Maria Gianetto," he said.

Pike looked into the old man's eyes and knew the name.

Fabrizio Senza saw the understanding in his face. Pike knew himself at that moment in a way he had never known himself. As a dead man. The muzzle of the Colt flowered white. Pike knew that it would. That was the way of guns. But the heat shocked him. It was the last thought he had as the round punched through his skull and painted the green glass mirror behind him in deltas and rivers of bright shining red. The heat—

Late in August, just around sunset, Claire Torinetti was found dead in the pool at their house in Rensselaer. Only one round in her lungs, but it was enough to keep her on the bottom until the cops arrived. Frank was sitting in a deck chair, drinking a Bombay Sapphire gin straight up, listening to "Midnight Sun," playing it over and over again. It's a Johnny Mercer song, which if you take the time to find and listen to real careful, you get a picture of how Frank was doing at the time. He died a couple days later, and they had a real nice funeral for them both, and buried them side by side on a little crest of hill with a view of the river there.

Greco nailed Marty Glazer's dick to a door and got all the credit for taking down a big Wall Street outfit. She's in DC now, a rising star, and did a turn on *Burden of Proof* last week. The camera still loves her, which you have to figure is enough for her.

Carmine DaJulia lived to take a plea and is now somewhere in the witness protection program. If there's a God, Carmine is working as a stock boy in a Wal-Mart in some rat's-ass trailer town way out in the middle of Nebraska. The mutt.

Fabrizio Senza had a heart attack while Nicky and Casey were taking him down to Central Booking, and died in the Rikers Island infirmary a month later. At the autopsy, they cut him open, his heart was like a brown paper bag. Here's a kicker. When they looked into it later, Casey found out that this Gianetto kid was no relation to Senza at all. Yes, his niece had died. In a hit-and-run up in Tarrytown. No connection with Pike at all. Frank Torinetti wanted Pike dead as a kind of insurance, and Fabrizio Senza was just playing with Pike's head while he shot him. The old guy was dying anyway, and what he said when he shot Pike took the official heat away from Frank. Maybe Fabrizio Senza just wanted to die like an old soldier. And he did.

Casey and Nicky took some heat for letting Pike get killed, but in the long run everyone was just damn glad the man was finally dead. He took a lot of things to the grave with him, which had to be a relief to his friends at CCS. Casey and Nicky are still an item, and they go see Morgan Rule when they can. No change there, but everybody has to have some hope. It's the thing with feathers.

About Casey's mother? Baby steps.

Jack's kid, Danny, was transferred to a medium-security facility outside Fresno as soon as he got out of the clinic at Lompoc, just the way Jack Vermillion had wanted it. He got himself killed two months later in a tractor accident while he was working in a big field of grapevines. It was a fine sunny day in southern California and he'd been out of detox a month and was clean and straight when he died, according to the prison medics who did the autopsy. Anyway, there you go. That's about it. No. Wait. There was one last thing.

ONE LAST THING . . .

Creek was watching the snow falling down over the campus grounds. It fell like apple blossoms, soft and white and into a perfect silence. The yellow windows glowed in the dark buildings, and the sound of a Christmas choir rose into the black night sky. Creek watched the snow come down out of the night. It was dizzying, like the stars falling. He looked at his pool, at the cover straining under the weight of the snow falling on it. The warm lights from his penthouse shone out into the patio and put a lovely amber tint on the snow that had gathered on his lawn chairs and his patio table, on the rounded dome of the barbecue where he had grilled steaks for his old friend Jack on the first day of the summer that was now long gone. Jack, who was coming home tonight. Creek had taken a call from Jack in the early morning, just as the snow had begun to fall. As he watched the snow falling into the deep dark below him, Creek thought about that call, played it over in his mind again and again.

"Creek, Jack here."

"Jack! Great to hear from you. Where are you?"

"I'm in Harrisburg. The airport. They let me out today."

"I heard. You want me to pick you up at the airport?"

"No. I'll take a cab. I wanted to say something to you."

"Sure. Yeah. Okay."

"You took money from Glazer, right?"

Creek had been silent for a long time then, before he said yes.

"Why, Creek?"

"How'd you find out?"

"Flannery told me yesterday. It came out in Glazer's plea bargain, during the full-and-frank-statement part. Flannery didn't want me to know. But now I do. Why did you take it?"

What the hell was there to say? How about the truth?

"I was into a lot of people. Carmine. His friends. Gambling. I made some bad calls in the market. I owed people. The cars weren't enough. I had talked to some Wall Street people about our plans to redo the pension fund, and I guess one of them talked to Galitzine Sheng and Munro. Glazer called me. He knew about my cash flow . . . my problems. He asked me to arrange a meet."

"At the Frontenac?"

"Yeah . . . Jack, listen—"

"How much did you take? To set up the meet?"

"A quarter million. I paid off Carmine a hundred thousand, but I still have some left. I can—"

"Nothing to do now, Creek. All done. Listen, what I wanted to say . . . you're my friend, Creek. My good friend. I understand. I understand how a man can do things . . . under the gun, a guy can do things and then be sorry for them later. I did that. It's . . . nobody's above it, okay? Anybody can do . . . anything."

"Christ, Jack . . . I'm sorry every goddamn day."

"Yeah . . . me too. Look . . . they're calling my plane."

"You want me to come and get you?"

"No, Creek . . . I'll give you a call. In the new year."

"In the new year? Promise? I'll look forward to it. Fly safe."

"Yeah. I promise. You stay safe too, buddy."

Then he was gone. That had been many hours ago. A very long time ago. Now Creek was standing at the edge of his roof, looking out over the low huddled buildings of the college, the yellow glow of the dormitory windows, listening to the sweet voices of the choir, and the snow continued to fall out of the black woolen sky in huge soft flakes that were just like apple blossoms.

Could a man fall like that, if he were to step out into the black woolen night? Would he fall the way the snow falls, into a perfect silence? How sweet it would be to have the courage to know.

A NOTE TO THE READER

My descriptions of the territorial and judicial conflicts encountered every day by the men and women of the NYPD are as accurate as my research and personal observations could make them. The operational details are based on my own experiences with working detectives on the streets of the five boroughs. The real-life consequences of the asset seizure laws, including their corrosive effect on the principles and conduct of certain city, state, and federal attorneys, are a matter of public record for those of you who care to look.

Although this novel is a work of fiction, and any resemblance to the living or dead is purely coincidental, Earl V. Pike is a composite of several men I have met in the course of my long and uneven life, many of whom are now safely tucked away in shallow graves in assorted third-world hellholes, and for whom no one mourns but I.

Carsten Stroud
Thunder Beach

ABOUT THE AUTHOR

CARSTEN STROUD is the author of the *New York Times* bestseller *Close Pursuit,* and the award-winning *Sniper's Moon,* both set in the New York City Police Department. He lives and writes in Thunder Beach.